A TAUREAN DRAGON

by

Bryony York

A gift from my Mum & Me

x

Lots of Love Tracy
You are an incredible and wonderful friend

Katey x

Copyright © 2017 Bryony York

Cover Design © 2017 Mairi Nolan

All rights reserved

All characters in this publication are fictitious and any resemblance to real persons, living or dead, is purely coincidental

Published as a Kindle eBook in 2016 under the title The Reunion, by Bryony York

PROLOGUE
The North of England – Two hundred years ago

Jed blanched as the old crone spat out her venomous tirade. If he'd had to guess, he would have said that her words saddled him with a short life and a painful death, but she spoke in the old patois and he hadn't understood most of it – only enough to get the gist.

He may well have been a doughty lad and unafraid to die, but Jed wasn't used to poisonous attacks like this. Maybe he should have told the old hag that her black magic was a load of rubbish, but to be on the safe side he just prayed to his own god that she had no talent for curses.

The woman's pregnant grand-daughter backed away in fright, as well she might. It was her own silliness that had caused all the commotion anyway and, to be honest, she was ready to let go of Jed Cook and never set eyes on him again. She and Jed were the only ones to know the truth. Oh yes, her pregnancy was genuine right enough, but Jed was not the father.

Leila Gray had a reputation as a trollop with a trail of misdemeanours in her wake a mile long, and when Jed refused her amorous advances, the little minx went off in a huff to search for another victim. It was only a matter of time before she got herself 'into trouble' as her mother would have said, had the poor woman still been alive.

A crowd of onlookers stepped aside as the old harridan walked away. She snarled at those who openly gaped at her, and made a point of frightening the youngsters by showing an ugly row of rotten teeth as she passed by.

She cackled loudly over her shoulder. 'Come, grand-daughter. We shall leave this place; the stench is not good for you in your condition.'

Leila and her grandmother moved away to another part of Yorkshire, and it wasn't long before a dry summer melted into a tempestuous October. Animals went into hiding at the first growl of thunder to escape the wrath of the gods, trees bent almost double as a vicious wind howled at them, and a torrential downpour soon turned the fields into mud.

There may well have been chaos everywhere but Leila had needs of her own that night. She stopped her pacing and took herself off to their crude hut where the straw mattress was hard and lumpy, though good enough for what she was about to do.

The infant cried with her first breath, which was when the wind paused for a moment to listen, as though the occasion itself was momentous enough to demand a little respect. After a while, thunderous rumbling took over again and flashes of white adorned the sky as the baby competed lustily with the elements to ascertain which of them could create the loudest noise. Eventually, the new-born child slept and her exhausted young mother relaxed.

Come dawn, the place looked like a battlefield. Fences and hedges had been cut down by the onslaught, rubbish had been hurled everywhere, and things that had not been physically strapped down were scattered far and wide.

In the soft light of a new day, Leila's grandmother stared down at the olive-skinned baby who showed all the promise of growing into a beautiful child.

Leila gave a small sigh of relief that the baby bore no resemblance to her natural father, but a trace of uneasiness showed in her own emerald green eyes when she fixed her gaze on the wise old woman's face.

The grandmother stared from mother to baby for a few moments, but held her tongue. Then, she placed a small stone amulet into the baby's tiny wrinkled hand and was rewarded by a tightening of small fingers around it, a gesture that made her smile knowingly. She muttered a few words of incantation under her breath and left the hovel.

Leila would have cast the amulet straight into the fire, had she thought it would burn to dust, but she knew it would only lie there in the embers until she could retrieve it later. In any case, she was scared of her grandmother's perspicacity. The night had been long enough and she did not have the strength to do anything except sleep. She felt too weak.

She closed her eyes. She would think what to do for the best when she woke in a few hours.

Her body was beginning to burn wildly in spite of the cold outside, and her head was pounding.

Perhaps tomorrow …

CHAPTER ONE
Present-day London

I still come out in goose bumps when I think about that lousy October day last year. Black Tuesday I called it: the day when our small computer firm lost its battle to stay independent and became part of a giant conglomerate.

In anybody's book it smacked of a takeover, although the new chief obligingly called it a merger. It was also the turning point of my life, though I didn't realize it at the time.

It was around ten in the morning when James, my long-standing manager and friend, began his staff briefings to reveal all, and I was first on his list. Up to that point, all the finer points had been kept secret, well, as hush-hush as anybody could make them in an environment such as ours that seemed to thrive on gossip. He made his way to my office in what could only be described as a pensive mood.

Office? That's a good one! For the past eight years, I had spent my working hours in a tiny glass-partitioned affair on the ground floor that the architects vaguely labelled 'office' on their drawings, but which was in reality an air-conditioned goldfish bowl. There was room for a table, a two-drawer filing cabinet and two chairs. Just.

My own chair was one of those black upholstered ones which swiveled and squeaked when it decided the moment was appropriate; the other chair was purposely hard and unyielding. I saved that for visitors.

Nice view from the window, though. One of the garden kind, which in reality meant that I looked out on a small patch of grass surrounded by well-established sycamore and silver birch trees, with only the occasional blur of traffic and a high-rise office block across the road to enhance the scenery.

I pushed my keyboard and paperwork to one side to give James room to perch himself on the edge of the desk (he always avoided the hard chair) as he went through the squiggly details on his notepad, word for word, adding a few comments he'd had the innate good sense not to write down. As his voice buzzed in the background, I glanced through the window.

An earlier mild wind had decided to turn blustery, and my lawn (for want of a better word) was now almost entirely covered in autumnal leaves. More wrinkled coppery leaves added to the pile as they fluttered gracefully downwards.

The lyrical half of my brain suggested that their metaphorical mother was discarding them in a bid to streamline the world for some important forthcoming event. The other half whispered sardonically that this was nature's normal playful refurbishment and not to get too keyed up about it.

Funny how an idea takes over. This speculative mode of mine convinced me that I could easily be like those crumbling brown leaves before much longer, after all, I had been dithering about this job of mine ever since my Personnel countdown interview three weeks ago.

Call it unknown foresight, call it autumn madness, but it only took me a split second to decide that I wanted to sever my link with the past, just as those leaves were doing: I didn't need James to join up the dots for me. Yes, you might say that my comfort zone was slowly dissolving and an indescribable urge to cut loose nibbled at my insides.

When the briefing came to an end, he paused and put his notebook down on the desk. Not difficult to guess what was coming next.

'What I really wanted you to know, Elise, is that there will be a spanking new office for you, too, if you decide to come with me.'

So that was it.

I met his gaze uncomfortably and his eyes narrowed slightly. He knew me well enough to be able to tell I was deciding how to phrase the next bit.

'I've been thinking about this—'

An understatement if ever there was one. I had been rehearsing this moment in my sleep, yea or nay, even before I heard the details. It wasn't James's fault if I decided to jump off the carousel and try my luck elsewhere. Might be a foolish move in the end, but there you go.

From humble beginnings as a tyro computer analyst, I had steadily grown into what James generously called an important cog in the wheels of his company, and some inner hubris fancifully allowed me to imagine that the job market would soon be wildly scrambling over itself to offer me alternative employment. Silly woman.

Naturally, I came up with pettifogging excuses, fundamentally because I am one of the 'why tinker with something that works well?' brigade. And, naturally, James the Friend tactfully tried to persuade me to accept one of the new jobs until I found something else, of course he did, but deep down he knew that once his star pupil had made up her mind, right or wrong, that was that.

But then, James the Manager steered the conversation round to my current workload and whether I would be able to get through everything in my in-tray before the new company imposed its deadlines. There didn't seem to be any problems when we'd looked at the details.

Picking up his notebook, he turned towards the door and cast a tired glance around as though he were taking a last look at the world of sanity as he understood it.

'I shall miss you. I shall miss this whole damn place, Elise. We have always been a good team, but I suppose it's time to move on.'

The nod had a kind of finality about it, then he left me to ponder my fate alone.

There was no one standing by the drinks machine when I got up from my chair and walked along the corridor on the first floor.

My daily fix was an unidentifiable brown liquid going by the code on the selection list as coffee and, as it squirted downwards, I glanced at my reflection in the glass panel on the front of the machine.

No changes of a noticeable kind; perhaps a bit tired; calendar catching up with me? I leaned forward to note the mildest of wrinkles round hazel eyes, and automatically fluffed up my dark spiky hair into a kind of halo that merged with the supplier's logo.

I have always felt that my hair reveals a fondness for the bizarre rather than a hatred of hairdressers. On a normal day, I apply gel to make it stand on end properly – the scarecrow look I call it – but I hadn't bothered today: the morning so far was anything but normal.

The coffee tasted just as repulsive as ever. At least nobody had spiked the machine. Yet!

Yes, you might say that it had been a stimulating day for changes so far, and it wasn't even lunchtime.

To be honest, I didn't know which was worse: the man with whom I had shared my life for the past five years walking out on me at breakfast time, or the second jolt of the day when a crazy October wind pushed me into a jobless existence.

Turner Cooper is his name, and his sudden departure from the flat left me feeling completely deflated. In fact, over and above the zigzagging of my career, I was still quivering from the impact of his sudden announcement that he intended to move in permanently with his secretary.

Permanently! His secretary! I ask you! It's like something from a soap opera.

That man is as slick as a poker player when it comes to intrigue, but his hanky-panky had been nimble enough to escape even my eagle eye, and his announcement that morning came as a violent shock. So much so, that I was unable to think of a single word of pejorative abuse as he calmly packed his bags and walked out of the door.

Perhaps my non-reaction stemmed from a gut realization that our relationship was already fizzling out of its own accord, and that I would probably have thrown him out in another six months anyway. The flat is in my name, after all.

The silence hit me forcibly when I got home and opened the front door. It was still blustery out in the street, but now it was cold and dark as well.

All the lights were off, which was something I wasn't used to, but I managed to pick up a few letters in the hall before I stabbed them with the heel of my shoe and cursed out loud. Even the clock in the hall seemed to tick like a time bomb. Strange. I had never noticed that before.

There was no Turner standing by the cooker with a smile on that rakishly handsome face of his. No

Turner holding out a glass of wine for me while I eased off my shoes and changed from systems analyst into housewife mode.

Usually home first, Turner normally prepared our evening meal – rice maybe, but more often than not some other delicious concoction of his own. I always brag to my friends that one of the good things about our lifestyle is that Turner is a dab hand in the kitchen and I like to eat well.

A quick look round the flat confirmed my mounting suspicion that the obnoxious man had decided to remove everything he personally owned. The bathroom still smelled of his sexy aftershave, but Turner's shelf was empty, as was his half of the wardrobe and the drawer where he untidily kept his underwear. It was as though the past five years had just gone up in smoke.

There was still a bottle of Chardonnay in the fridge though, which was a surprise. At least he'd had the decency to leave that, and I gloomily poured myself a large glass before perching on one of the bar stools in the kitchen.

What I really wanted to do was talk to somebody about work and, though Turner might be petty-minded about many things, he was always sympathetic when it came to listening to tales of mulish recklessness. It was only now that I suspected I probably hadn't been wearing my sensible head when I cut myself adrift to search for an elusive dream.

'Perhaps I should have taken that job,' I muttered as I abandoned the maudlin effects of wine and stuck the cold kettle under the tap for a cup of tea instead. 'Maybe I should have ignored my instinctive reaction and held on to James's escape route.'

Yes, that crummy October day ended by giving me a weird feeling of worthlessness I hadn't felt in a long time. It's at times like that when you come to realize that employment – or indeed romance for that matter – can be such a transient thing.

It was going to be a horrible evening.

I felt like kicking something.

CHAPTER TWO

Richard Mason is the kind of man who makes a lasting impact when you see him for the first time. He comes across as a perfect advertisement for men's aftershave: clean features, lean body, smouldering eyes. And the rest.

I first met him when he gate-crashed my party two months after Black Tuesday, though I didn't hold that against him. Nobody could have called our kind of malarkey a party anyway, not really. It was simply a reunion for a group of female friends who get together twice a year to dissect their lives and put them back together again in a different order.

It was always going to be a zany kind of day when we sorted out insoluble problems for a few hours without any interference from what you might call 'outsiders'. A day, in fact, when we home in on tasty titbits relevant to a group of new-age women.

This getting together all started as a lunch date for a few girls from school who wanted to keep in touch. Later on, we added catholic tastes to the mix by introducing friends from other walks of life into the group – college, work, that kind of thing.

The consequence was that membership bounced merrily upwards, and attendance at these affairs fluctuated sporadically somewhere between the original six and the current twenty-seven. A motley crew, we laughingly say.

It's strange really, or perhaps not so strange when you think about it: different from a family bonding, we're talking here about that unidentifiable tie that comes along through personal choice rather than genetic duty.

Only the ones who actually live within a radius of two hundred miles of the hosting venue are likely to turn up on a regular basis. Around eighteen if they all come.

This particular December was nothing special, except it was my turn to act as hostess. Never mind the exigencies of unemployment, it was time to forget whatever emotional baggage I was carrying around with me for a few hours and concentrate on what everyone else has been doing. Whether an attitude like that was going to put me in a better frame of mind on this occasion was a matter for conjecture.

Media gossip? No way! We modern women have far too much of our own stuff to talk about without doing battle with the rest of the world.

Hobbies? Of course. Not like those girlish days when some of us collected stamps or accumulated dozens of signed photographs of film stars: no, we are far more sophisticated now. We are into escapades that stir the brain cells a bit more: things like the intricate world of finance or the complex art of T'ai Chi.

We have a theme. We always have a theme. It helps to keep the momentum going and the juices flowing, as they say.

Slight difficulty this year, in that my lounge is a bit too small for exercising on a grand arm-waving scale (even without Turner's accoutrements), and large glasses of wine would most likely put paid to any discussion about the dollar or the euro.

This being the case, I gleefully decided at the planning stage to get down to a serious subject that was just as exhilarating, to me at any rate. My own absorbing passion: tea leaves and rune stones, or rather, the reading thereof.

Telling fortunes happens to be my hobby, which is another reason why I ought to have spotted Turner's little blob of dust blowing over the horizon. But, sad to say, I didn't. Or maybe I did, but decided to ignore the signs. All the clues were there, but even the rune stones and Tarot cards refused to let me in on the secret.

Traitorous devils!

When the detestable man disappeared into the great unknown, I took solace in reading tea leaves, but even this lifelong interest of mine in predicting the future seemed to have deserted me and, in a fit of pique, I changed to teabags. A state of obstinacy that didn't last long, I might add. I cast this modern answer to the teapot to one side only a week ago and reverted to my favourite kind of leaf tea so that the caddy would be well-stocked up for anything newsworthy today.

My reunion friends are perfectly well aware that I make things up as I go along, but they are nice enough to say that it is only a bit of light-hearted fun at the end of the day.

Strange really, this paradoxical interest of mine in the paranormal when I have years of technical expertise mounting up behind me from my job. Always supposing that I still have a job, of course, after the year end next March (the crystal ball is mysteriously tight-lipped on that one).

Anyway, back to Richard.

This particular day was the first Saturday in the month and the weather was trying hard to be sociable by not raining. You could not really expect anything other than low temperatures and a blanket of cloud at this time of year, but a harsh night frost had made sure that the bare shrubs were glistening prettily in the back yard, and the forecast talked about snow flurries later on. A typical December day, in fact.

It was almost noon by the time fourteen well-scrubbed-up women abandoned the perishing cold outside and turned my lounge into an aviary. We are all roughly the same age (thirty-five-ish, give or take a few years), 'Well into our prime,' is what we say each time we meet. Given that none of us wants to admit to getting any older, we blissfully ignore any wrinkles or strands of grey hair.

It might be cold outside, but my tiny ground floor London flat was delightfully warm, and I was keen to make sure that endless baking smells floated deliciously through to the lounge as I welcomed my guests and laid out their contributions to the feast on the dining room table. As usual, there would be far too much food, but it was natural to over-provide at these events, and I was mightily satisfied with my own efforts at the oven today.

Until I met the infamous Turner, I had been brought up to believe that food came out of a tin, and was taught by one of the best in the business how to be a whiz with a can opener and frozen peas, but I am desperately trying to break the habit and morph into a Cookery Goddess. Not sure why, except that I have this feeling that I might need all the skills I can muster in the not too distant future.

Actually, I am showing such an interest in my oven that I now have a row of books by celebrity chefs on the kitchen shelf. I might even bake a Christmas cake next week! Or perhaps not. I have a feeling that my new project might only be temporary.

The kitchen timer buzzed, which made me break off from newsy chatter in the lounge to check on the immediate problem of what was going one galley-wise.

I confess that my forays into cookery are still a bit touch and go, but this time there was no need to panic.

The apple cake definitely looked edible, nicely brown and rounded as opposed to sunken or flat. All I needed was for it to jump out of the tin, turn over, and land successfully on the plate like the picture in the book.

But then, just at that moment, the doorbell rang, breaking into domesticity of a culinary kind and startling me. I looked up, mid-thrust; knife poised like a murderer about to commit a crime, and peered along the passageway in the direction of the front door. A dark shape was outlined against the frosted glass, so I called out for some help, considering my hands were fully occupied.

Noise is one of the keynotes of these little meetings of ours and somebody had put on a CD that Turner had left behind. It was one of those '*Yeah, Yeah*' beat type of things that he knew I hated (probably why he left it in the first place) and the blaring noise would have been enough to give the tenants upstairs a headache if they hadn't heard about the party and sensibly gone away for the weekend.

'Chessie,' I yelled. 'Get the door, will you please. My hands are full. And find somebody to turn that ruddy noise down a peg or two, will you. They can probably hear it down the street.'

Give me Sinatra any day.

'Okey dokey, darling. On my way.'

Chessie is far better at multi-tasking than any of the others, though her name tripped off the tongue easily because she is one of the original six from school and we are growing old together. It is also a quirk of fate that we live only a couple of miles from each other.

The noise sank to a more reasonable pitch and the woman herself sashayed elegantly into the hallway.

She was wearing a red woollen dress that clung to her figure like a second skin, with a wide gold belt round her slim waist, an ensemble that worked well with her cascade of long, beige-highlighted caramel hair.

Her hand-made Italian black leather shoes zoomed her up a few notches to five feet ten, give or take a whisker, and at that precise moment she held a glass of Sauvignon Blanc between her beautifully manicured fingers.

Mondaine? You bet! Nothing tawdry about Chessie. She has an inherent gift for showing herself off whilst being completely unaware that she is doing it, and her lissom figure would make any couturier's mouth water. She is probably the most polished gemstone among the group, and certainly the nearest I shall ever get to having a sister.

Chessie is the one person I can ring in the middle of the night; that important person you can trust with anything. The two of us even finish sentences for each other when we speak.

Only Chessie could open a door with such panache, as she did just then – none of the others was in the same league – and a gust of cold air blew through the flat, causing a door to bang somewhere and make the kitchen curtains flutter wildly in front of the barely-open window. The apple cake was doing nicely on its own by this time, so I had the chance to pay more attention to the large visitor framed in the open doorway.

Actually, had I been asked, I fully expected it to be number fifteen of our happy band, another female of similar age and disposition, but I was wrong. This one was male and it threw me for a moment. I carefully wiped my hands on a towel and made my way down the hallway towards him.

As I approached, I thought for a moment that a Hollywood A-Lister had flown into town and had decided to put in an appearance, because here was a fabulous-looking guy, weak-at-the-knees stunning if I was being honest. Covertly taking in his appearance, I told myself that I ought to be taking more notice of what is on the inside of a wrapper at my age, rather than be taken in by silver paper and glitter.

Weighing men up on a scale of 1 to 10 hasn't done me one iota of good so far. Two serious boyfriends; no wedding ring. Turner Cooper and ... and ... Who the devil was the other one? Damn! I can't even remember his name. Drew something or other. Maybe I am trying to block him out because he was so awful.

Wrapper apart, this one looked, well, lost.

His head of thick grey-sprinkled hair might well have been completely dark at some time, and I put him in his mid-forties. A less-than-confident gleam in his pale brown eyes, he was effusively giving the tall woman standing in front of him the benefit of a set of exquisitely capped teeth, and obviously doing his best to win her over.

Worth mentioning here that Chessie is not the easiest person to get on with, but when she is on somebody else's territory it is noticeable that she tries harder.

'Hello, I am Richard.'

The stranger had a rich baritone voice and what most people, including me, would call a sexy smile. The boyish face gave a lie to salt and pepper hair.

Chessie's body language was more of a *'So what?'* but what she actually said was, 'Hello Richard. And what can we do for you?'

Elegant and assertive, she speaks with aristocratic vowels and has the natural confidence of a thoroughbred pony who can't stop winning races.

On a personal note, I pity anyone who has the temerity to cross her, and today she held herself ramrod straight and kept her poker face calm. Richard could not fail to be impressed – I know I was. His eyes widened slightly and he took in the dazzling female in front of him, a smile pasted firmly on his face.

'Richard Mason,' he said. He made it sound like a question.

Something clicked and I hurriedly smoothed my egg-stained apron as best I could and went to meet him properly, holding out my hand. The penny had dropped. I concealed my sympathy for Chessie's cool reception and allowed a big smile to lighten my face.

'Yes, of course, Richard. Richard Mason. Virginia's husband.'

It would be true to say that I probably went a bit over the top in my haste to be hospitable, but I wanted to show this man that Virginia's school pals knew how to conduct themselves properly in company, and that he had not suddenly encountered a couple of hostile Amazons. On the other hand, how were we supposed to know who he was? Neither of us had ever met him before.

'Please, come in.'

Behind our visitor's broad back, Chessie wrinkled her nose but magnanimously stepped to one side to allow him further access into the hall. This was when he came into full view, stepping over the threshold and making my miniscule domain look even smaller than it really was. He towered above us and offered a firm handshake with no sign of nervousness in his attitude now. He was evidently used to lots of attention.

Chessie was rather more reserved: she eyed Richard up and down before she would let him anywhere near her hand.

It was then that I realised the full implication of his being here. The door was still ajar and I excitedly peeped over his shoulder, fully expecting our well-mannered school buddy to emerge from behind the bushes and walk briskly up the garden path.

But there was no friendly voice, no stylish wave from a super-chic female coming up the drive, bottle under her arm and a carrier bag in her hand filled with fairy cakes. No refined giggle from the school pal we hadn't seen for two years because this husband of hers has whisked her off in his search for a new life on the other side of the world.

It all gave rise to speculation that this man's personal attitude to girlie events might be responsible for her non-appearance.

But of course, that was hardly likely to be the case, and somewhat uncharitable when you weigh it up. Virginia's mother had lived with them in the Lake District until her accident, hadn't she, so the man couldn't have been much of an awkward so-and-so to mind about female reunions.

By now, I was frantically hopping around on tiptoe so I could see over the hedge. It made Richard chuckle indulgently. Even his laughter was soft and warm as a hot summer day.

'Is Virginia still in the car?'

'No. I am awfully sorry. That is exactly why I am here: just to say sorry. We are only in England on a flying visit to see a cousin who is in hospital in Scotland. He is terminally ill y'know. Virginia has some legal matters to discuss about property that happens to be in both their names. I had to see somebody in the City yesterday, so I came down on the train and offered to pop in to see you before I went back to Glasgow. Actually, she did promise faithfully to ring while I was here.'

He didn't sound particularly perturbed about the cousin; but he retrieved his mobile phone from his pocket and waved it about to make sure he had a signal (presumably for our benefit). His attitude came across loud and clear that his wife was the important one here.

Chessie frowned. 'You could have come another day you know; it didn't have to be today. Virginia has already emailed us to say she was unlikely to make it this year as Canada has got a firm grip on her.'

Richard's smile remained friendly and his eyes softened at that, but it was obvious that he would not look forward to a journey from Glasgow to London, plus returns, twice in a few days. He looked contrite.

'We really don't have time, I'm afraid. We fly home tomorrow, but I'm sure she will ring.'

He couldn't have looked more apologetic as he put the mobile back into his trouser pocket. Chessie closed the door to stop any more of the chilly wind getting in, and pulled the curtain neatly across the glass, giving the hall a chance to feel warm and homely again.

'That's a shame. Never mind, tell her we will be in touch in the usual way.'

He flashed another friendly smile and nodded, then surprised the two of us by placing a large box of Belgian chocolates on the table next to the telephone.

He cast a doubtful glance at the box. 'I hope there's enough to go round.' Nice gesture.

'How very kind of you, Richard, thank you. Look, I am forgetting my manners. Do you have time to meet everyone properly and have a drink?'

He looked at his watch before casually taking off his thick camel coat.

The designer label suit and leather shoes looked expensive to my uncultured taste, but Chessie, who has a top-notch job in the fashion world and is at this point in her life on the highest rung of the couture game, probably knew down to the last penny what everything cost.

Richard was seemingly not in too much of a rush and I made small talk as I carefully – very carefully (and delicately) – draped his coat on a hanger and hung it on the rack in the hall. I would hate to spoil it. Who was it who said 'Clothes maketh the man'? Never mind who, just 'What a man!'

Chessie would have weighed up his appearance in a flash, of course: gunmetal grey silk scarf looped over a black roll-necked silk shirt, plus the fact that everything was one hundred per cent authentic. She liked a man to have flair, even though whatever charisma this particular man exuded, the individual on the inside was still not her type.

She took a sip of her drink and fixed her eyes on him over the rim of her glass. Charming. Yes, that was the word. Richard was a man who was at ease with himself and aware of others. We always said that Virginia deserved the best: liquid gold ran through her veins and her mother had brought her up to know that she could have anything money could buy, so he was just right.

Neither of us knew what Richard did for a living, and it would have been tactless to ask, even though we were both dying to know. I was, anyway; I can only guess that Chessie was just as curious.

For as long as we had known her, Virginia never talked about anything as vulgar as money, but by the look of things a healthy bank balance was part of Richard's overall picture.

On the other hand, she would not have been mean with her mother's inheritance: Flora Winters had provided well for her daughter.

Richard's entrance into the female-infested lounge caused a bit of a stir. Girlish chatter suddenly ground to a halt mid-squawk as he was introduced, and he became the cynosure of another thirteen pairs of eyes. He stood in the doorway and nodded Hello before entering.

It was like a flock of birds watching their male counterpart strutting his stuff, but some unspoken command eventually ended the brief silence. The murmuring began again, and Lucy (short for Lucinda) resumed her self-imposed role as head waitress in charge of all things edible. She usually keeps us in order. She teaches a class of six-year-olds Monday to Friday and says they are a doddle compared with a gaggle of women who never stop talking.

Brandishing a bottle in each hand, she looked at our latest guest and said in the didactic tones of her profession, 'Red or white?'

'Oh, all right then. Just the one. Red please.'

CHAPTER THREE

It seemed ages since male urbanity inhabited my lounge and, frankly, I found it intoxicating. Richard had the knack of speaking to each one of us as though she were the most important person in the room—some people have that gift, some don't – but he was good at it. He managed to give everyone a flash of twinkling eyes that made you want to melt into them and divulge all your secrets.

Not sure whether anyone else noticed, but even some of Virginia's mannerisms seemed to have rubbed off on him as well. Things like the way he held his head forward, eyebrows raised, and said '*Really?*' when he wanted to emphasise his interest in what one of us said. The hand gestures, the eye-to-eye contact: they were all a reflection of our absent friend. It was quite uncanny.

In point of fact, I was slightly annoyed that some of my friends became a little coy and flirty. After all, he was Virginia's husband and there are rules about such things, but I was glad to see that Chessie eventually put her skittishness to one side and joined in the general hubbub. She is always very protective of our reunions and Richard was an interloper, after all.

'Virginia is blooming,' he said when we asked how she was. 'Happier than she has ever been since the unfortunate events of the past few years. I'm convinced that life in Canada is having a therapeutic effect; it's one of the most beautiful places you could ever wish to see. She has made lots of friends and we regularly have people round for a meal.'

He was making me happier by the minute. Virginia has a master-class understanding of food and drink, so having friends round for dinner would allow her to shine. I found his words strangely comforting. It really did seem as though her bad luck had turned.

He went on to describe where they lived, miles away from civilization by the sound of things, and his tanned complexion spoke of an outdoor life. There was a thoughtful look on his face when he stared into space; it was as though he did not want to miss anything out.

As for me, I took time to picture what he was saying, and imagine a chalet-type house with a large garden, plenty of trees and a nearby stream (he called it a creek). Did his words conjure up for the others, as they did for me, a vision of our friend pottering around the shrubbery with two Pyrenean mountain dogs, or strolling down to the creek in her homespun gingham Sunday best? She would no doubt giggle and say, 'Oh this old rag.'

She had always been a bit of a nomad, even as a youngster, and would have accepted new life thousands of miles away from the land of her birth without a qualm.

Richard's mobile phone suddenly rang, making me jump out of my reverie. He gave a sudden shout of enthusiasm and shot to his feet immediately. He retrieved the phone and flicked it open, moving around the room to get a good signal. Eventually, he found his way into the hallway and we could hear the animated voice of a one-sided conversation.

'Hello! Hello! Are you still there?'

After a minute or two he came back into the lounge with an exasperated look on his face.

'A bit of bad luck there, guys. She is somewhere in the wilds of Scotland and there is a problem with the signal.

'Bad weather and all that, by the sound of it, but I'm sure she'll ring again in a minute. She has her laptop with her as well, so I think she will get in touch somehow or other before the day is out.'

He seemed a bit agitated underneath; perhaps he worried about her and was understandably anxious about her being on her own. I liked that.

For the second time that afternoon, Chessie involuntarily said, 'Oh, that's a shame. Let's hope she gets through properly next time.'

The day wore on and Lucy kept re-filling his glass with something that she insisted was non-alcoholic because he said he wanted to keep his head in order. After two glasses, he smiled genially at the blonde sitting next to him: she was holding an open photograph album on her lap.

'I don't usually drink this stuff, you know, but it's actually quite nice after a few glasses. I might get a few bottles to take back home.' He nodded towards the children who stared curiously out from the colourful pages of her album. 'No need to ask your name. You must be September Day. Lovely month, September. Lovely name.' He pronounced it slowly, rolling it around his tongue.

September smirked. 'Dad's choice, Richard, the name, I mean. Because I was born in September. My mother, bless her, said she didn't care one way or the other what month it was; she was just glad the whole ghastly experience was behind her. They never imagined for one minute that I would marry somebody called William Day, so here I am, lumbered with a name that gets me funny looks. It's dad's fault, really.'

I marvel at this woman, you know. She is the only one amongst us who managed to find her perfect future straight from school: six children all under the age of fifteen, and every one of them an angel to be admired. Typical sheep, too, Chinese astrologically speaking: kind to a fault and the biggest worrier around. She swells with pride when anybody admires her brood.

Somebody continued the theme about parents and children, and when the name 'Mrs Winters' came into the conversation, Richard's face shadowed a little.

'Ah yes, my mother-in-law.' Long pause and you could see he was choosing his words carefully. 'It took a while for Virginia to recover, you know, losing her mother in such a freak accident. It was a terrible shock to all of us. Myself as much as anybody.'

He shook his head, but the distraught look that came over his face was so slight I think I was probably the only one who noticed.

'I'm only glad she had people like you here to confide in.' He forced his lips into a kind of smile before saying, 'Now let me guess which one of you was close enough to be her special friend when she was at school. She used to talk a lot about a nickname. Bunter, or something. No, wait a minute. Bunty, wasn't it? Yes. That was it. *Bunty.*'

Lucy helped herself to another caramel slice and Richard glanced round expectantly as a roomful of blank faces stared back at him. Some of them would not have known Virginia at school anyway.

He pursued his train of thought. 'A lot of you had nicknames, didn't you? Now, I can figure out Carrots because that's easy.' He laughingly lifted a finger and pointed at Josephine (Sophe, to us), whose auburn hair had not yet lost the thick lustre of her youth.

Sophe looked round with a grin on her face. 'I remember that Chessie was known as Moody because, well, that's what she used to be, and Sam was Dodo because she lived in the stone age. Still gets a bit jumpy about anything new. Our private website is a traumatic experience for her.'

Samantha raised her chin tartly at that. 'I'm not happy with the jargon you all use. I know that Elise and Alexandra were really clever to design the program in the first place, but I find it hard enough to log on to the main page without having to deal with all the extras. You know I have an inherent scepticism for anything to do with computers; I even have a hard time programming the TV recorder.'

She received a sympathetic glance from Richard, and Alexandra said, 'My younger brother called me Andra when he was a toddler, and it's kinda stuck. I think he was trying for the full name but couldn't quite make it. You must appreciate, Richard, I wasn't born into this lot,' she waved her arms expansively at the others. 'I came along much later. I'm a colleague of Elise's from Business College in Speyside.'

This must have been the longest speech we had heard from Andra all afternoon. She was the least loquacious of our bunch and would most likely be throwing all these comments into the various cubby holes of her mind. A female version of James, in fact, if such an animal existed.

Richard gave us one his bonhomie smiles. 'You all took it in good part, but who *was* Bunty?'

I greedily helped myself to a third dish of the trifle that September had brought with her, before shrugging my shoulders and saying I had no idea. The others looked, in turn, equally nonplussed and Chessie furrowed her brow.

'It's not a name we used at school,' she replied eventually. 'Perhaps it was a friend from the playgroup where Virginia used to work.'

I had to smile as our memories floated to the top, and I homed in first on Chessie, my cerebral pal with the catwalk gait, aquamarine eyes and pear-shaped face that owes its glowing skin to gloriously expensive creams and treatments.

She uses fake tan, of course, we all know that, so she always looks as though she has just returned from a holiday abroad. The nose job has been a success, too. Cure for a breathing problem rather than for vanity. Definitely a little more retroussé since the op, but in any case, what was a little surgery these days?

I glanced at the others: All weathered rather well, come to think of it. An amalgam of interests and lifestyles, a couple of divorces and re-marriages, nobody was seriously overweight, and some of them grudgingly confessed years ago to having problems that had ended with the surgeon's knife.

And what about me? Well trained but jobless. No partner or husband. The class live wire at school and destined to be successful, or so they used to say. Look at me now: unequivocally scrap heap material. A pariah.

The gossip began as soon as Richard left and closed the door behind him.

'Wasn't it a pity that Virginia didn't manage to get through to us again?' Chessie said thoughtfully. 'I would love to have heard her voice. I really miss her at these get-togethers, you know.'

'We all do,' I sighed, 'but never mind. Let's have some more champagne. Nobody is driving home, after all.'

We screamed with laughter as the cork flew wildly across the room.

CHAPTER FOUR

September and Chessie had arranged to stay overnight, and it was just before eleven o'clock by the time the others had been whisked away by their respective partners, husbands, etc. September was in the process of saying goodnight to her eldest on her mobile, while Chessie absently paged through a fashion magazine on the sofa next to her.

I contemplated the formation of rune stones that was laid out on the table in front of me, and stifled a yawn that had been steadily building up since the others left.

To me, rune stones are similar to a logic puzzle: each symbol has a meaning, which, when put together, builds into a story. Least that's what normally happens, but my vibes must have deserted me tonight because they made no sense at all. It was so frustrating.

'My brain has gone AWOL, Chessie; I just can't see the bigger picture in this lot. I've been searching through my reference book for ideas as well, but it's no help. The job-changing rune keeps turning up though, which has got to be extremely fortunate under the present circumstances, don't you think?'

Chessie ignored the intended sarcasm in my voice and pointed across the table.

'That one looks like the kiss-cross you put after your name.'

Not much help there then.

'That's exactly what it is – the friendship rune. Except that the one next to it is reversed, which turns any sign of friendship into a problem.

'Whatever else you can say about all those soothsayers in the olden days, they certainly earned their keep.'

I gathered up my stones and put them into their velvet pouch. Chessie looked at her watch and then grinned wickedly.

'I noticed you cleared them away rather smartish when Richard was here, darling. Could it be that the gorgeous Mr Mason is responsible for your lack of primordial intuition?'

I gave her a sour frown. 'As you know perfectly well, I'm happy to have sceptics around, and I know it's all a bit of a charade, but normally I can turn it into a game and we can still have fun. Richard just had a strange effect on me: he made me feel I was doing something silly, that's all.'

She dropped the magazine on to the coffee table and her eyebrows rose in amazement. 'Don't prevaricate. You've never done anything silly since you fell off your bike when you were eleven. You just don't like showing off, that's your trouble.'

'That was kid-stuff. This is now. It's all a bit confusing when the stones don't add up. Tonight, to coin a phrase, they have gone barmy. I must be tired.'

'It's not midnight yet,' Chessie protested scornfully. 'I'm just waking up.'

Eyes skyward, I heaved another big sigh and carried our empty coffee mugs into the kitchen where the dishwasher was dutifully swishing its fourth load of the day.

'I'll go and make sure your beds are ready,' I said when I returned. 'Must say, I am ready for a good night's sleep myself. This crick in my neck is telling me it's been a long day.'

'Bring your photo box, will you, darling,' Chessie called out as I left the room, 'I feel like a good long delve into the past.

'It's Sunday tomorrow, so no one has to get up for work.' A theatrical groan from me only brought on the response, 'Oops! Sorry! That was thoughtless of me. I forgot.' Still no news on the work front for me, and Christmas was fast approaching.

I popped along the corridor, stopping first in the guest bedroom to straighten the duvets and make sure everything was tidy, and as I drew the curtains, I watched the first snowflakes of the year floating past the window, as promised by the weatherman.

I like this time of year: it reminds me of the warm feeling of woolly hats and thick jumpers, long walks with school friends in the countryside when we chatted eagerly about Christmas that was just around the corner, and then returning home, cheeks bright red, to buttered crumpets and a fire crackling in the fireplace. No worries about life's problems in those halcyon days.

I switched on the table lamp between the twin beds and fiddled unnecessarily with a couple of magazines on the shelf. Things have to be neat. James used to say, 'It is not so much where to *put* things, Elise, as *where you would like to find them later.*'

Turner, of course, had been to a different school; he didn't 'do' tidy. Even a pile of clothes screwed up on the floor was an art form.

Switching off the light, I then went to my own bedroom a little further down the corridor.

The large shoebox at the bottom of my wardrobe had originally contained a pair of knee-length boots but was now heavy with tatty scraps of memorabilia from thirty-odd years of my life. It contained all manner of important documents, as well as snippets that might be described as rubbish.

There were letters and school snapshots ... recipes ... newspaper articles ... newsy items about the reunion group. Stuff that would be of little interest to anybody else, I suppose.

I still don't know why I keep old train tickets and menus from restaurants. It's only sentimental scrap. I fully intended to sort out or even destroy some of it when I have time, but for the moment I was still busy at the office, frantically trying to finish projects and tie up loose ends before I left.

So, my cardboard box might be an untidy mess, but at least I know where everything is. I carefully fished out the items that were surplus to Chessie's requirements and dumped it all on the floor by the side of my bed, squaring up some of the letters with my hand as I went along. I could sort them all out properly later, so I turned off all the lights and carried the box, now containing only photographs, through to the living room.

September was domestically satisfied that her brood was happy when I posed the question and placed my shoebox ceremoniously on the table. I then went to brew more coffee: it looked like being a long night and those two were still mulling over the day as though it were the first reunion we had ever had.

I earwigged their conversation from the kitchen: it was obviously about Virginia.

'I remember her first husband because we all went to the wedding,' September's curtain of shiny hair hid her face as she stared down at her hands. 'I don't think any of us went to this second one, did we? She kept it quiet, as I remember. Love at first sight. I must say, she certainly knows how to pick photogenic blokes for husbands, doesn't she? I thought her first one was delicious, but this one is stunning. Poor Richard! Just fancy, having to contend with a roomful of women.'

'A computer geek,' Chessie said dryly. 'He seemed to know more about our website than I do, but then again I'm not particularly technical. Virginia must talk about us a lot: he seemed to know every detail about what we had all been doing for the past year.'

'Yes, I picked that up, too,' September remarked. 'He told some funny jokes, though. I really must write them down before I go to sleep tonight or I shall forget the punch lines and I want to tell Bill. He'll howl at the one about the wide-mouthed frog.'

Chessie riffled enthusiastically through the box and pulled the pile of photos on to her lap.

'Where shall we start? Oh, just look at this one—'

Raucous comments rang out over the noise of the singing kettle, and I returned to giddy laughter as I carried fresh supplies of coffee back into the lounge.

'I just hope you two realise how precious that box is to me, so don't you go knocking it about. It's already sticky-taped beyond recognition and it's one of the first things I shall pick up if ever there is a fire. I shall take my mother's lacquered writing box, as well. And her portable sewing machine. Always supposing I shall be in a fit state to carry them with all that smoke around. If I keep adding to the list at this rate, I reckon my arms will be full, come the day I launch myself through the flames.'

They were cackling like a couple of old hens as they ransacked the box and I joined in when we looked at the older ones.

'Speaking of Richard,' I picked up the threads of what they had been talking about. 'Virginia used to steer clear of mechanical things, she was more the domestic science type, so if he helps her to use our website then he's bound to become familiar with what we put on there.

'She was really in love with him when they got married, as I recall. Don't you remember how she told us she had met this fantastic man and they were a real together couple? A coming together of two minds and hearts, I think she said.'

Chessie treated us to one of her 'heard-it-all-before' looks and rearranged herself on the sofa so she could spread everything out properly. 'Know what I think?' she said. 'I think they are so wrapped up in each other that the rest of us have to take a back seat. Haven't you noticed that she doesn't go on the website to send messages all that much nowadays? Once a month at the last count.'

'Yes, but she's always bright and cheerful when she does,' September put in. 'They're like a pair of lovebirds; he dotes on her. He was so anxious when she rang.' Her face took on a dreamy look. 'Maybe they will have lots of children,' she added with a happy sigh.

Chessie received a quelling glance from me when she began to play an invisible violin, but September continued to ramble on, oblivious of any sarcasm floating on the air. 'Well, she must confide in him all the time. I don't think we said anything that he didn't already know. He must have an incredible memory; even I can't remember half the stuff I've written on my web page.'

I knew what she meant. We may have moved into the Twenty-first Century paperless, but I really ought to clear off some of the older stuff. There is loads of junk on there; it is getting very cluttered. 'I'll get Andra to give me a hand,' I said.

'Snail mail will never die,' quoted September in that judicious tone she sometimes adopts, but her words reflected the view of some of our friends who resolutely refuse to use the Internet (or even a computer in some cases) and still send letters by post.

Chessie picked up a photograph of a happy teenage Virginia: long dark hair, a fey look in her soft grey eyes that the camera always captured so successfully. September's brows knitted together.

'What exactly are we looking for, Chessie?'

'Virginia's first wedding photo, of course, darling. The one with all of us on it; don't be obtuse. Ah yes. Here it is. Tom and Virginia.' She held it out.

Virginia's first wedding day, almost thirteen years ago. The black and white professional print was blurred with creases and the groom's face was hardly recognizable. We were all dolled up in our best clothes and fancy hats, but it was so long ago that we looked outdated. The good part was that we looked younger: twenty-two at the time. Virginia had sent a copy to everybody in the group, but this particular photo had been manhandled many times.

'He was too young to die,' Chessie said compassionately as she accurately stirred four drops of milk into her coffee – always four, never three or five. No one liked to ask why. 'Tom, I mean. Burned to death in a car crash when he was only twenty-eight, along with their daughter. Little Jennifer was only three.'

September pulled a face. 'Then Flora Winters trips and falls down a rock face in the Lake District while she is out fell-walking. It must be awful to lose your family at any time, particularly in an accident, but to lose three of your nearest and dearest in such a short space of time must be shattering.'

'Puts my own dreary situation into perspective,' I said bitterly.

'You knew her better than any of us, Elise, didn't you?' September said.

'Hmn. Yeah. Her father died when we were both three. She lived with her mother in an enormous house, as I remember, but for some reason I can't picture Flora Winters all that clearly.

'What I remember most about her is that she used to drag Virginia off abroad, mostly at the end of term, but also whenever the opportunity cropped up. Cultural holidays, she called them: Egypt, Rome, Australia and such. She probably thought the girl would turn into a rebel if she saw too much of me.'

'I thought you used to go to parties at their house, darling,' Chessie said, and I nodded.

'Sometimes. They had a regiment of servants to look after everything: caterers, cleaners, conjurers to entertain us, that kind of thing. I remember once when Virginia somehow managed to get herself locked in a cupboard and almost screamed the place down.' I allowed a small detail that must apply to millions of people: 'Been afraid of the dark ever since.' A few unwholesome thoughts followed, till I pulled myself back on track. 'But as for her mother, you know, now I think about it, I only ever saw Mrs Winters waving us off from a window when it was time to go home.'

I directed my gaze down to Flora in her glamorous finery and a posh hat that would probably leave little change from a computer programmer's monthly salary.

'All I can dredge up is a lady in a hat. This occasion. This hat.' I tapped the photograph and handed it back. 'We never really knew her, did we?'

'She would have been in her mid-sixties now,' said September. 'Suicide, they whispered, though the Coroner decided it was a tragic accident. Virginia and Richard moved to Canada soon afterwards, didn't they? None of us could get to the funeral, as I remember, because we were on holiday at the time.'

Chessie shuddered and placed the photograph back on the top of the pile as though it had suddenly become hot. 'It's not fair, is it, for one family to have so much misfortune? Let's hope Richard brings her good luck.'

The following morning, we all claimed to have slept well, and it was a little shy of eight o'clock when September's taxi arrived to take her to Euston station.

There was no sign of last evening's sprinkling of snow. Bells pealed solemnly nearby, reminding the whole street that it was Sunday and the residents ought to be thinking of going to church, but apart from the odd muffled up person carrying a newspaper, there was a general absence of activity.

The knock on the door made September hurriedly spring to attention. For somebody who was used to sorting out the lives of six children and two dogs, plus organizing the diary of her dentist husband, she always got herself into a fluster when she was with us.

First her overnight case. Then her handbag. Where were her gloves?

Chessie and I threw on our coats as well so we could go outside and wave properly.

'Right girls. I'm off. Bill said he would meet me in Manchester and it will put him in a bad temper if I miss the train. Thank you for yesterday, Elise, I shall definitely have a go at Sophe's luscious broccoli salad when I get home. It probably won't be as nice as hers, but Bill will say he likes it anyway: he always does.'

We hugged and pecked.

'I'll give you a ring; let you know I arrived OK. And don't be depressed about your little stones playing silly devils yesterday. I thought they were very promising. There is something in the air, I can feel it.'

'Yes, darling,' Chessie replied tartly, wrapping her faux fur closer and pulling a grim face. 'It's called frost.'

September is my biggest fan when it comes to telling fortunes. She takes it for granted that there is something or someone out there in the greater universe that most people hadn't latched on to, but seeing as I am the nearest she will ever get to being in touch with the supernatural, she gives me the hat to wear.

She showed a row of beautiful teeth (courtesy of her husband's colleague) and blew strands of white breath into the air as we all hurried down the path.

The patient Mr Taxi-Man carried her case to the car. It had been a slow morning for him so far and he had nothing else worthwhile to do. Besides, this woman might be someone important. The clothes were like those in the magazines his girlfriend drooled over when she had nothing better to do – expensive – and his fare definitely looked the part of a celebrity.

She might be flying off to the other side of the world to sort out a diplomatic crisis for all he knew. She only had one case with her, though. Probably not. The girls back at base always laughed at his imaginings.

As though they hadn't exhausted all topics of conversation yesterday, the women were still sorting their diaries, much to his amusement. He twiddled the knobs on his radio, using his code name to the girl on the other end and saying something saucy that was unlikely to be understood by anyone listening in.

His passenger stepped out on to the pavement at last, blowing kisses into the air to the other two, so he cut the radio with a smart punch of the button, and got out to open the back door.

She was still waving to her pals out of the back window as they drove down the street and out of sight, which made him feel important. He loved this job.

Chessie left on foot half an hour later, with much less kerfuffle let it be said, and I prepared to go out for my daily jog.

Running used to be part of my weight-reducing regime, but that's all in the past now: previous diets and exercise would never have accomplished what Turner managed to achieve in thirty minutes. The inches have vanished from my waistline and my former pear-shaped hips have diminished dramatically by two sizes in less than three months.

My metabolism has taken up the challenge and now jogging is for fun.

It was afternoon by the time I sent an email to Virginia, who, Richard had emphasised more than once yesterday, had brought her laptop with her.

Her email reply came back within minutes, so she must have been online, and it was in the old-fashioned tone that was so much part of her character.

> *Hi Elise,* she had typed.
> *Yes. Seeing my cousin for what will probably be the last time was quite devastating, but extremely useful. We used to have joint ownership of some land on the outskirts of Windermere, and we were able to sort everything out this weekend so that it is all now in my name.*

Thank you for making Richard feel welcome. He told me about his visit and how nice you had all been to him. Perhaps I shall make it to the next reunion. Much Love V x

Some hopes. I wrote back. I was about to add a personal comment about Richard, but something held me back and I signed off in the usual way. Chessie was right, the woman had already had her share of bad luck. It was to be hoped that the jinx on her family had run its course with Richard's introduction into her life.

I picked up the box of photographs still on the table from last night and took it back into the bedroom, where I gingerly replaced the old letters and notes I had left on the floor, smoothing out the creases as I did so. The one on the top of the pile just happened to be from Virginia, written when we were both about ten, and I smiled at the childish handwriting.

We go back a long way, Virginia and I. Playschool back in Norfolk, before we joined infant-cum-junior school on the exact same day. Two wide-eyed five-year-olds with freshly scrubbed faces; two identical navy-blue tunics and red jumpers.

We seemed to get along so well, as I remember, even at such an early age: so much so that we spent many of our formative years declaring eternal friendship and sharing secrets.

In fact, the only difference that I can recall (apart from the size of our houses) was that a chauffeur-driven car would whisk her off to her parents' mansion at three-thirty in the afternoon after school on the dot and I would walk home with the other children down our street.

We used to write to each other often in those early days because we agreed that it was fun to listen to the exciting clatter of the letterbox when the postman pushed things through.

Lately, it is only the humming of a computer, because we haven't communicated either by post or even spoken on the telephone for about two years.

I couldn't help opening the letter quickly to remind myself of the contents. It was nothing special, only one of our regular little chats on paper, but it began:

My dearest Bunty ...

CHAPTER FIVE

Where were all these offers in reply to my job applications? Nothing landed on my doormat except junk mail. You could almost say that my credentials as a businesswoman with both feet on the ground had disappeared overnight, and, though I wouldn't say it out loud, I privately admitted to feeling mentally battered.

Christmas is usually the time when I move in with my uncle and aunt for a few days, and there was no valid reason why this year should be any different – certainly not because I was unemployed anyway. I still think of their lovely house in Norfolk as my retreat, if only because it was the peaceful sanctuary where I grew up.

My life would have been cut short prematurely had it not been for the fact that Charles and Millie had been looking after me on that disastrous day thirty-four years ago when both my parents got themselves killed by a runaway lorry during a thunderstorm. Their little car was a write-off but the other driver miraculously escaped unhurt.

It seems that we lived somewhere in the Midlands at the time, but we were on holiday with my father's younger brother and his wife at their house in Wells-next-the-Sea. At ten months, I would most likely have been indifferent to the accident that had mercilessly claimed the lives of my parents, and I have since looked on Charles and Millie as surrogate parents because I can remember no other.

My memories are their memories. *Speech Days … Sports Days … Amateur Dramatics*. It's all there.

Millie's cheeks would be flushed and she wiped her eyes a lot, whatever I happened to be doing, whether it be singing, running or play-acting. If she was proud of me, then I was doubly proud of her.

Having said that, my reminiscences of Charles are deeply embedded inside me, too, memories that are more of the DIY kind – the two of us tinkering with cars or mending watches, kind of thing.

My career tutor at school once said that I would have made a more than adequate garage apprentice by the time I left school, and I often I wonder if that was what led me to take computers to bits, to see how they work. Got to be a message in there somewhere.

Charles is now an enigmatic late seventy-something who looks good for his age: no bags under his steely blue eyes, tall and thin as a lat, hair that has changed from lamp black to an extremely handsome gunmetal grey over the years. He hasn't slowed down at all either, mentally, and the only medication I have ever seen him take is a ventilator for his asthma.

Charles only ever loved two women in his life: Millie and me. Not even his own mother, rest her soul, could compete, but then again, she made no attempt to cover up the fact that she preferred his older brother, John, my father.

My dad's premature death would most likely have come as nasty shock, an unforgivable blast from the gods from which she never recovered, and poor Charles was left to pick up the pieces.

Which he did. Without a murmur.

So, there they were on Christmas Day, cheering me on. It was good to talk about the upside downs and wrong side outs of life; they referred to my recent comings and goings as signposts.

We were walking along the pebbly beach after an enormous lunch at the local pub, followed by a good deal too much to drink. A chilly but lovely day. A good time to forget work and become utterly immersed in a world that did not revolve around my earning capabilities.

Charles had his scratched old binoculars round his neck and was wearing a battle-scarred green waxed jacket that amazingly still fitted him after all these years. Millie and I trailed alongside, shrouded deep in colourful fisherman knits (her) and sombre-hued waterproofs (me).

'Has he given you his key back?' Charles asked. His mind, protective as ever on my behalf, was on Turner.

'Oh yes, yes! No problem there. The landlord changed the locks as soon as I explained what had happened. He said he does it as a matter of course to prevent people sneaking back in to do nasties: I think he was just trying to stop me worrying.'

'I wonder how many tenants try to return for a bit of revenge vandalism,' Millie pondered absently, treading artistic footprints in the sand and then savagely kicking at a pebble that was in her way, 'That young man simply wasn't good enough for you, you know: we always said so. You should have had the gumption to throw him out years ago.'

She linked my arm and squeezed gently through two lots of padding and we dodged over the strandline on the beach, almost trotting along and giggling like schoolgirls.

'Things happen for a reason,' she said at last, and I could tell she was going to give me one of her well-worn pragmatic theories. 'Life is too short for you to stand still, my dear. A change of job will do you good.

'Think of it as an opportunity to develop your talents. Or is it to follow your star?' her face twisted into a thoughtful frown. 'I can never remember.'

As well as the outlandishly colourful jacket she was wearing today, Millie also had a bright pink nose and sparkling eyes; nothing to do with the four glasses of wine with lunch, she declared, it was just a bracing day. Actually, she drinks like a fish, but on the plus side, medically speaking, she has never smoked.

'Finding a new job isn't easy,' I sighed when we slowed the pace again. 'The right ones are in the wrong place, and vice versa, but I have plenty of scouts sussing things out for me. James is networking his old buddies, so I shouldn't have too much difficulty getting fixed up. Bound to be only a temporary glitch. What I really need is a modicum of good luck.'

I forestalled her worries about money by saying I wasn't flat broke, and that my bank book wouldn't be catching a chill just yet, thanks to Charles's financial wizardry at keeping an eye on my investments.

Between bouts of fresh-air silence and deep breathing, all three of us came up with ideas, some non-runners and most outrageously silly, although we all agreed that a regular income was of prime importance and high on the list. The near future was still a blur, though.

New Year frivolity came along soon enough with everyone's stubborn affirmation that the world was definitely not going to come to an end at the end of March.

I was not completely convinced. With each day that passed, I was becoming more and more certain that the great Administration Manager in the sky still had me on his list of '*Unemployables*'.

CHAPTER SIX

I must have perused the letter from the solicitor at least a dozen times before the mystifying message finally sank in.

It was early January when it dropped through the letterbox; the time when I had switched on to auto-pilot as far as work was concerned and was still trawling through the Sits Vac ads.

Three brief paragraphs on heavy-quality cream paper with the firm's name embossed at the top. Whoever had signed it was plainly unable to make his signature legible, but the paper itself was still in pristine condition despite being well-scrutinized by me and shuffled around so much recently in my bag.

My brain was jumping like a firecracker when I met Chessie in town for a bite to eat and said, 'To be honest, I thought it might be some silly prank of September's, just to give credence to her comments about premonitions in the air.'

She peered at me suspiciously. 'You haven't been at the fish paste again have you? If it's a practical joke, darling, I'm sure it isn't from any of *us*. That's ridiculous.' She broke off to accept her avocado and prawn salad from the waitress. 'What about Turner? Doesn't he still work for that stationery firm? He will have access to quality paper.'

'Not like him at all. He may pretend to be one of the lads and zoom around in a noisy sports car with the radio blaring, but he was never into practical jokes as far as I know. In any case, Turner is history. He ended our relationship three months, twelve days, five hours and three minutes ago. Not that I am counting.'

She looked at me thoughtfully and said nothing. Then she turned her attention to the beautiful arrangement of pink and green on her plate.

'Only one way to find out.'

'I knew you'd say that.'

Under cover of tackling my own herb omelette, I watched the dainty way Chessie handled cutlery, in the same calm way she handles herself every day of her life.

We met at Grammar School, let's see ... must be twenty-four years ago now, when we sat next to each other in class. Everybody sat alphabetically in rows and there was nobody else with a name that came between Elise Kent and the girl who would become my best buddy, Francesca Hamilton.

I was the jumpy one: new uniform, new deliciously-smelling leather schoolbag, fresh haircut. I remember it so well. Chessie, similarly turned out, was an enviable picture of composure. Been like that ever since.

Virginia Winters was cool that day, too, as I remember, even though she's a Chinese astrological sheep, (another worrier), but I remember she was happy enough to find herself sitting alongside September Wilding. Virginia was only with us for a few weeks before her mother whipped her off to the Lake District to some private school or other. I remember Millie muttering, 'Hardly worth the trouble of buying a school uniform.'

I detected a glimmer of excitement now in Chessie's violet-shadowed eyes as she pensively re-read my letter.

'Get real, darling. You have a rich uncle. Or,' she added reasonably, 'given the timing, you used to have a rich uncle.'

'Can't be. I only have one uncle and he is very much with us. I'm sure Millie would have at least mentioned something if Charles hadn't made it to the end of last week. I have no rich relatives, dead or otherwise. Interesting though, isn't it? What do you think I should wear? Do you think I should appear penniless, seeing as I am about to be made redundant in the next few weeks, or give the impression that I'm incredibly wealthy anyway and whatever cash this solicitor is about to hand over is only destined to be my slush fund?'

Chessie sipped her glass of water. I was having wine but she was the one on a diet. Correction ... *always* on a diet.

'Now, let's not be silly, darling. You know you haven't got anything that looks remotely wealthy, so I don't think that's on. To say you are handy with a needle, your entire collection of clothing is shabby. And not even shabby-chic. You neglect yourself terribly; you talk to computers as though the rest of the world doesn't exist. Just look at you—'

Justifiable. I was wearing my favourite cardigan: a thick stripy affair that Millie had knitted for me about fifteen years ago, pilled and matted round the elbows now and in the brightest colours imaginable. James wasn't the only one to wear woollen hand-knits at work.

If you took any notice of the ambiguous jokes Chessie throws out from time to time, I was born on the fringes of fashion and never likely to veer anywhere near the centre. Today, she even kindly offered to let me poke around in her fashion department wardrobe for my forthcoming visit to see the solicitor. I must be crisis material: it's not an offer she frequently hands out.

Mind you, it was an empty offer. I am a whole fashion rail away from her gang of stick insects, who could all wear thick tweed suits and still cover themselves in size X-Small overcoats in a blizzard.

When I explained this, she said, 'I thought you said you were down a couple of sizes. We have lots of things that would fit you, you know. Well, one or two, maybe.'

'I do have a decent suit, actually.' It sounded like a forgotten relic even as I said it. 'Paid a lot for it, too, and only wore it once. It put Turner into one of his moods. Blithering idiot!'

'Still bugs you, doesn't he? The degenerate rat.'

I think she might have been referring to Turner's astrological sign, but you can never be sure with Chessie's queer sense of humour. Turner is four years younger than us and comes under the sign of the Chinese Rat, which she has always found amusing.

'Sure. Put it this way, he's a bit like a Sat-Nav: nice to have, but something you can manage well enough without. I'm still looking for someone strong and protective; someone who will gallop down Harlingdon Road and carry me off on a white stallion into the great beyond. Virginia's managed it. Turner wouldn't even look good on a donkey.'

She fiercely shook her head and gave one of her ladylike snorts. 'That's a novel way of looking at romance, darling. Think that, if you want to sleep at night, but it's fairy tale stuff. The truth is much more primitive and down to earth. I've almost had two husbands. *Al-most*. Got out in the nick of time. Believe me, I should know.'

She did, too. You had to admire the way she dodged the matrimonial circuit, yet sailed through relationships like a film star on a mission.

On a more positive note, she graced magazine covers for a decade before she put her money into a modelling agency to help other hopefuls to achieve their dreams of stardom.

Put another way, my friend is a walking crash course in intellectual stability and common sense: everything is now calculated down to the last full stop and her money belt is bulging, which at the age of thirty-five is not bad in my opinion.

I picked up my own wine glass and quickly drained it. I didn't really feel like going back to my goldfish bowl but I had a lot to do.

'Anyway, never mind the toe-rag, what about Messrs Sugden, Sugden & Sharp. What about my windfall?'

'When are you going?'

'Thursday. I'm taking the day off in case it's a long meeting and I fall asleep with boredom. It's also a special time of year for us, remember.'

'Sorry? What's special about it?'

I sometimes get exasperated with my best friend. I must have told her a hundred times, but I decided to bore her again.

'The world will soon move into the Chinese Year of the Monkey. Our sign, Chessie. The year we turn thirty-six. The oracle says that it will be a year for speculating and gambling.'

She looked less than impressed.

CHAPTER SEVEN

Rain ran like crazy paving down my bedroom window on Thursday. The pelting noise brought me to life, which was a good job because I had missed the alarm on my mobile phone.

No, what really happened was that I forgot to take the phone into the bedroom, so it played a rousing march to itself for a couple of minutes on the kitchen table before automatically going into 'Reset' mode.

You-know-who took our proper alarm clock with him. OK, it was his, after all, so I have no right to complain, and I haven't bought another one yet. At least the kettle is mine, and the whole contents of the kitchen. I was still able to fill the percolator and have a cup of coffee and toast.

So that's what I did. Plenty of time before my trip into town.

It felt strange not having someone at my elbow to confide in and I tossed the meagre contents of my wardrobe on to the bed so I could decide for myself what to wear.

One of Turner's good points – and I do have the grace to admit that there were one or two – was that he used to calm me down when I was running late for work. He would always offer to wash the breakfast things before he set off for his own workplace.

Now that I think about it, he probably wanted me out of the way so he could telephone his secretary and say lovey dovey things to her in private before he got to work. Just call me naïve.

At Christmas, when we were talking about men in general and Turner in particular, Millie ventured to say, 'I wonder whether Turner misses your kettle as much as you miss his radio alarm clock.'

I said nothing at the time, but privately added a rider that I wondered whether his secretary bird was a frolicsome spring chicken or a wise old boiler. My fickle mind regularly conjures up an unsavoury picture of the two of them canoodling behind the filing cabinet in her office, but seeing as I haven't a clue what she looks like, the image tends to be a bit fuzzy and I can only see the back of her head.

I parked in a small yard behind the solicitors' office. The grey day persisted and in spite of putting up my umbrella, rivulets of rain ran irritatingly down my neck when I got out and ran round to the main street.

It was a horrid morning; I just hoped it wasn't an omen of more misery still to come.

'Terrible day,' conceded the efficient receptionist when I arrived at the third-floor office and signed in. 'Let me take your wet things, Miss Kent, so you can sit in comfort for a few minutes. Mr Sugden will be ready for you soon.'

She whisked my coat and umbrella away into a small cubby hole nearby, before returning to a busy telephone which never seemed to stop ringing. Must have caused her a degree of frustration, but you had to admire her skill at opening letters at the same time as she projected a calm voice over the telephone.

I looked at my watch. Ten minutes early. Always the same, I'd rather be early than late.

At long last, there was an insistent buzz on her desk and, with a friendly smile, she led me down a brightly-lit corridor to where a tall, thin man dressed in a black suit greeted me at the door of his office and shook my hand.

The jacket was rather longer than I would have expected and he stooped slightly, but although his hand was bony it was surprisingly warm.

'Good morning, Miss Kent. Do come in and sit yourself down.'

Mr Sugden (Leonard to his wife and friends) ushered me into the room and indicated one of the padded chairs by the side of the table.

What a change from the reception area I had just left. I don't know what I expected: lawyers are an unknown bunch to me, so my thoughts are naturally coloured by whatever the TV or film director decides to let me believe.

None of what I was seeing today matched the script. My impression of the man who now seated himself tranquilly opposite me was that he was from another era. Elderly – very elderly – with a scratchy voice and longish silver hair that made him look old-fashioned rather than simply old.

It was as though I had stepped back in time into a Dickensian novel. The room was tidy in a tangled sort of way: huge piles of brown manila files tied up with yards of pink ribbon; dark carpet and walls hidden by floor-to-ceiling bookshelves. An enormous leather-topped table dominated the room, and even the black telephone was one of the old sit-up-and-beg type.

The only thing that saved the office from being gloomy was a large window that looked down on to the main street from its lofty position.

You could see this man was happier with the past. 'Our senior partner,' the receptionist had whispered reverently, and I estimated that he must be at least ninety years old. What were the other partners like? Were they young or were they almost in their dotage, too? This one looked decades older than Charles.

There was no sign of a computer. Such nonsense had been dished out to the office down the corridor where younger mortals hit keys and pressed 'Enter' as though the future of this firm depended on it. They must have been competent; business was good by the sound of things down there.

He opened his file and began to talk. It was time for me to listen.

A million questions popped in and out of my head as my thoughts began to take shape, and Mr Sugden smiled patiently after finishing his astonishing tale.

'It is really not so surprising that the name Amelia Parsons should be unknown to you, Miss Kent. She was your late grandmother's elder sister and had shut herself away, by choice I might add, for the past thirty years. She was something of a recluse who was not, how shall I put it, entirely in full possession of her faculties towards the end.'

He peered over his half-moon spectacles like an indulgent grandfather at me, his innocent new client.

'Yes, that's right,' he agreed with himself when I didn't say anything. He nodded to the ceiling with a contemplative look on his face. 'She was ninety-nine when she died, you know, and quite frail. I hadn't seen her myself for, oh … what, at least twenty years, which was when she came up to town to give instructions for a Codicil to her Will. My young partner looks after clients on my behalf when they live some distance away from the City.'

Aha! Young partner. Would that be a Sugden or a Sharp? A Sugden would be a member of the family; a Sharp would be some genius they had discovered to join them and deliver the masterstroke that would make the partnership flourish. This time, I made a small noise that could have sounded either sympathetic or understanding. Take your pick.

Mr Sugden was not to be swayed from his train of thought. He assiduously went on to describe the documentation that had accumulated in his file, knowing full well that the person sitting in front of him was totally in the dark anyway.

'Although the Will was drawn up many years ago, we have no reason to doubt that the old lady wanted your mother, Frances, to benefit from her estate. There were no other children in her family to consider apart from Frances, to whom she was devoted.'

His voice had the kind of theatrical growl, but for all it was mesmerizing, it made me far from sleepy. He cleared his throat and allowed a shadow of a smile to touch his thin lips. To be perfectly honest, I was absorbed more by the way he spoke than by what he was actually saying.

He stood once or twice during our meeting and sidled over to the window, to look down on rain-soaked people in the street. Maybe his old bones were unhappy at being in one position for a long time, and I noticed he arched his back a little each time he returned to his chair. It made me want to fetch a cushion and settle him more comfortably, grandad-style, but there was none to be had.

Gradually he built up a picture and I was, in fact, quite startled when he got down to the real reason for his summons.

'It is equally clear,' averred Mr Sugden, 'that she wanted you, in turn, to inherit, in the event of your mother predeceasing her.'

Not sure whether it was the right moment to interrupt, but I tentatively put forward information I had given out so many times. 'My mother and father were killed in a car accident when I was a baby, Mr Sugden. I am only here today because my uncle and aunt happened to be looking after me at the time of the tragedy.'

My voice tailed off. I have what can only be described as an ambivalent attitude to being orphaned. It had all been so long ago and I didn't have any sense of loss because I was too young to remember. Mr Sugden must have thought it all very sad, but he had probably seen many instances like this in his lifetime.

He bestowed a grandfatherly smile on me and reached for another small file, while I tried to tame the wayward thoughts fluttering around in my head. I wanted to be able to concoct a sensible question or two, to show that I was interested in what he was saying, not just someone who sat there looking like a dumb scarecrow.

'Quite so.' He flipped through the pages, skipping paragraphs and speed-reading as he went. 'Your adoptive parents, Charles and Mildred Kent. An address in Norfolk.'

He had all the facts about my mother at his fingertips as well. Amelia Parsons had apparently left nothing to chance and had steadily built up a pile of paperwork over the years that she had left in his strong room for safekeeping.

He briefly read aloud a few salient points about my life to date and it only dawned on me later that my benefactress must have kept in touch somehow and had monitored my every movement. How had she done that?

Mr Sugden smiled broadly this time and gave me a version of steeple fingers I hadn't seen before, where one set of fingerprints gently rubbed the nails on his other hand. I noticed his knuckles were enlarged; a touch of arthritis, maybe?

He was almost beaming now, his soliloquy complete, and I had the amusing feeling that this was the point where I was meant to burst into spontaneous applause. He really was very nice, and I almost did.

So far, it had all seemed so unreal, but the play was only just beginning. What I had heard so far was quite bewildering and I was finding it difficult to put my thoughts into rational words. Coming as it did, just at this moment, was the most extraordinary good fortune – little short of a miracle, in fact – and I wondered whether there was going to be some nasty twist that he had not yet mentioned.

It was strange. Normally I would have had a lot to say, but I couldn't think of anything off the top of my head, though I knew I would probably come up with a surfeit of questions once I got outside. He took my silence in his stride and gave me a benevolent look over the top of his half-moon spectacles.

That was the point when he relaxed and spoke into a communicating device at the edge of his desk that seemed curiously out-of-place with the rest of the outmoded office. An orange light came on, which made his eyes widen with pleasure. He enunciated his words carefully as though speaking to a foreigner who had no command of English whatsoever, and I could hear an eerie echo when he spoke.

'Are you there, Miss Wade?'

There was some kind of a crackle on the line, so his next words were slower and louder. 'Do you think you could possibly bring two cups of tea and a plate of those delicious custard creams you bought at the supermarket yesterday?'

'I have the kettle already on the boil, sir,' came back an equally well-modulated voice, though maybe not quite as stilted. 'I shall be with you in exactly two and a half minutes.'

He smiled at the contraption, fascinated, and muttered something about a wonderful invention. Whether he meant the super-efficiency of the eloquent Miss Wade or the intercom itself, I was none too sure.

'So, you see, Miss Kent, I hope we shall be able to conclude our business today to our mutual satisfaction. And now to the details …'

CHAPTER EIGHT

It was almost afternoon by the time I emerged from Mr Sugden's office. Rain had continued to wash the streets while I had been sipping tea and coming to terms with my future, and my head was reeling. I decided to skip lunch and aimed instead for a coffee shop to use my mobile phone.

I made two important calls. The first was to Charles whom I knew would be waiting to hear all about my meeting and eager to listen to the results. There were too many unanswered questions flying around and I hoped he might be able to scrape up a bit more news about this unknown benefactress, now that I at least knew her name.

Unfortunately, he had little to add because he and Millie had gone through my background with me so many times before and uncovered nothing new, though he kindly offered to start at the beginning of his records and go through everything again. If there was anything to find, he would find it. He has a mind like an encyclopaedia and still has the doggedness he developed when he worked in the Ministry of Defence.

'Sorry, love. I haven't the faintest idea *who* she was. Your grandmother's elder sister, you say? Let me get a pencil and I'll write down the details. Millie's dancing around at my elbow, waiting for me to hand the phone to her. She might remember something even if I don't, and you can be sure we'll do everything we can to find out: you know how I like researching these things. I'll try one of these genealogy websites and see what I can come up with.'

Millie's squeaky voice in the background suddenly came on the line loud and clear, so I had to repeat everything again. She could add nothing new. When it came to my maternal family, Millie was the only one to have shown any interest in her sister-in-law by marriage. I was the daughter they never had.

The only reason I know what my parents looked like was because Millie had stuck photographs into the family album. She's a big softie: there is always a tear in her eye whenever we sit together and look through the pages.

Beyond that, there is a void. Frances had been a private person and not the sort to divulge personal details to anyone. Which was a shame because it means that no one knows much about her, apart from her physical appearance. A small lady, slender, pretty, dark-haired.

Someone who would have been a friend.

I know about my father because Charles quite often makes a point of talking about his elder brother's antics as a child: sometimes with pride in his voice, sometimes with a shake of his head, but more often, with sadness.

Millie insisted early on that I should take over every memento, every photograph or keepsake appertaining to the people who had brought me into the world. Which is all very well, but it means that my own photograph album starts with a large black and white collection of people and faces who mean nothing to me.

I would save it from the fire of course, because it is in my mother's writing box.

My maternal grandmother, Elizabeth, after whom I have been named (sort of) died the week before I was born, so that was another big black hole.

Having lost my parents as well, Charles always said that I had been cruelly robbed of three people who would have been special to me, had fate dealt a kinder hand.

With such an appalling lack of family, it was interesting to find that an elderly unmarried woman by the name of Amelia Parsons had evidently forgiven my lack of knowledge and left her entire worldly belongings to me – someone she had never met.

At exactly a quarter to six, I walked through the doors of *Café Sonata* in Harlingdon Road and up to their main restaurant on the first floor. The head waiter took my coat, my colourful wet umbrella and an assortment of logo'd plastic bags I'd picked up in town.

He pointedly looked at his watch to check whether it had stopped – our table was booked for seven o'clock – and I looked suitably apologetic at his puzzled expression.

'I'm early, but I thought it was better to wait here than trudge around the shops for the umpteenth time. Besides, it's raining.'

It had rained consistently, in fact, ever since I made my two phone calls, and by the time I had searched for appropriate travel guides I was soaked.

My second call of the afternoon had been to Chessie, who told me she had placed her mobile phone on the desk and been standing over her office landline telephone since noon, tapping her feet and waiting for news.

'Phew! Have I got lots to tell you? I'm across the street from the bookshop. I want to look for Ordnance Survey maps of Yorkshire.'

'Yorkshire? Why on earth—? No, tell me later. I'm sure you have a perfectly good reason.'

I could barely contain my excitement but I wanted to tell Chessie everything properly, rather than over the phone.

I added, 'I've booked a table at the restaurant for seven, like we agreed, so I'll see you there. Byeee ...'

I punched the button and broke the call, leaving Chessie no better informed than she had been earlier. Apart from revealing that it was something about Yorkshire, that is.

So, there I was, sitting on one of the squashy sofas in the lounge part of the restaurant. The champagne was on ice, and the waiter, 'Jake' to the staff, had thoughtfully placed a dish of peanuts on the low table. Which was no bad thing, seeing as I had eaten nothing since the custard creams in Mr Sugden's office.

Too excited for lunch.

Too apprehensive about the future.

So much to do.

I looked round at the still empty restaurant and at the blue-uniformed staff who were setting tables and polishing glasses.

This place has a musical ambience, which I like and which you do not get in their downstairs café. Up here, the walls are papered with sheet music from the fifties and sixties, and tables are named after famous composers. Even the menus are cunningly disguised as old 78 rpm record sleeves. A talking point for guests, as though the appetising menu itself wasn't enough. I have one of their old menus in my shoebox, actually.

Two gins down the road, I was already on to white wine by the time Chessie appeared, flushed from a brisk walk down the street.

'Brr! It's buggeringly cold out there,' (she has a wonderful way with words).

'Why are there never any parking spots when you need them? I've had to park in front of your house.'

I had to admire the way she looked: as though she had stepped out from the pages of *Vogue*, even on such a day as this. She smiled charmingly at the head waiter who helped her off with her thick designer astrakhan coat and slipped it carefully on to a hanger.

She nodded towards my white wine.

'How long have you been here? Or, put it another way, how many of me do you see?'

I moved my head from side to side and gave her a stupid grin.

She held out her hands and warmed them on my cheeks, making me jump, and I nodded to Jake, who produced glasses like rabbits out of a hat for the champagne, so the drinking could start in earnest.

'Right then, darling. Don't keep me in suspense. I'm all ears, and my diet has gone by the board for today. What are we drinking to? Thank you …'

Jake took her coquettish smile as his due reward and poured bubbling liquid into her glass, before placing the bottle in the bucket.

'My inheritance.'

Chessie's eyes widened.

'Wow! I was right then.'

'Almost. Not too far off the mark. I did have a rich relative, not an uncle, as it happens, but a very old woman born almost a hundred years ago. Wait for it, Chessie. She has left me her entire fortune, which amounts to a house on the east coast of Yorkshire and an obscene income that will enable me to become a lazy old cow, if that's what I decide to be.'

'You're kidding!'

I moved my head from side to side again, giving credence to what I had just said. Then I revealed the essentials, burbling of course, but it was excusable considering the months of pent-up gloom inside me.

Millie used to say, 'You have so much to do in this life, don't hold back on anything. There isn't enough time'.

'To quote Mr Sugden, who, by the way, turned out to be very nice, Amelia Parsons, from my mother's side, has made me into a woman of considerable wealth.'

'Well, darling. It's been a hell of a day at the office, and if I needed something to celebrate, this is it. Not just the best news of the week, the best news of a lifetime.' She stared at me, her beautifully mascara'd eyes bright with excitement. 'I must admit, I had a little "Ah-ha" moment when you rang this afternoon, and the champagne is a dead giveaway, but I never expected anything like this. Do you realise, you look ten years younger than you did at our reunion? I hope you don't want me to genuflect, you little parvenu, you. Cheers!'

'I'll drink to that.'

We clinked glasses and the waiter, who was watching from a distance, smiled at two of the happiest diners he had seen for a long time. Ear-to-ear grins on animated faces and toasting something special. He reckoned it was a good time to bring the menus.

'So, what's with the travel brochures?' Chessie nodded towards the carrier bag on the floor before looking at the menu properly.

'Oh those. I want to bone up on the east coast before I actually get there. I've never been so far north; it will be good to know my way round.'

'You mean you don't need a job after all then? You can say goodbye to James with an easy conscience?'

'He'll be happy for me, I know that.'

'It's a great pity, because it was a good little computer company, everybody said so, but I suppose the accent was on the word *little*.

'But you know, darling, you're bound to be a lot happier out in the sticks. You were never meant to be part of this rat race: you just aren't tough enough when it boils down to it. Besides, you will be able to fly anywhere in the world now and lash out on new clothes every other week.'

I gave her a caustic frown and she clucked happily into her glass. She and others of her ilk changed their outfits at a snap of the fingers from High Street know-all gurus, whereas I only throw things away when they are disgustingly worn out. The idea of filling my wardrobe just for the sake of it would bore me to tears. I took another sip from my glass.

'Life's like a balloon, isn't it, Chessie? You squeeze it at one end and something pops out at the other. You're right though: I might not need a salary after all, but I shall have to do something or my balloon will burst completely. Perhaps I might consider gardening. On the other hand, I could always set myself up as a business consultant. James said it didn't matter where you lived these days, it could be the other side of the world.'

Life itself is an endless gamble, I think. According to Mr Sugden, I now had more money in the bank than I had ever dreamed of, and the word 'insecurity' (or even worse – 'penury') was not going to be in my vocabulary after all. Not a Lottery fortune by any means, but certainly more than one person needed. I could not go wrong.

'I hope you're not going to let all that training go to waste, darling, now that you have inherited your pile.

'You will be able to put September's mind at rest anyway. She asked whether you had anything in the pipeline, and now you can say yes. I must ring round with your news.'

I thought about all the tea leaves I had read with such good humour at the reunion, and all the confusing runes. It seemed such a long time ago. In the space of three hours on a wet January day, everything had changed.

Chessie quickly glanced through the menu's lighter options, smiled dazzlingly at Jake and ordered one of their vegetarian specials. I ignored that page and ordered a rib-eye steak because I was ravenous.

'I have a problem with all this, Chessie. Amelia Parsons, I mean. I just cannot help wondering why I never heard about her before. It seems wrong to take over her entire possessions when I didn't even know she existed until this morning. I rang Charles before I came here and he promised faithfully to comb through all his old papers to see if he could come up with something.'

'A relative on your mother's side, you say?'

'Yes. It sounds as though she thought a lot about my mother. Charles is going to do a bit of research on the Internet as well, but I'm not holding my breath.'

'You always were inquisitive, darling, always looking for something to investigate. Are you certain you never wanted to be a police officer? The uniform would suit you.'

'Don't be silly, you know I hate hats.'

She gave me a perky little grin. 'Sticking to the point, though, there must be something in your past that we have overlooked. Something that Charles and Millie thought was dead and buried. Except that it wasn't.'

'Well! Could be, I suppose. Mr Sugden said there were lots of Amelia's possessions to sift through when I get to my new house, and that his junior partner might be able to help with the more detailed aspects of my inheritance.

'Amelia had apparently shut herself away for years and her only contact with the outside world was a daily help and a handyman gardener, plus a nurse, towards the end.'

'You won't be entirely on your own then, assuming they want to carry on? What else did he say, apart from the hermit bit?'

I paused when a different waiter came to place our glasses on his silver tray and show us to the table marked *Chopin*, the marquetry edges of which were decorated with black and white strips to resemble piano keys. When we were both sitting down, he lit the two candles in the centre of the table and I tried to dredge up every detail I had heard during the morning.

'She wasn't very nimble on her feet. And what was the other one? Ah yes, she might have had dementia.'

'Ninety-nine is a good age, but not good enough to get a telegram from HM. OK, you will be moving away. Where was it again? Whitby, did you say?'

'More north, actually, on the Heritage Coast. A village called Wraycliffe, not quite as far as Saltburn.'

'I think I might have heard of it,' she said without too much conviction. 'A rival for Scarborough at some point, wasn't it?'

'No, no, you're thinking of another village further south. This is nearer Middlesbrough and according to my book of Norse legends it means "remote place". I shall give notice on my flat tomorrow.' I helped myself to a bread roll and a pat of butter that was embossed with a treble clef. 'The funeral is next week by the way.'

'At Wraycliffe?'

'Apparently not. Amelia decided a long time ago that she wanted to be buried with her sister in a village called Ashford, just outside York.

'Mr Sugden excused it as being the romantic notion of a nonagenarian lady whose mind was intact at the time she made her Will but who still maintained the stubborn streak of her youth. He also said he admired her for writing everything down, so nothing could go wrong. He has a long list of instructions.'

Chessie nodded. 'You mean a Funeral File, darling. Leaves nothing to chance.'

'Well it's being followed to the letter: private burial soon after her demise, then a memorial service at Wraycliffe a few weeks later. She lived there for nearly a hundred years.'

Chessie looked well satisfied at the sound common sense of it all, and then murmured her delight as a waiter arrived with her melon and crab starter. It looked miserably small to me, a mouthful at the most, but she seemed happy enough with it and I buttered a second bread roll before tackling my courgette soup.

'My grandparents lived in Ashford for years and Amelia spent a fair bit of time with them. She fell in love with the church apparently, if only because it looks spectacular when the daffodils are out and it has a pretty garden. I went there once when I was in my teens.'

That was something I did remember: begging Charles and Millie to take me to Elizabeth and Robert Walker's house, where my mother had lived as a girl. I chattered on, admitting later that I regretted the trip because I thought it had been a bit pointless. The people who lived there by that time had no recollection whatsoever of the previous occupants. I bet they wondered why the devil we had gone to snoop around.

'I'll come with you if you like. I know a super little hotel in York, on The Mount, handy for the station,' said Chessie with a burst of enthusiasm as she placed her cutlery neatly on her plate.

'I've stayed there before, so I know it's good. We could travel by train and take in a few days' shopping.'

'Oh, would you? That would be much nicer than going on my own. I was going to ask Millie and Charles, but they will be on holiday on the Costa del Sol.'

'No problem. You sort out when and I'll get my team to do the reservations.' I smiled when she added, 'I must say, that starter was one of the best I have ever had. Perhaps I was hungry.'

Hungry? Her appetite is practically *lifeless*. She eats lots of raw vegetables such as carrots and fresh peas, when she can get them. The staff don't go in for much else at her fashion house. They're all the same. Carbs are deadly.

She gave the waiter one of her demure 'thank you' smiles and sent her compliments to the chef. Chessie is one of those people who always gives an opinion, good or bad, about service and satisfaction. Good customer relations she calls it.

'I am really going to miss you, you know. You do realise that you will be more than three hundred miles away and we won't be able to do this as often as we do now. I positively won't want to come here on my own.'

'You won't miss me at all, because you're going to come and stay. Often. Please say you will. Three hundred miles is nothing.'

'Goes without saying, darling, I shall turn up on your doorstep whenever I can. It's a pity that you didn't know about all this before the reunion; we could have come north and given you a proper housewarming party.'

'Maybe we could still do that in the summer. Perhaps Virginia might come and I could read my Tarot cards next time.'

Chessie's sardonic frown was distorted by the flame flickering between us. She's not exactly a non-believer: she just doesn't believe.

We were nicely into the meal when Chessie suddenly asked, 'Why didn't you tell Richard you were Bunty? You know, at the reunion?'

Chewing my steak gave me thinking time, not that it was tough, far from it, but I wasn't sure of the answer. Virginia had confided things that would remain secret until she said otherwise. I rewound my brain a few weeks.

'I don't know; something stopped me. Strange, isn't it, Richard mentioning it just like that? Put it this way: if he knew about the name Bunty, then he must also have known it was me: the two things go hand in hand. Virginia must have a good reason to keep half of the equation to herself.'

'Like she wanted to hang on to a little bit of her childhood privacy?'

'Perhaps,' I said evasively. 'It was so unimportant; one of those madcap things you do when you are little. Virginia called me Bunty long before we ever went to Grammar School: you were probably the only other person in the room who knew what he was on about. I ache to have a long chat with her, you know. Like we used to.'

Chessie nodded and expertly studied the ruby meniscus in her glass (she picked up the habit from a sommelier she was once keen on, and has never quite lost the knack).

She said, 'At one time she would have moved mountains to speak to us on the telephone. I know they don't use a landline back home and I must have tried dozens of times to get her on her mobile, but there's no reply. I end up going on to voicemail.'

'Me too. Strange. Like you said the other day: she and Richard seem besotted with each other. No time for us.'

Chessie patted my hand. 'Never mind them. I've just had this great idea when we come to your new place for our next reunion in the summer. We'll give the cards and runes a miss, if you don't mind, and try something outlandishly grand like a cruise along the Yorkshire coast on a chartered yacht. Not often I get to stay with a millionaire, you know.'

CHAPTER NINE

Amelia's funeral had all the dismal elements you might expect: appalling weather, congregation saying very little to each other and a feeling of depression hanging around like an unwanted guest.

Mr Sharp met us at York Railway Station. The 'young partner'. I caught a glimpse of his back view when we got off the train: even from a distance he was tall enough to stand out in the crowd.

He was waiting for us on the far side of the tracks and, for one idiotic moment, I thought it was Turner. It looked so much like him that I seriously thought about ignoring him and leading Chessie in the opposite direction. Churlish, I told myself crossly. I could at least greet him.

Briefly.

And *then* ignore him.

But, of course, it wasn't the egregious Mr Cooper at all. This man's eyes raked the line of passengers crossing over the bridge and came to rest on mine. Our black coats must have identified us and with only the barest nod of his head he lifted his hand in a gloved finger-stretching wave of acknowledgement. He was well-wrapped up in his own thick dark overcoat – a *covert* coat, Chessie informed me knowledgeably – and he had a bowler hat pulled low over his head.

'Typical solicitor,' she stated without elaborating.

By the time we got outside the station, the rain was pouring down. It was definitely not the sort of day to hang about, so we quickly introduced ourselves and my new solicitor shepherded us under his large black umbrella to a taxi that was waiting for us.

'Interesting weather,' Chessie commented with what might have been her version of a scowl as we climbed into the back seat. You never know whether she is being sarcastic or not. 'We have ploughed our way from King's Cross through a mixture of drizzle and cloudburst, then a speck of sunshine followed by more drizzle, and now this.'

I added some remark about our reason for being there and thanked Mr Sharp for all the arrangements he was bound to have made during the past few weeks.

'Whims cannot always be explained,' he replied vaguely as we drove through York itself and on to the A64. 'Miss Parsons was most specific about her funeral and she planned all the arrangements down to the last full stop. It was her express wish that she should share her final resting place with her sister. In fact, she often referred to the gardens surrounding Ashford churchyard as Xanadu, the nearest thing on earth to paradise. There is also to be a memorial service back at Wraycliffe ... at a time to suit yourself, of course, Miss Kent. Your involvement is a key factor in both events.'

He obviously knew the file off by heart.

He was in the passenger seat and I could see his inscrutable expression reflected in the mirror. I detected an underlying curiosity in his words, but his face gave nothing away when he momentarily turned to look at me. Chessie remained impassive at my side, but I knew she would be taking in every word.

'I understand you have a past connection with Ashford through your mother, Miss Kent, and hopefully a future with the people of Wraycliffe. Miss Parsons hoped you would turn her house into your home, although the choice is yours, of course. How soon do you expect to move into *Painter's Lodge*?'

In an instant, my heart unexpectedly did a little flip-flop, and all because he called my new home by its name.

Up to now, I had been trying to get to grips with some nebulous, elusive inheritance that was floating somewhere above my head, but the words *Painter's Lodge* suddenly whetted my appetite and brought the house to life. It felt romantic, albeit strange, because it had now taken shape as bricks and mortar, and all of a sudden, I wanted to see it first hand and get my somewhat turbulent life moving again as soon as I could.

I also wanted to curb my impatience, so I put a business-like smile on my face as the rain splattered on to the windscreen and the wipers thumped it rhythmically away.

'I thought about next week, actually. I have one or two things to do back home but it shouldn't take me long to deal with them.'

Chessie knew that we were only talking half a day maximum to sort everything out, but he didn't. She and I had already discussed it and she had offered to take time off work to help.

Not a big move: packing my paltry belongings would take only a few hours, and letting people know where I had gone would produce only a handful of letters at the most. I could send emails to everybody else. There was no job to worry about either; James had said he would cover things at his end.

'Good. I shall come and see you shortly then.' It seemed that I was not expected to answer, and his expression in the mirror never budged an inch. 'I shall bring all the paperwork for you to sign and we can talk about a memorial service at the village church at the same time.'

Legal procedures were things that belonged out of sight in a strong room as far as I was concerned, and now was not the right time to ask questions. I had had little to do with solicitors up to now, but even from this distance, I could see no difference between Leonard Sugden and Nathaniel Sharp, other than fifty-odd years. They would go through the business of the day by rote more than likely, using clever brains disciplined by all that legal jargon they go in for.

As well as what went on underneath, they both wore morbid black, so I had no way of knowing whether Mr Sharp was in funeral mode or not today. Their dreams probably all took place in Hansard-land, too.

Nathaniel Sharp was polite and attentive enough, although I couldn't help feeling that he did 'brisk' and 'efficient' rather better than Leonard Sugden, whose approach had been more fatherly. Not that Mr Sharp made me feel I was being a nuisance. I was his client, after all, and I could play the part as well as anybody.

The neat row of houses along Ashford's main road probably looked just the same as it did in Grandmother Elizabeth's day.

St Mary's Church was at least two hundred years old. I was told that willing local volunteers kept it tidy, and the much-vaunted gardens might indeed be beautiful when the sun was shining, but not today. No way! Miserable, relentless rain poured on a group of mourners who stood round a recently opened grave and slaked over the canopy of black umbrellas to land in large puddles at our feet.

Chessie and I had our own umbrellas but I was glad I was wearing knee-high boots and a long coat.

I was hard pressed to think of the churchyard as a paradise in its present state but if I were in poetic mood (which I could honestly say I wasn't) I would have said that the gods were weeping over the death of my benefactress. Apart from Chessie, I knew no one, nor expected to.

I was keen to meet the mourners who had travelled sixty-odd miles from Wraycliffe. These were going to be my new neighbours and somehow it felt important to meet Amelia's friends. There were at least a dozen people grouped together and all dressed in sombre gear. Mr Sharp sat with us in the same pew during the church service and I could tell I was being scrutinized by people behind us who were just as curious about the new incumbent of *Painter's Lodge* as I was about them.

It felt like the funeral was being held in the wrong place, and even the Reverend Clayton must have been wondering how he came to be officiating on this occasion. He was new to the parish and knew little about the deceased, apart from the fact that she wasn't one of his parishioners.

But he took it all in his stride and delivered a eulogy that suggested he had known her quite well. Vicars are prone to do that, I believe: they do their homework diligently and are used to the scenario. Must be page two in their training manual.

The small congregation was in lusty voice – no surprise, considering Amelia had pre-booked a choir to sing all her favourite hymns – and her mortal remains were eventually laid to rest next to those of her sister and brother-in-law.

I was standing in the porch when a tall elderly man broke away from the Wraycliffe group and came towards me.

I felt a sudden rush of sadness that these people would be mourning the loss of a friend and would most likely be feeling a greater grief than my own, whereas I had lost a relative without even knowing her.

Mr Sharp quickly stepped forward to introduce us.

'This is Ben, Miss Kent. A friend of the family.'

'Good to meet you Miss Kent.' Ben touched his trilby as men of his age tend to do. 'I'll miss her. We all will.'

He indicated the dark-clad group behind him and shook my hand, holding on warmly for what seemed an inordinately long time. I could see his eyes were moist as he stared down at me. His face revealed a bucolic life, weather-beaten and wrinkled, and for some reason I was deeply touched by the sorrowful look in his eyes.

We stepped forward together a few yards to stare down at the dozens of wreaths and flowers that had been carefully placed at the edge of the now-sodden lawns, and crowded together under the umbrella to prevent us becoming drenched. I automatically clasped my other hand over his to let our mixed feelings entwine.

'She'd have been happy to see you here.' The well-educated voice was deep and hushed. He kept his face averted, but his hand gave mine a little squeeze. 'Miss Parsons wanted a memorial service back home, so we'll be seeing you again soon enough, I expect.'

'I'm hoping to come next week.'

He nodded and patted my hand again before saying goodbye and re-joining his companions. I was on my own.

'Who was that?' Chessie had been watching from a distance and she now came and gently nudged my arm.

'A man from Wraycliffe, one of Amelia's friends, I think. A close friend. He was rather nice.' I stared at the line of cars and the dark outline of heads as the convoy slowly made its way out to the main road. 'It's all quite moving, Chessie. Amelia knew these people, probably quite well in some cases, whereas I feel as though I am the stranger. The fact that she chose Ashford must be a mystery to them, but I suppose she knew what she was doing. I think I'll get over to *Painter's Lodge* as soon as I can.'

Mr Clayton shook hands with me and said kind words of condolence as Chessie and I again sheltered in his porch to say goodbye. Then it was Mr Sharp's turn.

'Don't worry that some people have already left, Miss Kent. The memorial service at Wraycliffe will be more important to them, so I shall carry out Miss Parsons' directive and organize the service over there in a few weeks, as you decide. She didn't want to have a meal afterwards – "To be buried in ham and small talk" she called it – but you might like to arrange something yourself later on, when you get to know people better. As for now, the car is at your disposal for the rest of the day. You only have to instruct the driver and he will take you anywhere you want to go.'

A quick glance at Chessie to confirm. 'Only to the hotel, I think, but thank you for that.'

It was only when he had walked away that I wondered how he would get home himself and perhaps I should have offered to give him a lift. I need not have worried: I saw him drive off later in his large black Mercedes.

All of which strengthened my view that business was definitely good.

CHAPTER TEN

And so, I started my new life on Friday the Thirteenth. Naturally, I thought about travelling north on another, less ominous, day but other people had been primed to take part in all this, so I couldn't alter my plans. Besides, Chessie insisted that my inherent superstition surrounding a mere number was a load of tosh and I was stupid to worry about it.

Anxiety battled with impatience, and I could not shake off this idea that the whole venture was going to be one big lousy mistake. 'Starting afresh' I said to James, but let's face it, I didn't have all that many other options in the pipeline.

Well, none, actually.

Technically, from the monetary aspect, there were no uncertainties ahead of me, but realistically there was also no guarantee that things had changed for the better, and I was apprehensive. In fact, the only good thing about the day so far was that I had witnessed two magpies foraging in my yard back home (I really must stop calling London my home).

'Two for Joy', I shouted to Chessie as we packed the car and she filled a Thermos with decaf for me. I don't think she heard me, or if she did, she ignored my enthusiasm. She was programmed to hang around Harlingdon Road until Millie and Charles arrived.

It must surely have been the coldest February day northern England had seen for a long time. The sun was somewhere up there in the sky as I drove up the M1, but not enough to make any difference to the chill on the hard ground.

The miles zoomed quickly by. Even the possibility of getting lost, which had been high on my Friday the Thirteenth gloom list, did not materialise either as I drove further and further away from my familiar nest.

My Ford Escort might be old and a bit battered (a much-welcomed twenty-first birthday present from Charles and still going strong) but she is special to me and in dire need of a long trip such as this. The speedometer climbed and she ran like a dream.

Whitby Abbey was outlined starkly in the distance when I drove up Yorkshire's coast road. I'd only seen photographs of it before but I was too keyed up to take in the reality: my mind was bursting with the unexpected turn of events that had overtaken me. The move was more than welcome but there was still that little niggle at the back of my mind that comes along when big changes are just on the horizon. Like Chessie repeatedly says: 'Only one way to find out.'

I had a safety net, of course.

Mr Sugden had reminded me that I could always sell the house and move back south if I didn't take to it, but he also advised me, in that persuasive grandfatherly voice of his, not to make any rash decisions.

'Give yourself time to settle down and have a look round, Miss Kent. Amelia Parsons was very happy at Wraycliffe, I am told. Never been there myself, but it must have something going for it for her to get so enthusiastic on the telephone. A population of six hundred at the last count, very small place, very unified she always said.'

'Just a tad different from what I'm used to in London,' I replied, sitting in his office and gazing down at the picture of a country village pub. It looked appealing and cosy, with ivy-clad stone walls and an internal glow lighting up its Georgian windows.

Millie said much the same thing when I discussed my plans. Unsurprisingly, I got the usual, 'You only get one life, make the most of it,' speech from her, before she reached for the bottle of white from the fridge. To celebrate, she said.

Amelia Parsons.

I had done little but think of this generous old lady ever since Mr Sugden introduced her name into the conversation.

I had spoken to the daily help over the telephone before and made arrangements for her to let me in before she went home. I glanced quickly down at the dashboard clock; I only hoped I wasn't going to be too late.

She may well have had a pretty name – Bella – but it was a waspish voice that came down the line when we first spoke, and the nearer I got to Wraycliffe the more I tried to imagine what she would be like. Old, most likely. Someone who found it easy to put up with an elderly invalid.

Invalid? No, that wasn't quite right. Mr Sugden hadn't called Amelia an invalid: he merely hinted that she had been a bit peculiar, that was all.

My imagination can get a bit vivid sometimes, and I fervently hoped that 'peculiarity' had not rubbed off on the daily help. Old age combined with awkward is asking for a heap of trouble I always think.

The fifth set of temporary traffic lights made me groan and I wound down the car window to breathe in salty air that signalled close proximity to the coast. I had grown up near the sea and loved its changeable moods, but on this occasion, the chilly wind reddened my ears and made me shiver enough to close the window. That was February for you.

It was a long queue but my jazz tape mitigated the tedium of waiting.

The signals eventually changed to green and I hoped it was my last groan of the day.

The road hugged the coastline until fresh tarmac gradually became a main street, and a road sign announced that I had finally arrived at my destination.

Names of places often come with a picture to me, and anything to do with cliffs brings me out in a flood of blissful expectation. I love the sea. Always have.

Wraycliffe fit the bill exactly.

It was a small village huddled round a pond; one telephone box; a church set back from the road, and a shop with a red letterbox outside. The village green was ablaze with snowdrops trying to come to terms with a February sprinkling of icing sugar snow, and habitation looked sparse and elegant. Farms and large red brick houses indicated a community that was far removed from pauperism, and a smattering of elegant limousines on block-paved drives told the same story.

Apart from the sounds of high-pitched voices down one of the offshoot lanes – a school yard, I assumed – the only sign of activity was a lone walker with a dog and she gave me a studied glance as I passed her.

Nice to know the neighbourhood watch was thriving: I could feel, rather than see, that she took note of my car and number plate.

I drove slowly, taking it all in.

'*Painter's Lodge* is on the far side of the village, on its own,' Mr Sugden had read from the estate agents' blurb, adding expressively, 'with a commanding view of the North Sea'.

No poetic licence there, Leonard, and I had no cause for complaint.

The bleak coastline gradually unwound northwards and I could almost feel the emptiness across water over to my right that stretched as far as the continent.

This is what reminds me of my roots, you know: a wide expanse of water, and, in this particular case, it is the same sea that Millie and Charles watch from their window. We may be miles apart, but I was supremely conscious that we were about to share every wave, every stretch of foamy water, every message in a bottle.

Something told me to add all this scenery to my memory cells, just in case I decided not to stay, but for the moment, I was simply glad to have arrived.

The beach fell away as my car began to climb enough of a gradient for me to change down a gear. My new home must be around here somewhere. Mr Sharp had outlined the general direction before we parted, saying that it was perched on the edge of the village, and I scanned the terrain for signposts that might indicate I had gone too far.

Then I saw it. Well, the top half anyway, and a funny feeling fluttered inside me. I held my breath, stared upwards.

The house stood back from the road, almost hidden by a high wall and dense garden shrubbery, with only the chimney pots and attic tower visible from here, but I recognised its shape instantly from the file photograph. The reality was something else, and it was no surprise to see smoke curling from the chimney into the late afternoon sky.

No entrance to the house from the road, said the typed instructions, so, as directed, I followed the wall down a little dusty track to the left. It seemed to go nowhere apart from acres of farmland stretching into the distance beyond, and the main road continued its way up the coastline without me.

The seasonally leafless horse chestnuts at one side of the lane looked like dark skeletons in the dimming light and after about twenty-five yards I came to a car-sized break in the wall.

This, according to a sign with irregularly spaced black letters painted on it, was the entrance to *Painter's Lodge.* By the time I drove up the curved gravel drive, the day was past its best.

Something hit me in the stomach when I saw my house properly. It was almost as though I'd been here before, but I pushed the notion to one side as a childhood dream, something I had imagined when I was young perhaps. It reminded me strangely of Virginia's house with a grandeur that I never imagined I would own. I hadn't been born to know such luxury: she had.

I got out of the car, muffled with scarf and gloves against the cold, and simply stood there locking in a first impression that I was certain I would remember for the rest of my life.

The wall and shrubbery might have afforded a little privacy around the perimeter, but they were not high enough to shelter the house from its elevated position in a harsh coastal climate. I found myself looking at three storeys of blackened stone, sculpted and weathered by years of lashing wind and sea. It might even have somebody else's fingerprints all over it, but it was mine now. Mine to do whatever I wanted to do with it.

There were three steps up to the to the pilaster-framed entrance, and a door that had been freshly painted glossy dark blue smiled at me and begged me to open it.

Here I was, looking at my own front door. I still didn't know what I had done to deserve Amelia's fortune, which according to Charles was turning out to be considerably larger than anyone had expected.

I had left Mr Sugden's office with most of the estate agent's paperwork, numerous photos of the house and garden, and a touristy guide book of the local area.

The house had apparently been in the family for almost two hundred years, even longer if you took into account that a more modest habitation stood on the site before that. I had a little side bet going with Charles as to just how many dogs and cats were buried deep in the back garden (grisly secrets that would remain secret, as far as I was concerned.)

Now I was up close, I could see that newer renovations had been carried out fairly recently and that the photographs were probably about twenty years out of date. Instead of the wooden sash windows and tiny panes of antique glass, the house now had large white PVC windows and soffits. Quite a large house, Mr Sugden had described it, with a smallish garden and trees all round to give it seclusion.

Away from the bustle of London, it gave me a powerful feeling of peace and I stood there with what must have been a dreamy look on my face. I thought I was on my own until I heard a rattling noise on my right. A wheelbarrow, rusty and old, pushed by somebody who was so well wrapped up as to be unidentifiable.

He came nearer and I saw it was Ben. He paused for a moment to give me a nod and a courteous touch of his woolly cap; the gravelly voice was deep and welcoming.

'Good afternoon Miss Kent. Nice to see you again.'

'Hello Ben. My goodness, I hardly recognized you. All that winter padding makes you look quite different. I didn't realise last week that you looked after Amelia's garden. I'm really sorry I didn't make the connection.'

I would have pigeonholed him properly at the funeral if only I had known who he was.

I didn't recall Mr Sharp saying anything, but perhaps my mind had been elsewhere: there had been so much to take in. In any case, Ben looked vastly different today in workday clothes and rubber boots. He held out his hand after first rubbing it down the side of his jacket.

'How does cold weather suit you, Ben?'

'Oh, so so, y'know. We get used to it and there's more snow on the way, so they say. Been bad this year but we've had worse. Bella's expecting you: she's been hopping around with that duster of hers all afternoon.'

It was too cold for a long conversation so I said, 'Catch up with you tomorrow then?'

'Yes indeed, Miss. I shall be here.' He nodded and carried on walking; I turned back to the car.

As I glanced up to the rooftops, I fancied I could see someone standing behind the circular attic window directly under the eaves. Too shadowy now to make the figure out properly but another movement lower down in one of the bedrooms was real enough.

A light was shining and a female form busily poked one of those brightly coloured fluffy things on a stick into the corners of the window (the modern answer to the feather duster – Millie has one). Had to be my housekeeper. When she saw me, she bent her head in what I assumed was meant to be a friendly nod and moved away from the window.

I locked the car with the remote and dragged my luggage to the doorstep, fully prepared to meet the starchy woman I had created in my head. She would be an elderly retainer who would want the house to run exactly the same as always, without any interference from the new owner, and a 'townie' at that.

Noises on the staircase were followed by the sound of numerous locks and bolts being undone and the door finally opened.

How wrong can you be?

The person standing there looked so young I almost said, 'Is your mother at home?' but she forestalled me with, 'Hello, you must be Miss Kent. Do come in. I'm Bella Graham.'

The rumble on the stairs ought to have prepared me for a more agile pair of legs, I suppose, because the genuine Bella Graham was around my age, or perhaps a couple of years older. Petite and blonde, slim and energetic-looking, barely five feet tall, and much younger than I expected. She also had a calm voice that was nothing like the one that had come across earlier on the telephone.

Time to re-vamp your thoughts on senile old housekeepers, Elise.

CHAPTER ELEVEN

The warmth of the small storm porch was a welcome change from the cold evening air and I briskly rubbed my hands. Bella brushed past me to re-lock the outside door and slide the bolts (must remember that: *house rules*). Then she closed the inner door and we finally shook hands, making small talk about the advantages of storm porches in foul weather.

'Will the car be OK if I leave it just in front of the door? I'll move it somewhere else tomorrow if you point me in the right direction.'

'More heavy snow tonight,' Bella forecast cheerfully. 'You might not be able to see your car tomorrow, but don't worry about it. It'll be fine.'

She gave me a wide-eyed stare and a sniff when she saw me properly. I wondered whether she was studying my hair or just my general dishevelled appearance, because I knew I could easily have had a smudge on my face from handling maps and photos in the car. I quickly ran my fingers through my hair, knowing it would be a waste of time.

As you might expect, I was quick to do my own summing up as well. Worry lines around her eyes prevented Bella from being textbook pretty, but we all know that wrinkles are hard-earned, and these were relatively insignificant when you took in the glorious shiny mop of blonde hair that she had loosely tied back with a butterfly clip. I was none too keen on the black dress, but perhaps Amelia had liked it.

Of the two of us, I think she was the tidiest.

'Well that was a day and a half, Bella. You've no idea how glad I am to have arrived at last. Three hundred miles might not be such a long way for some people, but it's enough for me. I'm not used to it.'

She must have decided she didn't mind the hair because I saw only interest in her gaze.

'I'll show you to your room first if you like, and you can freshen up before dinner. I didn't know what time to expect you, so I made a casserole that could be ready whenever you came.'

'What a nice thought. Thank you so much, Bella, that's good of you. And if that's what I can smell, then I'm ravenous.'

Bella's strength was glaringly out of all proportion with her diminutive stature and she humped my overnight holdall and laptop upstairs as though they were filled with feathers. I struggled with the suitcase. I could have sworn both bags had weighed the same when I packed them.

I had crammed all my personal trivia into the suitcase, which meant that it now contained the trappings of my lifestyle: crystal ball, rune stones, Tarot cards and reference books. Not to mention items of lesser importance (such as clothes) that I thought I might need until everything else arrived on Monday.

Inquisitiveness showed on her face again as I lugged the suitcase to the top of the stairs and, taking a deep breath, muttered, 'Stuff I can't do without,' by way of explanation. She merely raised her eyebrows and sank her chin into her chest.

'I've switched the radiator on to the highest setting in your room, Miss Kent. Mr Sharp came this morning to make sure I knew you were coming and to have a prowl around, as per usual.'

This time she made a wry face and I frowned.

'Does he often come to look round?'

'Not lately, but he used to do it a lot when Miss Amelia was really poorly. Then she died and he went through her papers – with him being her executor an' all, I suppose. He only stopped nosing around when I made it clear I wanted to get on with a bit of spring cleaning.'

She wouldn't meet my eyes and I suspected there was more, but she clammed up. That was as much as the new owner was going to get on the first day.

'Executors have to make sure that things are in order,' I nodded. 'I'll give him a ring and make arrangements to see him again.'

Her loud sniff gave me the impression that Mr Sharp was not high on her list of chums.

She opened the door to a fair-sized room opposite the bathroom and announced that this was to be my bedroom. It was huge: larger than anything I had ever had before, and spacious enough to contain two large wardrobes, a tallboy and a dressing table. I didn't mention that it was more than adequate for my own meagre possessions; she would find out for herself eventually.

'Miss Amelia's own bedroom when she was a child,' Bella proclaimed softly in a voice that I would swear held a tinge of worship. 'I made up the bed for you in here because it overlooks the sea out front. Nicest bedroom in the house, according to my gran and I have always agreed with her, but you can swap for one of the others, if you like. Mr Sharp told me to carry on as normal until the new owner decided what changes she would like to make.'

It sounded just like him, organized and methodical, and I muttered something along those lines. She chose to hear, but not necessarily to listen.

'I've set the table in the kitchen, Miss Kent, but you can eat in the dining room tonight if you want to. Supper will be ready in ten minutes.

'I wanted to see you scttlcd in before I went home, but my ma plays pop if I'm late. Doesn't like being left on her own, you see. I didn't normally work in the evenings for Miss Amelia, but ma will understand tonight.'

'The kitchen will be fine. Oh, and by the way, let's start as we mean to go on, Bella. Please call me Elise; Miss Kent sounds so formal.'

It was like being in a foreign land up here and 'formal' was something I could do without. She nodded her head and gave another sniff (it was obviously a little habit I was going to have to get used to).

'I'll make it *Miss* Elise, then, if you don't mind. My ma always said it was the proper thing to do when she was here.'

That was a surprise. 'I didn't know that. You mean she was Amelia's housekeeper?'

'Oh yes, she used to bring me in my pram until I was old enough to tag along on foot. Then I went to school. It was only when ma started being ill about ten years ago that I took over. My gran lived here as a housekeeper as well, long before her.'

'Well now. Am I lucky or what? You'll be a godsend if you can fill in all the gaps for me. I have *so* many questions to ask I don't even know where to start. You see, this is all new to me, Bella, and I never even met Amelia Parsons. I only wish I had.'

She looked sad for a moment. Then came the sniff.

First things first. It only took a few moments to make a quick telephone call to Chessie to report my arrival and give my first impressions an airing.
I would like to have taken a shower as well and maybe get changed but I didn't want to keep Bella waiting because I felt duty bound to fit in with her getaway plans.

But timing wasn't the only reason to hurry: the aroma that floated up the stairs would have been enough on its own.

I tactfully removed the pilled cardigan in case my new housekeeper thought I normally looked like a ragbag (I noticed she had given it the kind of scrutiny I expect from Chessie when I took off my coat downstairs). I had almost thrown it away that morning, but then retrieved it at the last minute from the black plastic bag, much to Chessie's disgust. I now sported a tee shirt with a big red heart that said '*I Love Rome*' (present from James and his wife Gail – I've never been).

I halted on the bottom step for a moment. Not a big hallway; in fact, the crimson-carpeted staircase was the most impressive thing about it. The rest was dingy and old, though wall lights gave the place an intimate glow, and the mahogany panelling and thick timber doors hinted at a life from long ago.

The smart little antique table at the bottom of the staircase was Queen Anne, I decided. It was probably ancient and valuable, though I'm not well up on these things and I might have clocked it up totally in the wrong era. A slim-line telephone sat on top, incongruously out of time and place to my way of thinking, but it was a cosmopolitan touch that made me smile, and I stroked it gently with my fingertips as I passed.

Glancing at my watch, I saw that I had made my kitchen deadline with two minutes to spare.

Bella didn't exactly have her hat and coat on, but her slightly protruding eyes glanced up at the clock over the oven as I reappeared and I took it as a subtle reminder that she wanted to be off. She did an up-and-down at me and I could only hope that she approved of my freshened appearance and carefully combed hair.

The sound of my trainers on the squeaky-clean quarry tiles made me want to tiptoe but I couldn't hold back a little gasp of pleasure when I saw how Bella had set the kitchen table. Just for me.

Scrubbed almost white, the table was a butcher's block that that you don't often see nowadays, but it was now laid out with shining cutlery and a wineglass just asking to be filled. A couple of red candles flickered invitingly in a leafy centrepiece. It was obviously in my honour and I couldn't help congratulating her on how attractive it all looked.

'I'm more than ready to eat, Bella, and I can manage nicely on my own now if you want to get off.'

She nodded. She was holding a shiny red exercise book in her hand, the kind that most newsagents carry on their shelves.

'I've written everything down for you, Miss Elise, and I've left my telephone number on the pad in the hall in case I've missed anything.' She flicked her fingers into the air as she read. 'There's plenty of food in the fridge (I gave the enormous refrigerator in the corner a courteous glance) but there's always Mrs Hanby's post office shop down the road if you want anything else (a nod from me). She only keeps a small stock – things she likes herself, you understand – so you have to make do with that until you go to the supermarket out on the Industrial Estate.'

She went on: keys; cupboard contents; emergency telephone numbers … She brushed an errant strand of hair from her eyes. 'Ben has put wood in the scuttle to keep the kitchen stove going, and I'll be back tomorrow morning for a couple of hours, but I've got to take my ma shopping first.'

With a short pause, she proceeded to add a few more 'Not to be forgotten' items from her list, finishing with, 'I think that's about everything.'

I was relieved. It had been a long day, but not nearly as daunting as I had expected, and I felt that everything was slotting into place nicely. Well, I hadn't known what to expect when I started out this morning, and that's the truth of it, and I suppose she and Ben must have had the same feelings about me. I hope they weren't disappointed.

'You've been very thorough, Bella. And so very kind. Thanks for that. You've made things so easy for me.'

I watched her place the precious notebook in the drawer alongside the sink (noting its precise position because I was ninety-nine percent sure I was going to yank it out again as soon as she departed) then she turned and looked as though she might add another comment. But she obviously thought better of it and gave me a sniff instead, accompanied by a cheerful, 'See you tomorrow, then.'

'I'll see you out.'

It was relatively chilly in the porch, compared with the hall, which is presumably why Amelia had seen to its construction in the first place – assuming it had been her idea – and I was about to open the outside door when something caught my eye.

'Good grief! What's *that*?'

No one would argue that the vestibule was cramped with two of us in it, and to be honest it felt like an even smaller version of my familiar little goldfish bowl. There was scarcely enough room for cat-swinging, but it was large enough to house the large floor-standing vase that had suddenly caught my attention. Two feet high, it was a vase in a hideous shade of sickly green with loud orange flowers all the way round.

A repository for umbrellas? There was a walking stick in there at the moment. Bella allowed a glimmer of fun to dance in her eyes.

'Horrible, isn't it? Somebody told Miss Amelia that it might be valuable, so she couldn't bear to throw it away, just in case. She stuck it in here where she wouldn't have to look at it so often, but everybody who comes through that door gives it the same kind of look: just like you're doing now.'

'I reckon I'll just have to get used to it then. If it's valuable.'

We both fell about laughing, but this time Bella showed a neat row of small teeth and a genuine twinkle in her eye. I think that was the point I decided I had found a friend rather than an employee, and a minute later her tiny frame bustled down the street.

Large flakes of snow had begun to fall and the house felt quite empty without her.

CHAPTER TWELVE

My new rule book, as I called it when I told Chessie about it, stretched to roughly eighteen pages and I scanned the first few before returning it to the drawer because Bella had written things down in some kind of gobbledygook shorthand of her own design.

I found it hard going, which is saying something when you consider James's illegible handwriting, which I can just about tolerate because I know what it's about.

This scribble may even have been some childish lexicon she had gleaned from her mother way back, but whatever it wanted to be, it was difficult to decipher and would have to wait until she came to interpret it tomorrow. In the meantime, I would have to fend for myself.

I did more than that: I ate voraciously, and drank modestly. The casserole would have been big enough for two if I hadn't been so hungry, but I also managed to tuck in to homemade bread like a starving woman and a fruit salad to die for. I was replete.

Whatever magic that girl had sprinkled over the food, I vowed that her cookery skills were not going to get away from me so easily. She hadn't mentioned anything about leaving now there was a new owner, but you never know about these things.

Charles and Millie were in overall charge of removals at the London end and the plan was for them to despatch my worldly possessions on Monday, following the van for a holiday up here in Yorkshire for a few days.

In the meantime, they intended to soak up the City atmosphere and turn the escapade into a romantic weekend. They both loved London and didn't get to see it all that often.

Our plan was on target and Millie telephoned me to say they had been to a West End show and were having fish and chips out of newspaper, and wine out of plastic cups whilst sitting on top of a tea chest (what else?)

I had been wombling about, upstairs and down, trying to get my bearings and coming to terms with my new property, and was now sitting up in bed with my mobile phone in my hand.

'What's the housekeeper like, then, this Bella Graham?'

I had treated myself to another large glass of wine before I came upstairs, so alcohol was trickling nicely through my own veins by this time and sleep was close by, but my befuddled brain came up with a description straight away.

'Helpful without being over-talkative; active brain; ten years into the job, and tiny. So tiny, Millie, she's like a little blonde elf. Strong, though. You should see the way she yanked my luggage upstairs. I think we'll get along fine.'

'Not like the woman in that old black and white film then: the housekeeper who couldn't get over the death of the first wife? Not the most helpful character to help you on your way, I would say.'

'Oh God, no! Nothing like that. Younger than I expected, too, but it sounds as though she had a good rapport with Amelia and the Parsons family. Her mother and grandmother were here for a long time, as well. I didn't know that. I'll have to start writing an *aide memoire* for myself because I don't want to forget anything she tells me.

'If you think about it, she's my new link with the past: she and Ben, of course. Anyway, they will both be here when you come next week, so you can see for yourself.'

I broke off when my mind took a 'U' turn and landed on the delights of homemade bread.

'You will be able to sample her cooking, Millie. It's out of this world.'

I would never have gone to bed in London without drawing the curtains first, but it didn't seem to matter here. Hardly any noise outside to speak of: no car boots slamming, no voices or shouting from late night revellers. This was a coastal road and Amelia's double-glazing easily filtered out the gentle hum of the occasional car.

Besides, I wanted to gaze at the stars before I went to sleep; there were always too many street lights competing for the privilege of lighting up the sky back in Queen's Park.

I suppose I became used to illumination because my bedroom was on the ground floor. Here, there was nothing apart from the odd light bobbing in distant sea foam, and it felt as though I was on my own on the edge of the world. Bella had bagged me the best of a rather handsome bunch of rooms, not only the largest, but one with the 'commanding view' too.

I didn't sleep much that first night, but I put it down to noises off: noises like central heating firing up in the cellar and floorboards creaking. You expect old houses to creak, at least I do, but it didn't seem to be an old-house type of noise that woke me with a start just after midnight. It was more like a discordant whimper in my head and at one point I was convinced it was an animal scratching upstairs in the attic.

Warning bells!

Chessie told me once that she once lived in a house with an attic and she would lie in bed at night listening to mice scuttling around. Great! Thank you Chessie.

Just so long as I don't have to deal with rats. Charles says they are never far away, and I confess I don't get this 'all creatures great and small' loving feeling for them. In a terraced house, you get used to noise from other people, particularly when you have neighbours upstairs, but in a detached house like this, I guess all noises have to be mine, top to bottom.

I got out of bed and slipped on my cardigan and slippers (dressing gown still to come) before tiptoeing out on to the landing. I was trying to ascertain where the sound might have been coming from, although I admit I couldn't hear it any more. Must have been in my dreams.

The room directly opposite my bedroom was one I hadn't yet investigated, so I decided to check whether the window was open. I'd been round most of the others after reading Bella's specific note about locking doors and windows against burglars. A bit paranoid, I thought, but I had taken heed and followed her instructions to the letter. I was the new girl here!

I reached for the handle and pushed open the door ...

And couldn't help a loud gasp of surprise as my eyes slid round the room. The moonlight picked out hefty old-fashioned furniture and cast shadows on the carpet in what seemed to be an uncommonly large area, and I switched on the light to see properly. It was Amelia's studio.

At first glance, everything appeared to be rather more dilapidated than the rest of the house.

Huge bookcases and worn old rag rugs were flattened and shredded with time, mahogany panels of the same type as those in the hall lined one of the walls and an old-fashioned rocking chair with tatty chintz cushions faced a cold electric fire.

There was a tang in the air that I couldn't name.

Nothing minimal here. Not a bedroom either – no bed! A strange air of comfort reigned, though there was nothing that would account for the sounds I had heard. The windows were shut tight (and probably locked if Bella had anything to do about it).

I switched off the light and closed the door. Needless to say, I found nothing of any import when I padded my way downstairs either and, assuming I had been unnecessarily twitchy, I returned to the warmth of my bed.

Twice again during the night something brought me abruptly awake and I lay there, listening intently but hearing nothing of any consequence. I put it all down to strange surroundings and kept my fingers crossed for the success of future sleep patterns, hopefully starting tomorrow.

I don't think I was worried. Perhaps I should have been.

CHAPTER THIRTEEN

It was the electrically powered milk van that woke me properly a few hours later. That, plus the waves lapping down on the beach less than a hundred yards away. Both were long-forgotten sounds of my childhood and I felt a rush of something akin to contentment.

Something else, though; something I hadn't been accustomed to in the streets of London. Brightness lightened my bedroom and I looked out to find that an overnight fall of snow had turned my front garden white and the sun was shining brightly.

Ben's forecast never hinted at how picturesque it was likely to be when the snow came, but the front lawn glistened with slivers of rainbow colours and tiny footprints of birds, giving it the stillness of a Christmas card. I could only assume that my beautiful little car was somewhere snug and safe underneath the heap of white directly below my window.

The milkman was dressed for the climate in a thick duffel coat and large woolly hat, and his bottles rattled as he walked round to the back of the house and deposited three full creams on the step. So, they still had milk deliveries round here then? No tramping to the corner shop as I used to do, where tills clank twenty-four seven.

I watched him as he made a second row of deep footprints back to his van in the road, before shuffling his empties into crates and setting off with a steady hum. Muffled silence indoors was now interrupted only by the clicking of the radiator behind me.

All signs of sleep had blown away in spite of all the traipsing around I had done during the night, so I showered and spent ages rearranging the few toiletries I had brought with me, thoughts zigzagging through my brain as I pottered. Today I was in uncharted waters: nowhere to go; no goal to aspire to; no short-term aim or even a medium-term objective. Life had no noticeable purpose, apart from getting to know Wraycliffe, that is.

How long would it be before ennui kicked in without my nine-to-five routine? I gazed speculatively at the holdall in the corner that the office gang had presented to me two days ago; even that was new, with no memories attached to it. The bigger question was: now I am here, what am I actually going to *do* …?

Something nudged me into action and I placed the holdall tidily inside the otherwise empty wardrobe. All of a sudden, I was primed to give this new status of mine my best shot. After all, time was on my side, and if an old lady thought me worth the effort of bequeathing her life's work to me, who was I to question her trust? No doubt I would get into the swing of things when my belongings arrived, which in itself was likely to revitalize me.

A clattering sound from the kitchen made me negotiate the staircase quickly but skilfully, due to all the practice I had had during the night presumably. The house was warm and I was wearing the violet lightweight leisure suit Chessie had given me as a housewarming present (when she's in sales mode she calls it a fashionable shade of indigo).

I opened the kitchen door and immediately took a step back when two bright amber eyes stared at me from the draining board.

A black cat, completely black if you didn't count the white whiskers and a few stray white hairs on his chest. He also looked as though he had a perfect right to be there. I didn't move quickly in case it panicked him. I think I might have squeaked in surprise, but that was about it.

Glancing round, I saw that his entry point had been a small window in the walk-in larder. It was flapping wildly so I quickly went to close it, not for the cat, I might add, but because I didn't want cold air to penetrate the overnight warmth of the house.

The wood burner looked as though it contained too much grey ash to last much longer anyway, so I gave the coals a thorough rattle with the poker before stoking up again properly and soon had the logs sparking.

After taking account of my wanderings, the animal calmly ignored me and continued with his toilette, smartening himself up and licking his fur as though he owned not only the sink area but the whole kitchen. Had I inherited Amelia's moggy along with all her other possessions, then?

Now that gave me a problem. Nobody had thought to mention this little amazingly significant detail before, and I had two days to work out what to do about it.

Charles's arrival on Monday was now mightily inconvenient, the simple reason being that the poor love has been asthmatic and allergic to fur almost from the day he was born, and is careful to avoid all contact with animals in case they bring on vicious attacks of sneezing and sweating. Millie and I are OK, but cats and dogs were always a no-no in our house for as long as I can remember.

No, somehow, moggy would have to disappear for a while.

The cat jumped daintily down, his contortions complete, and did comfortable eights round my legs. I could feel the thickness of his fur through the soft velour of my leisure suit.

'Well, this is a surprise. Who are *you* then? Got your winter coat on still, I see. And what the devil am I going to do with you on Monday?'

Amber eyes watched me closely as I put the kettle on to boil and found bread to toast, before bending down to stroke him. Beautiful condition, he was. Well-fed, too. Perhaps there was something about him in Bella's notebook.

'You would like something to eat, I take it?'

He gave a loud purr and ecstatic neck stretch and I fondled a coat that was still slightly damp from a night of hunting. There didn't seem to be any cat food on the larder shelves, so I got the full fawning treatment until I opened a tin of salmon.

'You'll have to make do with this until I find out a bit more about you. Doesn't matter what your name is, I'll call you Stringer for the time being, after a coal man I used to know.'

Mr Stringer. Probably dead now (I must ask Millie) used to dump coal down our chute in Norfolk when I was small and he always gave me a sixpence for my moneybox when he came. Seemed light years away. Come to think of it, it *was* light years ago. I figured Bella would know all about the cat.

She did.

'Salmon!' She gave a moue of disgust when she arrived an hour later and had shaken off all the snow from her boots and put them tidily in the porch. 'That was for your sandwiches at lunchtime.'

'You mean he doesn't live here? He's not mine at all?' My big sigh of relief narrowed her eyes.

'Oh no, he lives with Jim and Diana down at the *Nags Head*, but he spends as much time here as he does with them. Miss Amelia never turned him out. I thought he'd gone for good when the place was empty and the food ran out, but he must have seen the light on and decided to come back.'

'If I am only part owner, I'm calling my half Stringer.'

Even as I said it, I pondered the question what Diana and Jim called their half. And did the cat care anyway? Two owners equal two tins of cat food. He jumped up on to the buffet next to me at the table and eyed my biscuit hungrily, sitting like a statue. Perfect manners; he didn't make a wrong move.

But as far as I was concerned, it was good news all the way and I explained as much to Bella. I could now quite reasonably pack him off to Jim and Diana for a week so that Charles would not have any problems. I might have to give the cushions an extra vacuum for hairs and stuff, but that would be the least of my worries.

Bella wagged her finger reprovingly and gave him a malevolent glare before she went to collect the post from the letter basket in the storm porch. I hadn't even heard the letterbox click, but she returned with a handful of junk mail and a letter that had been re-directed to 'Miss E Kent' by the Greenford/Windsor Mail Centre in London.

I recognized the handwriting immediately and surreptitiously placed it, unopened, in my pocket, while Bella stuck a handful of flyers and brochures in a pile and left them for me to browse through later. There was a distinct possibility that I might put them all in the bin when she had gone, including my pocketed letter.

I studied Bella as she fastened an apron round her waist and switched on the oven before gathering baking ingredients from the larder. I tried to follow what she was doing but she expertly wielded spoons and baking tins like an accomplished conjuror.

'Ma says I have to make a chocolate fudge cake for Monday. Save you wondering what to give your guests when they arrive.'

I made coffee for us both and sat down on one of the kitchen chairs as she worked. We chatted like old friends. I was glad about that because I wanted to fit in.

She told me she had spent most of yesterday evening describing the new owner to her mother, who, incidentally wanted to be introduced to me. She confessed she had struggled to recall every blemish, every wrinkle and just about every word I had uttered. I wondered whether she mentioned my cardigan, but didn't like to ask.

It also passed fleetingly through my mind why Mrs Graham had probed so intensely into my arrival or why she was keen to meet me.

Perhaps she still took an interest in what went on at *Painter's Lodge*, to keep in touch, so to speak. No doubt every single one of my possessions would come in for scrutiny and onward reporting when they arrived in the removal van on Monday, too. Hope they wouldn't be too disappointed.

Seeing Bella this morning gave me a different impression of my daily help. Cream slacks and coral tee shirt made her look more feminine than the dreary garb of yesterday. Even the worry lines around her eyes seemed to have shrunk and turned into laughter lines, and she was wearing light makeup that suited her. Her long hair was still anchored loosely at the top of her head, and she had left attractive tendrils to dangle casually down the back of her neck.

Blossomed overnight, I decided. Her pale face yesterday had looked ghostly and ethereal against the black dress, but she was a pretty little fairy this morning.

My younger solicitor was obviously a talking point this morning, too – a 'bally nuisance' she called him. She had put up with a lot lately: first the high and mighty Mr Sharp throwing his weight about and giving her a lot of flak, and then the new owner turning up sooner than she had expected.

'Just when I wanted to clean the carpets and take down the curtains to show the house at its best—' She broke off and bit her lip when she saw the rueful expression on my face. 'I don't really mind, Miss Elise. I'm not overly fond of spring cleaning at the best of times.'

A wave of my fingers brushed her excuses to one side; her resentment seemed to be aimed more at Mr Sharp's interference than the upheaval Amelia had unwittingly created by her untimely demise. I detected some underlying grudge or problem that she would keep under wraps until she knew me better.

Even though the lady of the house herself had provided her solicitor and her housekeeper with a common bond, I could tell there was no *entente cordiale*, and when I tried to delve a little deeper she sniffed and merely said she didn't like being bossed around. That was apparently what Mr Sharp tried to do.

I didn't want to interfere at this stage. They didn't necessarily have to like each other but some kind of harmony would have been nice.

I decided I was on safer ground talking about her mother and she wrinkled her nose when I asked how she was.

'Physically, fine, but sometimes her mind drifts into the past and you never know quite what she will do when I'm not there. I've lost count of the number of times my neighbours have found her roaming around the streets and brought her home. She remembers the past very well: it's the present she has problems with.'

I understood that. Chessie said her grandmother was the same: cognitive impairment, she calls it. But she gets by. I told Bella I couldn't even begin to imagine coping with such a debilitating condition.

'She's been much better lately: the lady next door keeps a close eye on her for me, and I have my mobile phone switched on all the time. It's quite strange really. There's been a complete turnaround since last summer. She used to wander off, but now she seems to be too frightened to go out on her own: stays indoors and locks herself in.'

I was woefully out of my depth here but we came to an understanding that Bella would rush off at a minute's notice whenever there was a need. She told me she hadn't planned to give up her job but if I was happy with flexible employment, then it suited her fine.

I detected a slight glisten in her eyes as she popped the cake into the oven, but she was in control again when she glanced up at the clock and turned around to reach for her coffee.

Change of subject. The time had come for me to learn all about somebody called George, a local electrician who had been hoping to make Bella his wife for the past ten years.

'We ought to be married by now, but we have always felt that the cost of a wedding would be astronomical, well, the kind he wants me to have.

'You don't even want to know the lowest quotation we've been given, Miss Elise, and the highest is completely out of our reach. But we have a little more money in the bank now, of course. You will know all the details better than I do, but Miss Amelia was generous to me in her Will and we can easily afford the deposit on a house. George is forty, the same age as me, though I still think of him as a young man. *My* young man,' she finished proudly.

I fell silent as I stared into my coffee mug and contemplated my own single situation. I was the last person to offer any opinion on marriage; Turner and I had never talked about a trip down the aisle because neither of us expected it to happen. I was going to tell myself that he's probably just as glad about that now as I am, but after my inheritance I am not too sure.

What I did know was that Amelia Parsons had left bequests amounting to approximately ten years' salary to both Bella and Ben. Mr Sugden had gone into the details with me thoroughly, but it was nicer seeing it from the beneficiary's angle.

'Right then,' she said as she slipped off her apron and hung it on the peg behind the door. 'Let me show you round properly.'

CHAPTER FOURTEEN

What I soon came to realize was that this was not a house for a single person: it was far too big for a start. What I had inherited was a family house, a house that needed a large brood of children to bring it to life.

Amelia would have seen it as that when she was younger, and September would know all about play space on a vast scale, but in my present state of singleness, I had still to be initiated.

I have always felt that marriage doesn't have to be a family thing: lots of my reunion pals are comfortably married without offspring. Parenting, on the other hand, is a whole different ballgame.

Do I want any of that, I often ask myself, or do I see myself growing into an old spinster? I confess I have never felt the urge to be a mother, and I often wonder whether that might be some psychological trauma buried deep inside me. You know, things happen to parents that shouldn't. Accidents, for instance. And who would take care of the children then?

Perhaps I just haven't found the right man.

I was already fairly familiar with the first floor, although I must confess I hadn't taken too much notice of the décor yesterday. Dozens of paintings hung along the landing from end to end, and Bella chuckled when she caught me peering at the signatures.

'Miss Amelia painted all these, but not recently. Her eyesight wasn't so good as she got older.'

So, my benefactress was a talented artist as well as an almost-one-hundred-year-old mystery woman.

I stared appreciatively at the creativity surrounding me: large, small, watercolour, acrylic, oil; she was a prolific painter right enough.

'She wanted to move into one of the smaller rooms at the end when she became seriously ill. The far one on the right.' Bella pointed a finger in the general direction, and we walked the entire length of the landing to a single-sized bedroom at the far end. This was what you would describe as a long-by-narrow house. I call it landscape, but that's just me.

'She died in here.' It was said matter-of-factly, though Bella stared at the small bed with its silk coverlet, now looking like a lounger. I let the moment linger.

'She was lovely. Always cheerful and talkative when she was with other people, but she liked to paint and just be herself when she was on her own. She was so kind to us, Ben and me, even towards the end when she became more and more withdrawn. It was just like living with my grandmother; we used to sit and chat until she fell asleep. I couldn't even go to the funeral I was so upset, I just went to bed all day and cried.'

Like many others I knew, Amelia must have been one of those gregarious animals when she was on show, but with a hankering for peace and solitude inside herself.

'I wish I'd known her,' I said.

It was a superfluous comment when I thought about it later, but it received a slight nod and a sniff. Bella pointed to a second door in the far corner.

'That's where the nurse kept all her medical equipment. I dismantled all the extra shelving and cleared it out when she left.'

I opened the adjoining door and saw how the tiny pharmacy had reverted back to being little more than a clutter cupboard.

Not much bigger than the porch downstairs, at a guess. We went out and she closed the door with a soft click, presumably because she saw it as a special place.

'Was she ill for a long time, then? Really ill?'

Bella continued our tour and seemed to take a while to consider the point. Illness is such a vague thing; you can be ill without it showing until 'Wham!' the doctor comes in with a non-negotiable verdict.

A trace of sadness came back into her voice. 'Only a few months. She had a series of strokes but lapsed into a deep sleep at the end. That was after she started to say odd things, although her speech wasn't very good by then and I had to listen really carefully and watch her face at the same time.'

'Odd? How do you mean?'

She stared into space to collect her thoughts and then eventually said in her soft voice, 'Not odd, particularly, just different from normal. She'd been talking to herself for years, but this time it was as though people from way back were in the room with her and she was having long conversations with them. None of us could see anybody and the nurse said she was delirious. She mentioned your name a lot, too, Miss Elise, before she stopped talking all together. It was as though she wanted nothing more to do with any of us, even my ma, who popped in to see her once or twice. She only wanted her family. You, in other words.'

And there was I, not even knowing she existed. I felt bad about that.

'Five bedrooms, one studio and two bathrooms,' she declared, pushing open each door as we walked from room to room.

In my mind, I was already installing family and friends when they came to visit. *If* they came to visit.

There were paintings on the walls everywhere (naturally), and the furniture was the kind of mismatch that had been handed down through generations. It was becoming clear by this time that Amelia was the kind of person who didn't actually get rid of anything.

The whole house had a cheerful warmth about it and Bella told me that she had taken it upon herself not to switch off the boiler, so I would not find it too damp when I arrived.

'I have to say, it was all the Mr Sharp's idea.'

Her tone suggested that she hadn't needed to be told; she would have done it anyway, but she had evidently trudged back and forth along the main road in all weathers, to make sure the Lodge was presentable. She didn't mention what was going to happen to her mother when she married George and moved away, and I didn't like to ask.

When we got to my bedroom she opened the window wider and chased a bluebottle outside that had been clever enough to live indoors throughout the bad weather. I hardly noticed, I had taken off my slippers and was re-testing my squashy bed.

'I must say, this is much better than the one I have just left in London. I'm going to ask the removal men to put all my things into here when they arrive, by the way.'

Her sniff didn't sound quite so fierce to my ears this morning, and I made no mention of the fact that there wouldn't be much to occupy the available space in the bedroom anyway. Or anywhere else in fact. No fitted carpet in here, I observed; only polished wooden floorboards with large shag pile rugs in a pale cream colour. I wasn't sure at this stage whether I even wanted a carpet.

'I can see now that my flat was quite ordinary compared with all this.

'I'm still struggling with the sitting room downstairs, you know, trying to get my head round how modern it all is. I never expected to inherit anything like it, Bella. Amelia must have been a modern miss down to her socks.'

When I had opened the door of the sitting room yesterday evening, my guess would have been to see flock wallpaper and a large ornate mirror on a wall somewhere. Maybe three ducks flying to some mysterious destination, and heavy furniture that would be more at home in an antique shop. But it wasn't a bit like that.

Bella's smile was indulgent. 'Almost right, Miss Elise. She didn't have modern tastes herself, but she brought somebody in to design it and I could tell she was pleased with the results.'

'Why do you think she went to all that trouble? I would have enjoyed looking at period furniture, but I suppose she wasn't to know that.'

'Oh, there's plenty of that around as well,' Bella laughed. 'It's only the front room that Miss Amelia wanted to look fresh and new. She wanted everything in there to be up-to-date so you would fall in love with it when you came. None of us knew when that would be, of course, so she had it decorated every year, just in case. She wanted you to like it well enough to stay.'

I couldn't find an answer to that.

'Was she getting a little senile by that time, do you think?'

'Senile? Good Lord, no. Miss Amelia used to laugh about dementia and say she hoped she would be whisked off before her brain started to go crazy. Sharp as a razor blade right to the end, she was, and far from decrepit. Not that we didn't suspect something, or someone, was troubling her.'

'That sounds ominous. What was that about?'

I slid my feet back into my slippers, straightened the quilt and walked over to stand next to her by the window.

'Well, like I said before, she talked to herself, but it became more noticeable as she grew older. I don't mind admitting, it scared me a bit.'

Perhaps Bella felt a little disloyal by talking this way, and she nervously pursed her lips. We both turned away from the window.

'Maybe she was poorly, maybe something was going wrong inside her head?' I suggested.

She frowned. 'I don't think so, because she was completely all right when someone else was around. She was good at telling stories. I used to sit with her for hours while she told me about things she used to do when she was young: you know, when she was a child. It was like history at school, but more special than that because she had lived through it and been part of it. I did wonder, afterwards, whether she'd made it all up, well ... some days the stories altered slightly and I think she embroidered the facts until she didn't know which bits were true and which weren't.'

'Old people get like that, Bella; some events are not worth remembering so they add little embellishments to make them interesting. Mind you, talking to herself doesn't sound so bad; I talk to myself most of the time.'

'Well, yes. Difficult to explain, really. Take Ben, for instance, talking to his plants. He's not big on conversation at the best of times, and you can tell by the way he looks at them that he doesn't really think they will talk back to him. I heard him having some sort of barney with his asparagus once; it's all part of the job to him, as though he's talking to a child.'

'Isn't that what gardeners are supposed to do, Bella? I did hear once that it encourages shoots to develop quickly. Perhaps their hearing is not so good and they need to sprout upwards to listen.' Don't know where I got that from, but she smiled anyway.

'But it was different with Miss Amelia somehow. She shouted at people who weren't there and it was as though they were having an argument. I even saw her turn sideways and point her finger once, but nobody was there.'

She gave a vigorous shake of her head, to reconstruct the memory with a more realistic image. I was paying avid attention by this time.

'You should have seen the two of them, Miss Amelia and Ben, when they walked round the garden together. You couldn't decide whether they were talking to each other sixteen to the dozen or just to themselves. It was like an old black and white film with the sound turned off. I never really got used to it.'

With a sigh, Bella quickly put on her tour guide hat again and we crossed the landing. She glanced over her shoulder at me.

'I recognized you straight away from your photo, you know.'

'My photo?'

'Yes, the one in Miss Amelia's studio. In here.'

I thought at first that I might have misheard, but I walked towards the door opposite mine, curiosity making my nose twitch. It was the room where I had heard noises off last night. She opened the door with the flourish.

'My *favourite* room,' she declared, almost proudly. 'Miss Amelia's, too. Used to be two rooms years ago when they had seven large bedrooms in all, plus the box room you've already seen.

'Miss Amelia knocked the place around a bit when she was on her own. Said she didn't need so many bedrooms and that these two would make a better studio for her painting, seeing as they overlooked the garden. A big studio now, of course. Brighter too.'

The furnishings didn't seem quite so dilapidated in the daylight as they had done during the night. Emergent sunlight now picked out the lighter colours of the rag rug, and the contents of the bookcases looked neat and tidy.

A mammoth building project that had added a sunroom extension to the dining room directly below had been duplicated up here, such that this southwest-facing studio also had a bay window that ran the entire length of one side. A panoramic view of woods and acres of currently snow-covered farmland stretched as far as the eye could see.

Perfect for an artist.

Pretty good as a computer workroom, too.

The rest of the fixtures were the kind of old-fashioned muddle I had expected – padded footstools, small tables, china ornaments. Nothing like the expensive things Amelia had put into the sitting room especially for me. These belonged to a rich lady who didn't feel the need for change and hadn't even bothered to buy a new carpet for herself.

I was drawn to the enormous window where a few brightly coloured gemstones and crystals hung on threads to catch the sunlight. The snow was just as thick even on this sheltered side of the house, and I took a moment to watch Ben through the window, pottering about before going into his shed.

The pretty stones cast sparkling lights on the ceiling when I gently pushed them with my finger. I had a book somewhere amongst my collection back home about the magical and healing properties of crystals.

Back home? That's not right. This was my home now and, so far, it was sensational.

'Did Amelia collect these for a reason?'

'Don't think so. I guess she just liked the colours when the sun shone on them. She liked little knick-knacks. If you look outside, you'll see wind chimes hanging on hooks and posts. She liked the tinkling noise they make, but she told Ben they were to ward off evil spirits. She started to say things like that, later on.'

From up here I could see at least half a dozen sets of chimes scattered in strategic places across the garden where they could catch the breeze. I've always liked the idea but my back yard in Harlingdon Road, such as it was, was too closed in for them to be active.

A rather handsome piece of French-polished furniture over in the far corner caught my eye. It would have been a gentleman's wardrobe in its day, I think, with fretwork panels and little brass loop handles on the door. You could tell it was old: anything younger than forty years would be relatively new in this house anyway. I tentatively tried to pull the doors open, but found it locked.

I was about to ask Bella about keys when she called out, 'Here it is. Here's the photo I was telling you about.'

She was standing next to a brown roll top bureau of a style popular in the forties. She picked up a photo frame and handed it to me.

'I could tell it was you.'

Of course, it was me. I remembered the coloured snapshot from way back. It was the hair that gave me away: dark and unruly in those days just as it is now, though longer.

Taken on my eleventh birthday, it showed me standing centre stage in the back garden in Norfolk surrounded by a handful of friends who had been invited to my birthday party. We were all wearing posh frocks.

I think I said 'Aww' as I held the frame up to the light. Chessie and September were grinning like happy Smileys, as always, and there were a few girls from down the road whose names I couldn't even remember. Virginia looked her normal picture of tranquillity. I recalled that the woman who took the photo was the mother of one of the little girls. What I couldn't understand was how it came to be here.

'This is so strange, Bella. I have an exact copy of this in my own album. Do you know how Amelia came by it?'

'I have no idea; it's before my time. Ma might be able to tell you, but she will only remember if she's having one of her good days and taking all her tablets. I wouldn't bank on it, though. All I know is that Miss Amelia said it was appropriate for it to be in this room.'

Appropriate? An odd word to use.

The kitchen timer started to buzz at that moment and Bella seized the opportunity to flee downstairs, leaving me alone.

Paintings were dotted around me again, which was no surprise as it was an artist's studio after all, but one complete wall caught my attention and I went to take a closer look. Amelia had come up with a special kind of display, and the spotlights above each ornate frame came on individually when I pressed the switches.

Three large portraits, three ages of women by the look of them, with Amelia's signature clear enough, bottom right.

The earliest said '1969' alongside her name, and I couldn't help my quick intake of breath when I read that. It was the year my parents died, and I quickly calculated that Amelia would have been in her early sixties at the time.

Oils, I think, although she may well have been trying her hand with acrylics by then and I wasn't familiar enough with art to be able to tell the difference. Mr Sharp might know; I could always ask him.

The date would have been important to both of us, Amelia and me, and I knew without being told that she would be grieving at the time. Within twelve months she had lost both a sister and an adored niece. Perhaps it was understandable that she had cast her eye in my direction, a ten-month-old baby, and had thrown herself into her painting. Both our lives changed rapidly at that point.

I knew all about milestones, though, in retrospect, I think I came off better. After all, the disaster had given me new parents, whereas Amelia had probably retrieved nothing.

CHAPTER FIFTEEN

I was as proficient as any country house tour guide by the time the big cream and red removal van trundled north two days later.

My guests arrived first because the van driver and his mate stopped somewhere *en route* for a sandwich and a pint, whereas we, on the other hand, tucked into a more delicious option: Bella's cottage pie and chocolate fudge cake.

In the event, I didn't have to worry about Charles's allergy, because my half cat mysteriously vanished into the night. It was as though he knew he wouldn't be welcome, but I had twice-vacuumed the entire house thoroughly, just in case, and there wasn't a cat hair in sight.

The contents of my life had been held fast with ropes and covered with large canvas sheets in the back of the van, but there wasn't much for thirty-five years, I thought sorrowfully when it all arrived and we unpacked everything.

The whole lot seemed a paltry load, primarily because the furniture back in London had not been mine anyway. Mr Shackleton throws a lot of money at his properties and rents his flats furnished – fitted wardrobes, complete kitchen – which accounted for the paucity of my own *objets d'art*. Chessie had made sure all the landlord's fixtures and fittings were left exactly as they were on the day I moved in: clean and orderly.

'A little gold mine,' she commented over the phone when she was preparing to abandon the empty flat and hand back the keys.

'He could give this place a makeover while it's empty and re-package it as bijou, if he wanted to.'

She always did go the extra mile.

Millie is a chronic picture-straightener, so she had a fine old time putting my own possessions in what she called 'their proper place' and making sure Amelia's paintings were displayed for best effect. At one point, she tried enthusiastically to help in the kitchen but complained that Bella had brushed her aside like an unwelcome bee (on account of diverse inclinations with the cooker, I assumed).

Charles trailed after us everywhere with his little black notebook and made sure that my new acquisition was a sound investment. I didn't ask him to, but I was grateful for his seal of approval.

He poked around in the utility room in the cellar, he checked the gas meter, the electricity meter, and then the security alarms. With his eagle-eye he even pointed out little things I hadn't had time to discover, such as the remote device in the kitchen that controlled the central heating system. 'Working Perfectly', he ticked in his book. Mostly he nodded, sometimes he frowned, but I noticed he made copious notes all the time.

In the end, there was nothing to complain about. He pronounced my new home fit and well and gave me a verbal MOT certificate.

Millie might have been shooed out of the kitchen but she had a bit more luck in Ben's domain. She had ooh'd at Bella's cookery skills, now she aah'd at my garden which was now relatively snow-free. My taciturn gardener was doing his own thing and probably wouldn't have minded if she had chosen to ignore him, but, as it happens, they got on famously because they both have green fingers.

'He spends most of his time in the potting shed,' I told her when she came back in, 'but he's not into dialogue in a big way. Talks to his plants on a regular basis and he'll only smile if he beats me at snakes and ladders.'

I had to explain that Amelia used to sit in the shed with him, playing the board game for hours on end.

'He's a formidable opponent by all accounts, Bella says, and he'll probably expect me to carry on playing, once he gets to know me.'

'He's certainly agile for his age,' Millie commented.

'Eighty-five, with no aches and pains that he admits to. Started about the same time as old Mrs Graham, and has been coming here almost every day since. His wife died three years ago. He was an electrical engineer when he was younger, and only came to look after the garden and take care of odd jobs around the house when he retired. He can fix anything.'

'Really? You can see he's smart.'

'They're both smart, Millie: Bella and Ben. And thankfully neither of them trusts me to be let loose on my own, so they look as though they will stay.'

'Well, you've got yourself a real treasure in the garden. Knows more than I shall ever know about gardening. In return for his advice, I sorted out the contents of his shed for him, just to say thank you.'

My insides cringed a little at that and I glanced through the kitchen window at my lovely garden: first contemplating all the work I would have to do if both my helpers left, and secondly, wondering whether Ben would change his shed back to normality again once Millie had gone home.

It was later that same afternoon when we found something of immense value – to me at any rate.

We managed to drag Charles from the garden where he'd been discussing some clever feat of engineering with Ben that involved lengths of wire and a plank of wood, and I gave the attic an exciting build-up as we climbed the rickety old wooden staircase.

It was a bit like Blackpool illuminations on a low-budget day up there. Half-a-dozen coloured lamps came on at the same time (would have been more, but most of the bulbs needed replacing) and a single overhead light had a cream parchment shade covered with roses and silk fringing – circa the thirties, most likely.

I've never lived in a house with an attic before so I don't know an awful lot about them, but mine was wall-to-wall open plan with stupendous views from large round windows at each end. The view coast-side was a higher version of the one I could see from my bedroom, while the window on the opposite side overlooked the back garden and miles out over the Yorkshire Dales to the distant Cleveland Hills.

'It might be a caboodle of bric-à-brac at the moment, but I want to turn all this into my boudoir – a boudoir in the sky. What do you think, guys? I can visualise a central spiral stairwell from the floor below instead of the wooden steps.'

Charles looked amazed. 'What's so special about a boudoir? And why the devil do you need another bedroom when you have five already? That's what I'd like to know. Not to mention your studio which is big enough to house three cars.'

'Nonsense, dear.' Millie was always up for something new. 'Just think of the views from up here, and apart from anything else it will keep Elise occupied for months. Besides she will be having lots of people to stay, won't you? We shall certainly want to spend a lot of time here, that's for certain.'

She didn't even wait for a reply, and Charles gave in by valiantly taking measurements for his notebook. He didn't stand a chance against us. You can tell when Millie gets keyed up because you can catch a faint whiff of French accent, courtesy of the years she spent in Paris with her mother's family. It's hardly discernible until she gets excited.

She is indefatigable, my aunt (she never lets on about her age) and she continued to give unsolicited opinions on refurbishments, even though the top floor felt more like a des res for a large mouse at the moment than a lavish boudoir for me.

I don't find it easy to throw things away, but, on balance, I think I am better at it than Amelia. What on earth was I going to do with her enormous pile of old magazines? Or the tailor's padded dummy … the stack of old gramophone records … the numerous rolls of carpeting. It would take me weeks to clear such a melange of discarded property. And these were only the things on the front row!

I had already taken a cheval mirror (with much puffing and panting, I might add) downstairs into my bedroom, and had left all the detritus of one era chasing another up here.

Time for our big discovery.

Charles suddenly called out. 'Ah, this is nice, Elise. Come over here and look at this.'

He had been going through the mound of paintings over by the window and had obviously found one he liked. I clambered over the obstacle course as he extracted a large framed portrait and held it up to the light.

A remarkably pretty girl stared back at us out of the frame. She was dressed in a frothy pink lace ball gown and wearing some kind of white smock over the top.

About twenty, I would think, winsome, with reddish-brown Grecian curls that were swept elegantly away from her slightly chubby face and hanging down her back.

She was standing in front of an easel and holding her paintbrush while she posed; the roguish light in her eye suggested her smile was for the artist alone.

I had seen her before, of course, through the round window when I first arrived. It was an almost life-size portrait, roughly four feet by five, I estimated, and signed, though I didn't recognize the name as anybody famous. It simply said 'Fleming'.

To make it easy for future admirers, Fleming had thoughtfully put a clue into his picture that would tell everyone the name of his model. A leather-bound book lay on the table by her side with the words 'Amelia's Journal' printed on the cover.

A little shiver ran down my spine and I gave a small gasp.

'Oh, my word! It's got to be Amelia as a girl. Look Millie, just look at her, she's beautiful.' Then I whispered, almost to myself: 'It's the first time I've seen her.'

At last I knew what she looked like. As a girl, anyway. Okay, this might only be a painting but it was impossible not to return the provocative smile. The three of us stood back in order to have a better look at an episode in Amelia's life when she was gay and happy.

'It's a bit dirty.' Charles wrinkled his nose and peered closely at the frame. 'But nothing that can't be put right.'

'Let's take it downstairs,' I was full of eagerness now. 'It will look magnificent in the sitting room.'

It was heavy, but between us we managed to get it to the ground floor where Millie got to work with dusters for the picture itself and a wet cloth for the frame.

Charles hung the painting over the fireplace, replacing the one that was already there, and stood back to check whether it was straight. I would have to get it cleaned professionally soon enough, but for the moment Amelia had come to life and was firmly ensconced in my sitting room.

I swear Amelia's lips curved a little when I said, 'Hello, Amelia. Welcome to your new home.'

Millie sought out a bottle from the fridge and was soon pouring drinks all round.

'We used to have corks in France,' she said in a distant voice that was full to the brim with memories, 'but these screw caps are so much handier, don't you think?'

We raised three glasses. 'Cheers, Amelia.'

CHAPTER SIXTEEN

I certainly wasn't at a loose end during those first few weeks, and it didn't take me long to spread my DNA all over my new home.

Every room had smiled at me from the moment I arrived. Even the contents of the drawers were to my liking, although I remember hesitating to re-arrange anything in the kitchen because I didn't want to interfere with Bella's routines. Privately, I cherished the idea that we could maybe swap things around a little together – not just yet, but over the coming months.

Inevitably, it was the studio that became the focal point of my new life. I say inevitably because I knew when I first saw it that it was perfect for me – my own personal space – and it occurred to me that Amelia must have felt the same.

Now that I had my own belongings around me, I was able to turn this enormous area into the kind of workroom I could only dream about when I lived in London. My guests had gone back home earlier in the day and it was mid-afternoon by the time I had arranged and rearranged everything in there to my satisfaction.

I even found a place for the housewarming gift that Turner had unexpectedly sent for me. Or perhaps it was not entirely unexpected: it was the sort of thing he would do. He had sent me a rather nice digital clock via Millie, and I put it on one of the bookshelves – not to remind me of him, but because it was a good-looking timepiece that deserved to be on show.

Millie described him as a shadow of his former self when he turned up with it on their doorstep. Thinner and drawn, she said. I didn't tell her that I had also received a Valentine card from him at the weekend that I had since turned into ashes. No way was I going to be pig-headed about the clock and dump it.

'He said he regretted walking out on you.'

'I'll bet.' I replied tartly. 'Look at it this way, Millie. If he feels any kind of remorse that he screwed up, which incidentally I am certain he will, now that I have all this, then that's his problem. As you know, he was on a short piece of string with me anyway.'

Charles put it more succinctly. 'Put the tin hat on it old girl, eh?'

Amelia would never know how much I loved her studio, even more than her designer sitting room, but I did. Like Charles said, it was as big as a car showroom so I could get everything that was important to me into here and not be cramped.

Amelia had fortuitously installed a telephone socket under the window, so there was no problem with an Internet connection. Fibre-optic broadband was super-efficient in the village, for which I was grateful because we had good reception in London, so the speed was good. I might be alone, but I didn't feel lonely.

Stringer padded in there to watch me adjust my computer equipment so the screen didn't catch the sunlight. He had discreetly come back through the pantry window again almost as soon as my guests had driven out into the main road and had never left my side since. Almost as though he knew the score. Amazing!

Sunshine had begun to creep round this side of the house, streaming past lacy curtains that Bella had gathered into swathes, dappling patterns on the threadbare carpet square and the rag rug. The wide border of floorboards surrounding the carpet must have been varnished black some time ago: maybe they were original ones, I don't know. All you could say for them was that they were well-scuffed.

I had the weird feeling that Amelia would be looking over my shoulder for my own reaction to my surroundings. I only hope she wasn't disappointed.

With a little bounce on his back legs, Stringer jumped up on to the windowsill and draped himself comfortably next to a dish of rose scented *pot pourri*. I was tempted to brush him off, but I didn't; this had been Amelia's personal space and anyone could see he was used to sitting there.

While I tickled the back of his neck, I happened to glance out of the window and see Ben working in the vegetable patch. His lips moved as he walked up and down the paths and occasionally stopped to give the shrubs a good talking to. He saw me watching him and we waved.

Well, I waved and he nodded.

It was a smell of painting materials that led me to the far end of the room, a fugitive odour that no amount of fragrant dried rose petals or cleaning fluid could disguise, Maybe Bella had become so used to the smell that she never noticed, but there was definitely turpentine or varnish, mixed with powdery paint, somewhere in the air.

Probably ingrained in the carpet, the smell was not exactly noisome, but nose-ticklingly present. I was surprised to see that the large cupboard at the far end now had a small brass key in the lock.

Interesting. I was positive it hadn't been there on Saturday, but I now turned it and pulled the door open.

It was a typical man's wardrobe. Hanging space on one side with drawers at the bottom, and shelves on the other, all filled with painting materials rather than clothing.

If I had originally toyed with the idea of using it as a stationery cabinet when I first saw it, I quickly revised my plan. I had more than enough shelf space for my own stationery needs, now that I had my computer table and cabinets around me.

Stringer jumped down and joined me for a snoop. After flicking through the used sketchpads that filled the top two shelves, I took out a wooden easel that had been propped up at the back. Aprons and smocks still hung on pegs, and the boxes of pastels and dried-up tubes of paint lower down were clearly labelled.

I decided to search through the contents more thoroughly later, but a rusty old biscuit tin caught my eye and I heaved it out, amassing its contents on to the carpet. Amelia would no doubt have found what she was looking for blindfold, but I was more cautious. No such scruples from the cat, though. I was in the throes of doing some in-depth sorting when he playfully dived into the pile of rubbish, as cats do.

I would have been annoyed with him if anything had been broken during his antics, but that wasn't the case. A small porcelain jar fell over, luckily without being damaged, and a pile of what looked like trash spewed all over the floor.

All of which provided Stringer with unscheduled entertainment as he noisily rolled rainbow coloured marbles from one end of the room to the other.

A long day, all in all, but a lucky one for me.

Finding that jar was like finding a carefully hidden geocache without clues; one that had been long-forgotten.

It was getting dark by the time I finally held the fine piece of white porcelain in my hand, now clean after its gentle scrub in soapy water. It was about twelve inches high with a delicate tracery of tiny purple and gold flowers all over it – not chipped, either, which was a bonus.

Even later, I set up a makeshift cleaning stall in front of the electric fire in the studio and set about sifting and sorting the other debris. I suppose I could have left it till morning, but patience doesn't feature to high on my list of personal attributes.

Ninety-percent of my booty was beyond help. Clarty old chains were encrusted with something that looked like paint but could just as easily have been glue, and buttons that were dirty with age still had threads hanging through the holes. Like I said before, Amelia must never, ever, have thrown anything away.

It was all past its best and needed far more attention than I was prepared to give. You never know, Sophe from our reunion might be able to make use of it. She happens to be a jeweller and can make incredible things out of something and nothing.

I put anything for her to one side, leaving myself with a small heap of scrunched up metal which I had purposely left until last.

Which was when I claimed another treasure, my second serendipitous discovery in my new home. It was a chain of some sort, delicate, and a bit more attractive than anything else I had seen so far. I concentrated on disentangling it slowly and carefully so as not to break it.

The knots were finicky and took an age, even though I had a bright reading lamp shining over my shoulder, and I had almost decided to leave it for another day and go to bed when the final loops magically fell apart.

A tarnished silver chain was threaded through an engraved locket that looked antique and I gave a sigh that I suppose was a combination of satisfaction for my rigorous efforts and admiration for what I had uncovered.

I had a good feeling about my first week, actually. As well as a beautiful portrait of my benefactress, I had now been rewarded with a handsome vase, plus a prize that might well be a valuable piece of jewellery when I got the cleaning fluid on it. Underneath the grime, it bore no sign of damage in spite of its long association with a mountain of buttons and pins, and I felt satisfied that my efforts had not been in vain.

The sepia photo on the inside was so dimmed with age you could hardly make it out, but an undeniably handsome face smiled at me: the cocksure gaze of a man who was confident with his life. A man who still had youth on his side.

I frowned and looked at it closely but it wasn't until I woke up the following morning that I realised just where I had seen the locket before. It had been niggling me. And if I hadn't known better, I could have sworn that the man in the photo was Mr Sharp.

CHAPTER SEVENTEEN

Amelia wore the locket in the portrait that was now ensconced in my sitting room, of course. You could attribute its current lack of glitter to sitting alongside dross in a dirty old jar, but by the time Bella came it was a seventy-year-old piece of sparkling silver round my neck. And so it should, with all that polish. Sparkle, I mean.

'No idea where that came from,' she shook her head when I asked. 'I haven't seen it before.' She was as keen as I had been to look inside.

'Do you think he was somebody special?' I asked when I opened it, careful not to mention any resemblance to my solicitor, which, now I looked at the photo in the morning light, was really nothing like him at all. 'Amelia wouldn't be wearing it in the picture otherwise, but it is rather lovely, isn't it?'

I caressed the patterned surface gently and enjoyed the feel of the engraving beneath my fingers. Bella looked thoughtful.

'My ma might know. There's something familiar about him; maybe this isn't the first time I've seen that photo. Ben might even remember; he's been here a long time. He once told me she had been engaged at one time.'

Bingo! 'That's it, then. It must be her fiancé. Quite a good-looking chap, don't you think?'

She peered down at the sepia features. 'Not as handsome as my George,' she said reasonably. 'Where did you find it?'

'Stringer found it, actually. In an old biscuit tin in the cupboard upstairs. The tall one at the far end.'

'Has his uses, I suppose.'

I got the usual sniff and she stared suspiciously down at the animal who was now languorously stretched in front of the stove.

'That's the strange part, Bella. I'm sure that cupboard was locked when I first moved in, but it was open yesterday.'

She stared evasively at the floor and then grimaced.

'Uh-oh! I can see I shall have to come clean. Ma says I should have told you when you arrived. But I thought I was doing the right thing and protecting Miss Amelia's possessions.'

'Told me what?' I could see I was going to have to concentrate. 'Let's have coffee and you can tell me properly.'

Apparently, it all stemmed from the time when Amelia became really ill a few months ago. Mr Sharp had been a regular visitor to *Painter's Lodge* for a few years: by that time, he was more of a friend than a solicitor and he and Amelia seemed to get on quite well. But towards the end, Amelia took to her bed, and it was then that Mr Sharp began to prowl around.

'Sometimes I would hear him go up to the attic, when Miss Amelia was fast asleep,' Bella said. 'He was looking for something, Miss Elise. I'm sure of it.'

'He must have had a legitimate reason to search,' I offered reasonably, though a chill was starting to spread through me.

'That's what I thought at first, but then one day I was sitting in Miss Amelia's room, reading to her, and I mentioned that he wandered around the house a lot and that he seemed to be looking for something. At first she said that everything he needed when it came to sorting out her estate was already in her box file in her bedroom.'

'Her Will, you mean?'

'Yes, plus all her investment certificates and bank documents. He knew all about all her papers because he had been keeping everything up-to-date and making sure it was all right. He'd been doing that for years.'

I was trying to get a handle on the situation. 'What else would he be trying to look for?'

'Well, that's just it. I'm not sure. Miss Amelia smiled at me in a funny kind of way and said that she knew exactly what he was looking for, but that he wouldn't find it. She never told me what it was; she didn't even tell me where it might be. Then she made me promise to keep her old journals safe so no one could find them until you got here.'

'Journals?'

'Yes, she was quite clear about them. They are yours – all five of them. I remember the way she looked at me and patted my hand.'

Bella knew exactly where the journals were, of course, but it sounded as though Amelia's confidential requests kept her on her toes. She'd already told me about the ranting and raving, but this was something extra that involved being vigilant. You have to admire the way she kept pace with the old lady's wishes.

Mr Sharp apparently went up to the attic over and over again, but if the journals were what he was looking for, then he was looking in the wrong place. Amelia had apparently squashed them at the back of her painting wardrobe in the studio years ago, and the door was locked. The only key was on Bella's keyring.

'Of course, he might have been searching for something different, but then Miss Amelia died and he started to explore the studio instead. He was still looking for something, I'm sure of it, but by that time I had moved the journals to a big trunk in the attic before he could get his hands on them.

'I figured he was unlikely to bother with the top floor again, and that would be the safest place until you came.'

'Where are they now?' I asked.

'Back in the studio, locked in the cupboard. I stuffed them right at the back and covered them with sheets. I only remembered to put the key back in a few days ago.'

It all seemed a bit of a pantomime to me. An old lady's paranoia about protecting something that was valuable to her but probably to no one else. Thinking about it, though, I do it myself. Amelia's journals were no different from my obsession with my ma's writing case, which incidentally now sits elegantly on a small table in the studio. Or the shoebox of photos in the bureau drawer. No difference at all.

CHAPTER EIGHTEEN

A couple of weekends later brought one of those crisp mornings where things are bright and you feel that spring is here, but it's only when you go outside and start to shiver that you realise it isn't like that at all. I abandoned my plan to go for my daily run-stroke-walk and took the opportunity to work on the computer first thing instead.

Strange how a place feels silent when there's nobody else clattering around. Back in my employment days, I would always be aware of people going up and down the stairs, or visitors signing in at reception. All I could hear now was the occasional whirr of the external hard drive, drumming radiators and the gentle tapping of my slippers on the wooden floorboards when I moved around the room.

For a while I played around with my fortune-telling file, the one I wrote for myself, and began to shuffle a few runes around on the screen – not as much fun as doing it in real life, I admit, but it has something going for it.

The word 'fun' made me think of Virginia, for no other reason than Richard had told us how much fun she was having in Canada.

Naturally, I had already posted photographs of my new house on to our website – every room, every crack, every stick of furniture – and had exhorted all my reunion friends to come and stay. Loads of replies bounced back, including one from Virginia saying that she and Richard looked forward to seeing it in real life.

I took a fresh look at her postings and digital photographs of their own house. Sometimes I get a real longing to speak to her like we used to do on the telephone; we would talk for hours.

Even when she was married to Tom we remained good friends and we gossiped a lot. Still do in a smaller way, via the Internet, but I haven't had a snail mail letter from her for ages, and I must have sent at least two to Canada during the last twelve months.

I did a Tarot reading for her and included it in an email. I knew she would like that, though I also knew she wouldn't reply immediately because they are seven hours behind us at this time of year. September isn't the only one to be hooked on clairvoyance: Virginia used to pander selflessly to my hobby, too.

So, all in all, it had been a busy morning. As well as our website, I had also been messing around with a small system I have written for Sophe. It is only in its embryonic stage at the moment but I have no doubt that a few hours will turn it into what she wants, and clinch her enthusiasm to use it.

It was the kind of day destined to become the norm if Bella moved away as a married woman. She had this morning taken her mother to see an elderly relative down in Lincolnshire, so I was on my own for the weekend – apart from Ben in the garden, that is. He was most likely in his shed next to his paraffin heater, and as for Stringer ... well, he could be anywhere.

Ben had a habit of popping into the kitchen each day to make sure I have everything I need in the way of logs, but Bella told me that she usually took him a pot of tea around ten o'clock.

Clearly time to wander down the garden, I think. I didn't know where the snakes and ladders board was, but I could manage a mug of tea.

The shed is very small and it was like an oven this morning with the heater turned on full.

I set the mug down on Ben's old chest of drawers and sat in the only available chair opposite him. It reminded me of my goldfish bowl office. He was rolling cigarettes. He nodded his thanks for the tea and spread tobacco on to a paper he held in his hand. Fascinating routine, and one I wasn't used to, but as I watched his concentration, it gave me the advantage of admiring the hand-knitted thick jumper that his daughter made for him. She must use the same patterns as Millie. Talk about bright and energizing!

I might be able to provide hot drinks and lunchtime sandwiches for the inner man, but I have no clout when it comes to lungs.

He only smokes three cigarettes a day according to my all-seeing daily help, but looking at the pile of tobacco he was working with today, I think she must have under-estimated his usage. But then again, what do I know? He probably revels in the physical pleasure of making them and has a stash waiting to come on duty somewhere back at his house.

Of course, he could always have an entrepreneurial bent, and be selling them to his mates down at the *Nags Head*.

'I keep all my old tins,' he pointed to the oblong yellow-edged box by his side. 'You never know when they'll come in useful. Masses of them at home, I have. Filled mostly with garbage,' he added with a half growl, half chortle. 'Miss Parsons used to give me her old tins as well.'

'Did Miss Parsons smoke then?' That was a surprise.

'Oh yes. She used to roll her own, except she used one of those silly little machines and filter tips. Ruddy amateur,' he said fondly, as memories curled his lip. 'She was a funny-ossity and no mistake.'

I picked up a hopeful gleam in his eyes as he looked across at me and the bushy eyebrows lifted slightly. I solemnly told him I would continue the tradition of handing over my tins if and when I started to smoke. He gave me a nod, and the deal was struck. His eyes met mine for a fraction of a second, presumably to make sure I was taking notice of his nimble demonstration.

'And how do you like *Painter's Lodge* then, Miss Kent? Do you think you will stay? Or is it too soon to say?'

I had the feeling that he was thinking about his own future, and the question seemed innocuous enough.

'To be honest with you, Ben, I hadn't decided what to do before I came here, but as soon as I arrived, I just knew I wanted to stay. I love the house, and the people in the village are more like the neighbours I was used to in Norfolk. For all I've only been here a few weeks, I feel that this is my home. Not simply somewhere to live; a proper home where I belong.'

Even as I said it, I realised how much it was true: I wanted to stay and make a go of life here. For some reason, I began to tell him about my childhood and how much I loved life in a small village, particularly one that was near the sea.

'I could go on for hours,' I told him, suddenly breaking off, slightly embarrassed. 'Don't get me wrong, I like the big City very much, but the landscape is so perfect here it gives me goose-pimples every time I look around me. I bet I could see Denmark across the water on a clear day.'

Not quite true but he laughed anyway.

'Besides,' I mused aloud, 'I can do my job anywhere.'

I sounded like James when I said that, but Ben looked at me keenly and nodded his head.

He understood what I meant. He was a clever man and I had the impression that a lot went on beneath the woolly hat than he ever let on about.

A few more cigarettes were added to his pile while I rambled on about fresh air and country living. Talking to Ben made me realise the full impact of my situation. I was the next generation of Parsons and I was the blood tie with this family home. The only one left, in fact.

As I fell silent and warmed my hands on my own mug, he nodded towards the vegetable patch and pointed out parts of the garden I had yet to discover. Seeing as it was all new territory for me, he knew he was on safe ground. Showed me where the old summerhouse used to be, over in the far corner, where Amelia used to sit and read. And a few yards further on, where her father's joinery workshop used to be.

'Bit before my time, but the old lady showed me sketches she had done when she was younger.' His eyes stared into space, seeing the garden in its heyday, perhaps.

'This used to be a garage,' he nodded down to the floor beneath his chair. 'But that was only a recent change. Only five or six years ago. She thought you would prefer the other one round the front.'

I did, even though my car looked tiny when it was parked in the large structure at the far end of the front lawn. I could open all the car doors and still have room to waltz all the way round the car.

What really confused me, though, was how this lady had been in no doubt that I would get here eventually, and I was overcome yet again by her forward planning. I found it strange that she never thought to get in touch with me.

After a few minutes he said, 'What would you like me to do with the basket Miss Parsons left with me?'

'Her basket?'

He turned a little and indicated a high dusty corner. 'On that shelf over there. I didn't want to bother you before, seeing as you had plenty to do, acclimatising yourself, so to speak, but Miss Parsons asked me to let you have it as soon as you were settled. Said she'd leave you a note.'

The tobacco tin was closed with a kind of finality and he got to his feet. I must say, he was so sprightly that I wondered whether Bella had been wrong about the years.

'I'm afraid I don't know anything about a basket,' I told him, perplexed by yet another little twist, 'but I'll take a look if you show me.'

'She used to use it when she came outside. Full of gardening stuff, it is.' He smiled warm-heartedly as he once again voiced his memories. 'She regularly wore her rubber boots, plus a daft little hat, and she used to sit for hours over there.' He indicated a far corner up against a high wall. 'She used to talk to herself, y'know.'

Takes one to know one, as Millie used to say.

He nodded towards the far side of the garden. A pergola now stood where the joinery shop had been, with a kind of arbour and rustic seat, plus a rose garden that apparently had been Amelia's favourite place. It was definitely the prettiest part of the garden in my opinion, though I didn't want to start any arguments with Ben so early in the game if his neat rows of vegetables were part of the contest.

I imagined the two of them, Amelia and Ben, each chuntering away to themselves, he talking to his plants and she talking to herself peacefully in the sunshine of her garden. I told him I hadn't found a note yet, but that I would look for one and he gave me his customary nod.

'I reckon she must have forgotten about it,' he muttered matter-of-factly, reaching up for the basket.

Amelia had given a large picnic hamper into his care and he had deposited it high on the metal shelf behind watering cans and clay pots. I have no idea whether Millie had shifted it around while she was doing her organizing, but I know for certain he would have put it back when she had gone.

It was full of old wiping cloths and gardening gloves. Digging a little deeper I found a scarred old wooden pencil box containing a dried-up fountain pen and a few pencils, plus the 'daft little hat' which was actually a rather nice straw with a gaudy green ribbon round the brim. I immediately plonked it on my head at a jaunty angle, and Ben grinned hugely when I asked if I looked countryish.

I had no need for power dressing now: no high heels and suits – my smaller derrière looks much better in jeans anyway these days. Well, I think so. Camouflage has gone out of the window and, in the future, I intend to wear baggy sweaters that would fit King Kong simply because I like them. The hat looked perfect for sunshine, I thought.

I know people hang on to carrier bags and bubble wrap but there was enough of it in the basket to keep me going for years. It was only when I heard the telephone ringing that I hastily re-packed what I had taken out, said cheerio, and hurried outside, lugging the fairly heavy basket with me.

I should point out that the telephones inside the house (one up, one down) have dainty little trills, suitable for a genteel lady with perfect eardrums, but all you get outside is the insistent clanging of an extension bell just outside the back door.

Today, it sounded like an old fire engine and made me quicken my step, which is probably why I dumped the basket in one of the cubby-holes in the kitchen and forgot all about it.

My new number is still a bit strange to me, so I have to read it carefully from the sticker on the receiver.

It was Sophe. She must be telepathic. I had completed everything I intended to do for the time being on her file, until I tested it with data.

'I finished your spreadsheet this morning, Sophe. How about getting together and I'll talk you through it. Let's see, today is Saturday. I'm trying to get Chessie to come and stay but she says she has a few fires to put out before she heads north, so it is an on-off-on arrangement. Could be any time. How about meeting up Wednesday week? I'm up to my ears with sorting things out and finding my way around here, but I should have written some kind of manual by then.'

We talked for a while. Sophe lives near East Midlands Airport, but we are both quite mobile – only seventy-odd miles apart after all. I would meet her and her laptop at a Service Station on the A1 where I could load the program and give her some simple instructions.

Anyone in my line of business loves to capture a client like Josephine, someone who is fascinated by little extras, even though her oh-so-simple system has to be easily controllable for her work.

She makes jewellery at home for craft fairs and she wants a way of keeping track of her finances. Her business might be small, but she insists that her computer system has to be modern. What she means is that it has to be technology at the press of a button.

'I'm no computer buff,' she admitted when she gave me her instructions at the reunion. 'Whatever you come up with can be as slick as you like on the inside, just so long as you make it nice and simple for me to operate, Elise. Please.'

CHAPTER NINETEEN

It was destined to be a busy day. No sooner had I put down the receiver than the front doorbell rang.

I have managed to get into the habit of closing the inner glass door of the entrance porch for warmth, but Bella keeps reminding me to lock the front door as well, just in case. 'You don't want people wandering in, do you?'

And so it was, after I had dealt with numerous, *absolutely essential* locks and bolts, that I found Mr Sharp on the doorstep.

I hardly recognized him. A camel coat this time, and the scarf and winter padding made him look even larger than before. Could always have been muscles, I suppose, but who can tell under that lot? I always think that a bowler categorizes a man, but it rather suited him in an odd way. Not many men look good in hats, but I have to confess he does.

'How do you do, Miss Kent.'

He leaned to one side, emphasising the point that I appeared to be hiding behind the door, which made me self-conscious, and I automatically opened the gap wider to invite him in. I guessed he had parked his car in the lane outside, but the way he stamped his feet on the mat suggested he had hammered the matting dozens of times before and could probably outdistance me with footprints on the carpet easily.

Bella's heads up came immediately to mind.

He gave the brolly vase a frown and a wide berth. If he was surprised to see it still there, he made no comment. Perhaps he likes it; there's no accounting for taste.

'It's good of you to come, Mr Sharp. I never expected the day to be so eventful when I got up this morning. Please come in.'

I closed the outer door and he casually hung up his coat in the hall, almost as though the peg had his name on it, and placed his bowler and gloves on the table. As usual, presumably.

The dark suit reminded me of James on one of his formal days, but I suspected Mr Sharp dressed in three-piece pin stripes and silk tie all the time. He definitely wouldn't look right with a punk hairdo or flowery shirt, but then, neither would James. Oh, I don't know, though!

Tall and gangly this man was, as though he had spent the early years of his life hanging from the rafters with weights on his feet. Chessie is tall but he had a good six-inch view over her head, I recalled.

'I assume we have business to discuss?' The leather briefcase had his initials embossed on the lower corner - NFS - and he nodded. He gave me a courteous solicitor-client nod that had a kind of military touch to it. 'Would you like a cup of coffee?'

'Black, please, if it's not too much trouble.'

'Have a seat in the sitting room then, and I'll be with you in a minute. It won't take long to boil the kettle.'

He hovered a bit, looking temporarily confused, and it made me wonder whether he felt awkward here, now that I was the lady of the house. He might even have been used to homelier chats with Amelia in the kitchen, which I doubted, or in her studio (more likely). But that was in the past; I preferred my elegant sitting room until I got to know him better.

His eyes missed nothing: they swirled around the hallway and came to rest momentarily on the open kitchen door and the rack of clothes I had ironed late last night.

But then I left him as he followed my instructions and made for the sitting room. It was like entertaining royalty in my best room.

'I hope my visit isn't inconvenient,' he said when I had everything under control in the kitchen and joined him. 'I can always re-schedule and come back some other time, but Saturday is a working day for me. I'm usually quite busy, but I happened to be in the area so I thought I'd come on the off-chance.'

I confess I had been waiting for him to appear in Wraycliffe. He must have been wondering about me, too. Whether I had settled in properly and what kind of impression I give out when I'm not on my best behaviour – funerals are such an illusory guide when you want to see what a person is really like. I wasn't keen to divulge anything so I just shook my head.

'Now is as good a time as any, Mr Sharp. As a matter of fact, I've had quite a busy morning on the computer, but I've had enough of that for a while.'

'Ah yes. I saw a file note that the beneficiary used to work as a computer analyst.'

Ordinarily, I would have flinched at the words 'used to', but I didn't over-react this time. I was still a bit prickly about having no job but I didn't let it show; I had so much more to occupy my time now.

He glanced appreciatively around him before taking up a position with his back to the fireplace. I had a log fire going this morning; the room was large but pleasantly warm.

'Do you like the way Miss Parsons refurbished this part of the house?' he asked, turning his head to examine the paintings. I have always thought she had excellent taste.'

'I certainly do; I think it's fabulous. Bella told me Amelia's reasons for keeping pace with fashion, but it must have been extortionately costly.

'It would have been nice to tell her how much I appreciate the gesture. To be perfectly honest with you, Mr Sharp, I expected something more old-fashioned. Nothing like this, but I'm more than happy with it.'

I lifted my hand to indicate the plasma screen TV, the sumptuous cream leather sofa and the hardly-walked-on carpet. A room that had nothing to do with the past.

'The last few weeks have been quite a jolt for me, you know. My world has already been turned upside down on the work front, but Amelia has made it spin a little as well and I haven't come to terms with my new life yet. I am not used to having nowhere to go every day and it's quite daunting not to have a busy schedule when things won't budge from your 'in-tray' however hard you clatter your keyboard and work long hours.'

So much for not divulging anything, Elise!

He narrowed his dark eyes as he studied me, but he said nothing and turned back to the fire to warm his hands in front of the slumbering logs. I could tell he had done it before. Charles used to do that on a cold day.

I took the opportunity to go and attend to the coffee, and when I came back with a tray of best china and some of Bella's delicious home-made cake, he was studying the painting of Amelia over the mantelpiece.

Stringer followed me in and brushed up familiarly against Mr Sharp's legs. I worried about cat hairs on the pin-stripes, decided to ignore it, and said instead that I hoped he liked strong Colombian. He merely said 'Mmn,' and continued to stare at the portrait.

'I see you found Miss Parsons then?'

He was obviously acquainted with the portrait, and, if Bella was right, he would definitely have come across it in the attic.

'Yes. I might have it cleaned professionally later, but I wanted to hang it somewhere now and keep it on view. I can't seem to find any modern photographs of Amelia anywhere.'

He sat down opposite me, striding round the cat who had stretched out in front of the fire and was now fast asleep.

'She was a painter, not a photographer,' he said. It felt like a rebuke.

As I poured coffee, I noticed his attention was on all the other paintings in the room. He was spoiled for choice.

'Some of these have been worked earlier in her life,' he said. 'You can see the beginner's meretricious perspective in one or two of them, but a gradual coming together of talent and technique that infuses the later ones with increasing ability.'

Well! That was a long-winded way of saying that some were better than others, but I could see what he meant and my eyes followed the direction of his long pointing finger. My own analysis would have been to say they looked like a lifetime's work, painstakingly carried out to the best of her ability as she learned her craft.

After about half an hour I was used to the clipped tones and serious legalese, but I now understood what Bella meant by bossy. I wouldn't have called it that: no, I think he had cultivated an assured manner in his job so that people would take notice of him. It wasn't arrogance; I think he was just being careful never to put a foot wrong.

'Well then, Miss Kent. Down to business. Now that Miss Parsons has passed over, we have a few details to tie up.'

Passed over? How biblical. I gave one of Bella's sniffs (must be catching).

'I run the northern branch of our firm based in Leeds,' he explained, 'although I do spend a fair bit of time in the City, when I get around to it.'

He fished in his briefcase and pulled out a few typewritten sheets which he sorted in some kind of order and placed in front of him on the glass table. He began quoting from the notes Mr Sugden had already talked about, and I tried to sound as though I remembered everything off pat. This was a list of bequests, and the one on top had pencilled sketches interspersed with handwritten notes.

I was glad I had done my homework and that I knew about the bequests to the local school. They were all paintings – local views, all of them – but they were not mine. Not now, anyway. Never had been either, by the sound of things. I could see he was impressed by what I already knew about them, and he ticked his sheet before turning his attention to the rest of the pile in front of him.

'If it is convenient then, I'll have someone call round to collect them on Wednesday. In the meantime, perhaps you wouldn't mind signing these.'

I put on my reading glasses and he explained each of the forms in meticulous detail. Much of it was about finance, which would inevitably find its way into Charles's domain even though I was well-versed in my own situation. My mother's assets had been in interest-bearing accounts that had dwindled in a strange marketplace after the Second World War, whilst my father's estate was almost entirely in shares: all of which came to be absorbed into my own portfolio.

Now, of course, it required a complete overhaul, although Charles tells me that he has everything under control, bless him.

A lot was about tax and insurance and I listened carefully because I wasn't as clued up on this as I was on investments. If it hadn't been for the way Mr Sharp explained everything, I would have found it quite incomprehensible, and for the next half hour we covered a lot of ground. I suppose a legal brain dared not make mistakes when giving advice in today's blame-culture world.

Even when he was silent I got the distinct impression that the gears in his head were crunching and sifting before he spoke. He referred to all his mass of papers as legal loose ends, but I'm sure they were more important than he made out and I had no hesitation in signing everything he put before me.

I was glad to have such a knowledgeable person in tow. He had a way of looking at me directly into my eyes when he wanted to press home a particular point. In no way could I have called it patronising, and I had already pigeonholed him as typical of the legal world: effusively polite and well on the way to becoming a clone of Leonard Sugden. If he wasn't already!

The benign smile he kept throwing in my direction must be something solicitors learn to do when there is a breathing space, because his boss had done exactly the same thing, and he even managed to persuade me to draw up a Will somewhere along the way, the clever man. That must have been around the time I lost my powers of concentration.

At closer quarters, I saw that I had been right about the muscular body; he was probably a gym freak and worked out every morning before he went into the office. Personally, I thought that his nose was a shade too large, but as Sadie (a woman back at my office) used to say when she spoke about gentry: they always look well fed.

'And what do you think of Yorkshire then, Miss Kent?'

I abruptly left my thoughts about him hidden and took off my glasses. We had evidently completed the official stuff, so perhaps it was time to open up a little.

'To be honest, it's the first time I've been to Wraycliffe. Quite a new experience for me, Mr Sharp. I wasn't even sure whether I wanted to keep the house when I first found out about it. It sounded rather large, and a long way from where I think of as home.'

His eyes narrowed and the clean-shaven jaw tightened slightly, or was it my imagination?

'You would get a good price if you put the house on the market. We would be only too pleased to act for you. Houses of this size are selling extremely well just now.'

It was the way he said it, slowly and deliberately, that bridled me. He sounded a shade too interested and I felt my face burn. His eyes were trained upon me as he waited to hear more, but I smoothly backtracked.

'Oh no. I haven't seriously thought about selling since I got here,' I said, hoping I sounded pleasant, though it was irksome to think I had confided in him so easily. 'I like it so much now; I don't think I shall ever want to leave. A carapace for the rest of my days, as the poets say.'

It was galling to think that anyone should be so eager to take all this away from me so soon after I had acquired it, and something inside me wanted to be truculent.

'I promise to let you know if I ever do decide to pack up and go.'

With exaggerated patience, he searched in one of his inside pockets and handed me a business card showing office and mobile phone numbers. Then he looked at his watch, clicked his briefcase shut and stood up.

'Right then, I must go. Thank you for the drink, Miss Kent, and please call me if there is anything you need, or want to know.'

'I will. Thank you.'

Then, an afterthought, perhaps. 'Oh yes, we shall soon be holding our annual Investment Presentation in this area in conjunction with a local Financial firm. An evening with cocktails, I think, though the format hasn't been finalized yet. Early April as a rule. Would you like to come?'

'What a good idea. That would be very useful. Thank you, Mr Sharp.'

'Nathaniel, please.'

'Nathaniel.'

'My office will send you an invitation in due course then.'

This time he gave me his best S.S.&S. smile and the deep voice echoed majestically around the hall as I followed him and helped him into his coat. He turned and held out a hand that was cool and firm. Those intelligent eyes and expression were hard to read, but it suddenly occurred to me that his surname was most appropriate. When he had gone, I turned his name around in my head.

Mr N. F. Sharp

Nathaniel Sharp

Nathaniel.

I have no idea why I was quick to lock the door behind him. I had no intention of letting Bella influence me in any way, but I suddenly felt I wanted to be on my own with my newfound Parsons family.

CHAPTER TWENTY

The school caretaker turned up a few days later, as promised, and it was a bit of a surprise to see that Mr Sharp – Nathaniel – was with him. I had expected him to be on his own and it caught me a little unawares.

I had just put the last full stop into Sophe's instruction sheet and come downstairs to watch one of those breakfast programmes on TV that I never had the opportunity to watch when I worked.

To be truthful, it didn't take me long to realise I hadn't been missing much. Flames hissed in the fireplace as the logs burned and re-settled, which I thought was frankly a more interesting show than what was on the box.

The script was lightweight, and it wasn't until the presenter introduced a dark-haired woman sticking flowers into a vase that I sat up and took notice. She was tall and willowy, and looked so much like Virginia that I did a double take. Virginia had done her best to show me how to arrange flowers years ago, but I had been useless. They say you get better with practice, but it isn't true: you just give up after a while and hope it all looks good after you plunge everything into a vase.

It was on Virginia herself that I homed in. There was something I had been meaning to do for a few weeks, but had put it off. Today, for some reason, the urge took hold of me and I immediately went back upstairs to the workroom.

I still think of the writing box as my mother's. I'm not a hoarder – well, perhaps I am – but I do keep my most secret papers in there so I know where to find them when I need them. Important stuff like birth certificates, medical cards and such.

The box is fairly heavy and I opened it warily because I didn't want to damage the delicate hinges. The sloping, green baize writing surface came adrift slightly a few years ago so I stuck it back with superglue (which probably does nothing for its antique value) but I reckon it will last my lifetime if I take care of it.

I squeezed the secret panel to reveal the compartments underneath, one of which is a drawer where I put Virginia's grown-up letters to me. I have kept them for no other reason than that I thought they might come in useful some time. I winced a little when I saw my parents' death certificates and pushed them back into their own drawer, but I eventually found what I was looking for.

It was Virginia's last letter to me before my friends and I climbed into the next technological era and began to communicate using the website. For some reason, I had also kept the envelope – her handwriting was remarkably beautiful by then and I saw that the letter had an Ambleside postmark on it, where she lived at the time.

Four pages. I quickly read them, not really knowing what I was searching for and finding nothing of any consequence until I came to the last page. She had been writing about her mother's funeral for most of the letter; telling me all about it because I had been unable to go.

I have read this letter over and over again from the day I received it, seeing it differently each time and not quite grasping its meaning.

As far as I knew, no one else knew its contents, not even Chessie, but the letter was all about the day Virginia's mother died.

She wrote that she was confused, which I put down to normal depression from her mother's sudden death and recent loss of her husband and child. She had hardly any family left, but she kept mentioning a man called McGovern. Inspector Silas McGovern, who was looking into Flora's accident. Towards the end, she wrote:

> *But enough of this rambling, my dearest Bunty. What I really want to do is to ask you a favour. If you ever have any worries about me – anything at all – then I want you to contact Inspector McGovern. Please, please say you will. He is a clever man.*

Not Richard then!

I glanced at the date on the first page and saw that for all she had only been married two years, this detective seemed to be more on her mind than her husband. He had been Tom's friend at school and had been at their wedding. I couldn't remember him, but she mentioned Silas in just about every other paragraph.

I stared down at the letter in my hand and carefully folded its abstruse contents back into the envelope.

Something was scratching away at the back of my mind; something that I knew was important. What should I do? What ought I to do about Virginia?

I had written a long letter to her only yesterday – not using our pet names, of course, because some inner voice told me it would be unwise.

I had said nothing about Richard, either, nor his visit to London. No, I wrote about Wraycliffe, about Mrs Hanby's shop and the cup of tea she had given me when I went to place an order for my regular morning paper.

It was the kind of chatty letter we had written to each other down the years, only now I was addressing it to Canada.

I begged her to write to me with news of a more personal kind rather than with the openness we share on the website. Truth to tell, I miss getting something from her where my address is written in her own handwriting, though I didn't actually say that in the letter. Only that I missed her.

The doorbell rang. Two men stood on my doorstep: Mr Sharp (in mufti this time) and a younger man whom I took to be the school caretaker. I had only seen my solicitor in his office gear before, but he was showing me another elusive facet of his personality this morning.

Without the bowler, his dark hair shone in the morning sun. Yes, it was slightly long, and yes, he had long eyelashes any girl would die for, but the fact that he wore a sheepskin jacket over his checked shirt and cream cord trousers befuddled me for a moment. He looked less formidable somehow.

'I assume this is more of a social call?' I pointedly looked him up and down before smiling hugely and inviting them into the hall.

I was glad Bella was downstairs. Knowing her antipathy towards Nathaniel, it was something of a relief to know she was busy sorting through sheets and pillowcases in the cellar, and that she would hide herself away until he left. I wasn't quite ready to referee any sparring just yet.

'Half and half, actually,' he said cheerfully. 'Business here first, and then lunch with my mother in town, when "casual" gets the upper hand. She's a cantankerous old dear who makes her opinions plain: she likes me to look less of a solicitor and more the country gentleman.'

I pictured a little grey-haired old lady in twinset and pearls who would become apprehensive if her son were late. Not so. A few more questions from me turned her into a very active woman who played golf to a reasonable handicap at the age of seventy-eight.

'She will have been playing golf this morning – Ladies' Medal Day, you know – so she will be either in a good mood or disgustingly cross, depending on how she played.'

He locked those rather interesting eyes with mine and I detected a note of irony, but I quickly looked away. This was a new side of my solicitor I hadn't seen before.

'Gordon,' he introduced his companion. 'He has come for the paintings, and I have brought some papers for you to sign.' He raised his eyebrows and held his briefcase aloft.

Gordon tipped his cap and then held out his hand as though he hadn't been quite sure which to do. To be on the safe side, he was doing both.

'I was sorry about the old lady, your grandmother, miss.'

I thanked him without putting him right about my true relationship with the Parsons family, and he refused my offer of coffee, saying he was in a hurry.

'Busy day,' he declared, tipping his hat again and lodging the paintings carefully in his truck. 'Thank you, Miss. And thank you Mr Sharp.'

My solicitor sniffed longingly at the smell of freshly ground coffee as I brought a couple of mugs through from the kitchen and placed them on the coffee table.

I was glad I was wearing my leisure suit instead of jeans this morning and I only hoped Mr Sharp hadn't noticed that I had also run my hand surreptitiously through my hair while I was out of the room.

The business part of the morning was apparently the signing of my Will, and I casually wondered what the 'F' stood for when NFS bent down to open his monogrammed briefcase. He brought out a double sheet of parchment-type paper.

'Only a short Will. Very basic, until your situation changes,' he explained (which I suppose means until I marry). For the time being, I have left everything I own to Charles and Millie.

'In the unfortunate event that you die before they do, they will adhere to a list of gifts that will be set out on a separate sheet of paper, which you can alter at any time without the need to make a fresh Will. It's all very straightforward.'

It was, and I told him I could find nothing to change when I had read it through.

'That's all right then,' he said, taking out his fountain pen and jotting a few notes on his pad. 'We shall need another witness. If we can persuade Bella to spare a few minutes of her time it will save you a trip to the office. Or Ben, perhaps?'

He must have heard the washing machine thumping away in the cellar and I managed to catch Bella as she came back up the stone steps with an empty washing basket in her hands. This had to be handled with tact.

'Bella, Mr Sharp is here,' I whispered. 'Do you think you could come in and witness a document for me?'

I felt without looking at her that she had screwed up her eyes. 'Please. It won't take long. We could ask Ben, but I don't want to trek down to the shed.'

'I still have to see to the tumbler dryer,' she said repressively. I raised my eyebrows with a persuasive smile on my face. She cleared her throat and her eyes registered her disdain as she cast them to the ceiling. 'Oh, all right. Just let me put my basket away and I'll come straight in.'

I went back into the sitting room with a feeling of apprehension which I thought I hid rather well. Bella gave him a brief and very correct smile when she joined us a minute or two later. There wasn't one iota of resentment in her voice; she was sweetness itself and I sneaked a quick wink at her that suggested I was on her side.

The man was more amiable than I expected, good-naturedly completing the business of the day and nodding appreciatively when Bella brought fresh coffee. The tin of chocolate biscuits was a miraculous extra she had found from goodness knows where, and I mouthed an 'Ooh!' in thanks as she quickly disappeared from the room.

'These were always a favourite in this house,' NFS said with an indulgent smile, once again asserting his right to be here. I drooled over my choice of biscuit and eventually selected a chocolate cream. The thoughts that flickered across his face were invisible to me as he circled his forefinger over the tin and eventually homed in on one himself.

'How many years have you known Miss Parsons?' I was prompted to ask.

I wasn't sure whether social conversation was going to be easy, but I could probably manage twenty minutes without a problem.

I found myself wondering what his mother was like when it came to personalities, the golfing lunch lady. Were there any similarities?

He stood up and walked over to look at the painting over the fireplace as he mentally totted up the years.

'Let me see. I joined the firm fifteen years ago, but I didn't come to the Leeds office straight away. Leonard passed the Parsons account to me about five years ago. Yes, that's right. We are talking roughly five years.'

'What was she like?' A pent-up enthusiasm was building up inside me. 'Really like, I mean. Not just on the surface. What was she like underneath?'

'You must remember that she was old by the time I knew her,' he replied with good humour. 'An inimitable lady who kept me entertained with tales of her youth that I personally found fascinating. In her own words, she said she had been a high-spirited if not wilful child. I can add to that by saying that she grew to old age as a feisty woman with a massively fertile wit.'

'If we are lucky enough to get to ninety-nine, we are supposed to be special,' I reasoned with a wry grin.

He turned towards me from the painting. 'I see you found the locket.' He nodded towards my neck and I automatically lifted my hand to stroke the silver. 'Miss Parsons thought she had lost it, but I always assumed it had merely been misplaced. Where was it?'

'In the studio. Actually, the cat found it in an old jar, intermingled with lots of other tarnished bits and pieces – chains, key rings, stuff like that.'

'You didn't find the other necklace, then?'

'What other necklace?'

'The black amulet on a ribbon, the one that appears in all the studio portraits.'

I shook my head and murmured something like 'Not yet.' Surely, he hadn't been looking for old jewellery in the attic? Back on track I then said, 'Go on then, tell me everything you know about Amelia Parsons.'

He laughed. 'That's a big question. My word. Where to begin?'

'Anywhere. Anywhere at all. I want to know every detail.'

'Amelia Parsons as a child, then, I suppose.' He smiled at my eagerness and went on, 'A proud little girl; an impetuous scallywag who went for walks in the middle of the night and climbed trees with the village urchins during the day. She could get away with whatever she liked, as long as it was accompanied by a winning smile and a shake of her dark brown curls. Er ... her words, not mine.'

He was warming to his subject – a born storyteller – and I found I was having a hard time remembering Bella's warnings.

'Well, her romantic aspirations blossomed when she learned that boys eventually grew into men. The Parsons sisters were regulars at County Balls and parties, you understand, and Amelia in particular grew to be an outstanding beauty. By the way, did you know that Miss Parsons had two sisters, both younger than herself?'

My eyes widened. 'No, I only knew about my grandmother, I hadn't realised there was anyone else.'

'No? Well, Elizabeth was the next sibling in age, but the baby of the family was called Harriet.'

Three girls? That was a surprise. Wait till I tell Millie that I am accumulating relatives thick and fast this year.

'It's all documented in her journals, I believe. Have you discovered their whereabouts yet?'

Aha! Now I was on my guard but I managed to shake my head. I've never been good at lying, but this part was true: I hadn't actually seen these journals although, unlike the man sitting opposite me, I knew where they were.

'Miss Parsons only showed me the early volumes, but I understand that she kept the last one separate. She started it forty years ago, and told me she had destroyed it by accident later, which, incidentally, I don't believe. Her choice, of course, whether to show it to me or not.'

'Now you really have got me confused,' I said with a frown. 'Is the last journal important? Does it contain anything of significance?'

'Probably not,' he said with a sigh. 'Just some old lady's imaginings.'

I knew what he meant. I suffer with that myself sometimes.

'Well I can tell you the gist of what the early ones contain,' he said easily. 'Amelia told me that she had numerous boyfriends, but something happened in the summer of the year she was twenty-three that suddenly made her grow up. She met the most perfect man in the world and fell in love. One minute she was a giddy teenager and the next, a flirtatious young woman who found a man with whom she wanted to spend the rest of her life.'

'The man in the locket? Mr Smiley?'

He laughed at my description.

'Well yes, you could call him that. The man who turned her head was the artist who painted that portrait of yours above your fireplace – Nathan Fleming.

'She first met him at a friend's party and, Whiz Bang! That was it. She somehow persuaded her father to commission a set of paintings, so he could come to the house regularly.'

'Wow! I knew he had to be special. You can tell by the way she looks at him on the canvas, and his rascally grin in the photo.'

'She believed they were made for each other, but unfortunately, her plan fell apart when young Harriet, who was her junior by five years, made a play for him and they ran away together. It caused quite an uproar. Amelia was devastated and dear old papa was furious.'

'How awful. Poor Amelia!'

'The deal was for Fleming to paint Mrs Parsons and three daughters, not to whisk one of them off from under the old man's nose. But what made it a whole lot worse was when they discovered that the Nathan already had a wife – going through a divorce procedure, I grant you, but a wife nonetheless.'

'All these goings-on don't seem to matter nowadays,' I cut in. 'Running away with an artist wouldn't be such a catastrophe today.'

The solicitor in him nodded wisely. 'Multiple-layer families are quite common and need a lot of sorting out. But, as you might expect, Amelia displayed the tenacity for which she was famous and boosted the family's morale by getting engaged shortly afterwards to an American by the name of Josiah Shaw. The marriage was arranged by her parents, which was quite common in those days, but I gather she wasn't entirely smitten.'

'I'm not surprised. She was probably still reeling from the artist fiasco.'

Amelia apparently had great moments of lucidity by the time Mr Sharp came on the scene, and though her early life might be an open book, it was though she put a blanket over her later years.

I said, 'By the way, how do you know all this?'

He looked thoughtful for a moment. 'Miss Parsons had business affairs that only needed the occasional tweak, so for the most part, my visits here were quite informal. She saw me as someone to confide in when I came to get her to sign her Codicil. Old people like to be sociable, you know. One thing led to another and she allowed me access to the journals that included quite a bit about Harriet, the black sheep of the family. Well, one of the black sheep anyway,' he added carelessly.

'Did Harriet ever come back then?'

'Apparently not. She married Nathan Fleming and they went to Europe. They had a child, but all three of them died in a fire. There's a grave somewhere in France.'

'So that was the end of that particular branch of the family?'

'Yes, which was a pity because it would have added a spark to the later chapters.'

'Chapters?'

'Of my book,' he explained. 'I am writing a biography of my family.' He gave a loud sigh that contained an element of frustration and told me that his writing was not going all that well. 'Unfortunately, my book and I are not friends at the moment. One day I shall pick it up again, but for the time being I am throwing myself into work of a more lucrative kind. At least, that's what my mother calls it,' he added, rubbing his finger and thumb together as he spoke.

'What has your family to do with Amelia Parsons?' My brain was struggling to sort out what he was telling me.

'Oh . . . didn't I tell you that part? Nathan Fleming was my grandfather.'

CHAPTER TWENTY-ONE

It has taken a few days for it all to sink in, but apparently, I come from a long line of market gardeners. In fact, the only reason I am here at all at *Painter's Lodge* is because of a gambling debt.

All this fascinating news set Charles off on one of his Internet trawls straight away when I told him; Millie, being of a more romantic persuasion, simply became imaginative and unnecessarily romantic in my opinion.

Amelia's grandfather (the first black sheep?) went to Canada as a struggling carpenter and came back a rich man. He went out there to make his fortune sometime in the early eighteen hundreds and he did just that. Not, as I understand it, as an artisan, which had been his original intention, but as a gambler who happened to strike lucky. He was the one who started the market gardening business next door to the main house.

Even further back than that, we were gypsy paupers, which personally I found a lot more exciting than having a rich man in my family tree who knew how to play cards (and probably cheat!) From gypsy pauper to wealthy landowner in a couple of leaps is quite a feat.

Buoyed up by Mr Sharp's summary and doing my best to get Bella's negative attitude towards him in perspective, I discovered all this when I started to pore over the journals.

Amelia was thirteen when she began the first journal, and as for the amulet, Nathaniel was right.

The black stone necklace was in every one of the paintings in the studio, and I broke off from my reading to stand in front of each of them in turn.

First the one with the child in it. A thin little waif with a daisy chain wrapped round her long-tousled curls. She was wearing some kind of rough cotton shift and was leaning against what looked like a sundial. You could see the outline of her ribcage through her shift, though whether that was imaginative brushwork I couldn't be sure.

The stern-looking woman in the next portrait was wearing a purple and green striped gown with a matching hat, and the last portrait was of an old woman who was sitting in a chair, looking gentle and rather shy. They all looked vaguely alike, but again I put it down to predilection of the artist rather than accurate representation.

I peered closer at the chunky amulet.

In the waif picture, it was at her feet, discarded next to a wooden doll; purple and green had it dangling from her hand on a piece of string and the older woman wore it as a pendant on a black velvet ribbon. There was nothing elegant about it: it could easily be a rock or a pebble from the garden.

Amelia had been honest and forthcoming in her writing and I felt an outsider's guilt about reading her words until I realised that what she had actually produced here was her autobiography. Mr Sharp had described her perfectly and I even contemplated writing a biography of my own. Maybe at some time in the future.

I admit to feeling a certain sympathy with her mother, who must have found this 'infuriating little minx' rather tiresome.

Her dear papa on the other hand (I noticed that she always referred to him as 'dear') seemed impervious to the danger of her escapades and was probably secretly proud of her. After all, he was the one who had descended from a maverick card player from way back.

The beleaguered servants who had to mop up after her messier escapades must have thought she was a downright pest.

Whatever text she had written about Nathan Fleming in the mid-Twenties was now illegible because she had scribbled heavy black lines over her words so no one could share her (presumably derisive) thoughts. That would have been when she discarded her necklace and stashed it in the jar.

Her teeth-gnashing script about the worthy American Josiah Shaw who came afterwards was still visible, however. She described him as 'obnoxious' and a 'pompous ass'. A bit like Turner, I decided nastily.

He probably did her a favour by ending his own life – with a revolver, would you believe – when he came a cropper in the stock market crash of Nineteen twenty-nine. Yes, Josiah the financial genius had sunk his own family fortunes into the red and had forfeited his life as a result. Mind you, he wasn't on his own; the world at that time was falling about while everybody panicked.

What was strange, though, was that Amelia's words were quite impersonal about his death, quite matter-of-fact and aloof.

The one I liked best was one of her earlier entries. She would obviously be referring to the woman in the portrait, and for me at any rate, it summed up her character magnificently:

I have the most affinity with my mother's sister, Aunt Rosie, who is in the Women's Social & Political Union. She is a suffragette who is intellectually brilliant and a close friend of wonderful Emmeline and Christabel.

I heard that she stormed up Downing Street with a few friends and threw vegetables at the Prime Minister. Mama was terribly shocked (I don't suppose Mr Asquith was all that impressed either). Even dear papa said Rosie was an embarrassment to us and the last thing he wanted was for his family to be tainted with such ignominy.

How I wish I had been born earlier. I could have been a suffragette, but it is to my lasting regret that I am not old enough.

Women have at last been given the vote - Hurrah! But only if you are over thirty. Mama called it a triumph, but Aunt Rosie only called it 'a start'.

Looks as though breaking away from her father's traditional values was an acme of achievement.

CHAPTER TWENTY-TWO

In retrospect, those early weeks were like being on holiday and I almost felt ashamed that the idea of spending my days in a glass cubicle glued to a works computer didn't even offer a glimmer of attraction any more.

Leap year day had been and gone without anything exciting happening, and Wraycliffe continued to smile at me. I think it always will: its coastline glistens in the sun, the people are so friendly, and the foamy North Sea waves stretch into nothingness, which gives me a feeling of serenity that I haven't felt for a long time.

I have no qualms about the proximity of my house to the cliff when it comes to erosion. It isn't near enough to be in danger and is unlikely to crash into the water below, at least not in my lifetime, although people further south have not been quite so lucky of late, I hear.

I got up early in those first weeks, simply because it was routine, an unbreakable habit from my lost working days, but instead of collecting dodgy coffee from a machine first thing in a morning, I now enjoy a brisk walk along country lanes or a jog down to the pebbly beach. The exercise freaks are there, of course, with their dogs, throwing sticks or simply prancing around, and we chalk up the yards with 'Mornins' and agree that the day is either 'lovely' or 'horrible', as appropriate.

The path along the cliff top follows the contours of the coastline; it's a bit of a climb in some parts, but challenging when I want to blow away the cobwebs.

The cliffs in this area may well be high, but nothing compared with the dizzy heights of Bempton further down the coast. Council notices warn walkers to keep away from the edge as the rocks are notoriously dangerous and slippery when wet.

The local bird-watching society donated money about ten years ago to erect a seat and a bird hide on the highest point looking out to sea, about half a mile from my house. It looks more like a wooden bus shelter (without a bus stop) and is a cosy little affair when the weather is inclement. Known locally as *Dixon's Hut*, because he was the chap who designed it.

I sometimes take a packed lunch and simply go and sit in it, just to watch gulls forage and swoop overhead. I like to think that Amelia probably did exactly the same as well. I haven't started talking to her portrait yet, but sometimes I am pretty close.

It was towards the end of one of my jogs landside that I made friends with the man who has pastoral guidance over the people of Wraycliffe, the vicar at the Church of St Nicholas. On this occasion, I had stopped to watch children at play through the railing of the school yard, which is in the lane opposite the church.

He wandered across the road to welcome me to his parish and introduce himself, before walking with me back to the lych-gate and through to his notable area of interest, the garden.

He apologized for not getting in touch with me sooner, he had been away on a conference, but he was pleased to meet me at last, and would be happy to arrange Amelia's memorial service for a few weeks hence. He also asked me to call him Geoffrey, which I think I might have a little difficulty with, but we shall see.

Personally, I thought our churchyard was every bit as pretty as the one where Amelia had chosen to be buried; perhaps the wild daffodils and tulips added atmosphere, contrasting with the impression I had gained of Ashford. He seemed buoyed up by my observations when I told him so.

'It is rather beautiful, isn't it? It's a wildflower garden, you know, where everything has been planted to attract wildlife. Not quite looking its best just yet, but just wait till you see it in April/May when the bluebells and forget-me-nots are out: it will be a riot of colour. The wild garlic, by the way, has no special significance. We don't have vampires in Wraycliffe.'

He chortled at that and his face glowed with pleasure as he pointed towards some of the patches of less well-known wild flowers and named them for me.

'Our final resting place is quite immaterial, you know, Miss Kent. Miss Parsons was born in Wraycliffe and her spirit will always be here with us. We are simply sharing her with Ashford.'

'Yes, I hadn't thought about it like that, vicar ... I mean Geoffrey. Please call me Elise (he courteously nodded at that). I hope I shall be here myself for a very long time.'

'I hope so, too, young lady. Have you discovered all there is to know about the village? You will be fascinated when the weather is warmer and we get a sea fog that makes it so easy to get lost. Be on your guard and extremely careful if you find yourself out in it. The North Sea Haar is *very* unpredictable.'

'I think I read about that somewhere.' I couldn't remember where or when, but it had to be somewhere in the brochures I had brought back from the tourist information office. 'Quite something along this coast, I understand.'

'Our residents are far more exciting,' he whispered with confiding glimmer in his eye. 'You have only to spend a few minutes in our little village emporium each day to find out everything you want to know.'

He laughingly called the shop the 'gossip centre', but then put his hand to his mouth as though he had just said something he maybe shouldn't have.

'Mrs Hanby is the most charming lady you could ever wish to meet, but my parishioners will insist on going into her establishment to chatter and rubberneck, rather than to buy.'

CHAPTER TWENTY-THREE

Bad weather was the key feature of March, all in all. It was stormy on occasions, and I frequently ate soup and a roll for lunch to the tune of howling rain rattling the workroom window. I think I shall have to stop calling it Amelia's studio because there is more of me in it now with books all around me and all my belongings scattered around.

On this particular day, radiators rumbled to prove the central heating was working, but I still switched on the electric fire for the warming effect of imitation coal rather than the heat. It would have been a good day for working on the Internet but I didn't like turning it on if a storm were in the offing, and in any case my mind was on other things. I wanted to spend another day with Amelia's journals.

Ben was conducting a battle with his daughter's car in Saltburn. I had offered to lend a hand but he said he had everything under control (I think he has doubts about my car-maintenance capabilities) and Bella had stayed at home. She rang to say that her mother had sprained her wrist when she fell against the bathroom door, so she needed to look after her.

'George happened to be here at the time and we drove her to A&E to get her sorted out, but the poor love played the whole thing low-key because that's the way she is. Always has been. No fuss, no nothing. Went the whole day without so much as an aspirin.'

You had to admire the way some people have a stalwart acceptance of accidents: Margaret Graham had apparently scalded herself badly with a pot of tea only a few days earlier as well. The list goes on …

I was still only halfway through the journals, even though I skipped through some of the pages. I must admit, I got a vicarious thrill as Amelia spun an entertaining yarn and I laughed out loud at some of the comments she had made. Without giving away details of any adventures of an amorous or sexual nature, Amelia embarked on her career as a heartbreaker, and her journals were carefully edited, I suspect, to exclude the juicier bits.

Here was a girl with a piquant wit who was a boisterous tomboy as a child, played board games with her gardener as an older woman, and made a confidante of her solicitor in her old age. She was a Chinese Dragon, and because she was born in the year of the Wood Dragon, she would be fiery, outspoken and fearless. Seems true.

But her life was not all to her liking, even though she sounded the sort to take rough bits in her stride. By the time I got to the time she was twenty-five, she had loved and lost a talented painter who was devastatingly good to look at, and become engaged to a manipulative tyrant, to whom she gave no brownie points whatsoever.

I was so engrossed in the past that I decided not to have a proper dinner and to make myself another sandwich instead. It was quite late in the evening when I got to the last journal. The overhead light emphasised a growing blackness outside and I was unable to see anything through the window, save my own reflection and that of the room behind me.

Turning sixty was not a particularly auspicious occasion for Amelia, who was by then spending a lot of time with her sister in Ashford.

She mentioned my own mother a few times as a quiet teenager who was good at school, but showed no predisposition for lively nights on the town: a girl who preferred to read in her bedroom every evening, in fact. Imagine how that went down with Aunt Amelia!

Towards the end of the last book, she mentioned something that jogged my memory.

A hat.

Yes, that was it! The straw hat in the basket that Ben had given me. I had even tried it on. Now where had I put that ruddy basket? I had dumped it, intending to go through it thoroughly when I had time. And then forgotten all about it.

I put the journals carefully back into their new home on the second shelf of the bookcase, gave them a flick with a duster and a look of approval, and then made my way downstairs. Another storm was brewing overhead and it was dark so I switched on the hall lights. Fickle weather.

My memory must be slipping. The basket ... large ... heavy ... now, where was it? And then it came to me. I delved into the kitchen cupboard and took it back upstairs.

The basket was deep and I carefully lifted things out until I got to the bottom: hat, gardening gloves, pencil case etc. etc. Right at the bottom was a tin box.

Nothing surprises me any more in this place. The box even had my name on it, painted in large white letters on its blackened lid.

I thought that the secrets of *Painter's Lodge* had been revealed to me when I found Amelia's portrait and her locket, but that was only the start. The box promised to be the real beginning, and my hands were trembling as I lifted the lid.

My one thought was that Amelia must have intended me to find it all along. It was like a treasure hunt, one clue leading to another, before I finally won the prize.

Whatever that might be ...

There were three things inside. One was a little bundle safely wrapped in a lace handkerchief with the letter "A" embroidered in blue thread in the corner; the second was a small envelope addressed to me (naturally) and, finally, there was a leather-bound notebook.

The storm was working its way towards us from the north and I could see a louring sky through the window as the rain began to lash once more against the window. Lightning suddenly forked in the distance and I counted the seconds till I heard the rumble of thunder. It's a perfunctory habit of mine, something I always do, and I calculated that the trouble was about four miles away.

I have no fear of storms for their destructive habits, but I must confess I am usually a bit on edge and glad when they are over. Not like the lady who used to live next door to me in London who was so terrified that she would rush to be with anyone who was at home at the slightest sign of a squall. Virginia always said that I probably feel jittery because my parents died during a thunderstorm.

I ignored what was going on outside and turned my attention to the contents of my tin box.

I opened the envelope first. There was a thin piece of lined paper inside, the kind that might have been torn from Bella's red exercise book with the date "1981" scribbled on the top line. I quickly calculated that Amelia would have been in her late seventies by then, so I made allowances for the large scrawl and held it up to the light so I could see better.

Her earlier journals had been easy to read, but this spidery handwriting was in pencil.

By that year she would have lost most of her family; her sisters and her brother-in-law were dead and I would be the only relative she had left. It was not exactly a letter, it was more of a private little message for my eyes only, something she wanted no one else to know about. This must be the note Ben had meant. It was short.

> *I am glad you have come across this letter, Elise, because it means that Ben must have decided to hand my most treasured possessions over to you when you told him you wanted to make Painter's Lodge your home. You cannot possibly know how happy that makes me.*
>
> *The amulet is our oldest family possession. It came from 1790 and belonged to Leila Gray's daughter, Linnet. It was given to her on the day she was born to enable her to differentiate between good and evil.*
>
> *The unwritten rules are that it should be passed only to a blood relative, so you see, my dear, it is yours by right. Linnet's painting is in the studio; the old lady in cream is your great-great-grandmother, Charlotte, and the one in purple and green is my aunt Rosie.*
>
> *I hope that you and I shall meet one day, but for now,*
> *All my love,*
> *Amelia*

It brought a lump to my throat and I re-read it. In the event, the opportunity to meet hadn't presented itself, but I assumed all would become clear when I started on the journal that was at the bottom of the box.

It began with an entry in 1965, and I thought it was a scrapbook at first glance because there were torn bits of paper sticking out where she had begun to glue items cut from magazines. Not a bit like the others.

Indeed, this was where the final journal had been all this time, not destroyed at all. No wonder Nathaniel never found it: Ben had been keeping an eye on it until I got here. It occurred to me just then that Amelia had been just as wary of her solicitor as Bella had been, and I couldn't help wondering why. He has been perfectly courteous and charming to me.

Glancing quickly through the pages, I could see that Amelia continued her normal practice of drawing pictures and making little sketches alongside the text. Her handwriting was less well-formed than before, but there were recipes for sauces, and ideas for party menus interspersed with dates when she planted seedlings and the time of day when she took her medicine.

She had drawn a caricature of a man with a long nose and a bald head with a stethoscope round his neck and waving his arms angrily in the air. Obviously, it was the poor old medic who had the misfortune to deal with a recalcitrant patient like Amelia, and a caption underneath said 'Does the silly man think I don't *know* when to take my tablet? Does he think I might *cheat*?'

I decided to read the rest of the book later because I was keen to see what else she had left me. Not difficult to guess what I would find within the folds of the dirty handkerchief.

I could see that the edging of lace that had been conscientiously worked in its heyday was now torn, but cleanliness wasn't of prime importance in my current state of impatience. I wouldn't have minded if everything had been covered with red paint.

Frankly, I do not know whether I was disappointed or not when I unwrapped the necklace. I had seen it in the paintings, of course: a dark stone in the shape of a crescent moon, smooth and worn with age. Maybe jet, maybe not. Had I used my imagination, it could also have been a banana, but my thoughts careened towards the crescent moon idea because it was more appealing than a piece of fruit.

I picked it up and held it to the light. It was quite ordinary: a black pendant hanging on a grubby black velvet ribbon. Heavy-ish.

Under normal circumstances, this type of jewellery would be far too chunky for my taste, but there was something about it that I liked. Perhaps age came into it, or maybe its background.

Or maybe it was because it was yet another possession of Amelia Parsons that had become mine.

The stone was shiny with wear, even though it had been in the dusty depths of the basket all these years, and I fancied that it warmed slightly in my hand. Perhaps jet has properties like that; I'm not too well-versed in geology. I will ask Sophe when I see her.

Now that I actually had the pendant in my hand, I recognized the marks cut into the surface as runic symbols, though they were nothing like anything I had seen before, and I made a mental note to translate them with my reference book material. Amelia hadn't bothered to paint the symbols too accurately in her pictures, and they were not all that clear now because they were covered in gunge. The narrow ribbon was threaded through a small hole at the apex of the moon.

I put the ribbon over my head on an impulse and went to look at myself in the mirror on the inside of the cupboard over by the window. I happened to be wearing a green cotton tee shirt that day, and I could feel the shape of the moon through the flimsy material on my skin. Strangely, it still felt warm and I gazed at my reflection, smiling at the face that stared back at me.

I was quite surprised. It looked far nicer round my neck than I thought it would, so I decided to keep it on. A new length of ribbon could do no harm; I probably had something suitable in my sewing box already.

It was at that moment that a flash of lightning broke into the room and all the lights suddenly went out: everything, including the electric fire. Actually, my first instinct was to unplug my computer, but then I began to worry about damage to other items in the house.

Did I know how to switch the electricity back on? Probably. If only I knew where the electrical consumer unit was? It sounded like a direct hit by the thunder god and I tried not to think about fires.

The room was in total darkness, and my eyes were taking their time to adjust, but as another bolt of lightning shot through the sky, I glanced up at the mirror and froze.

There was someone standing directly behind me.

It was only a transitory flicker, a quick flash of a figure in purple and green, but enough to make the hairs stand up on my arms and a shiver run down my back. I could feel my heart pumping and if my feet hadn't felt like lead, I would have dashed to the doorway and tried the light switch, but I didn't. It probably wouldn't have worked anyway.

Instead, I closed my eyes for a moment and then blinked them open again, only to discover that the light had come back on. A temporary blackout, then? The electric fire clicked and started up again.

The handkerchief that I had been holding had slipped to the floor and as I bent to pick it up, I saw that Stringer had come into the room and was standing by my feet. No doubt he had been unsettled by the weather as well and was looking for a comfortable knee to sit on. I didn't even know he was in the house.

He must have sensed my unease because he came pushing against my legs and I picked him up and took him over to sit with me in Amelia's rocking chair. I don't know whether he felt the tremble in my fingers or not, but he purred into the silence and I made a show of fussing over him with the handkerchief still in my hand. He sniffed at it, turned up his nose at grime coupled with the bad odour of old paint, and kindly clawed at my knee for my efforts.

He didn't seem to like our situation any more than I did and, after a minute or two, I stood up and coaxed him to the floor while I went downstairs to inspect the outside and see if there was any damage. The rain had abated, but the security lights came on to show me that there were plenty of puddles in my back garden. Fortunately, no slates off the roof or anything like that.

Ben would have his work cut out tomorrow when he turned up to see what the rain had done to his vegetables. Must ask him about the electricity box.

It was almost midnight when I was getting ready for bed that I tried to re-live my experience of the evening, if only to put a logical interpretation on it and not place any more importance on it than it deserved.

In my dressing gown, I tidied the workroom and went to stand in front of the mirror, looking for answers. I turned slightly this way and that, and came to the preferred conclusion that I had seen the painting behind me in the mirror at the exact moment when the lightning startled me, and it was only because the perspective had become disjointed that Aunt Rosie had appeared to be only inches away from me. The portrait must have come into my line of vision when I jumped.

Talk about letting your imagination go into overdrive!

On the other hand, I could easily have fallen asleep for a few moments without warning. Millie told me about an aunt of hers once who had such a condition and there's a name for it if only I could remember. Not something I could associate with, but then again, it was Millie and her words of wisdom who had given me nightmares about chimney pots tumbling down during a thunderstorm in the first place. She's a bundle of laughs, my Millie.

CHAPTER TWENTY-FOUR

Sophe treats her laptop suspiciously as though it were a precious ornament instead of the workhorse Mr Dell intended it to be.

We met as arranged; I loaded my system on to her laptop and showed her the rudiments of the game. She was delighted with it and we celebrated with a kind of sandwich lunch that these motorway restaurants do by the million.

'The tax man will love it,' I told her, 'and I am on hand, so to speak, if things go adrift. You'll be able to add up your earnings, expenses and allowances and it will produce an ongoing report at a keystroke.'

It was a '*Press a button and Bingo!*' affair with all sorts of devious machinations in its belly. I had programmed in a few extras for fun, giving her things such as fancy letterheads and invoices, and she was thrilled to bits.

'More to the point,' she told me smugly, 'it's fool proof. You know how I'm no fan of technology.'

'You navigate through our website OK.'

'But that's easy. I talk to you all as though you are in the room with me and I know that only my friends can see whether I make a fool of myself.'

We had exhausted all the intricacies of my little system and were on to our third cup of coffee when Sophe broached the subject of paying me.

'Look, how much do I owe you for this? You must have put a lot of work into it and it's exactly what I wanted. I bet it would have made a big hole in my profits if I had gone to someone else.'

'Not at all, but how about a quid pro quo? I need a big favour.'

She looked interested when I produced my package of treasure from my bag and laid it carefully on the table. 'This is worth more than any piddling little computer system. What do you think of it?'

I unwrapped the tissue paper gingerly to reveal Linnet's stone. I don't know why I treated it in such a fragile fashion – it was only a nondescript hunk of rock after all – and I placed it in front of her so she could see it properly. She picked it up.

Sophe's long enamelled Yin and Yang earrings (home-made) bobbed around in the sunlight as she bent her head to take a better look.

'Oh Elise, this is a little beauty. Where did you get it?'

'I found it. I thought it might be jet, but seeing as I know nothing about these things, it could easily be something totally different.'

Personally, I wouldn't have called it a beauty exactly, quite a sorry piece, in fact, but it meant a lot to me.

She took her dad's old jewellery loupe from her handbag and examined my offering closely. As a former watchmaker, her father had needed the small magnifying glass professionally. He may well have lost his enthusiasm for timepieces but his rabid interest in gadgetry had survived intact and he had a whole roomful of trivia at home.

His wife moaned that the things he brought back from car boot sales were steadily filling the spare room, though he hadn't responded positively when I asked if he wanted a computer system to keep track of it all.

Sophe peered closely at the object in her hand, gently turning it over and over and relishing the feel of it. People who work with their hands often do that.

'No,' she said with certainty. 'It's too heavy to be jet. It is probably some kind of granite, though it's nothing I recognize.' She frowned and surveyed it from all angles. 'Looks like something I saw in a museum once; a meteorite type of thing. It could be very old. You found it, you say?'

'In my house,' I laughed. 'It probably needs a good clean, but I thought it might make into something wearable. It used to hang on a ribbon; it was threaded through the hole at the top.'

I had removed the black velvet because it was scruffy and crumpled. I didn't like it anyway.

'I think it will clean up quite well. There's a lot of dirt in the carving, but I should be able to wash that out. Lord knows what the symbols mean. That's more your line of business. Runic, aren't they?'

'Yes. The message isn't very clear but one of them is meant to heighten insight, feminine insight, to be more specific. That one.' I pointed to the sign that looked like an arrow with one of its prongs missing.

'Oh yes. I see. How interesting.'

'The crescent moon itself has the power to see into the past—'

I suddenly broke off, embarrassed. That was something Amelia had written in her journal.

Sophe looked at me with a frown.

'It's only a good luck charm, Elise. You don't really believe in superstitions, do you?'

Did I? What a silly question. Yes, I did. The old-fashioned variety, anyway: white rabbits, throwing salt over my shoulder, not walking under ladders. You know the kind of thing.

'No, of course not,' I lied.

Sophe was still turning my amulet over in her hand, feeling its weight.

'Yes,' she said with conviction. I'll willingly sort it for you.'

I was wearing Amelia's silver locket, so I took it off, dangled it in front of her face and watched her eyes light up.

'Don't tell me you found that as well,' she said in surprise, taking hold of it when I took it off. 'Have you moved into Aladdin's cave?'

'Another little treasure from the lady who left me the house. She was my grandmother's older sister; did I tell you that?'

Sophe shook her head, but I could tell her brain was fully occupied with the silver in her hand. She expertly sized it up for its weight and dimensions.

'It was tarnished and filthy when I found it. I *have* cleaned it,' I told her when she looked through her loupe again. If I was hoping for a bit of praise, I was disappointed.

'Not very expertly,' she said sourly. 'You had better let me have this as well.'

In the end, I let her take both of my trinkets away with her. She promised to return them when she had done what she called a 'proper job' on them.

'You may as well have these, as well,' I told her, passing over some of the contents of Stringer's jar.

There were agates, a few broken chains and a couple of old wristwatches that hadn't worked for years and probably never would again. Her dad might even be interested in them for his collection. She was delighted and scooped them into the side pocket of her handbag.

'I can make good use of these. Thank you.'

'Well, if you find they come in handy, they're yours. Throw them away if you don't want them.'

It was yet another horrible day, weather-wise, when the postman knocked on my door a week later. Rain dripped off the end of his nose.

In addition to normal mail, he had a bubble-wrapped package in one hand and an electronic gadget that seemed to have replaced normal Recorded Delivery as I have always known it, in the other.

The rain had poured down since early morning, staving off my run for another day and I had spent the last hour doing physical jerks that bore little relation to T'ai Chi and thinking how much nicer it had been with Chessie when we went to evening classes in Kilburn. Perhaps someone here would be interested in starting a group. Out of the six hundred or so denizens of Wraycliffe, there must surely be someone who would join me in the village hall every week.

I greeted the po-faced delivery man on my doorstep with a friendly smile and he did his best to pass it back. He looked like a mobile tepee this morning in his waterproof gear cape.

His name is Lionel.

Sometimes it is a girl on a bike who delivers small packages, but more often than not it is this man in a red van who has a larger area to cover and larger parcels. On a good day, he whistles and walks jauntily up my path, but today he screwed up his eyes and hunched his back against the rain-swept gale.

I knew that the package was from Sophe by the postmark, so I invited Lionel to stand inside my storm porch while we sorted things out. He didn't have time for a coffee, he said, because he wanted to get back to the depot before he got too wet. He handed me my normal post and then tapped away at the little screen in his hand before I signed my part.

'People are always happy to see me,' he said gloomily, 'I wonder why.'

I was glad now that I hadn't been out when he came and I carried all my post upstairs to the workroom.

One of the envelopes contained a thick printed card with wavy silver edges, inviting me (plus guest) to a cocktail evening and financial presentation: the one Nathaniel had talked about. Quickly discarding the guest idea, I entered the details in my desk diary anyway. I might learn a lot that I could pass on at the next reunion.

Sophe's package would be far more interesting and I eagerly scraped my fingernails at the sticky tape where she had secured the bubble envelope. She was going to a lot of trouble on my behalf and I was astonished to see the results.

She had made a first-class job of the silver locket and had cleaned it up much better than I could ever have done. It looked like new. She had even given me a little blue velvet-lined box for it.

A second box, also blue, contained my amulet and I couldn't believe what a difference she had made to it. The stone was now cleaned and polished and she had inserted a small piece of rock crystal where the hole had been. To me, it looked like a mystic eye and somehow added to its charm.

The whole thing was now re-mounted into a shiny silver setting which kind of matched the locket, except that this one hung on a strong sterling silver chain, long enough to go over my head without a fastener. Silver and black went together beautifully. It was the most eye-catching piece of jewellery I have ever owned and I couldn't wait to thank her personally over the telephone.

I immediately rang her number and waited for her cheery voice, but she must have been out and I only got the answer machine. I rarely leave messages on these darned things, it's all right listening to the chatty bit first, but I come over all tongue-tied as soon as I am invited to speak.

Must be something to do with the magical qualities of a bleep and the hypnotic words 'after the tone'.

There was a flyer folded up in the box, the kind of paper that she gives out when she goes to craft fairs, which listed the attributes of the stone itself.

The moon was the shadow side of the sun, it said, and the crescent moon is a feminine sign connected with wisdom and truth, which will give the wearer intuition of a psychic nature. In trade jargon, it was supposed to induce a state of clairvoyance and was a good luck charm of the highest importance.

Sophe wrote:

> *I haven't been able to find out anything about the inscriptions - you are so much better at these hieroglyphic things than I am anyway – but it sounds as though you have discovered your mojo, Elise, for when you delve into the future.*
>
> *I hope you like what I have done with it. I tried to copy the locket's setting in case you want to wear both necklaces at the same time, but if you need a different length chain, please let me know and I shall be only too happy to oblige. Cheers. Sophe.*

I consulted Amelia's Book of Fortune straight away, but it only confirmed what Sophe had already told me. There was an extra bit about foretelling death, but I am not into doleful news so I took no notice of that. I still couldn't make sense of the symbols, even though Sophe's cleaning brush had made them clearer. It must have been a message of some sort, written by whoever created the talisman in the first place. I shall never know.

So, there it was: a blessing or a jinx connected with women. Part of me didn't believe it, the logic part, but something told me I ought to keep an open mind.

CHAPTER TWENTY-FIVE

Getting the regulation seven hours' sleep has never been a problem for me, ever, but somewhere down the line I think my brain must have received a message not to shut down so easily here in Wraycliffe.

Delving into Amelia's past must have caught hold of my imagination in a big way, such that I found myself waking regularly at odd times during the night, simply to read her journals and wander down the next chapters of her life. An idea was already taking shape, in fact, that I might write her biography (not an original idea, and presumably triggered by Nathaniel's own project), and I even started making notes of my own, to supplement hers.

So, it wasn't a complete surprise when a loud cry disturbed me one night. I had been asleep for a while and it was only when the dark world of nightmares faded and I returned to the safety of my bedroom that I realised the cry had been my own, and that perspiration was trickling down my back.

I turned to look at the clock beside me. I thought I had been in bed for ages, but it was only ten to two – less than two hours! Some instinct told me that my deep sleep had been almost unnatural, and I knew full well that on this occasion it had been nothing to do with Amelia at all.

It was about Virginia, or rather her mother, Flora Winters. She had been so clear to me in my slumberous state, and it didn't make sense because I hardly knew the woman. I had only ever seen her face to face at Virginia's first wedding, although I do look at her photograph from time to time.

In my dream, she was wearing the same wedding outfit and the same hat, but whereas she had been smiling in the photograph, this time she was sobbing. She cried out to me, but I couldn't catch what she was saying as she waved her arms frantically in my direction.

Each time I tried to hold out my hand to her, she slipped away, as though she were leading me to a different part of my dream.

Now wide awake, I closed my eyes and tried to hang on to the pictures in my head as I lay there, but they were fading fast, and it was only because a raging thirst became paramount that I pulled back the sheets, turned on the light, and made to swing my legs out of bed.

The amulet was on my bedside table, glittering under the lamp, and I picked it up yet again, trying to interpret the symbols and wondering why such a dull piece of stone had triggered Amelia's imagination. It is one of those things that is nice to hold, and feels even better now it is in its silver setting. It fits snugly into the palm of my hand and its shape makes me want to stroke it.

I put it round my neck and made my way down to the kitchen to get a cool drink of water from the fridge. I couldn't remember the last time I had a nightmare, but there was no way I would get back to sleep straight away, so I went to the workroom when I returned upstairs, just to potter about. I find I spend more time in there than anywhere else, day or night, and I stared at my three ancestors in much the same way as the current incumbent of a stately home might occasionally ogle oil paintings as he climbs the enormous staircase on his way to bed. A bit like looking at Millie's photograph album, only bigger.

What really gave my ego a boost was that I had added three new names to my family tree. And what elegant ancestors they were, even Linnet, in spite of her poverty-stricken clothing. It was something about the eyes and the way they all held their heads in a kind of arrogant, condescending manner, almost as though they felt superior to the artist who had created them.

But what I had also discovered during my frequent sojourns into this room, (and it wasn't something I realised when I first arrived) was that each picture had been painted to a kind of formula. It was a technique that was becoming more and more conspicuous each time I looked at them.

The main figures were positioned dead centre with a kind of bright aura around them, whilst the contrasting backgrounds were dark and slightly blurred. It was a simple approach that gave each model an ethereal, almost three-dimensional effect and I concluded that Amelia had wanted to concentrate on the model and had left the background to sort itself out.

What also interested me was that each one of them was standing or sitting in my back garden near the arbour, and this was something I hadn't paid much attention to before. Presumably that was because in the early days I was unsure what my back garden looked like. But now I was certain.

Perhaps Amelia loved that particular corner so much that she decided to let her figures pose there. Slight changes had me fooled for a while, but once I knew what I was looking for, the topography was the same.

I was wide awake by this time, not to mention curious, and I moved over to the window where the moonlight shone brightly over the garden.

The night was cool and clear and I could see the outline of everything I needed to see. I stared for a few minutes – there was a lot to take in – and then shuffled back to the paintings.

The urchin child, Leila's daughter Linnet, was framed by sombre russet-coloured mountains in the distance. Definitely artistic licence there, because they were twice as large as the gently rolling hills that were actually outside.

Aunt Rosie was surrounded by meadow flowers – licence again and more picturesque than vegetable tops, I suppose, although there may well have been flower beds over there in Amelia's day. The elderly Charlotte was sitting in front of what looked like an apricot tree, which may or may not have grown there at some time so I wasn't sure whether it was fact or fiction. But in spite of those differences, the tell-tale wall was there, next to the arbour, plus the dusty path through the archway.

I homed in on Linnet because that particular painting was the one I liked best, and I reached out to touch her on the cheek. She was a pretty little thing in an unkempt sort of way, but she had such a serious look on her face that it brought out a tender instinct I didn't know I had.

Feeling not the slightest bit embarrassed, I said, 'I hope you don't mind my wearing your necklace, Linnet. I think it's quite beautiful, even though I don't know what the symbols mean.'

An uncanny feeling came over me – not excited exactly, but curious – and time seemed to stand still.

Narcolepsy, that was the word I was looking for earlier.

I wouldn't call the picture a masterpiece, but it was one of those that makes you want to stare at every brushstroke and analyse more deeply what the painter had intended.

For some inexplicable reason, Linnet's two-dimensional world seemed more real to me than my own at that precise moment, and I was weirdly transported into her garden, seeing it through the painter's eyes.

The room around me transmogrified into the fresh air of a summer day, the sun was shining overhead and a breeze blew gently on the back of my neck. Linnet's eyes seemed to stare mischievously into mine and the hem of her cotton shift stirred slightly in the wind until I glanced anxiously away and wondered what was going on.

It all seemed so real for a moment, but when I looked down at my own clothing I saw only my towelling dressing gown. I was back in the workroom in the middle of the night, staring at a portrait of a scantily-clad child of the eighteenth century.

CHAPTER TWENTY-SIX

My morning jog passed in a blur. I spoke to a few people down the main road, but I was so preoccupied by my extraordinary nightmare that I was on autopilot and I couldn't recall later whom I had seen.

Thinking about it logically, I ought to have been exhausted from lack of sleep, but I wasn't. Clouds hovered in a moody sky and common sense told me not to venture too far, but seeing as I was already outside, I felt the urge to seek peace and quiet in the churchyard.

I suppose my brain was still revolving around my ancestors and, ultimately, my reason for being here at all, but I had been meaning to look for headstones belonging to my family ever since I met the vicar ... er ... Geoffrey. I just hadn't made the effort yet.

The church was only a few hundred yards from my house so it seemed like a good idea to cut my run short and head that way. It was indeed a quiet place, with a number of bench seats scattered around. The wildflower garden was enhanced by mature trees and secluded corners that somehow gave it a feeling of history and the unknown. Larger than I expected, too, when I wandered round to the back.

I noted that some of the graves had little vases of flowers on them. Somebody still cared, then, about whoever was in the ground beneath? Not Amelia's first choice, I know, but I had moved on since her funeral and was looking for other members of my family at this point.

I found what I was looking for in a quiet corner well away from the road, adjacent to the sea, and I ambled under the shelter of a group of windswept hawthorns to read the names on the headstones.

I encountered Amelia's mother, Alys, her dear papa Henry Oliver Parsons, and her grandmother Charlotte Carter. Older stones ravaged by time bore different surnames and might well have been part of the family, but I hadn't a clue who they were.

Having said that, the names I was familiar with were here right enough, and I decided there and then to bring flowers on a regular basis to show my respect. In that crazy moment, it occurred to me that I, too, might end up here. And who would leave flowers for me?

The vicar's voice interrupted my sobering thoughts.

'I thought I saw you arrive, Elise. I see you have found some of your ancestors.'

'Yes indeed, Geoffrey. They lived to a ripe old age by the look of things,' I replied amiably. Perhaps the sea air round here is conducive to a long life.'

'Perhaps,' he agreed in his calm, singsong voice, so suitable for a vicar. 'Actually, I was going to come and see you this week, so I'm glad to have caught you.'

I moved away from the well-tended plots and walked towards him.

'That's nice of you. What about?'

If he looked self-conscious for a moment, the expression quickly disappeared.

'Might as well get straight to the point,' he said with a cough, 'without any flannel. The ladies of the WI are short of a stall holder for our village fête, or garden party, some call it. They have already co-opted me to their ranks. Can I tempt you to join us?'

I was about to open my mouth when he briskly continued and gave me no chance to opt out, 'Not a great deal to do: it's more a question of salesmanship, at which, I have to confess,' he said with a self-deprecating smile, 'I myself am rather backward, if you know what I mean. Persuading people to part with money is not my strong suit, but the committee would indeed value your assistance, and their chairman has appointed me as your interlocutor.'

How could I refuse? He made it sound too easy, so I asked a few pertinent questions about where and when exactly, before putting his mind at rest and agreeing to go to a committee meeting next week to learn the ropes.

'Oh, I'm so glad you have accepted the challenge,' he said, breathing a sigh of relief as though it was a load off his mind, and pumping my hand. He walked me to the gate.

'I shall see you in the Village Hall on Wednesday evening then,' he said cheerfully, before giving me a munificent finger-wave and disappearing through the large wooden church door. He hurried a little, perhaps in case I changed my mind.

It was at that moment that the rain decided to put in an appearance and as I ran up the street, it began to bite into my cheeks like knives. I had a hood on my jacket but it was not a snug fit and the wind made it useless anyway. The weather had been so changeable since I arrived up here and, frankly, I was looking forward to summer.

When I got back, hunger took precedence over getting out of wet clothes and I went straight into the kitchen for toast and marmalade. Stringer decided to join me on his kitchen stool and I stroked him until he purred and stretched. It was good to chat with someone who hadn't a clue what I was talking about, so I told him about my dream.

Bella rang a few minutes later.

'I saw you running home, so I gave you time to get back before I rang. I wanted to catch you before you got to your computer.'

I gave a little chuckle at that, more at myself than anything. Was I so transparent, then, that she knew my daily routine?

What she wanted to tell me was that her mother had been feeling so much brighter since she sprained her wrist, and that she had been on a spending spree to the Designer Centre during the week. 'Can't work that one out,' she said with dry humour.

'She has been asking about you as well, so I thought it was time for the two of you to meet.'

She invited me for afternoon tea.

'How kind. I'm looking forward to seeing her. Around two?'

'That will be fine. Oh, and by the way—' (I do hate it when people say that. It usually presages something I might want to forget) 'I don't want to worry you but I think someone might be watching *Painter's Lodge*. Nothing concrete, just a feeling I get. He was there on Wednesday afternoon when I drove past with my mother and I remembered I had seen him the Wednesday before. If he's there again the next time I come, I'll get his number.'

'Where do you see him?' I asked after she had gone into some detail about his hair, his clothes and his apparent interest in the house. It could have been anybody.

'Sitting in his car overlooking the beach,' she replied, 'next to the old stone seat and the wastepaper bin. Seems to be filling in forms; my mother said he had lots of boxes on the back seat. I just thought it was strange that he should be there twice.'

Couldn't disagree with that, but she was flummoxed when I asked her what kind of car. She managed a vague 'Dark blue ... hatchback ... I think. Small. Not new.'

It didn't amount to much and I guessed it was just some salesman filling in his paperwork after a busy week.

'Not a car I recognize, but thanks for that, Bella. I'll keep my eyes open.'

I didn't expect to see him, but it showed our neighbourhood watch spirit was alive and well.

CHAPTER TWENTY-SEVEN

Margaret Graham was known to have moments of irascibility, due for the most part by her exasperating inability to control her memory, but today she was in fine fettle, and the brain cells showed no signs of wear and tear. It was obviously a good time to pay a visit.

She looked spry and bubbly when I got there, although her arm was still heavily bandaged and she held it guardedly close to her. Grannyish and homely in her new flowery dress from the Designer Centre, she opened the front door even before I knocked. Same elfin stature as her daughter.

The weather had changed radically during the morning, so that the lady herself stood in a doorway that was now bathed in sunshine. Silvery grey hair was done up in a tidily-folded plait at the nape of her neck, reminiscent of the fashionable thirties. One or two age spots decorated her cheeks and she had a peachy complexion that had never seen so much as a finger-full of makeup. Apart from the damaged arm, there was no sign of old-age frailty in the old bones at all.

Bella came to the door as well.

'This is Miss Elise, mum. You remember, I was telling you. The new lady up at *Painter's Lodge*.'

'Ah yes. The Lodge. I used to work up there, did Bella tell you? Do come in.'

I was shown into an open plan living room and Margaret indicated a comfortable seat that had fat cushions at least two feet thick along the back. Bella busied herself with the kettle and a large banana cake.

'It's lovely to meet you at last, Mrs Graham.'

'Margaret, please. You know, you are the image of your photograph in the studio. Miss Amelia will be so pleased you have come.'

I ignored the present tense as a momentary lapse and said, 'You probably recognize the hair.'

She laughed at that and graciously said that my style suited me. 'You look just as pretty in real life.'

Bella served tea as I sat with her mother on the sofa. I already knew they both shared the luckiest of all the Chinese signs, the rabbit, so I was prepared for similar characteristics. I was not disappointed: Margaret was charming and hospitable, with a gentle laugh that made you want to join in.

We chatted for a few minutes about her recent accident, which she shrugged off as unimportant, but then she began to talk about her work at *Painter's Lodge* in the Sixties and into the Seventies. Her memories were phenomenal and detailed.

After about half an hour she said, 'Will you excuse me for a moment, dear?'

It was as though she had suddenly thought of something and she quickly went out of the room. Bella poured more tea and gave me a quick grin at her mother's seemingly exuberant mood. We had already devoured plenty of the banana cake and I remarked how well her mother was looking. She nodded happily.

The door opened and Margaret came back in. For a moment, she looked confused and then looked at me in surprise.

'Oh hello, I didn't realise we had a guest. Bella, you didn't tell me we had company, dear. Why don't you introduce me?'

Bella narrowed her eyes at me and gave me an almost imperceptible shake of the head. She introduced me and again we shook hands.

Again, we spoke about life at *Painter's Lodge* in the Seventies, but this time I took things a stage further and brought her back to the question that had been plaguing me.

'Where did it come from, Margaret, the photograph, I mean?'

She put her head to one side and recalled the occasion clearly.

'That particular one arrived just after your birthday party. They always come from Norfolk.'

Even after all this time she was able to comment on the detail of our party dresses and the excitement on a group of young faces.

'Oh yes, Miss Amelia was thrilled to bits when she opened the letter and found your photo inside. I remember the day so well.'

Apparently, my party coincided with Amelia's own birthday, May the sixth. Which would make her a dazzling Taurean Dragon with no hang-ups whatsoever.

Mrs Graham had total recall of other details as though they had happened only yesterday. Her mind was full of Amelia, of her happy days at *Painter's Lodge* and of a young Elise, miles away in Norfolk. The past was amazingly vivid.

'I don't suppose you have a photograph of Amelia?' I asked, expecting and receiving a negative answer, even though I had hoped otherwise.

'I don't believe I have, dear,' she said. 'Strange, isn't it? Frank took one of us all when we went with the WI on a coach trip to the seaside, but now that I think about it, Miss Amelia slipped away so she wouldn't be on it. She said that she looked awful on film and preferred not to have to look at herself.'

'Oh dear! It doesn't look as though I am likely to know what she looks like at all, apart from in the portrait.'

'The girl in pink?' Margaret smiled. 'Alas, that was before my time, but I know the one you mean. Miss Amelia treasured that painting for a very long time until she decided to stick it in the attic out of the way.'

Now that Nathaniel had told me the background, I understood why. She probably never really got her artist out of her head.

I learned a lot that afternoon, thanks to a bit of gentle prodding. Margaret Graham's memories of yesteryear were spick and span, and at last I was able to discover many of the answers that had hitherto eluded me.

'How did Amelia know so much about me?'

She thought for a few seconds, as though she wanted to present the data to me in proper order.

'I suppose it all began because your mother kept in constant touch with both her and your grandmother. There's a heap of postcards and letters between the three of them somewhere in the attic if you look. But then your grandmother died and Miss Amelia was distraught, but she kept up her communication with your mother. Until the accident, of course.'

'So, Amelia knew about me from the day I was born?'

'Oh yes, of course, dear. There are *lots* of baby photos; they must still be upstairs somewhere. But then Miss Amelia was overcome with grief when she lost your mother as well. It upset her so much that she made herself ill thinking about it and had to go into a sanatorium for a few months. But she was never down for long. She seemed to come to terms with whatever had been bothering her, and she came home no worse for wear.'

'More tea, Miss Elise?' Bella was doing a first-rate job of keeping the teapot filled. Most of the banana cake had been eaten.

'Well, she still wanted to know everything about your progress and she used to confide in me. You see, while she had been in the hospital with nothing to do all day except lie on her bed, she had worked out that what she needed was a private investigator. I remember her being enthusiastic about it, but that was good. It meant that she was better. So that's what she did when she got back home.'

'What, you mean she employed a detective?'

'Yes. She engaged someone to keep track of you.'

'You're kidding!'

Margaret chuckled at that. She was revelling in her tales of exciting times gone by.

'Not at all. I told her I thought it was a clever idea.'

I did, too. It was exactly the kind of thing a lady like Amelia Parsons would have done. I don't know whether they had Yellow Pages for Private Enquiry Agents way back in those days but, if they didn't, then they must have had something similar. Whoever she found, she persuaded him to earn his keep and take himself off to Norfolk. It was the making of him by all accounts.

Evidently, he enlisted help from a lady who lived near us in Norfolk. It all started as a business arrangement but they hit it off well and the woman was happy for their relationship to develop into something more. They became quite good friends, though Margaret's memory started to wane at that point and she was none too clear about the outcome. It was all falling into place now. Photographs came out of Norfolk like a flock of geese at Blakeney Point.

'Do you remember who that lady was?'

I was curious, because nobody had mentioned this before. Margaret didn't even have to think twice.

'She ran the grocery shop in the High Street when the detective first got to know her.

'After a while, he found he liked the idea of being a shopkeeper so much that they got married and ran the shop together. Miss Amelia thought it was terribly romantic.'

'Mr and Mrs Crisp!' I said it almost to myself. 'I *remember* them. I used to go to school with their daughter, so it would be easy enough for them to take pictures at school events. Well, I never.'

'The two of them kept the link going between here and Norfolk. They passed on everything they knew. The way Miss Amelia used to go on about you; she was so proud of the things you did.'

Not that they would know much about me after I left Norfolk. Maybe a word from Millie here and there, when Mrs Crisp might casually ask, 'How is Elise?' The scenario had endless possibilities.

We were on to our third cup of tea when she commented on the amulet that I wore round my neck.

'We found that when Miss Amelia re-vamped the garden. It was a sheer fluke that she unearthed it; it might still be buried if she hadn't.'

I was suddenly all ears. This was new terrain.

'How do you mean?'

'Well, let me see. I suppose you know that the Lodge used to be called *Button House*?' I shook my head. 'Miss Amelia decided to change the name the same year I started working for her. Her mother had just died.' She put in a little diversion here, but it was easy enough to follow. 'The older Mrs Parsons was eighty-five.'

'She was my great grandmother.' I am sure there was no need to explain because she would know that. 'I saw her gravestone only this morning in the churchyard.'

Margaret was still in the past.

'We called her Mrs Parsons because she was a married lady. Anyway, Miss Amelia wanted to make drastic changes when she took over and the new name seemed more in keeping with an occupant who spent most of her time with a paintbrush in her hand.'

'I can well understand that.'

'It wasn't just the name she changed, either. She organized a lot of building work to the dining room and the studio. The garden came in for a makeover as well.'

'Ben has been telling me about what used to be there,' I said. 'I couldn't picture the house too clearly, but the garden was easy.'

'Yes. Ben was there, too. Did he tell you about the statue? No? Well, there used to be a statue at the bottom of the garden of that goddess ... now, what was her name? Ah yes, Aphrodite. But Miss Amelia hated it. She said she had always thought it unseemly: a semi-naked young woman was extremely bawdy and not quite right in a Yorkshire garden where she sometimes entertained young people. She asked the builders to knock it down, and put up a rather more refined, robust pergola.

'It's still there.'

'Well, all the building work went according to plan and it was only a few months later when Miss Amelia and Ben were planting honeysuckle and passiflora around the base of the new wooden posts that the box was discovered. It had been buried deep.'

'What kind of box?' I held my breath.

Margaret's response was instantaneous. 'An old tin box, wrapped in sacking. The amulet that you are wearing today was inside. She told me years later that her Aunt Rosie had taken it into her head to bury the necklace under the statue of Aphrodite at the turn of the Twentieth Century, velvet ribbon and all.

'It had lain there in that little tin box all that time until Miss Amelia dug it up.'

Talking about gardens and property in general must have stirred Mrs Graham into showing me round her cottage. She took hold of my hand and led me through to a conservatory that overlooked a small Italian-style courtyard. Paving stones were drying quickly, and an early azalea against the back wall looked freshened after its wash.

When we came back into the main room, she was talking knowledgeably about flowers and the work that had to be done to keep her garden beautiful. But then she looked at me with a puzzled smile on her face.

'Do I know you?' she asked. 'Have we met before? Bella, you haven't introduced me to our guest.'

Bella's shoulders slumped. Her mother was patently tired, so I whispered my goodbyes with a crook of my thumb and made my way towards the doorway.

'Perhaps I could come again some other time?' I suggested, and she nodded, putting her finger to her lips. She must be used to her mother's vacant expressions but I didn't want to cause any distress to Margaret by the stealth of my departure.

'I think it's been a successful afternoon,' she whispered. 'I hope so, anyway. You do realise, though, that she may not even remember you were here? You could be a total blank by tomorrow. Thank you anyway; I am sure she would love to see you again.'

Then she frowned. 'She said something last week that I thought was a bit strange, though. She asked whether the *other* girl was still there; the one in the studio. I have no idea who she meant, so I just said yes.'

CHAPTER TWENTY-EIGHT

There was a note in the final journal about the time Amelia and Ben discovered the amulet.

She was tempted at first to throw it away but then she stuffed it into her painting cupboard along with her other paraphernalia. A couple of years later (unwisely perhaps) she decided to wear it. Which was when her life changed.

I made a point of remaining upstairs in my workroom over the weekend so I could get a handle on the events Amelia described in her journal uninterrupted by television or radio. I wouldn't call them exciting as such; to be honest, I found them rather dark and gloomy.

After about ten or twelve pages of diary-type trivia, she got down to the nuts and bolts of life at *Painter's Lodge* and I could tell after the first few lines that she was in sombre mood. This was not the effervescent girl I had come to know so well, the one who hadn't a care in the world.

The journal was getting more gruesome page by page, and by Sunday morning I was finding the entries quite depressing. Within eighteen months of starting to wear the amulet, poor Amelia had lost the two people closest to her: her sister Lizzie and my mother Frances.

I could tell by flipping back through the books that she had begun to choose her words more carefully, more secretively, as though she wanted to be alone with her thoughts but couldn't stop herself putting them down on paper. As Millie would have said, she was more 'within herself'.

The details of how she came to create the paintings in the studio made me blow hot and cold.

For a start, she claimed that these three ancestors had come to her, physically, when she had been in her garden, but I had no way of corroborating her story because she told no one, neither Margaret nor Ben. She had been frightened at first – as anybody would – until they became friends, that is.

I didn't know what to believe. To be able to talk to one dead ancestor on a regular basis shows that you have a good imagination, but when you talk to two, or even three, it begins to look more like an obsession.

I *want* to believe that there is something we don't appreciate in a lateral world. Honestly! Life would be far more interesting if we could see into the past, but I have been programmed to believe that things *always* have a rational explanation.

Being an imaginative woman, Amelia had soon linked the uncontrollable events that were overtaking her with the black stone she had discovered in the garden. So much so, it was understandable that she soon began to believe it was cursed because dreadful things happened whenever she wore it.

A few months later, she wrote:

> *I am glad I did not give the amulet to Frances because it is unsettling to have visions and I would not want her to go through that. My grandmother gave it to Rosie because my mother wanted nothing to do with it. Perhaps she saw it for what it was.*

And so, I have come to a decision. I shall protect dear little Elise by cutting the connection completely, which my own death will accomplish. She can have the amulet as a bauble for its history rather than its secrets, and she will never know the distress I have discovered.

The doctor says I must rest and has arranged for me to go to hospital. I did not tell him that I have seen women from the past. I do not think he would believe me. Nobody would believe me because it is unbelievable.

They should not talk to me; they should send noises in the night or rushes of wind in a chilly room, like the poets and writers say. I never expected to see them so clearly.

My poor Lizzie
My sweet Frances
My beautiful baby Elise

She must have gone into the sanatorium shortly after that, because the entries were spasmodic and she covered the next twelve months in irregular little bursts. In some cases, I think she must have got the dates muddled because her words travelled back and forth inconsistently.

The doctors, of course, would have thought that it was grief caused by bereavement that pushed her over the edge. Mrs Graham said much the same thing, but I knew better now.

Stoicism was part of this lady's constitution: it was unlikely that she would allow death to upset her to such an extent that it would put her in a sanatorium. She had seen three people from the past and she needed space to work out why – away from the scene of the crime, so to speak.

Her entries were now scruffy and her thoughts incoherent, but after twelve months she came out of the sanatorium and everything had improved (apart from her handwriting).

Gone was the beautiful copperplate of her youth, and an ill-formed script that was spidery and awkward to read had taken its place. I even wondered whether someone else had written it on her behalf, but no, the entries suggested that she still wanted to keep her secrets very much to herself.

It was, therefore, for that very same reason that I decided I did not want anyone to know I had found her last journal.

With the kind of spunk I had come to expect of her, she jumped back into life at *Painter's Lodge* and dealt with whatever problems she encountered, now that she knew the rules. The visions remained, but she accepted their presence, maybe not with alacrity, but certainly with acquiescence.

She had even drawn a family tree on a separate piece of paper that had been folded and tucked inside the back cover. A sheet of thick cartridge paper we would call A3 today, it dated back to Seventeen ninety and began with a girl called Leila Gray.

A normal ancestral tree, but that's where convention stopped and artistry took over. Generation lines were in watercolours with proper tree branches bearing intricate lines of greenery and small birds hid between the leaves. She had gone on to fill the pages with miniature flowers and decorative vignettes.

Leila's bloodline had flourished: Linnet – Abigail – Cecilia – other relatives who had not seen fit to enter Amelia's esoteric world, or those not registered properly in church records in the first place perhaps. Presumably the mystical value of the stone had been handed down through the female line until it came to myself two centuries later. We were all there.

The minute I saw this pictorial record, I just knew I had to have it framed, professionally, with the creases straightened out if possible, because it was, in fact, my family 'Who's Who?' and definitely part of Amelia's biography.

A year ago, I had only dear old Millie and Charles: now I have a family consisting of literally dozens of people. How crazy is that in this changeable new world of mine?

She was shrewd, the Amelia I was getting to know. She painted things she liked, but only her journal was witness to the fact that she befriended her new female visitors and asked them to pose for her while she committed their images to canvas.

Linnet and Aunt Rosie must have been considerably older when they both died, but they appeared to Amelia in the likeness they preferred, and she painted them in situ, costumes, black stone and all. She chatted to them as she painted, and it began to seem normal to her. But that was the old lady's secret, and it was a secret that she now shared with me.

Her words were quite explicit: the amulet was the catalyst to whatever Amelia got up to, but she was adamant that she had been on good terms with Linnet and had spoken to her regularly.

Now I had reservations about that.

She might well have remembered the other two from real life, but not the little girl. Aunt Rosie had been around when she had been an impressionable girl in her teens and Charlotte was her grandmother – no doubt another reality of her younger life.

Amelia painted the grandmother first. The portrait showed her as a woman in her middle years, old, but not yet wrinkly as she would have been when Amelia knew her. 'Because that's how she appeared to me in the garden, in front of the apricot tree', Amelia affirmed. I still didn't know whether to believe her or whether this was just a tale of fiction.

Charlotte must have passed the pendant down to her youngest daughter, the irrepressible Rosie, who wore it for a while but then quickly hid it when she discovered that, far from being a simple adornment, it had a more bizarre side to it. She buried it, hoping that it would be lost for ever, but she had obviously been blasé in her assumption, because her wilful, inquisitive niece dug it up years later.

If Amelia were to be believed, Rosie was the second model to pose for her portrait at the bottom of the garden, and from the words on the page, I could picture the two women having a friendly altercation about the contents of the tin box.

'You should have left the bloody thing where it was, Amelia. It was feckless of you to revive it; you have probably done irreparable damage. I refused to wear it, but you can paint it in my hand if you like. I'm not in a position to care anymore. It's your problem, not mine.'

'Please keep still, Auntie, you will make yourself sweat in this heat and I want to paint you looking cool and calm.' (Amelia wrote that her paint was drying rapidly in the warm sunshine, almost as soon as she applied it.)

'Hurry up,' Rosie said through her teeth. 'Get the suffragette colours right: purple for dignity, white for purity and green for hope. And stop waffling, Amelia, you always did take too long to paint a picture. Mr Fleming would have finished by now. I hate standing here for your amusement.'

'I am going as fast as I can, Auntie. Besides, Mr Fleming had better brushes than mine. *And he worked to a different agenda,*' she said quietly as an afterthought. 'You, more than anyone, should have known that painting wasn't necessarily what he had in mind when he came here. Keep still, Auntie, there's a dear.'

The repartee would account for the beginnings of a smile that I had noticed in the portrait: a slight twitch to the corners of her mouth.

Personally, I think it far more likely that Amelia had dreams that she remembered the following morning, unlike those that float away long before the alarm clock rings. But according to her notes, she had not painted the portraits from memory. *Definitely not.*

I returned to the journal later and it was only when I paged through to the back that something fell out. A document so new that its crisp whiteness and sharp creases stood out against the yellowing pages of Amelia's writing. In spite of its pale condition, it turned out to be an even darker piece of the puzzle.

What I had in my hand was a new Will – Amelia's new Will. And what did I find? A document that would have left a large portion of her assets to one Winifred Fleming Sharp. She was the sole survivor of Nathan Fleming's children from his legal marriage, and I needed no reminder that Winifred was also Mr Sharp's mother.

This must have been what he had been looking for all along and it raised questions. OK, Nathan had ingratiated himself with the Parsons family, and Harriet in particular, but Amelia had discarded him as a scoundrel from her life years ago.

Another notch against Nathaniel. Who had decided that this was the right thing to do? Was it Amelia, was it Winifred, or was it Nathaniel himself? Anyone other than Amelia must have had sinister intentions.

But it didn't matter anyway, because the Will was unsigned. To push the point home, Amelia had even scribbled her loud objections across the front page in words unbecoming to a lady of culture. The words were in her latest, spidery hand but written in thick black felt pen, and the language she used was clear enough.

Put in less volatile fashion: No thank you. I want no part of this.

I locked it away in my writing box.

Well, well!

CHAPTER TWENTY-NINE

I began working again quite by accident. Diana wanted urgent assistance with her Internet connection at the *Nags Head* (she didn't know what, because she was baffled) so I lent a hand. I didn't mind at all, but refused any payment on the grounds that I had hardly done anything apart from linking a few loose wires and getting her to invest in a new mouse.

I would have been embarrassed to tell her the truth, that I no longer needed a working girl's income, and that any worries about cash flow were all in the past. She gave me a bottle of expensive wine instead. Much more useful.

From then on, the grapevine started up and work began to chase me. People continually asked how I had settled in and so forth, and I got the impression that my lovely neighbours would let me have anything I liked, anything at all. I only had to ask.

It was just the same at the village fête committee meeting when the WI Chairperson finagled me into having a look at her laptop and tidying it up for her. She was one of those women who had been on enough committees to know every method of persuasion known to mankind; someone who has one of those engaging smiles that could suck you into her plans within seconds.

I succumbed and found myself agreeing a 'To Do' list I would never have believed possible.

She had friends with similar requests: many friends who needed assistance.

James fell into this category as well. He had taken my lead and resigned from the 'hellhole' as he described his workplace, the one I had abandoned in cavalier manner without even experiencing. Time to rebel against the new management and some of their revolutionary ideas, he told me.

One of James's strengths, I have always felt, is his ability to absorb facts quickly and rearrange them in logical order, which is what he did in this case. It wouldn't have taken him long to realise that being a small fish again didn't suit him at all. We are only talking weeks into the new job.

'You are well out of it,' he grumbled over the telephone. 'Admin is top-heavy and unrealistically demanding, and the old workforce is intent on mutiny. You should have stuck with us, Elise, then your life could have been equally fruitless.'

You couldn't blame him for starting up another small company where he can write bespoke systems: a small computer firm is more to his liking and it is what he has done before anyway.

'So, you left, just like me?'

'Much the same. Too much input from the top, or shall we say too much interference by non-computing people who talk poppycock. They wanted to cut the most amazing corners, even though they gave me a fair amount of wriggle-room when I argued. You knew that would happen, didn't you?'

'Didn't you give them that bit about technology only being a tool to accomplish a job?' I asked in a voice loaded with syrupiness.

James guffawed loudly. He was no different from any other technical manager I knew, but the bottom line was that he was being asked to take orders from people with less experience than himself.

He would find that working to someone else's plan was restrictive. Couldn't blame him: we both liked to see a whole project through to the end.

Adept colleagues had followed him out of the front door, including the young office boy, and he had easily managed to recruit a couple more from outside who wanted the independency of a small company with a boss dedicated to the job in hand rather than a balance sheet.

There was a pause before he said, 'I don't suppose you want any programming work yourself, Elise?' I knew what was coming next; I could hear the animation in his voice. 'I have been inundated with new customers and could sure use a little help.'

It was obvious I had never disappeared from his radar, whatever my circumstances, and tempting me back to a bit of consultancy work was definitely worth a try. To be honest, I liked the idea of being employed again in a completely flexible arrangement, and James needed help, so my offer to cope with his overload ticked both boxes.

I made positive murmurings, and a satisfied chuckle landed in my ear. James is a clever person. Gail just needed to rub miracle cream on his shoulders from time to time so he could grow an extra pair of hands. He preferred to include me on his payroll as a consultant, he told me, even though I said I would work for the fun of it.

'No, no! It will make me feel better when my accountant looks at the figures if we do it my way.'

The following morning, he rang again.

'I have a little job for you,' he announced. 'Just a little job; it won't take you more than a couple of days.'

Which probably meant a week in my new, lazier, lifestyle. I said yes.

'That's my girl. I shall send you a few manuals down the line in a few minutes (I bet he had been working on them all night). Go through them, will you, and see if you can spot any anomalies.'

Sure enough, my mailbox began to fill and the new James Link & Associates logo shone out at the top of the screen – his personal initials surrounded by a silver circle. I remember he used to doodle it on his pad all the time.

The work was no sinecure: the operating manuals amounted to around a hundred pages all together, though without delving too deeply into the programs themselves, I couldn't decide whether the keystrokes were workable or not. Basically, I had to take the instructions on trust, but they were helpful and descriptive, which was the main thing.

So, that's what I did for the rest of the morning. I was already on Page 56 and was thinking that he had described everything pretty well. To be fair, I felt a little guilty about the consultancy fee, seeing as I didn't seem to be doing anything worthwhile.

I changed a couple of sentences around, just to earn my keep, and even suggested that a diagram or two might not come amiss. It was good fun and I enjoyed doing something productive again.

My relationship with James, far from growing tenuous, had actually strengthened, and we were back in business. I am a valued consultant to a promising business and with the best of both worlds: the sort of work that I adore and a level of solvency that means I don't have to worry if the enterprise dries up.

A long way from the neuroses of last winter.

The instructions were getting quite complicated. It might be nit-picking, but I needed a clear head, which, by late afternoon, I didn't have, and I was in need of a break.

I heaved a sigh and broke off to have a chat with Linnet.

I know, I know! But this is something I find myself doing these days. My little one-sided discussions sometimes help to brush away the trivia that's got stuck at the front of my mind. On this occasion, it miraculously helped, as it usually does, and I went back to the computer.

After a while, I found myself irresistibly segueing to my own website. I entered my password and watched the fancy logo appear, the one Andra had designed, together with the familiar graphics Chessie had come up with in one of her humorous moments: -

Old Girls, (Not so much of the old …)

The front page grew from a tiny dot as the familiar lines and pictures came into view and I drummed my fingers on the desktop. The words on the screen had become unaccountably blurred, so I took off my glasses and cleaned them. As the minutes ticked by, I almost forgot what I was looking for.

What was I looking for anyway?

I clattered my way through the pages and concentrated on reading what was in front of me. The usual photographs were there, plus recipes and my dire warnings every month when I try to save all my friends from the unknown with rune-casts.

There was a silly joke that Sam had picked up from somewhere and a new entry from Virginia, telling us about a cat she had discovered in her vegetable patch and how she was going to take him to the local vet the following day because he didn't appear to have an owner.

Not like my Stringer then, who had literally dozens of owners if Diana had her facts right. There was no one else on line for a chat.

Apart from her stray animal, which Virginia could never resist, now that I thought about it, her page was quite full and she talked about all of us in her usual chatty manner. I scanned everything else that was on the site: all the pages, all the photographs.

I was growing irritable. Something had been on the periphery of my normal comings and goings for a few weeks now. I couldn't get it out of my head that something was wrong with Virginia's cosy little world, because that's what it was: cosy. Too cosy and far removed from anything I had ever known. Think laterally, Elise, come on girl!

I could hear Bella singing in the kitchen and a mouth-watering smell floated temptingly upstairs, marmalade cake this time, I think, based on her mother's cut-and-come-again recipe, she says, though I confess I haven't met that one before. She would probably be bringing me a cup of coffee any time now, but I'd have to wait for a slice of the cake until it went cold.

The sun streamed through the window and caught the silvery shine round Linnet's stone that was hanging round my neck. It sent a rainbow-like coruscation on to the ceiling that had me spellbound, and I stopped typing for a moment to watch the colours dance as I coiled it through my fingers.

Then something seemed to come from the screen, just a faint, weary moan, like somebody crying. Whatever it was, it brought a dream to mind, my dream that involved Flora Winters on the night I first found the amulet.

I stared in front of me, only to find that the words I had typed had become jumbled up with the pictures.

I used to get eyesight problems when I stared at a screen for too long, but that was years ago, although I did wonder whether this might be something similar because I couldn't concentrate on what was supposed to be there.

Bright colours swirled with centripetal force and disappeared down a hole at the end of a tunnel. Unusually bright colours, like the rainbow I had just seen on the ceiling.

It was also uncannily like my dream. Here was Flora again, floating backwards into infinity like a cloudy brushstroke. I couldn't hear what she said: it sounded like 'Richard', but I think she was imploring me to help Virginia. She was still sobbing.

It must have been a good twenty seconds later that I heard Bella's dainty footsteps tapping up the stairs, and the screen fell back to normality on its own.

'Here we are, Miss Elise.' She placed a tray with coffee and biscuits on the small table. 'The cake is still warm, so I've left it on the kitchen table for later. I'll be off now, if there's nothing else. I'll lock the door on my way out.'

Whatever I uttered must have sounded vague because she looked at me and her eyes narrowed. My face had become hot and I must have looked dazed.

'You don't look too bright; is everything all right?'

I nodded and pulled myself together, and she carefully placed my drink on the desk.

'I can ring the doctor if you don't feel well.'

'No, no, Bella. I'm fine. Just a bit tired probably. I've not been sleeping well.'

Sniff. 'Well, if you're sure now. Make sure you eat properly when I'm not here. And don't give yourself headaches staring at that screen for too long.'

Not a fan of the computer, our Bella.

She would be back tomorrow afternoon and I smiled at her gentle reminders to look after myself. Even though I try to hide the empty tins, I think she is perfectly well aware of my penchant for canned food, and she certainly knew that I sat at the computer for long stretches at a time.

With another sniff, she was gone and I fancied that my fingers moved faster than usual over the keyboard as I heard the front door key turn and she locked me in.

I was on my own.

CHAPTER THIRTY

My thoughts chased erratically after that and I glanced through all the good things Virginia had written about Richard; how loving she seemed towards him and how he doted on her. I could see nothing untoward at first, until his own words at my reunion began to stride through my brain.

Virginia would ring again. The reception was poor. I have been trying all morning, but they are out of order—'

I began to work through my long-standing 'Why?'

I imagined my friend visiting the sick in a bleak countryside cottage, miles away from civilization. Had something or somebody prevented her ringing? It was only a small point, but why send an email later when she could have spoken to me on the telephone?

When I was working (something from the dim and distant past it now seemed) I tended to analyse things with a pencil in my hand, which is what I did now on the pad I keep handy on my desk. It helps me when I am fumbling around in my psychic jungle.

This time, I methodically jotted down everything I knew about Virginia, because she was the one who was causing my confusion – particularly after my dream.

We had bonded on the issue of parentage: cancer had robbed her of a father when she was young and her mother was still a woman in her twenties. The incident had served to forge a mother/daughter relationship into something unbreakable, and she had wonderful grandparents who had allowed her to grow up in a loving environment.

I had a similar environment, but an aunt and uncle, Millie and Charles, to share it with me instead.

Our mothers had both been born in Yorkshire before marrying and moving away, although the sadder distinction was that mine had died at the age of twenty-five when I was only ten months old. Virginia had lost her mother in a terrible accident only a few years ago. Again like me, I suppose, but Flora had been an older woman and had died much later in life.

That was when the young Mr and Mrs Mason moved to Canada. It was a loss to the reunion group as a whole and me in particular because it meant that we didn't get to see each other anymore.

Another thing about Virginia: Flora Winters had sent her daughter for elocution lessons as a child, so she spoke as beautifully as a titled lady might, just in case she might ever become one. I used to tease her about that and sometimes mimic what she said. She never mentioned whether Richard did the same.

Even computers don't come up with answers if you don't ask the right questions. I switched off with a sigh and took my notepad across to the armchair by the fireplace, where I added other things to my list and drank my coffee.

No brothers or sisters.

Wealthy.

Reserved.

My tenacity for statistics has a jigsaw effect where I move pieces around until they fit. This time I was on the lookout for something out of the ordinary, the extra special piece that is easy to miss, but it dodged me, whatever it was. I waited for an idea to float by like a hot air balloon, but I waited in vain. Nothing stirred the clouds. It was like being in a maze with no exit.

I must have dozed in the armchair for an hour. I know it was approximately an hour because I remember looking at the time on the computer before I switched it off, and I stretched and glanced down at my watch when Stringer jumped on to my knee and woke me up.

I was catnapping yet another crazy dream, but a pleasant one this time, and the strange thing was that I could remember all the details – I don't normally. And if I hadn't read Amelia's account of how she painted Linnet, my brain would have thought of something else to ramble on about, I'm sure.

It was a really mixed-up dream. There I was, sitting on a wooden bench underneath the pergola in my garden on a balmy summer day. The occasion was so real to me that I could actually feel the heat of the sun on my bare arms; there was a cloudless sky and I think I was reading a page from one of James's manuals that I had printed earlier. I had a black felt pen in my hand and was jotting notes on a scrap of paper.

Amelia was standing in front of me, sketching at her easel, and Linnet was doing her best to stand still. I knew I was witnessing the creation of the painting which was hanging in the studio.

Amelia worked silently, and I could hear Linnet's gruff voice clearly. The dialect was probably Yorkshire-based, but she had broader vowels than I had ever heard before. She also dropped aitches as though she didn't know they existed and had the boldness that I expected of a gypsy girl.

But it was the eyes that attracted me the most. They were darkly sexual with what seemed like years of experience hidden in her gaze; the kind of eyes that betray nothing; permanently bright and inquisitive. This vagabond child of the Seventeen nineties was quite breath-taking.

'I want you to put my grandmam's stone in the picture, Amelia, but I'm not going to hold it, and don't forget to paint the daisy chain round my hair as well. When you have finished my portrait, I want you to hang it next to Rosie. I don't know what a suffragette is because we didn't have them in our camp, but she makes me laugh.'

The two of them apparently couldn't see me, and Linnet blithely chattered as random topics popped into her head. She seemed to delight in telling gruesome tales about her grandmam being a witch who was able to cast spells to make people horribly ill.

Whatever was she going on about? Sickness was rife in her day, a state of affairs that historians would no doubt put down to seasonal malady or the natural course of events. The way she told it, her grandmam was personally responsible for the demolition of whole populations.

The old woman had most likely been a shaman of the village where they lived, a kind of soothsayer who concocted potions to heal the sick and frighten the life out of those she didn't like.

'They said my mam was a witch as well and it was a good job the devil took her the day I was born because, if he hadn't, the people of the camp would have buried her alive.'

There again, Leila had died in what was probably childbed fever, as so many of them did in those days, but this youngster had been brought up to believe the folklore of the day, plus the idea that her poor benighted mother had been destined to take over the mantle of 'chief mutilator' when her time came. Had she lived.

I felt an immediate affinity with this young girl, real or not, and my fingers tightened round the wooden seat beneath my knee.

Losing a mother is not a good move. At any age.

Her father, too, came in for close scrutiny and, in his case, condemnation. He was wicked and conniving, by the sound of it: a man who sold herbal potions and learned a few tricks while he was at it.

'He came from London,' she said, as though Amelia knew nothing about geography. 'That's the biggest place in the world and a long way from here. Good things can happen to you in London. Or bad, depending on which spell you are under.'

Said it all really. A foreign land filled with people casting spells and playing tricks. Reminded me of Turner.

Funnily enough, I liked her, this anachronistic child. It wasn't her fault that she had been indoctrinated in another time zone and was so entrenched in black magic that she was almost from a different universe.

I sat there, watching a performance that brought Amelia's journal and her paintings to life, a stage production which had somehow become entangled with James's paperwork.

At that moment, I felt a pricking sensation on my knee and the sunny day started to fade. The last thing I heard was Linnet's hypnotic little voice saying, 'Take another look at your website, Elise.'

That was when I woke up. Stringer had decided I had been asleep long enough.

The cake that Bella had left for me was delicious. And the shepherd's pie.

I was half way through watching an old black and white film on television much later (I am a sucker for old films) when an idea suddenly hit me and I snapped to attention.

It was getting on for midnight by this time, but I quickly left the squashy sofa and hurried upstairs. I booted up the computer and found the place I had been aiming for.

Mixed thoughts buzzed in my head. At last, I knew what I had been looking for earlier. It was simple, and if it hadn't been worrying me for such a long time I would have laughed out loud.

The film actress (doesn't matter who she was) played the part of a princess and spoke with perfect enunciation as one might expect from the elite. Her voice came across like Chessie's, though her hairdo was more like mine. But that wasn't the point.

My fingers flew over the computer keys: I was absolutely sure everything would be revealed in a few minutes.

The brightness of the screen made my eyes water; perhaps I really do need new glasses for computer work. Or, maybe I needed a tot of whisky more than spectacles. If I had mentioned any of my midnight meanderings to Millie she would have told me to go and see a wine merchant rather than an optician.

I quickly found my way to Virginia's Blog and, when I got there, I almost whooped for joy. She talked about 'Sam' and 'Chessie' and 'Andra' and 'Lucy', just as we all did. I stared at the screen, not really reading anything, but trying to get a fix on what I was thinking. I even tried to hear her voice in my head speaking the words I was looking at.

But that was the part that was wrong.

Virginia, well brought-up lady that she was, would never, ever, abbreviate our names. Even at school, she scorned such an idea. As an adult, she always spoke correctly and called us Elise ... Francesca ... Samantha ... Alexandra ... and so on.

She even used to be the same when she was typing on the site.

It was such a slip of a thing to home in on, but something told me I was on the right lines. I was sure of it. I rolled back a few months into the system, to about the time she and Richard moved to Canada. That is when it started; it was plain enough. For some reason known only to herself, she suddenly began to use our shortened names. Weird or what?

It was well past midnight by then. I rolled back my chair, hardly worrying that I might scrape the floorboards in my haste, and quickly moved over to my writing desk to have another look at Virginia's last letter to me. It was the one where she talked about her policeman friend and I read it once again, as I had so many times.

At the end of the letter was an address in the Lake District where I could get in touch with this Silas McGovern, and I think that was the point when I saw clearly what my next step would be.

I took my own letter addressed to Inspector McGovern down to the post box the following morning before I could change my mind. If nothing was wrong, then it sounded as though this kind man would not mind my interference.

On the other hand, if I had uncovered a nasty smelly trail, then Silas was the man to help me.

CHAPTER THIRTY-ONE

Now that I had set things in motion as far as Inspector McGovern was concerned, each new day seemed to have more hours in it than the last. I watched out for postman Lionel. I waited for the telephone to ring. I looked regularly at my emails. Even though I had given contact numbers for each, there was no word from Virginia's policeman friend.

'I need my hair doing,' I told Diana when I was sitting on a bar stool one lunchtime. 'I'm going to a financial presentation on Friday and I would like to look better than this.'

I shook my head from side to side, showing her that my hair was now long and straggly instead of short and spiky.

They do a nice cocktail of elderflower fizz and fruit at the *Nags Head*. Not busy that particular day, either: one or two walkers were sprawled in a corner taking the weight off their feet, and a young man who tapped away on his laptop computer was oblivious to everything except what was going on in cyberspace.

'I usually have mine done in Helmsley when I go and see Jim's dad. Do you want the number?'

Nothing untoward about that, except coincidence. It was the second time in a week that I had heard of a place I hardly knew existed when I came here.

First, one of the ladies at the village fête meeting had given me a glowing testimonial for a hairdresser called Jacqui who had a salon in Helmsley, and now Diana was doing exactly the same thing. Not too far away for me to have a day out and do a bit of shopping while I was at it, either, by the sound of it.

'I'm sure I have one of her cards upstairs. Hang on a minute and I'll get it for you. She's very good.'

When I got home I fed our cat and looked at my emails. There was one from Silas, who now lived – I couldn't believe this – in the little market town of Helmsley. The point of his message was to say that he would ring me tonight.

You know what they say about happenstance and coincidence. It must surely be time to take notice.

'I'm sorry for the delay,' he said that evening in a voice that oozed investigative friendliness. 'It's taken me a long time to reply because I've moved house and your letter eventually reached me by quite a long-winded and circuitous route.'

He was now a Detective Chief Inspector with the North Yorkshire Constabulary, having been promoted from the Cumbrian Force. It transpired that he had accepted a job on this side of the Pennines soon after Virginia had left for Canada. He had a wife at the time, but the breakdown of his marriage came only a few months later when she left him. I sympathized with his need to get away and make a new start: it is something I know a lot about.

Destiny had played an unfair game with the man. As well as a change of address, he was temporarily assigned to lighter duties in Yorkshire because his knee was giving him trouble.

'Not serious,' he insisted, 'but I've no doubt it will end in an operation sooner rather than later. I'm trying hard not to think about it.'

He did his best to put a bit of humour into his voice. I gathered that he was heading up Cold Cases based in Northallerton and his knee didn't prevent him from being a busy man.

His blunt manner had upset a few folks on his way up the ladder, but he had an honest and trustworthy attitude, which, coupled with significantly astute results, had caused him to be head-hunted by those who knew more about real life across the Pennines.

Few had been surprised by the promotion. His academic prowess had never been in question: he was a well-educated guy whose only fault was that he was outspoken.

We met at the *Castle Tearooms* in Helmsley the following day. He ought to have been familiar to me because he and his wife had been guests at Virginia's first wedding and would be on my photograph. But my information was sadly lacking on that one; it was nearly fourteen years ago, after all.

My first impression of the man was that he was huge, well over six feet, clean-shaven with short, almost skinhead (but not quite) iron-grey hair. The expression on his face was pure stern contemplation, but I think that must have been one of his interrogation techniques. I got the impression he didn't just listen to what we told him: he interpreted it as he went along.

He wasn't text-book handsome either (I'm sure he wouldn't mind my saying that) with the most wonderful soft brown eyes that you felt could see everything inside you right down to your socks and probably missed none of the bits in between.

He had the strong physique of a rugby forward, though he told me it had never been his game, and that he and Tom used to play golf in their youth. Navy blue fleece and jeans completed the off-duty image.

I liked the way his ears were flat to his head, too. Not like Turner who kept his hair long to cover his sticky-out ears.

Yes, Virginia's detective friend had a 'Wow!' factor I couldn't put a name to. She certainly has a knack of latching on to good-looking blokes.

'I had long black hair in those days,' he chuckled when we shook hands and I mentioned not remembering him from Virginia's wedding, 'but I remember *you*. You were with a bunch of raucous school friends who never stopped clucking.'

That must be the blunt approach appropriate to his copper background, but how could I mind? It was true. Late nights and hard work had left its mark on this man and his face was lined, though not unattractively so. He would be, what, early forties? Same age as Tom. He looked at me keenly.

'I bet you still turn heads.'

I decided I liked blunt.

Shyness must have shown on my face and I self-consciously raised my hand to flick my new hairstyle.

I had managed to get an appointment that very morning on Diana's personal recommendation, which was a stroke of luck. Apparently, she was a much-valued customer who had seen fit to send dozens of her acquaintances in this direction in the past.

Treated like royalty, I was – tea and biscuits under the dryer, plus a manicure that cost extra but did fantastic things for my morale. Silas McGovern couldn't see the pedicure, of course, but my toes were a matching shade of coral. I went from sooty scarecrow to fashion-plate in just under three hours, courtesy of Jacqui the miracle-worker, and came out of that salon with the most becoming streaks of gold and ruby in my hair. A slick smooth style like that would have cost twice as much south of Watford Gap.

My recent outdoor exercise regime had given my cheeks a kind of weather-beaten appeal, not like the monster tan Chessie shows to the world throughout the year, but a decent brownish glow nonetheless.

DCI Silas McGovern never knew what he had been missing for fourteen years; he only saw the new me.

Young, to say he had achieved so much. For the past twelve months, he had been living with his sister Ruth who ran the gift-cum-book shop up the road from the main square – a dinky little money-spinner by the sound of things – and they shared a nice cottage nearby.

In spite of being work-busy, Silas was not so much in demand that he couldn't take time off to look after Virginia's welfare: meeting me was a diversion from the office that he welcomed.

'I didn't know whether to get in touch with you or not,' I blurted out almost as soon as I arrived, 'but I am worried about Virginia.'

The soft brown stare narrowed.

'Look, let's go and sit on one of those comfy chairs over there. Would you like a coffee?'

He guided me to a seat in the corner and then went to the counter. There was hardly anyone in the café because it was still too early for lunch, but the coffee machine was bubbling merrily away to itself and he brought a plateful of home-made tiffin back with him to the table.

'You had better tell me why,' he said in a matter-of-fact tone, after he had hung up my coat on one of the pegs on the wall and sat down opposite me.

'It's all a bit muddled,' I sighed. 'As I told you on the telephone, it's just a feeling that I have. I know something is not right, but I don't know what.'

How could I tell him about my amulet? How could I tell him that I have nightmares about Flora Winters, a woman I have only spoken to once, and even that was a long time ago.

How could I present a tale about manifestations that Amelia had written about? He couldn't even begin to understand the dreams I have or that I get a kick out of talking to a precocious girl from way back in time.

Being me, I had jotted down a few notes so I wouldn't forget anything. I dug them out of my bag and for the next twenty minutes I told him about the name-changes on the Internet. I told him about Richard turning up in December, and I told him about the telephone calls that never materialised.

I knew I was wittering on a bit. It all sounded shallow and more like a grumble when I got going, but he didn't seem to mind (he already knew I could be talkative anyway, so my babbling was only confirmation). With acute perception befitting his station, he nodded as I filled in the details.

'The trouble is, these are not hard facts,' he said with a professional twist to his mouth when I had finished. It was the put-down I had expected, after all, but I had saved the best till last.

'That's what I thought at first. But listen to this. After I had posted my letter to you, I sent a harmless message to Virginia, something about Turner – he is my ex-boyfriend by the way – and I said I was well-rid and that even Charles's cat didn't like him.'

I could see Silas was having difficulty following my drift on this one, so I explained that Virginia would know it was a completely fatuous remark.

'How so?'

'You see, my uncle Charles never had a cat, or a dog for that matter. He has always been allergic to furry animals, so we never had one anywhere near the house. Virginia knew all about that, but her response was strange.

She replied at great length about animals being very perceptive and what a pity Charles didn't have a dog, because they could be friendlier, et cetera, et cetera. She now has three dogs and nine cats and they are all doing nicely. Actually, I wouldn't have expected her to have any, but that's by the bye.'

Silas whistled faintly through his teeth (beautiful teeth, by the way) but whether that was because our pal seemed to be running a pets' home or not I couldn't decide. He had the exaggerated calmness of someone who had a knack of getting at the truth, and I could see I was in the presence of a quicksilver brain that was pushing all the data into their proper positions.

He looked at me with the beginning of a fond smile on his face. 'I know all about you. She used to talk about you a lot.'

This was news to me and I waited patiently for more, but all he said was 'She called you Bunty.'

'You see!' I cried out triumphantly, making him jump back in surprise. 'That's exactly what I mean. She wouldn't tell somebody close without saying it was me. She didn't let on to Richard. She told you and Tom, but not him.'

He looked deep in thought and I sighed again. 'It's not much to go on, is it? A hunch, I mean.'

'Don't worry about it,' he shook his head slightly and looked directly into my eyes. 'Intuition is worth more than gold.'

I had to remind myself that this policeman was likely to be a smart interrogator, but what I found endearing was his habit of raising his eyebrows and nodding his head to one side as he stared at me. It drove the point home nicely. Virginia may well have told him about the reasons for our pseudonyms, but I felt I had to explain more.

'I used to be a bit on the plump side, and she was stick-thin, so she called me Bunty and I called her Olive, after Popeye's sweetheart. You know the one I mean? They were names we came up with when we were at infant school and they stuck, although we drifted apart a little when she moved to the Lake District with her mother. And even further apart when I went to Business College in Scotland.'

Seven years of age is too young to envisage the future importance of what we do; little did we think that our anonymity would act as a cover for a far bigger game in years to come. I had always thought that Chessie was the only one outside our families to know about our aliases, but obviously Virginia had shared it with the man sitting in front of me. I was telling the tale quickly now.

'I have the feeling that Richard came to our reunion to discover which one of us was Bunty. I didn't appreciate it at the time, but now I think I know better.'

Silas looked into the distance with shrewd eyes.

'I wonder why he was looking for Bunty. For you, I mean?'

'I have absolutely no idea. I've churned over all the possibilities and come up with zilch.'

The time had passed quickly. He looked at his watch again and seemed to come to a snap decision.

'You've hit me hard with this one, Elise. I need to think this through carefully before I decide what to do for the best. Look, tomorrow is Friday. Are you doing anything in the evening?'

'Well, I was, but I can cancel. This is more important.'

'Whatever it is, give it a miss. Let me take you to dinner instead. I should have come up with a plan by then.'

An idea. 'Why don't we do both? You can be my guest for cocktails and I will be yours for dinner. OK?'

I told him about the cocktail occasion and my invitation from Mr Sharp. Frankly, I was in no mood to see Nathaniel on my own, now I knew a little more about him.

'I'm up for that. Right then. We don't want to waste a fantastic hairdo, do we? Let's go show it off. Cocktails first, then dinner. Pick you up at seven. You'd better give me your postcode so the Sat-Nav can find you.'

CHAPTER THIRTY-TWO

I had been trying to decide what to wear ever since the moment Silas mentioned dinner. Not that I have much to choose from.

I have two dresses for occasions such as these. One is red silk, which is a bit on the short side, even though I consider my legs to be my best feature and should be shown to whoever would like to take a peek at them. The other one is a low-cut, slinky black number reaching down to my ankles that I bought on a sudden impulse at sale time when I was in Oxford Street last year.

One for cleavage; one for legs, Chessie calls them. She likes the black one best, but I feel good in both.

I confess I chose black tonight because the low neckline showed off the black pendant that I was wearing, along with Amelia's silver locket. They look rather good together, thank you Sophe.

My choice must have been the right one because I saw the DCI cast a sneaky gleam of approval in my direction as he helped me into his dark green Jaguar. Beyond saying that the combination of two necklaces went well with my hair, he offered no further comment. Didn't understand the reasoning on that one.

We drove through the gateway of *Bolton Manor*, a Country House Hotel about ten miles inland from Wraycliffe, and found a convenient parking space under the trees. Judging by the number of cars around, the place would be heaving, but we only planned to stay a short while before moving on. Silas parked near the exit.

'I know this place quite well,' he said, before going on to tell me its history since the Eighteenth century: private house, TB Sanatorium, a hospital during the war, and now a successful hotel. 'Wedding packages swell the coffers, of course. We used to have our annual regional dinner here. Good food. Staff changes a lot, but they are always helpful.'

We walked up to the stone pillars of the impressive doorway that must have appeared on dozens of wedding photographs and entered a plush foyer enhanced with a subtle murmur of voices. An electronic notice board in the doorway indicated that the financial presentation was being held in a private suite down a long corridor. A relatively large function room.

We signed in and accepted canapés and a drink from a blue-coated waiter, whereupon I was immediately pounced upon by an intellectual-looking woman who came towards us with a glass in her hand and an impish grin on her face.

She was a leggy redhead wearing short green silk that clung tantalizingly to her figure and showed every curve she possessed. It suited her wild hair to perfection, but she was a million miles away from my impression of a solicitor. She glanced down at the name badge I had been given.

'Miss Kent! How lovely to meet you at last: I have heard so much about you from Nathaniel that I feel I already know you. I'm Laura Andrews, Family Law.' She shook our hands warmly and peered at Silas's name badge. 'And Mr McGovern. How are you both?'

We did the pleasantries and apologized that we couldn't stay for the actual presentation as we had booked dinner elsewhere. She rubbed the apology out in the air with her fingers and shook her head.

'Good for you. In the meantime, let me introduce you to our team. We're not all here yet, but it's understandable because there's the usual traffic jam out of York at this time on a Friday.'

She walked us over to the bar and pointed to a flurry of colour: black and white for the men, shades of rainbow for the ladies. 'Just so you will know who you are speaking to when you ring the office. You will have to forgive the dressing up but a few of us are having a meal afterwards. I don't suppose you can stay? No? Of course not; you want to be alone. Leonard doesn't usually turn out to a junket like this, but he's made it this time.'

My two solicitors were standing at the bar and I quickly identified them for Silas's benefit.

'I've seen your file, of course,' Laura went on. 'Don't let Nathaniel monopolise you, though. There are dozens of legal bods here who already know who you are and they will be falling over themselves to meet you.'

She reminded me of Chessie, although I detected a smidgeon of fire in her cleverly made-up eyes and I wondered whether her courtroom expression was one she had cultivated for her job. Such a gift would be useful for ferreting out facts.

We were both treated as valuable clients by our hosts. Mr Sugden insisted that I call him Leonard and treated me like a long-lost daughter; his charming wife insisted I call her Caroline, and Christina Barclay (a priceless administrator that no office should be without) asked me firmly to call her Mrs Barclay. I think she was Nathaniel's PA and saw me as a potential rival. There were one or two others whose names I instantly forgot.

It was small-talk and mingling after that, but I confess my mind had been on other things for most of the time and I wanted to move on to our next stop.

Voices around us talked shop, but I was mildly surprised that the snatches of conversation I was hearing around me were about the world of tennis and golf, art and computing – not orientated to finance or legal matters at all.

But then chairs began to fill up as the time drew near for the presentation. Silas and I made our excuses and I shook hands with Leonard before we backed quietly out of the room.

'Have to take a look at their toilets before we set off, Silas. 'Meet you in the foyer in a few minutes.'

'Plenty of time. Our table is for eight-thirty and it's only ten minutes away.'

Laura Andrews was repairing her lip gloss when I came across her in the Ladies. Her own crinkly ringlets gave her a touch of élan by being artfully uncombed and she gave me a friendly grin in the mirror as I washed my hands.

Nathaniel had mentioned that she played golf somewhere along the line, so it was my opening comment.

'I hear you're a low-handicap golfer, Laura. Lower than two, was what Nathaniel actually said.'

'Only on the day,' she shrugged modestly.

'I used to caddy for my uncle years ago. All I do now is a little jogging and T'ai Chi. I went to classes with a friend in Kilburn for about five years, more for the exercise than anything else, and I was hoping to find something similar up here. Not been successful so far.'

'Well now, that's a coincidence,' she raised neatly plucked eyebrows and tugged a titian curl into position. 'I might just be able to help you there.'

'How so?'

'I go to a weekly class near where I live in Saltburn. Well, I say weekly, but my work takes me away so much of the time that I suppose I am more of an "as and when" person. Why don't you come along? You'll enjoy it.'

'I'm only looking for the discipline; I'm not very good. I don't want to join a group of experts when I am only a beginner.

'Same as me. To be honest, I only go to lower my stress levels, but Mingh – he is the guy in charge of the group – is a T'ai Chi master. He would love to get his teeth into something more advanced if his pupils showed an interest. Loves to talk about martial arts during the break, but for the most part we concentrate on slow movement. All to do with Yin and Yang, apparently. Are you OK for next Tuesday?'

'Love to. Thanks. Just what I'm looking for.'

I thought I was being subtle when I said, 'Nathaniel's mother is supposed to be a good golfer, too.' I was trying to shuffle my bits of information into position without making it too obvious. 'What's she like?'

'Golf, you mean, or as a person?' Eyes narrowed shrewdly. Obviously not as subtle as I had intended. Best to come clean.

'Both. Nathaniel told me her father used to be sweet on one of the Parsons sisters. Do you know the background?'

She put the lip gloss and comb back into her bag, which gave us both thinking time.

'Actually, yes, I do, but only because I worked on the file before Nathaniel took it over properly. Now, don't quote me, but he once let on that his mother is obsessed by your property and wants some kind of retribution.

'She has no case, so don't worry about it. The Will is airtight and they both know that. I don't think he cares one way or the other, but he's a mother's boy, our Nathaniel, and will do as he is told. Does that help you?'

It did, and I vowed to destroy the new draft Will as soon as I got home, but I got the feeling Laura didn't know it even existed. I wondered whether perhaps Laura was close to NFS or just a colleague. When I tactfully danced around the question, she rolled her eyes and gave a loud chuckle.

'Put it this way, Elise. I might have a lot to offer a devastating bachelor like Nathaniel but there's a big minus in my CV.'

'What's that?'

'Wrong gender.'

CHAPTER THIRTY-THREE

I was still speechless when I got into the car and we drove away from the hotel, but if Silas noticed anything untoward then he didn't say anything. Information like that stays between my ears.

The rest of our evening was for planning and scheming, and the *Crab and Lobster* restaurant was only a few miles from Wraycliffe down the coast. I covertly studied my 'date' as the car purred along and we talked about the evening so far – nothing yet about Virginia, I noticed.

The passenger seat offered a measure of proximity with the driver that I wasn't prepared for, even though I confess I liked it. He had been wearing jeans and a fleece yesterday, but the dark jacket and cream shirt looked equally good tonight. He wasn't wearing a tie, but he told me that he hates formality, although he usually carries one in his pocket, just in case.

Conversation paused for a moment as he negotiated a roundabout and turned south, but I eventually carried on, 'I was quite taken with Caroline Sugden, you know. Perhaps she makes a point of being friendly with all the clients, but she told me she had actually met Amelia Parsons years ago.'

I let my mind wander a bit, without saying anything to Silas, but it was interesting that Caroline had seemed to know all about me. Well, she would, I suppose, but being sworn to secrecy she had kept the details of my background to herself while Amelia was alive.

Just little things that she mentioned gave me clues; asking after Charles and Millie, for instance, and giving Norfolk a positive commendation of her own.

She even knew about my job as a Systems Analyst. I was glad that Amelia had been able to confide in the Sugdens because her later years must have been a lonely time for her.

What am I saying? Lonely? Not on your life!

This old lady had friends all over Wraycliffe and had conjured up a collection of ancestors to talk to whenever it suited her. I don't call that lonely.

'Seemed particularly interested in my pendant,' I said out loud now, 'and we talked about its background dating back to the late seventeen-hundreds. She was probably just being sociable, but she was very pleasant. Actually, I didn't think she looked well tonight.'

I saw Silas glance momentarily in my direction and then back at the road.

'Now that's an interesting observation. What gave you that idea? She looked OK to me. Another of your intuitions?'

'I really don't know. Something in her eyes. They looked …' I searched for a word, not knowing what I was looking for. 'Cloudy,' was the best I could come up with. 'Perhaps she's coming down with a cold.'

'I didn't notice,' he replied with a quick shake of his head, and I detected his frown rather than saw it.

He roared with laughter, though, when I said, 'There's one thing, Silas. I don't think I shall ever be able to call Mr Sugden Leonard.'

The restaurant car park was almost full when we arrived. We definitely needed a reservation, but Silas had been there many times and was almost a blood brother of the owner.

'I gather you've enjoyed the evening so far?'

'Yes, I've learned a lot,' I replied guardedly, and he chuckled.

'What you mean is that you managed to have a private chat with the delightful Miss Andrews and came up with a few answers of your own. Not to mention a head-to-head with Caroline Sugden that made your eyes light up and your face glow with pleasure.'

Sometimes I think I am surrounded by people who are too clever by half. He must have had his eye on me all evening – had even seen Laura and me coming out of the Ladies together.

We got out of the car and he put his hand under my elbow to guide me through the doorway.

He knew his way around and asked for a specific table in a small alcove away from larger tables. The menu was superb but we chose something off the specials board and Silas made a jocular remark to the waitress as he ordered with breezy familiarity. She replied with a smart retort that showed she knew him well enough to understand his humour and he broke into a loud guffaw before settling back in his chair.

It was only when we had completely finished our meal and were on to the coffee that he came to the part of the evening I had been waiting for.

'Let's continue our conversation of yesterday, shall we,' he said. 'I think I need to put you in the picture properly.'

The waitress carefully poured coffee and intuitively left us alone.

'My own marriage broke up years ago. Both our faults, I'm afraid. The hours I work are not particularly favourable for a happy home life and the strain was getting too much for both of us, so my wife left me. She married a doctor, and I think she realises now that the grass is no greener on *his* side of the fence than it is on mine. I wanted to make a success of my job and she wanted a nine-to-five husband. Bad casting on both our parts, I think.'

I didn't reply. There was a philosophical expression on his face and I felt sorry for two people who had been desperately trying to find something that wasn't there.

Silas related the saga that was Virginia, and the worry that had built a home in his head ever since she had stopped replying to his text messages which, more to the point, he thought she would never answer again.

'I last spoke to Virginia, if that's the right word for a text, just before they moved to Canada, oh, what, two years ago. She and I have been friends for years, long before her first marriage in fact, but she chose Tom because she fell head over heels in love with him. Then she became dewy-eyed with Richard, but it wasn't long before she talked about divorce. This second marriage had all been a rotten mistake, you see, and after her mother's accident she voiced her uncertainties.'

'Uncertainties?'

'She thought that Richard had somehow caused her mother's death out there on the fells.'

I must have looked aghast at that, but he went on to explain that for all it had been newsworthy at the time, the papers had reported it as a bad weather tragedy.

'Things did not add up, but the crime scene held on to its secrets in the end and we had no way of proving otherwise. The coroner brought in a verdict of accidental death.'

The professional barriers between us were happily down by this time and it seemed that Silas wanted someone to share his own fears, as well as take on mine. His face was a mixture of grim determination and realism.

'She probably changed her mind when the prospect of making things work with Richard on the other side of the world cropped up. You know what she is like. Always did fall for a sob story.'

'Poor Virginia. I had no idea. She never confided any of this in me at all. She is a sheep,' I said. 'It's what they do.'

Which made him give me a strange look until I explained.

As though he hadn't heard me, he went on, 'After a while our phone calls stopped. We'd only been using mobiles, of course, so I don't think Richard had any inkling. I lumbered myself with a drink problem around that time, not that anyone guessed because I managed to cover it up.

'But if you think logically about it, I had already lost my best schoolmate in Tom and now I was losing both our wives. I suppose I was trying to console myself. The cartilage problem followed shortly after. There was an address in Canada, a Post Box, but you probably know all about that.'

He looked up at me enquiringly and I thought I caught a fleeting glimpse of sadness before the waitress brought more *petits fours* to the table.

'I saw her new address on your website,' he went on, 'plus the photos and all the news items she puts on.'

'How on earth did you do that?' Wide-eyed now. 'Nobody outside the group can look at it: it's a closed site. I know, because I built it and it has all the latest security devices I could come up with.'

I had, too. I was chief administrator with Andra as my backup, and we had installed every scrupulously important tweak we could think of at the time. Silas looked indulgently at me and his mouth twisted a little, but he simply shrugged his shoulders.

'I knew her password and regularly looked at the site. Not daily perhaps, because I was busy, but every other day. I knew about September and the children getting lost in the Dales,' he said with a chuckle, 'and Samantha losing her wedding ring down the drain.'

'You and the rest of the world! Richard mentioned a few things when he came to our reunion.'

I expanded on the intricacies of our system, though I don't know why I bothered: this man couldn't care less. Unless someone was invited specifically, they couldn't even get on to the system as a registered user, but that didn't stop people looking over a shoulder.

Passwords were never a problem. We thought it was a fairly safe loophole, and in any case children learn so much at school now to be able to bypass them if they are curious enough. It's no bad thing for future teenagers to help if any of our group needed a hand.

I grunted. 'I'm glad for your sake Silas. It must have helped you to get over her.'

'It didn't actually. It made me even more annoyed to think that she had grown to like Richard Mason after all he had done to her.'

I looked up at that. 'What do you mean, done to her?'

I thought he was about to clam up but then he signalled to the waitress to bring a fresh pot of coffee. I didn't prod him about it until she had gone. He ignored me and carried on with his personal opinions.

'Richard is a measured individual who meticulously covers his tracks. I shouldn't say this, but I believe Virginia was right to be suspicious. Just a gut reaction of mine, like yours, Elise, but I've met his type before and something simply doesn't ring true.

'Before she went to Canada, we arranged little signs for each other: silly little expressions that we made up to use on the website or in the email messages that she would send privately to me. I set myself up as a DVD subsidiary to Ruth's shop.'

I knew the sort of shop he meant: a web address rather than a delivery one. He said he had spent quite a bit of time getting a friend from work to set it up, using the gift shop as a cover.

'My sister has always been business-like enough to send paperbacks and knitting wool to customers, but we had this arrangement that if they asked for a particular DVD – which doesn't exist actually – she would say they had run out, and pass it on to me. She was quite happy about the lucrative side of book sales. They weren't as good as the big boys, of course, but requests flooded in and she was making quite a packet.'

'But nothing, I take it, from Virginia.'

'No,' he said, shaking his head, 'nothing from our friend across the water.'

He stared at the sugar bowl as though he expected it to jump in the air, but I could see his mind was elsewhere. A puzzled look came over his face when he said, almost to himself, 'What is she playing at?'

'Please tell me, Silas. I promise it won't go any further than the two us but what did you mean by, you know, what you said. Done to her?'

I saw trust in his eyes and I would stake my life on him not having told anyone before. Not even his sister.

'She had bruises,' he said grimly.

That was good enough for me.

CHAPTER THIRTY-FOUR

As a background to a moonless sky, the security light came on as we drove up to my front door. I made some passing comment about Amelia's forward planning when it came to installing the light, but it seemed irrelevant because my mind was elsewhere.

The plan we had discussed earlier.

To be honest, I didn't know whether to invite him in, seeing as it was almost midnight. Didn't matter; he solved the awkward situation for me with the dry humour I had already come to expect.

'I have a long drive to the Midlands ahead of me tomorrow, Elise, so I won't have that coffee you were thinking about offering me.'

I looked up and we both laughed, which relieved the tension. 'I was going to suggest a cup of tea, actually,' I said, a throwaway remark that made him laugh even more.

He got out of the car and walked round to open the passenger door before I had a chance to click the handle myself. The cool air was refreshing and there was a slight breeze as I stepped out. I must confess I have become unaccustomed to little courtesies such as this of late, but this was the sort of gentlemanly thing he would do.

He hadn't drunk much alcohol, not when I had been watching anyway, and no way was he a secretive person. I found myself fancifully wondering again what his birth sign might be because this evening had shown me even more of the real DCI McGovern. I shall ask him next time I see him.

I walked to the front door and opened my bag to give him the key. As I turned, he caught hold of the cashmere stole that slipped slightly from my shoulders. With a 'Whoops!' he wrapped me up again inside the cuddly warmth, but somehow forgot to release his grip and bent to kiss my nose instead.

I wasn't prepared for such closeness – anything but – and it was a surprise for both of us, I think. A spontaneous gesture. We stared at each other in the shadows created by the security light; I don't know what was going through his mind but my hormones were doing a hop, skip and jump all over the place.

He put the key in the lock. The door swung open, but my eyes were glued to the key that he handed back to me.

He waited until I was safely inside before he went back to his car and switched on the engine. I knew I would see him again soon, but it wouldn't be soon enough. I watched from the doorway as he did a finger salute and the car moved slowly out into the lane. Then I shot all the bolts and turned out the hall lights.

Yes, it was late, but I wasn't tired. Happiness creating yet another little compartment inside me, perhaps? It has been a long time since a man looked at me the way Silas did a few minutes ago. Probing deeply into my mind and, hopefully, liking what he saw.

I knew I shouldn't read too much into it, but I had been thinking about the man instead of the policeman ever since I first heard about him; tonight just brought it out into the open that's all. Virginia and Tom thought a lot about him, I'm sure of that. Perhaps I was seeing him through their eyes. I wrapped the cashmere closer and went outside to sit under the pergola.

Sleep was a million miles away that night. The stars were waiting for me and I listened to the magical tinkle of my garden chimes as the night breeze gently wafted over them.

I received an important telephone call the following day. My new investigative partner, DCI Silas McGovern, had booked tickets for a trip to Wynyard, Canada.

Yesterday evening, he told me he had a friend in the Canadian Police Force, and had intended to pay them a visit last year and maybe find out how Virginia was doing at the same time.

'But until you wrote to me,' he added, 'I thought I was wasting my time. Now, I am convinced it is more urgent than I had realised.'

He had been examining his rough hands up to this point as though he had never seen them before, but then he looked up and stared into space.

'I'll set things up,' he said eventually, and his eyes were reassuring as he turned back to me. 'Let me go and take a look. Give me a fortnight. I just hope I have some good news for you and I'll get in touch with you as soon as I get back.'

A fortnight seemed an age, but I managed to inject conspiratorial low-key into the coffee as I stirred.

'Let's hope there's nothing to worry about,' I replied. 'And in the meantime, I shall set you up with a password so you can look at our system legitimately. I have an uncanny feeling about all this, Silas. Please be careful.'

Eye contact was steady for a long time and then he said, 'I shall. And you.'

It only took a few minutes to fix the website so that Silas could log on anonymously, and I followed it with a quick phone call to Andra.

'Seeing as you are my tekky buddy, you ought to know, just in case something goes wrong. Silas McGovern is a policeman who is interested in watching Virginia's movements for a few days. I don't suppose he'll want to stay on for long.' Almost the truth.

'Spare me the details, honey,' she replied in those clipped tones of hers. 'You wouldn't do it if you didn't have to, and I'd rather not know the ins and outs, thank you.'

I wandered round the workroom with our communal fluffy duster when I had put the phone down, and stopped in front of Linnet's portrait. Strange how I could see little changes each day, small nuances that I hadn't noticed before. She was becoming a friend.

'Not like any Mr Plod I have ever met,' I told her, as I needlessly stroked the frame with anti-static hairs. 'But he ticks all my boxes.' Ticking boxes would not be in her vocabulary, but it didn't matter because I knew she wouldn't be listening anyway.

'Mr McGovern might not have the suave sophistication of Richard Mason – I call that wrapping paper, Linnet – but he has something else that is far better and lasting. He's an honest man who would care for the woman he loved till death. He knows no more than any of us about all this palaver, but he's going to visit some friends in Canada and suss things out a little. Shouldn't take too long and he has our telephone numbers.'

Okay, it was another conversation of the one-sided kind, but you can't have everything.

I didn't mention the warm flush that swept over me when I first saw him. I didn't tell her about the tingle I felt when we shook hands, or the look in his eyes that sent my nerves sparking as we said goodbye last night. It was none of her business.

Instead, I said, 'There, Linnet my dear. Now you look fresh and clean.'

I whispered words of comfort to Flora in the dark that night as well, telling her that I was trying to sort out whatever mess Virginia was in. But there was no reply: no moving bedclothes, no weight of someone sitting at the foot of the bed, no dramatic billowing of curtains.

I fell into a dreamless sleep.

CHAPTER THIRTY-FIVE

I just knew it! I had a hunch that Turner would turn up sooner or later, and I was right.

I must admit I kind of suspected he might be the voyeur Bella had spotted out on the main road, because it was the sort of thing he would do: his motto was never to knock on the front door if you can climb through an upstairs window.

I allowed him as far as the vestibule, but he didn't stay long because I was curt and inhospitable. I like to think it was out of character but I just didn't like the way his eyes greedily took in my new possessions, and I just didn't want him here.

Anyway, enough of him.

Goodbye Turner.

Chessie finally managed to get here late Friday night. The fires she had been fighting back home had turned to sodden ashes, so she said, and she finally landed on my doorstep for a long weekend.

Hugging came first, followed by carting her expensive luggage indoors, plus superfluous comments about appearances.

It was lovely to talk to her properly again, to see the dimples in her cheeks and smell her signature perfume – a sexy little number that was designed especially for her by some French couturier or other.

She always wears this powdery perfume called *Francesca*, a subtle concoction of oriental flowers with woody notes and musk. Least, that's how she describes it. Smells good, whatever it is.

'You look wonderful, darling.' She held me at arm's length. 'Yorkshire agrees with you, I do believe you have put on a little weight since I last saw you.'

She means well.

'Testament to Bella's cooking,' I flicked her comment away. 'Only a couple of pounds, but enough to feel my waistband is taking the strain.'

We had coffee in the sitting room and I could see she was terrifically impressed by my house. Which pleased me a lot because I had given it such a glowing commendation and she can be quite pernickety when things don't come up to scratch.

'I can see now why you are so chipper, it's all so beautiful, inside and out. This place agrees with you.' She nodded without rancour, staring at the new me. 'The hair's good too.'

I pirouetted so she got to see the streaks at their best. She could see now that my enthusiasm over the telephone hadn't simply been pretence and that I hadn't regretted the move for an instant.

'I can't wait to see this attic you've been telling me about. All your anguish last year seemed a high price to pay at the time, but you have definitely landed butter-side up wouldn't you say?'

'You know, Chessie, I'm convinced the air is cleaner here. I get a heady blast of salty tang every morning when I go for my run and I find myself wanting to take deeper breaths. It's really strange, you know, but I just sense that Wraycliffe has been waiting for me all my life. Infinitely more salubrious than my flat, that's for sure.'

We spoke most days on the telephone, but I still missed seeing her. I missed her being part of my daily life and it was good to watch her kick off her shoes and pad about in her slippers as though she belonged.

Bella had left us a delicious fish salad (specially for my diet-conscious friend, she said) but we went to bed late that night because Chessie needed to see everything. *Absolutely everything.*

Friday evening, therefore, saw her investigating like a property dealer with only my peripatetic and sometimes non-existent cat to take an interest in what she did.

'Natty little utility room,' Chessie declared as we walked the length and breadth of the house below ground before moving upstairs, where she was aflame with ideas for my attic venture. I left her beavering about on her own, not in the least surprised when she came back down to the landing with cardboard boxes in her arms.

'Just look at these,' she said, holding yesteryear silken garments up against her Twenty-First Century figure. 'She was a slender little thing, wasn't she?'

'Hmn! Might not all be hers, you know. She had two sisters so we have no way of knowing who wore them. Beautiful, but not my style.'

Her face became flushed with pleasure as she tried them on and twirled and posed in front of the long cheval mirror in my bedroom. They were the sort of garments you might give to a Drama Group for their old-time productions.

That said, there is no chance of giving anything to a Drama Group when my friend gets into her stride. Clothing of any sort has a value to Chessie and I offered her the lot, as a present from Yorkshire.

She accepted with all the eagerness I expected, and then asked for the cheval mirror as well (she has a passion for antiques and knows a good thing when she sees it). I categorically said no, so she drooled over her new silken treasures instead.

'Amelia Parsons must have known more about you than Mr Sugden is letting on, to let you take on all this.'

I nodded, flicked lights on and off as we moved from room to room. It was like watching a butterfly settling on flowers as Chessie glided and admired. She homed in on the bureau and studied our photograph for a long time.

'Tell me again all about Silas. I hope you didn't wear your *très chic* cardigan when you went to dinner. You really should throw it away, you know.'

I told her not to be facetious. I'd already told her about him over the telephone, of course, but I told her again, including a few of my own observations this time.

'Interesting,' she said ambiguously.

'Which part?'

'The way your face lights up when you talk about DCI McGovern.'

'He was Tom's friend, and best man at Virginia's wedding.'

'Yeah, so you said. Four times. Or was it five?' She raised her right hand and stared into space, nodding each time she punched the air with her fingers – one, two, three etc.

I think my face flushed a little so she changed the subject. She smoothed the surface of the bureau as though she hardly dared to spoil it with fingerprints.

'These drawers don't have locks on them, darling.'

'I know. Amelia had an abomination of locks, so Bella says. Never used them. It was only when the solicitor warned her about the validation of her insurance policy that she called the joiner in to do something with the doors and windows.'

'Obviously a burglar could pick and choose anything he liked. Not that he would know that until he got inside, of course,' she pointed out reasonably.

We moved over to the portraits and she looked critically from one picture to another and then to the black stone round my neck. She knew exactly what it looked like because I had already described them to her over and over again.

The bookcase came in for detailed examination and she stood with her hands clasped behind her back, reading the titles.

'Chessie?'

'Mmn. Yes, darling.'

'If I told you I have been hearing things since I came here, what would you say?'

This was something I hadn't had the courage to talk about before. I had been saving it up until she came here and I could tell her face to face. James taught me this; it's so you can see what kind of response is really in there. She looked up from the book she had picked out and turned to look my way.

'What sort of things?'

I wasn't sure how to put it into words, but came up with, 'Would you say I was a reality kind of person?'

The answer came back without any hesitation and she stared me in the eye.

'Of course. Well, apart from your odd forays into predicting the future, which might be considered by some to be a bit quirky. But not me, I might add, because I take them with a pinch of salt. Why?'

'It's just that I've been hearing things: voices and the like, in here.'

'Voices?'

'Yup! They stop as soon as I come in, but I hear them as clearly as I hear you when I'm on the other side of that door.'

She thought for a moment, then said, 'Look. You're not trying to spook me, are you? It couldn't just be something simple, could it, like hearing the TV downstairs or creaking floorboards?

'These old houses do grunt and groan a bit, you know.'

Even as she spoke I watched her studied gaze bounce from corner to corner.

'I've considered that possibility but it doesn't fit what I've heard. More like whispering. Bella says she doesn't hear anything.'

She busied herself straightening the spines of the books she had been looking at and I could tell her mind was working overtime.

'We're talking ghosts here, darling. Right? All stately homes have them.'

'Hardly a stately home, Chessie. Come on!'

She rounded on me again and peered over her designer spectacles in a way that I suspected made her staff cringe.

'Stop splitting hairs. Your attic is a dusty old mausoleum, your cellar is large enough to stable six horses and this room is enormous. I'm a non-believer when it comes to spiritual things, as you know. I have never, ever, personally experienced such a manifestation, but I do know you pretty well. You are normally practical and intelligent, and if you say you hear things, then that's good enough for me.'

What a friend.

'That's the trouble, Chessie. I'm not sure myself any more. It sounds silly when I put it into words, so perhaps I'm being over-imaginative. You were always the sensible one, remember.'

She stood back to admire her re-arrangement of books on the bookshelf, held up a finger to silence me, and then took me out of the room.

She closed the door behind us and we wandered to and fro on the landing for a while ending back at the workroom.

The floorboard gave a loud creak at that point, which made me curl my nose, but then Chessie cocked her head towards the door to listen. The way she lifted her shoulders indicated 'possibly, but not convinced'. Then she bent down.

'There's a dirty big gap under the door. Apart from the whine of old wood we both heard, it's more than likely that you are hearing a draught whistling through, particularly if you've left a window open.'

We went inside and she tried the handles on each of the small windows in the bay. When she got to the one at the end, she pressed it hard.

'Did you know this one isn't locked? It doesn't fit all that well, either, which means that when you open the door you get the through-draught. You should get somebody in to fix the window, or maybe get yourself one of those draught excluders.'

I wasn't convinced, but I let it rest and she continued to walk the floorboards.

'Interesting,' she said again, leaving me none too sure what she was talking about without explaining why. 'Let's go downstairs and open a bottle. Then I can watch your face when you tell me about Silas McGovern again.'

CHAPTER THIRTY-SIX

It was a beautiful day for a garden party. Blue sky promised plenty of sunshine, and trees were beginning to show a healthy green haze that makes you want to catch your breath and admire nature's ingenuity. The days were lengthening and my garden was coming alive.

We had an hour or two to fill before I was due to stand behind my stall. Time enough for Chessie to examine the back yard of what she constantly referred to as my stately home.

Ben was captivated by this effervescent southern flower blowing in the morning breeze across his vegetable patch. My friend looked thoroughly out of place in her cream designer trousers and sloppy sweater as she bent down occasionally to admire his five-a-day veggies.

Her peregrinations through my herbaceous border and rose garden gave her ample opportunity to follow him doggedly round the network of paths that I proudly call my garden, and I thought it highly unlikely that he had ever met anyone like her before.

I watched them roam around together, he showing her every nook and cranny and she apparently asking question upon question, judging by all the gesticulations that were going on between them.

'He says he can't come tomorrow,' she announced brightly when she came back into the house. 'He's still trying to fathom out the problem with his daughter's car; some gubbins under the bonnet, he called it, and it could take all day.

'Goodness me! I haven't heard that word for years. I offered your help, by the way, but he seemed a bit chary about that. I wonder why he doesn't simply take the car to a garage and have done with it.'

I burst out laughing. 'You're too posh for plebs like us, Chessie. He's like Charles and me; he likes to tinker.'

She shrugged and gave me a sly smile, which made me think I had missed a point somewhere.

Every room smelled fragrant that day, and it wasn't just *Francesca*, it was the flowers she brought from outside. She took the small pots of hyacinth that Ben had been nurturing in the greenhouse and carefully placed them on the sunroom windowsill, taking tremendous pride in setting them out carefully so he could see them from his end of the garden.

It was no surprise when she came up with an eye-catching table decoration based on roses with a few bits of greenery scattered round the edges for good measure. Even though she is one of those people who treats flower-arranging as a science, I viewed the dreamy look on her face with suspicion.

'He knows a lot about horticulture,' she told me by way of explanation when I mentioned that she was somewhere on a cloud. 'I only used to like those plants that put weight on quickly, but now I like to watch every stage of their growth, every millimetre, every bud.'

I pricked up my ears and didn't need to feign surprise. Sub-text is not usually my speciality, but I could hardly miss it today, the way it was winging its way under my nose and clinging like a bat, and I honestly didn't believe that Ben warranted such an accolade.

It wasn't Ben, of course, and she eventually told me that there was a new beau in her life, a horticulturalist from Buckinghamshire called Charlie.

He is some clever consultant who has a client list that includes people I have only ever seen on television, much less met in real life.

Chessie is used to hobnobbing with famous people and simply doesn't understand why I come over all of a dither when I see a superstar. Charlie Barrington is the outdoor type, apparently, but soft and gentle when it matters.

And with that, the rest was left to my imagination. Chessie and I don't share sex confidences; we have always managed nicely with innuendo rather than detail. Consequently, she filtered out the more erotic bits but eventually admitted that Charlie has a magnificent body combined with a magic touch. She didn't say whether that was for her or his plants.

'I don't suppose you would like any new landscaping in your back yard, darling? He is very good. A snoozy little fruit garden in the sunshine beyond your pergola would be perfect, or have you thought about goldfish in a kidney-shaped pond somewhere in the middle. It would look like a garden centre brochure.'

'It's more a case of talking to Ben,' I said with a touch of irony. 'He's the one who has a firm grip on my soil.'

'And with perfect results, but he's not going to be around indefinitely and some of the work must be high maintenance. He must be knocking on a bit. A bit of paving and a courtyard will take some of the strain.'

I was amazed. She even sounded like a garden consultant!

The village fête saw Chessie and me delegated to the task of standing behind a stall in one of the larger village gardens that somebody had kindly offered to open up for the day.

We were raising money for the village hall which also served as a Brownie Hut, and the local newsletter suggested that a new extension was a distinct possibility within the next six months.

Patriotic bunting added to the carnival atmosphere, and visitors were arriving by the minute from surrounding districts. The vicar had taken a long time to inflate dozens of silver balloons, to be launched skywards by customers (at a price, naturally), with return addresses attached to see how far they had gone. Some joker had labelled the stall 'Communicate with the Galaxy'.

Never mind the Galaxy, I thought, what would these people say if they knew about the communicative skills of the previous owner of *Painter's Lodge* and her mystical interaction with her ancestors? If her journals were true, she had led a double life they knew nothing about.

I found myself looking for clues in seemingly innocent conversation when people spoke to me, but there were none.

The vicar saluted our arrival with a broad smile. His chair, I noted, was strategically positioned at the entrance to the garden. He was delighted to meet Chessie and welcomed her as though she were one of his flock rather than as a weekend guest, adding that we would both be most welcome to join the committee for a celebratory drink at the *Nags Head* in the evening.

From his prominent entrance position, he could waylay our paying customers who were already queuing, without actually tripping them up. You could tell it wasn't the first time he had done this, and he knew his stuff.

To enter into the spirit of the occasion, I tentatively offered to host the autumn event similar to this at my place.

His acceptance on behalf of the committee was unhesitatingly quick, which made me wonder whether I had let myself in for something difficult. But no, he went on to tell me that Miss Parsons used to open up her gardens regularly for events such as these and I was merely continuing the tradition.

I noticed he had a gleam of triumph in his eye and a huge smile of success on his face as he relayed the news to the organizer.

'Good job you suggested it,' Chessie whispered. 'You'd be an outcast by now if you hadn't.'

The WI Chairperson opened the proceedings with a little speech.

'I heard the cuckoo, this morning,' she announced briskly, pulling off her spectacles and dangling them casually in her hand (as she invariably did at committee meetings). 'Not only the harbinger of spring, but an omen, ladies and gentlemen, that signifies prosperity.' She beamed at all the faces looking up at her and there was a general titter when she added sagely, 'Prosperity for the organizers of this garden party, I hope. So please try to enjoy yourselves while we take your money.'

She replaced her glasses, the vicar gave Chessie and me a thumbs-up and the selling began.

It was late afternoon by the time the garden party finally ground to a halt. In addition to selling everything on my table, we made a handsome profit that would certainly pay for a few roof tiles and a cupboard for the Brownies.

'I didn't know you could play dominoes, Chessie,' I shrieked as we trotted our giddy way back to *Painter's Lodge* that same evening (it was almost the early hours of Sunday).

She giggled at me over her shoulder. 'Darling, I have never played in my life before. I just got lucky.'

It would have been about a quarter to twelve at night and we ought to have been walking on the pavement, but unwise children often goad each other into doing idiotic things, I suppose, and we had caroused with our new friends in the pub far longer than we had intended. To avoid some of the patchy bits on the tarmac caused by recent frost, we swerved and danced like a couple of drunken fools.

I cringed when I thought about it afterwards; it was a good job nobody could hear us. Most of the night owls were still at the *Nags Head* and those who weren't were hopefully in holes in their trees. The security light sprang to life when we made our way through the side gate.

Chessie's grasp on her pot azalea had been somewhat precarious when she clicked her high heeled boots up the road, but she clutched it firmly now, trying to protect it from whatever chill was around that night. I opened the door and we reached the safety of our bolt hole.

Ben goes to the pub every Saturday night and she had happily teamed up with him to play dominoes, whereupon the two of them had beaten the rest of us to a pulp. Hence the prize.

It was the first time I had ventured into the *Nags Head* at night, and I was surprised by the welcome I got when we walked in. I must be quite a celebrity, if only because I am a Parsons, not in name, but certainly in lineage. After all, I am the 'almost' granddaughter of a beloved local.

It seemed irrelevant that my true biological grand ancestor was Amelia's sister and that the lady of the home team herself had never married. No matter, they treated me as one of their own, someone who belonged. Someone, moreover, with a burgeoning reputation as a computer egghead.

I spotted old Ben at a corner table with three even older cronies, all of them nursing pints of ale and doing their best to hide the all-important dots on their dominoes from each other. When he saw me, he nodded, and Diana pointed to our reserved table next to the fireplace where Jim was poking the coals and freshening the fire.

That was a memory in itself and I nodded towards the fire.

'When I was old enough,' I said to Chessie, 'I used to do that every morning and spread the ash at the bottom of Millie's vegetable patch. Riddle the clinker, Charles called it.'

'Good for soil, potash,' she explained (what she doesn't know about horticulture now could be written on my thumbnail). I decided to shut up and not mention anything to do with gardens for a while.

I was well aware of the many pairs of eyes that followed Chessie as, buffed and toned like the professional model she used to be, she gracefully found her way to her chair and sat down. Diana provided us with a tasty home-made fish pie, which we enjoyed along with a bottle of her house white and I introduced Chessie as my pal from London.

She was an instant success to the gathered assembly, some of whom had been no further than Doncaster racecourse, and they seemed to relish the delights of her whirlwind existence when she filled them in.

I noticed she embellished bits of it by dropping a few famous names and I honestly don't remember whether she had ever met any of them, but it went down well.

To prove the validity of our Chinese astrological sign of the monkey, she has absorbed the 'confident showman' bit which is inherent in our simian personality (the original Miss Sparkle) whilst I have inherited an abundance of another of our traits – the love of a challenge.

Thus accepted by the local populace, we quickly finished our meal and cautiously infiltrated the domino match that was about to begin. I got the impression they may even have been waiting for us because there was a dearth of competitors desperate for a game, though no lack of enthusiasm from those who were milling around the bar to watch. Perhaps our presence was a bit of a novelty.

I managed to have a word with Diana at some point of the evening about our cat, but it seems that the little tinker has moved around the village like a gypsy from the day he was born and I was not to give him another thought.

From what she said, I didn't even own half of him, probably less than a leg, but it fleetingly registered that Mrs Hanby must be doing well out of the arrangement, stocking up on cat food for half the village, and I mentally added tins to my shopping list.

I agreed to partner the vicar, an unlikely presence in the *Nags Head*, I agree, and he was obviously no better at dominoes than myself. He was as much a stranger to the mysterious game known as Fives and Threes as I was, though I think he was trying his best, bless him. Lager flowed ceremoniously at this point and the worthy man of the cloth and I were well on the way to losing badly, much worse than anyone else apparently.

We spent most of the evening listening to sympathetic noises on either side of us. I don't know about the vicar, but I think I was a little squiffy, and by this time was calling him Geoff as though I had known him all my life.

'Drinks all round, Mr Innkeeper,' said Chessie, beaming broadly as she plonked her credit card on the counter.

I always knew she could handle booze!

My Big City friend was fast asleep when I went for my jog the following morning. I vary my route anyway on a daily basis, but dark clouds warned me to run down the main road to the far end of the village rather than on the beach where it can be a bit squelchy after a cloudburst.

I could smell grilling bacon when I returned and I slotted the newspaper with its colossal number of inserts into the magazine rack in the lounge. Chessie, who abhors running and sidesteps any of my attempts to get her to join in, had promised to produce something tasty by the time I got back, provided I didn't pester her to come with me.

I quickly changed into my leisure suit and towelled my hair as best I could before I joined her in the kitchen and mashed the tea.

'You know, I really ought to congratulate myself on having a guest who is not only nice to talk to and spend time with over breakfast, but who can also cook decent food.'

She scooped bacon from the grill pan and loaded my plate with bacon and egg sandwiches while I looked on greedily.

'Don't make rash statements,' came back the curt reply, 'you haven't tried it yet.' She was happier with fruit and yoghurt.

While we ate, Chessie graciously allowed me to see fortuitous things in her teacup, including a really good one that I made up about gardens. Then we took a fresh pot up to the workroom so I could put the photographs from yesterday on to the computer.

Do you really think I should ask everybody to come here for the next reunion?'

'Of course, darling. It will give you the opportunity to show it off.'

'That's all right then. I'll put a note on the site now and see if they all agree. Sophe liked the idea when I spoke to her on the telephone to thank her for my jewellery.'

'She's a bit like me, a novice when it comes to the computer, but we both realise we hold the future in our hands. I do hope Virginia can make it next time. What else did Sophe say?'

'I asked her what she thought about Richard, apart from stonking gorgeous, which we all thought. She said she wasn't sure. Didn't want to comment.'

Chessie cocked her head to one side and pursed her lips. 'I wonder whether Sophe's husband would know as much about all of us, like Richard seems to.'

'Funnily enough, I asked her that and she said not. I remember her words exactly, come to think of it. She said that David would never take such an interest: he hardly knows that we have a website, never mind who uses it. Richard must have brushed up on all our comings and goings before he came to see us. The poor man must have been terrified when he came into the room.'

Chessie cooed when her photographs came up on screen and we chose the best ones for the site. She had taken her point-and-shoot camera to the pub, and there were only two pictures worth uploading.

I added a caption appropriately for *"The winners, Chessie and Ben, holding their prizes"* but didn't label the one of myself and the vicar, because I thought we both looked a bit bleary-eyed and it wouldn't do either of our images any good. I left her to do what she wanted with the rest.

Virginia's latest information told us that she was now helping out at the local library three days a week and she was enjoying meeting some interesting people – 'local' being forty minutes away by truck.

'Library?' Chessie snorted in disgust as she poured more tea. 'Virginia never read a book in her life. She was more into embroidery and painting, as I recall.'

'Not quite true,' I reminded her. She read non-fiction when she was younger, but I remember she struggled with the booklist at school. Maybe she wants something to occupy her time.'

I fell asleep that night with one of Amelia's earlier journals in my arms, open at a particular page for Nineteen forty-four.

Before she left earlier in the day, Chessie had remarked on how beautiful the handwriting was, but I was more interested in the content of this particular entry.

> *My sister Lizzie gave birth to a seven-pound baby girl in Ashford today. I hope Robert appreciates all the effort she went through to bring the poor little mite into this world. I must surely be grateful that I shall not have to endure such an horrific experience, for I shall never marry now.*

Mama and I were with Lizzie the whole time during her confinement, and Doctor Race said he had never delivered such a bonny baby. I bet he says that to all the new mothers. Personally, I thought the baby was incredibly wrinkled and most unattractive, but then, aren't they all…

They are going to call her Frances.

I must have read those words at least a dozen times, but they still made me sad.

CHAPTER THIRTY-SEVEN

Caroline Sugden came down with a viral infection, or so Laura told me during one of our T'ai Chi sessions. Pleased about that – not the infection, you understand, but the fact that I predicted it.

I now had a regular spot in Mingh's group, almost out of sight on the back row, and had signed up for the rest of the year. Novices were most welcome, he said, and his classes were popular, almost to bursting point. I think I managed to get in because I had 'connections'.

Laura was justly curious when I said I wasn't surprised about Mrs Sugden, so I gave her a short lecture on the reliability of the sixth sense and the fact that my ancestors were gypsies who knew a thing or two about ailments.

I believe my obscure utterances must have alarmed her a little, because her powers of concentration made her grasp the bird's tail and gather her Chi with gusto from that point on.

I must say, after the initial jaw drop, I felt quite clever that I was developing this extra-sensory gift. I even told Linnet all about it because I thought she might be interested, woes and illness being her grandmam's line of business, you see.

I began to look at people more intently after that and stare at them for clues. Mrs Hanby, for instance; Lionel; Ben when he wasn't looking. Were any of them looking peaky? I couldn't honestly say. Table-top fortune telling I was used to, but a bit of ESP was new to me.

In spite of Amelia's own view that the amulet had a juju's power to trigger visions, I decided that the real thread running through all this mumbo-jumbo could be summed up in the word Silas used – intuition. It goes without saying that I never thought to question my own eccentricity in talking to myself when I dusted the paintings.

As well as my weekly trip to Saltburn, Bella enrolled me officially into the WI, reducing the white space in my diary even more and making me feel busy. I think I would have been invited to local parties and such if there had been a Mr Kent alongside me, but the well-bred ladies I had met so far were less enthusiastic about allowing me access to their husbands, seeing as I was a *feme sole*.

There wasn't a squeak out of any of my ancestors when I switched on the computer a few days later. Probably as well, I don't know what I would have done if I had heard anything, but I rabbited on regardless and went through the motions of booting up as I chatted to Linnet.

'The WI Chairperson has roped me in to be wardrobe mistress at the local dramatic society,' I said, loud enough to be heard at the other end of the room. 'That's ... er ... what you would call "mumming", Linnet. I have a week to get a book on Fashion in the Thirties from the library.'

I felt a silly sense of frustration at the empty silence; I was on my own.

The computer screen sprang to life.

April has always been a busy month on the website and it had steadily filled up with photographs. September's eldest daughter was the image of her mother at that age, and Lucy was pregnant.

All of which made me think about biological clocks and what might be happening to mine. I took a minute to break off and consider my surroundings: the workroom; Ben through the window; Bella doing the ironing in the cellar. Was I destined to become another Amelia Parsons? Unmarried? Dreamy?

Amelia had me for a descendant, of course, whereas I had no one to take care of my beautiful home when I had gone. I was happy with James's children and with September's, but what about my own? The runes say my future is bright, but they would, wouldn't they? They are in the hands of an optimist.

The only thing from Canada was that Virginia's library work experience continued to be a great success. She had made new friends and was even thinking of putting pen to paper and writing a kind of diary-style 'Journeys across Continents' about her travel experiences.

Plenty of data there, but what I did find a little strange was that she never mentioned Silas's visit. I kept quiet about it in case he was playing a watch-and-wait game in the background. He might still be finding his way round Canada.

Then, at last, came his email. A message loaded with mystery from a man of few words.

> *Elise – News important but can wait till I see you.*
> *Will return 27th. Silas*

He didn't want to say too much over the telephone, either, when he arrived back in England: just enough to say he was on his way to *Painter's Lodge*.

I was upstairs when I heard his car arrive, and couldn't decide from the way he got out and walked to the door whether his news was good or bad.

There was a deadpan look on his face, but I knew I shouldn't be deceived into thinking that it proved anything. It was a look he would undoubtedly have cultivated in his job and there would be a lot going on behind it.

I dashed downstairs and opened the door before he had chance to ring the bell.

'It's good to see you back in this country.'

I was at a loss to know whether to kiss his cheek or shake his hand. Were we friends now or did we merely have a business arrangement? For me, my feelings for him were growing rapidly, but I was none too sure about his.

He apparently had the same reservations, so we missed that bit out and simply smiled at each other instead. I pushed aside my eagerness to hear what he had to say because he looked worn out. 'Jetlag?' I asked.

'Not really. I've been back in England for a few days now, but there were things I had to do before I came here. God, I could do with a drink.'

He lifted his shoulders in careless fashion when I asked whether he had eaten.

'I had something yesterday, but only enough to survive. Can't even remember now what it was. And I didn't fancy breakfast this morning because I wanted to get here as soon as I could. Ruth gets cross when I miss breakfast. She's right, of course. She usually gives me some of those crunchy breakfast bars to take to work, but I didn't even fancy those.'

I looked quickly at the wall clock in the hall. Nearly lunch time. 'We could go down the road to the pub, if you like. They do a nice menu at this time of day. You must be famished.'

He seemed to have lost the roundness I had seen before, and instinct told me that he hadn't exactly enjoyed the last few weeks.

I collected my bag and keys and we set off to walk down the road. He walked vigorously; there was no sign of a limp.

'Knee all right, Silas? It doesn't look quite so painful today.'

He raised his eyebrows at that. 'Good days and bad, mostly good. Pierre's wife gave me some gel, which seems to have worked wonders. It's no miracle cure, but it will stave off the quack for a while longer.'

He looked around him appreciatively as we passed the church and neared the pub.

'Here we are then. I hope you can whip up an appetite. Diana takes a great pride in her menu; if you leave anything on your plate she will take it personally.'

CHAPTER THIRTY-EIGHT

Silas was sticking to tonic water he said, which I thought at first was because of the driving, but apparently, he was in no mood for alcohol. He wanted a clear head. And food.

I was conscious that he had said nothing yet about Virginia. We took our drinks to a quiet corner and sat down with the menu. I could wait no longer.

'So, you found her in Canada?' I said hopefully when we were both settled and Diana's young waitress, Meg, had taken our order.

He gave me a look of scorn. 'No, I didn't, but the truth will blow your blood pressure sky high.' He looked around him to confirm that we wouldn't be overheard. 'We could probably talk better at your house if you want to wait, but I'd rather not keep you in suspense any longer.'

'No, here's fine.'

'The trip was worth more than I can ever say.'

He finished his drink like a nomad who had just found an oasis in the desert. Then he stood to get another and nodded to my glass, but I declined a top up. My spritzer was almost untouched. Hiding a discreet burp with a shake of his head and a fist on his chest he added derisively, 'Don't know why I bother drinking this rubbish; I can't stand the stuff!'

When he returned to the table I said, 'It wasn't a wasted journey, you say.'

'On the contrary. Let me start at the beginning. As you know, I flew to Toronto and then on to Regina to stay with an old friend of mine in the RCMP. Pierre and I go back a long way, so when I told him what the problem was, he couldn't have been more helpful.

'Nice guy. I first met him when we were both in uniform on a law enforcement exchange.' The memory must have been agreeable enough judging by the smile. 'Their dress uniform is quite grand, you know.'

'I've only seen photographs,' I said. 'And musicals.'

He rolled his eyes at that. 'Yeah! Anyway, I don't suppose you've ever been to Wynyard, but I should point out that it is literally miles away from anywhere, same as everywhere else in Canada. The day after I arrived we motored a couple of hours to where Virginia and Richard are supposed to live. When we got there, I don't know what I expected to find and, to be perfectly honest, I hadn't made up my mind what I was going to do if I saw them.'

'You found their house?' I supplied. Wide-eyed. Eager now. This was what I had been waiting for.

'Nope! We tried, believe me. We looked everywhere, but there was nothing. They may have chosen Saskatchewan to live in isolation, but there is a communicative spirit among the residents that is second to none. Everybody knows everybody else, and if the Masons were there, someone would have known about them. This house of theirs is a load of eyewash. You have to understand, Elise, that Wynyard doesn't have addresses in streets like we do, so it was a matter of relying on neighbours.'

I could see he was anxious to find reasons for the things he was telling me because they were difficult to believe. His attitude was not agitated, more dynamic. I was genuinely puzzled.

'But it's a large house,' I interrupted. 'We have loads of pictures of it on the website.'

We were interrupted when Meg brought steak and ale pies and we spent the next few minutes organizing our food and cutlery.

'Yes, I know. But think about it logically. Those pictures could have been anywhere. And look at it this way: did you ever see Virginia anywhere near the house? Did you ever tie the two together?'

'Well ... '

'No. Right? Wherever it is, it certainly isn't in Wynyard,' he said almost defiantly.

He shook his head as he recalled his own feelings, but it emerged that he and Pierre traipsed over the gritted roads and found one question leading to another, but no answers.

'Anyway, after a bit of nosing around, we eventually managed to talk to a woman at the Post Office, a Madame Boulanger. Remember, we're talking small town here, very small town, with happy and contented people and not many shops. Between us, Pierre and I hoped we could persuade this postmistress to give us some information.'

Definitely hungry, this man. He cleared his plate long before I did, and began to relax. The little grey cells remained alert and his eyes were bright and sharp. He gestured towards Meg for another tonic. This time I joined him.

'Yes, there is a Post Box. That part is true – Elena Boulanger showed it to us. A lovely woman she is, very efficient and eager to help. She prides herself on giving the community a first-class service. Well, Pierre flashed his badge and got out his notebook for effect, and I threw in my best DCI smile for good measure, but Elena insisted that the box in question only had a forwarding address to England. No one ever collected anything from it in Canada, she said. There were hardly any envelopes to send back to the north of England anyway and she didn't know why Mr Mason even bothered to keep the system going.'

I was numb. I had so many questions to ask that I thought my head would burst, but I kept quiet until he had finished. Apparently the two policemen then asked Elena if she would mind checking her records again, while Pierre made copious notes to pretend it was an official enquiry. She had been looking after the box for almost three years and again was keen to insist that she obeyed the rules implicitly.

Meg came to clear away and we ordered freshly-made apple pies and custard. I hoped one of them would be a large portion – not mine, I must add.

'It would have been hilarious if I hadn't been so worried,' Silas said now, 'but we wandered into the shops and tried to find people who knew them, but there was nobody. We even went to the vet in Yorkton but there was no record of any transaction involving dogs or cats like Virginia had talked about on the website.'

That had been one of my questions. Virginia would have been keen on keeping her animals healthy with up-to-date vaccinations and so forth.

His voice was full of incredulity as he recounted the events of the past fortnight. There was no sign of the Masons in Wynyard now, but Richard at least must have been there to set up the Post Box in the first place. Elena Boulanger hadn't imagined it, and she had forms with Richard's signature on them to prove it.

Turning a beady eye towards me he said, 'Eventually we went back to Regina where I was looked after like a king. Joelle, that's Pierre's wife, did a better job of putting nourishing meals on the table than I did trying to put a smile on my face.

'I must have added more lines than you could count, with the interminable frowning I did. My leg was playing up, too.'

He stretched his foot out from under the table. 'That's when she came up with one of the wonder ointments she makes. Tell you something, Elise, I'm not going to dismiss herb potions in future.'

It crossed my mind that Linnet's grandmother would have concocted things like that as well. Never mind the recipe or the mystic incantations that she no doubt performed as part of the cure: it worked. That was all that mattered.

As an aside, he told me that Ruth was fully supportive of what he and I were doing, as he knew she would be. Life on his own home front still had a rosy glow, even if Virginia was making hard work of hers.

'So, I came home. All I had to go on was the return address to the UK that Elena had given me, somewhere in Grasmere. To a young teenager called Nigel whose parents own a home there.'

'I'm not too familiar with the Lake District,' I interrupted. 'I wonder if it's near where Mrs Winters and Virginia used to live.'

Hardly surprising he knew the answer to that.

'Fairly near. Actually, the town is well-visited as a walking spot, with its claim to fame revolving around its scenery and famous residents. The travel guide euphemistically calls the lake a "Water Feature". Some water feature, eh?'

He pushed his empty plate away and Meg came to clear the table. Did we want coffee? Yes, please. And we could manage whatever fancy chocolate truffles she could come up with. She smiled knowingly and came back with a plateful of goodies. I groaned and Silas winked at her.

'So that's where you've been for the past few days, Grasmere,' I said thoughtfully.

'That's about the size of it. God, it's good to get all this off my chest. Trekking across town, talking to villagers and calling in on friends of mine who still work over there takes it out of me these days. Richard's terrace house is stone-built, typical of the area, and the locals believe he's a businessman who works in Leyburn. He's supposedly a hard-working bloke who looks after things over here while his wife flies back and forth to Canada. The tale is that she is on some kind of contract for a translating company, but they don't know any more than that.

'Nobody takes much notice of holiday homes these days and Richard keeps himself to himself. He keeps his BMW in the yard at the back of the house when he's there, and gets to it down a back road that's no wider than an alleyway. None of the houses seem to have garages.'

'What about the letters that turn up in Grasmere?' I was thinking particularly of the ones I had sent myself, which must have taken weeks to get back to England. 'Does this Nigel deliver them anywhere?'

'Oh yes. He gets occasional packages from Canada, which he personally pops through Richard's letterbox. I am assuming that Richard pointlessly sends letters out of the country addressed to himself, which Elena dutifully forwards back to England in a large envelope.'

'A workable scheme, I suppose. But absurd. But what about letters for Virginia? I send Christmas cards and I'm sure other people must do the same because she was always popular. She has lots of friends.'

'I asked about that. Nigel told me that the large envelopes were only ever for Mr Mason.

'Mr Mason?' I asked quickly. 'Only Mister? Not Mr and Mrs?'

'He said they were only for the gentleman. So, where is she?'

He stared into his empty cup and I refilled it.

'You know, Elise, what we ought to do is to go and take a proper look at their house in Grasmere. But I need to do it when Richard isn't around and the place is locked up.'

'Can you get in?'

His bland expression told me not to be silly: what a DCI got up to in his spare time was no business of mine. I had to keep reminding myself that he was no fool, and that Grasmere had been part of his stamping-ground until a few years ago.

'I am only going to get into the house and have a look round,' he said in a placating tone. 'I promise not to disturb anything and Richard won't even know I have been.'

I could see he was coming up with a strategy, and that he was relatively unruffled about putting it all together. He was determined to get to the bottom of it, even more so than me. It was good to have him back. Like the saying goes: a problem shared is a problem halved.

Yes, he was keen to discuss a workable line of attack, but not necessarily the one I suggested, which I freely admit was a bit on the courageous side. I outlined what I had in mind and waited for a reaction.

'I don't like it,' he said when he had thought it through. 'You are only an amateur at this type of thing and you do realise you will be putting your own safety in jeopardy? I can foresee a lot of dangers.'

I had reservations, too, but we chewed things over and neither of us could come up with anything better. He was slightly mollified when I said I wouldn't be on my own, but still wasn't entirely convinced.

'If everything goes according to plan, Chessie will be with me, so that's a bonus, and when you are satisfied with what you find, you will be able to contact us. Don't worry about us. At the first sign of a hullabaloo I shall yell as loudly as I can.'

He still looked unconvinced. 'Give me the weekend to think about this, Elise. Please. I'm as concerned as you are, but we have to plan these things properly and I would like to talk to a friend of mine over in the Lake District first. I'm only asking you to put the brake on for a day or two so we can go firm on our arrangement when we have slept on it. Look, Monday is my day off. How about if I take you to York and we wander around for a while. Are you familiar with York?'

'A little.'

'OK. York on Monday then. I should have fine-tuned your amazing proposal by then and we can dot a few I's and cross a few T's.'

A delay for a few days sounded reasonable. He gave me one of his eyebrow-stare nods and I agreed.

I didn't say anything about Virginia, because I didn't know what to think; I just left my thoughts hanging mid-air. What I really expected, I suppose, was to find my friend reasonably happy with a life I didn't quite understand. She loved Richard, I was certain of that, but why all the subterfuge about living abroad?

I had built up several confusing pictures in my mind. I didn't want to intrude on her privacy, and if she and Richard wanted to be on their own, then that was fine by me, but things simply did not add up, and these lies about Canada didn't help.

I had already considered the possibility that bad investments had put paid to whatever wealth had come their way since Flora died, giving them a less affluent lifestyle than before.

Perhaps Richard had gone through her money the same as Josiah Shaw had managed to do seventy years earlier with his own family's fortune.

Amelia's words about the catastrophic financial crash of the thirties were imprinted on my brain, but I couldn't believe that Virginia would have allowed her friends to think one thing and then live a lie without letting us know. Well, without letting me know at least. We had always been closer than that.

Another possibility entered the equation: whether in fact she had been as rich in the first place as we all supposed. Children get these things into their heads and I admit I had been bowled over by chauffeurs and servants when I was younger.

The worst scenario was that these two were so wrapped up in each other that they wanted nothing more to do with us, and what easier way to do that than not coming to see us?

So many possibilities.

'So, run that past me again, darling, then I know what's going to happen,' Chessie said later that same day when I passed on all the details. I was having my almost-nightly chat with London.

'Silas wants to take a closer look at the house on his own, or maybe with this friend of his, whoever he is – I didn't dig too deeply on that one. We both think there must be something of Virginia's there but we can deal with that when we see what there is. We just have to make sure that Richard isn't around when Silas gets there. I didn't like to ask what he intended to do; frankly, I don't think I really want to know.'

Only a moment's pause before she said, 'You know you can count on me. I'm not given to heroic performances, but I can manage anything within reason. What do we actually do?'

I love the way she said 'we'.

'I was hoping you would say that, because I'm going to get Richard to come to *Painter's Lodge* for the day, and having you here as well is a plus. It will be a load off my mind if Virginia is with him, but we shall have to wait and see.'

'And Silas is OK with this?'

Pause. Long pause.

'Not exactly gung-ho, but, sort of.'

'I shall be up like a shot. You only have to name the day.'

CHAPTER THIRTY-NINE

I started the ball rolling and sent an innocent little email to Virginia's private email address, together with a copy to Silas and Chessie so we all kept pace with the game.

> *Hi Virginia*
> *You are not going to believe this, but I forgot to post your Wedding Anniversary card. It is still sitting on my desk and I am so sorry. I know I sent you an email message, but that's not the same and I apologise.*
>
> *How is the weather in Wynyard? It's like a summer day over here. I do wish we could meet up – I would love to show you my new house, and there are so many other things I want to talk to you about. Private things.*
>
> *I found a letter from your mother the other day which didn't make a lot of sense, but I will show it to you when I see you. I'd rather not talk about it on here.*
> *All my love, Bunty*

That should do the trick. I winced at the email address with the Canadian extension and added my new telephone number for good measure, because I wanted to leave nothing to chance.

I was looking forward to bringing things to a head and convincing myself that Virginia was all right, because, ever the optimist, I still believed there was a simple explanation to all this.

I spent a lot of time with my runes last night, seeking answers to questions that seemed silly when I thought about them later. They say that for every action there has to be a reaction and the very next day it turned up. I got an email from Virginia within twenty-four hours of mine, which bounced into my personal inbox rather than on the website.

She began –

> *My dear Bunty*
> *What a lovely surprise. It so happens that Richard and I had planned to come over to England to see his mother, so this gives us a marvellous opportunity to come and see you ...*

A perfectly normal communication? Of course it was, unless you knew that his mother died a long time ago.

She went on to say that she and Richard would come to England some time during the next two weeks; he had business in London but it would not stop them coming to see me in Yorkshire. She chatted about the weather in Canada and said she would let me know the exact time and date, etc. etc.

Surprised? I nearly laughed out loud. I quickly forwarded the message to Silas and Chessie to give them time to digest it and then waited for the telephone to ring. I heard from Silas first.

'This can't be right,' he growled impatiently. She says it's cold and blustery in Wynyard, but I know for a fact that there's nobody there.

'Not only that,' I replied sourly, 'I happen to know that Richard's mother is dead. I have a letter in my writing box saying that she died of pneumonia ten years ago. His father left them to fend for themselves long before that. I am convinced that Virginia is trying to tell me something, Silas,' I added in desperation. 'Let's hope we don't have to wait too long to find out what it is.'

They were the longest two weeks of my life. I kept in constant touch with both my accomplices and at last I got the expected telephone call from Richard, ostensibly from London, but it was a mobile number so it could have been anywhere.

As soon as I heard his voice I felt a shiver run down my neck. It was Richard, jovial Richard, who sounded completely at ease and wanted to come and see me. Virginia was here in England with him but had gone shopping, so she couldn't talk.

I dutifully asked about his mother and received some preposterous tale about her being in a nursing home, which, of course, elicited a sympathetic response from me before I completely dismissed it from my mind as fantasy. The god-like Richard had feet of clay.

'Can we come and see you on Sunday?' he asked. 'We are coming to Middlesbrough to see a few friends and would love to call in.'

'How lovely ... Yes, that will be fine. It will be great to see you both again.'

I was ninety per cent certain that Virginia would not be with him, but a hidden hand was pulling my strings so I played along. He rang off and I telephoned my partners in crime to fix everything up.

The audacity of our plan was so appealing that it never even occurred to me to question it.

It was straightforward enough: I would lure Richard to Wraycliffe while Silas went to Grasmere. In the meantime, Chessie would travel north to be here with me and between us we would keep him entertained until either Silas or the police arrived, whichever was appropriate.

Silas had tried to dampen my spirits with a few sarcastic labels for my scheme (I think 'hare-brained' was the kindest) but seeing as he couldn't think of anything better, it was all we had.

Intrigue and duplicity didn't come easily to me but I was convinced we were doing the right thing. On verra.

CHAPTER FORTY

The day finally dawned when I knew things would come to a head.

It felt like a normal Sunday morning, except that it was destined to be anything but, and I got up in a strangely apprehensive but euphoric mood. It was the kind of feeling you get when you know your adrenaline is working overtime. Whether that was a good thing or not, I couldn't say.

It also happened to be the day my mother would have been sixty – her birthday – so it was special to me for that reason alone. The prospect of a happy day looked good, so why was I fidgety?

The temperature dropped severely during the night, bringing on the boiler and resulting in a ground frost outside. I was wide awake by five thirty with no hope of getting back to sleep: too elated by thoughts of the next few hours, I suppose. The day hadn't yet woken up, and it even felt as though the birds had decided to turn over and go back to sleep.

Inner turmoil curbed any breakfast routine I had unwittingly cultivated, though Stringer had no such problems. He gave the day a spot of normality by demolishing a can of something disgusting that purported to be cat food while I managed to force down a spoonful of muesli and swallow a warm drink.

Today was a waiting game.

Waiting for Richard and Virginia.

Waiting for Silas to ring.

Waiting for Chessie to arrive.

A two-way game, waiting, I always think. Tedious when you are desperate for results, yes, but it also gives you time to think. (As though I hadn't already done plenty of that.)

Come on everybody. Let's get started! What are we waiting for?

Chessie's plan had originally been to travel yesterday, but an important meeting with a valued client had put paid to that and she rang yesterday morning to say that things had radically changed at her end.

'It's an infernal nuisance but it can't be helped, I'm afraid,' she said apologetically, 'but Bella will be with you when Richard arrives, won't she?'

I noticed she didn't suggest that two people would be arriving: Richard and our friend.

'Sadly no. George is taking her and her mum to the seaside for the weekend. But Ben will be along later in the afternoon.'

'Nothing to worry about then, darling. If I set off tomorrow first thing I can be with you mid-morning. I don't mind setting off in the dark.' Jovial. She's a pal.

So that's what we arranged.

She would be well on her way by now, and probably only an hour or so away. Richard and Virginia were supposed to come for a late lunch around one o'clock, and it was still early.

I needed some fresh air, if only to calm my nerves, so I pulled on my anorak and trainers. Just an hour or so of jogging would get me back in time to meet up with Chessie. Kitted out in sweatshirt and thick trousers, I dragged my woolly cap round my ears, to take off later, if and when the sun decided to emerge. I didn't need reminding to zip my mobile phone into my pocket.

Chessie said she would look underneath a pile of upturned plant pots in the back garden for my front door key if I was out. Not very original, I know, and probably the second most common hiding place a burglar would look after fumbling under the doormat, but it would serve its purpose.

The plant pot had been her suggestion, undeniably because her mind had been on gardening at the time (dear Charlie was a constant). However, an overnight frost had stuck the pots together and by the time I had prised them apart and re-arranged everything to my satisfaction, my fingers were stiff.

It was eerily still out there this morning. I don't remember May being as wintry as this, but the comfortable shape of my *vade mecum* amulet felt snug and warm next to my skin.

The runes last night had been what you might call *ultra-positive* about today's outcome: in fact, the Norse Gods deigned to promise 'a new beginning' – whatever that might mean. Perhaps Odin hadn't cottoned on yet to the fact that a fresh chapter of my life had already begun and I was having a great time treading a new path anyway.

Millie used to say that things had a way of working out properly. I just hoped that today was one of those occasions when her vocal expressions had some substance to them.

A favourite walk of mine is to turn inland outside my gate along the dusty path through the meadow. You come to a copse about half a mile away and a dense wood beyond. It is a walk that I could make last all day if I had the time – which I hadn't on this occasion. I only intended to burn surplus energy this morning because there was too much to do. I bounced along the path for a minute or two, after which, I settled down to a brisk walk.

What I planned to do was to circle round from the wood and come out on to the coast road not too far away from *Dixon's Hut*. A couple of hours maximum. The beach was out of the question because the tide would be rolling in, and it would be too cold on the cliff top, even for me, until the sun came out later.

It had been a grim morning so far, weather-wise, but a gust of wind was livening the scene by swirling wild grasses into waves across a field ablaze with bright patches of cowslips. Eventually, the sky lightened to a dull grey and I met no one, which was perhaps not so surprising on a day like this. I pressed on, glad I was wearing my hat.

To an observer, I could easily have been taking notice of the things around me but I was immersed in my personal memory space. My thoughts dallied around Christmas week, before any of this wonderful new life clock of mine had begun to tick.

A failing Amelia would still be at Wraycliffe, alive, but slowly coming to the end of her fascinating life. And me. What was I doing? Wallowing in self-pity because I couldn't foresee a future for myself. No inkling about today's shenanigans whatsoever.

Even last week's trip to York had been special, and that little memory gave me a contented buzz: Silas helped me climb the stone steps dotted all over the walls and held my hand as we walked round after an intimate lunch – if you can call a marketplace lunch stop intimate. He had reluctantly fine-tuned today's plan, and I could tell he was just as anxious as I was about finding Virginia again.

'Where the hell are you, Virginia?' I now called out to indiscriminate patches of yellow in the field.

If there had been a reply, it would have blown away on the wind.

CHAPTER FORTY-ONE

Maybe it was my internal clock that told me I had gone far enough, further than I had intended, because I found myself on the far side of the wood, a spot where I had never ventured before.

It was a pretty enough place, and one that looked like an enormous wildflower garden. It crossed my mind that it must surely belong to the farmer and that I had inadvertently left the public footpath and was trespassing on his land.

Rather than turn back, I reckoned that once I had ploughed my way through all the tall greenery, I could make my way out on to the coast road and then follow my nose home. I hadn't exactly worked up a sweat, but plenty of thin layers of clothing were working their magic and I was bearably warm.

Skirting round the edge, I made for the outer thicket and caught up with a path that was still crisp with frost towards the coastline. Slight panic, in that I thought I had veered nearer to the coast than I intended, and a quick calculation on my watch told me that I must be at least a mile north of my house. No matter, I still had plenty of time for the master plan.

At last, I chirpily broke through all vegetation, expecting to find water as far as the eye could see on the horizon.

But evidently not today, Elise.

Definitely not today.

Someone up there had decided to celebrate my mother's birthday with a visit by the North Sea Haar, the local phenomenon that the vicar had warned me about when I first arrived. It was a blanket of fog.

It was at that point that I wished I'd had my proper camera with me, but I'd left it in my bedroom and had to make do with a photo on my mobile phone instead. A better photo from further away would have allowed me to look back on the experience later, but for me, on this special day, any photo was better than none.

I couldn't even begin to describe the masochistic pleasure I felt, knowing that a curtained-off cliff edge was close to my feet yet dangerously invisible.

When I had researched the Haar back home, Internet data said it was likely to disappear as suddenly as it had arrived; it all depended on how long the sun took to penetrate through the layers of grey mist. That would no doubt come soon, but what made my pulse quicken the most was the sudden change from my sylvan surroundings of a few minutes ago.

People in the village said the mist had been known to come as far as my front door, but when I told them how keen I was to be a part of it, they either stared uncomprehendingly, or openly laughed at my simple-mindedness. 'A pest,' they called it. 'Just you wait and see.'

I didn't dawdle; time was rushing past me.

The earlier warmth I had worked up was beginning to lose its charm so I bounced up and down a little more briskly on the footpath and pulled my gloves higher up my wrists. Being slippery underfoot, I stepped off the path, road-side, and geared my regular stride up a notch until the shape of *Dixon's Hut* eventually came hazily into view – a long way in the distance, I might add.

Another glance at my watch told me I had plenty of time to sit down before Richard arrived and enjoy a non-view that was as much of a puzzle as anything else about today. Not sure when I would get the opportunity again.

Chessie would no doubt be in the vicinity by now, maybe even waiting for me at the house with a cup of tea, and just as anxious as I was to find out what the third member of our gang had discovered.

Whether Virginia was also close at hand was questionable, knowing that Richard's whole gambit was a sham.

A quick phone check showed I hadn't missed a call.

I had no doubt that Silas would be already timing his part in the plan to the second at his end, and when I had voiced my fears that he might be spotted, he calmed me down by promising to hang around the streets of Grasmere until he was sure the coast was clear.

'Not like this coast,' I muttered to myself with as much flippancy as I could muster.

It seemed ages, but I eventually came to the hut. I was beginning to chide myself for my carelessness in wandering further than I had intended, you know how it goes, when I became aware of a noise coming up behind me. It was the purr of an engine slowing down.

A sleek black BMW Z4 drew level with me and then slowed to a stop a few yards ahead. Without breaking my stride, I jogged towards it, thinking it was likely to be a driver who needed directions in what might be considered foul weather. A gentle buzz told me that the passenger window was winding down.

I sort of half-recognized the voice. Sounded like one of my neighbours at first, though I couldn't be certain. Might even be somebody who was kind enough to offer me a lift home and I primed myself up to say thank you and yes please.

'Elise!' A male voice called out. 'I thought it was you. What a dreadful day to be taking exercise. You can hardly see your hand in front of your face back there.'

I turned to look behind me, towards the north. He was right: it was more of a fog blanket up there, but my expression changed to well-disguised apprehension when I looked back at the car again and saw who was driving.

'Richard?'

Two things instantly sprang to mind: first, he was early by at least two hours, and secondly, he was alone.

Being early was a surprise. Being on his own was not.

The biggest bombshell of all, of course, was that his presence in Wraycliffe as early as this meant that our master plan was starting to go adrift – the plan my co-conspirators and I had so carefully orchestrated.

On the plus side, it also meant that Silas would be unhampered when he went ahead with his reconnoitre tactics. He had purposely kept the unlawful details to himself, but had talked about setting off mid-morning, which suggested he would probably be well on his way to his objective by now, and unless there was a Doberman in situ he might even have made it inside the house. Whether or not he had managed to co-opt this other guy from Cumbria into his scheme, I had no right to know.

This was to be the first roll of the dice then.

A deep breath from me brought me nearer the car. I fervently wished Chessie had rung to let me know she had arrived, but not to worry: I could entertain Richard on my own for as long as necessary. Something told me I would rather be alone with him out here than back at the house.

I peered into the car and carried on with the charade.

'Hello there, where's Virginia?'

'Middlesbrough,' he called out cheerily from the depths of the car. 'Having her hair done.'

Plausible. Maybe I would have done the same four months ago, and after all, he was travelling in the right direction. Part of me wanted to believe him. But not now. It was my metanoia moment.

Still the same undeniably sexy Richard that I remembered from December. His movements were graceful as a cat as he carefully folded the map on the passenger seat and opened his door to get out. He unhooked an expensive-looking leather jacket from the peg behind the driver's seat and slipped it on, remarking that for all it was chilly here, it had been pleasantly warm and sunny further north.

The notion floated across my brain that if financial difficulties were at the root of all this, they were well-disguised by his well-to-do appearance this morning. But a bank balance was no concern of mine; I only wanted to satisfy myself that my friend was all right.

He came towards me and I braced myself for the perfunctory peck. An idiotic thought popped into my head that my nose was cold against his warm cheek.

'Nice wheels, Richard,' I observed, quickly taking a pace backward.

'Borrowed from a friend, actually. It's only six months old. We use a four-wheel truck back home.'

Offhand.

Nice touch.

Liar!

'Ah yes, of course. For all that snow.'

What a load of balderdash. I felt like asking just how much snow they got in the Lake District in a bad winter, but didn't want to bring disingenuous trivia into the game just yet.

We both knew the car belonged to him, and I didn't begrudge him having a quality car for one moment, so long as he had the funds to support it. Unfortunately, all these untruths unveiled a side of his character that I neither liked nor expected.

'I'm early, but Virginia wouldn't stop pestering me to come. You know what she's like; she simply couldn't wait until this afternoon,' he endowed me with a pearly smile. 'In any case, she always describes you as an early bird so I knew you would be up and about somewhere. Not here, I might add,' he gestured into the fog with a laugh. 'I've come to escort you to the hotel. She's looking forward to the three of us having lunch.'

'Oh dear, that puts all my arrangements out of gear, Richard, and I wanted to show you both the house. Chessie is back there now, waiting for me.'

I didn't rightly know if that last part was true, and if it threw him a little, it didn't show. He leaned casually against the bonnet of the car and adjusted his scarf.

'Then we'll have to go and pick her up first. It will be a party for four instead.'

There was something different about him this Sunday morning: something indefinable. Still extrovert, yes, but my newly-discovered intuition detected an unpleasant hardness behind his words.

'I am in no hurry,' I told him, motioning in the direction of non-existent water. 'I have never seen the Haar before and it fascinates me. What do you think of this?'

He walked into the shelter with me and civilly took an interest in the fog-laden North Sea. Once inside, we sat down.

Personally, I could see the comical side to this.

A complete wall of fog with the precipitous edge of the Yorkshire coast only twenty feet away was not quite what I had arranged. But for some reason I was reluctant to take him to *Painter's Lodge*, just in case Chessie hadn't arrived. I just felt I would be more vulnerable there.

'We don't get anything like this at home,' Richard drawled conversationally. I cast a glance at his profile and he explained, 'Canada, I mean. Wynyard is mostly flat farming country. This is something to do with warm air over cold sea, isn't it?'

I almost came up with the comment that Grasmere had a water feature but I held my tongue. Sarcasm is not normally my forte, but I could see I was going to get plenty of practice to brush up my technique today.

Smooth mendacity like this was beyond belief. He settled back companionably with one ankle crossed over his other knee and we made small talk about their journey from abroad. The lies fell glibly from his lips and not once did he trip up. He even had the gall at one point to ask desultory questions about life in England and Yorkshire in particular – still bent on carrying on the masquerade.

The wind was blowing quite forcefully now, making a whistling noise through the gaps in the wooden sides of the hut, and Richard casually rested his arm round the back of the seat, near enough to touch me if I had settled back. The seat was only built for two, three at the most. Our eyes battled with each other.

'*Bunty*!' he said almost reproachfully when we had come to a pause in any coherent conversation. 'Well, well! You little rascal; whoever would have guessed it was *you?*'

I returned his gaze steadily.

'You don't deny it?' he said quizzically and I pulled a face.

'Why should I? We never told anyone; I don't even think Mrs Winters knew. Incidentally, why did you want to know?'

'Because I am certain my dear wife confided in you,' the quick answer volleyed straight back like a tennis ball. 'She told me that much, though she would never divulge exactly who you were.' I still held his eye but he was the first to look away. There was a long pause before he said casually, 'What exactly did you talk about?'

I lifted my shoulders carelessly.

'Oh, you know, girlish chitchat; this and that. Nothing that would interest anybody else.'

'Girlish chitchat my foot!' he mocked. He paused for a moment or two and then said, 'You don't want to believe everything you hear, Bunty. Virginia always did have a tendency to exaggerate … for effect, you understand.'

Well, that was wrong for a start. To my long-standing knowledge Virginia never exaggerated about anything, she had no need, but this man was paranoid about something and it was a safe bet he believed I was privy to information that was personal and private. I only wish I was. At least I would have some idea of what I was up against.

He watched my face carefully, though I didn't give him the benefit of a reaction. Frankly, I thought all this was a bit farcical. Where was it leading? I had the horrible feeling that I was caught up somewhere in a marital dispute, though instinct told me otherwise. Something was dreadfully wrong here, and I desperately wanted Silas to ring my phone and tell me what he had found. I shook my head, bewildered.

'Virginia no longer confides in me, Richard. Not since she married you. She speaks only of you in glowing terms on the website; in fact, she does nothing but praise you.'

His reaction was astonishing.

He raised his head to the wooden roof and laughed uproariously, his voice so loud that I swear they would have heard him in down the road in Mrs Hanby's shop. His shoulders eventually stopped shaking and he gave me a cheeky schoolboy smile.

I frowned. 'What's funny?'

'What you just said. That's really good, Bunty, really good. I suppose I can tell you now, because you're not going to be in a position to pass it on ...'

What was that he just said? Panic alarm started to buzz. Chessie? Where are you? He came up with a goodie, and I had difficulty with it at first, but then things slotted into place.

'Virginia doesn't read or write anything on the website; I do it all on her behalf. She doesn't care a fig for you lot. All those stupid photographs you pass round; all that meaningless drivel you write. Did you never work it out? The reason why I know so much about you all. And why everything about me is so perfect.'

He continued to chuckle at some dark thoughts of his own, and my body suddenly turned colder than the weather. Unease persisted in creeping up my back and into my shoulders.

This was my dear friend he was talking about and he was telling me that the lifestyle they had shared for the last two years was a total cock-and-bull story.

This was a Richard I hadn't encountered before, and I didn't much care for the newcomer sitting next to me. Gone was the debonair charm and striking persona as his demons took over. He clicked his tongue in exasperation and let out an infuriated grunt.

'You know, the thing that annoys me most about all this is that she will insist on going on about you.'

He mimicked Virginia's ladylike way of speaking. 'Bunty will come looking for me; Bunty will know that something is wrong.'

My stomach muscles clenched at the implication of what he had just said.

'What do you mean – wrong? She's all right, isn't she?' I was amazed how quietly my words came out.

He looked affronted. 'Certainly, she's all right. I take extremely good care of her.'

'So where is she then? You can cut the waffle about Middlesbrough and try again. How about *Grasmere*?'

That shook him.

'What do you know about Grasmere?'

'I know you don't live in Canada.'

A flash of sneering respect lit enraged eyes.

'My, my! You have been busy, haven't you? Bunty the Busy Bee. Now how did you find that out?' He raised his eyebrows and sat forward in the seat.

'Friends. I have friends in Canada.'

No untruths there. Well, so I had, a couple of weeks ago. A sudden feeling came over me that I needed help with this one, and I glanced down at my watch. Silas had been right to be concerned; even Chessie hadn't been completely convinced this was the right thing to do and I was slowly beginning to agree with them. Bit late now, old girl.

'I used to live in Canada,' he said conversationally, and the only relevance as far as I could see was that he knew enough about the place to bamboozle us.

'Enough!' I shouted, stamping my foot on the floor. 'I don't give a toss whether you live in England or on the moon. Just be straight with me, will you. Why isn't she here?'

God knows where she was. I glanced seaward, noting that instead of the fog retreating, the wind had blown it a little further inland and it had almost reached the hut. You couldn't see the cliff at all but I was angry enough not to pay any heed to my miasmic surroundings.

There was a coldness about this mist that went right through to my bones, but I was determined to wait until Chessie rang before I took him back to the house. A thought annoyingly floated past my brain: perhaps phone signals didn't work in weather like this anyway.

He must be psychic. He said, 'Let me give you a ride back to the village. You must be quite worn out after your exercise and we can talk better in the warmth. The Sat-Nav says it isn't far.'

'No.' Emphatically no.

I was disenchanted with the way things were going, but if he decided to leave and go back home, then I would have to put Plan B into operation. Silas needed more time.

Big problem there. We hadn't formulated a Plan B. None of us had even thought about one. Stupid, eh?

The wooden seat had been concreted into paving stones, and I don't know whether Richard felt nervous, but he began to tap his heel rhythmically on them. It sounded a bit like a dripping tap and the tension grew inside me. This was body language I had learned years ago: he was ill at ease but trying not to show it.

I glanced down at my wristwatch. Surely somebody would be trying to get in touch with me by now. Almost on cue, the mobile jangled and I took it out of my pocket. It was Chessie and I held it close to my ear. The news was not good.

'There's been an accident, darling. The road is closed and I'm going to be another half hour because of the blasted diversion. I'm stuck in a queue north of God knows where. Is everything all right?'

'No!'

I tried to sound calm, even though I wanted to yell louder. Richard was doing his best to hear, so I pressed the receiver closer to my ear while she spoke.

'Can't talk eh? Right, darling, I'll be as quick as I can.'

The connection crackled and finally died. It could have been either end, and whether she heard me say '*Dixon's Hut*' I couldn't say.

Half an hour! Not that it mattered any more: my part in today's objective had already been accomplished, if only because Richard was here in Wraycliffe and not wrestling with Silas over the other side of the Pennines.

I could almost feel his hot breath on my neck and only hoped he hadn't heard the disgust in Chessie's voice as she ranted. He looked at my sickened expression with interest when I flipped my mobile lid shut.

A faint grin came to his lips and he asked, 'Was that Virginia's lover?'

I didn't know how to respond to that, but I felt the colour drain from my face.

'Don't look so surprised, Bunty. I know all about Tom's school pal. Oh yes, the worthy detective McGovern,' he carried on scathingly. 'She thinks she's in love with him.'

Even if I could have thought of a suitable reply, it didn't rate one, although it put a different slant to my theories about 'reasons why'. Richard must have been raging inside, because what he did next was so bizarre it took me off my guard and a full twenty seconds to sink in.

He reached across and grabbed the mobile phone out of my hand. Mounting incredulity must have shown on my face when he stood and hurled it into the fog, saying cheerfully, 'You won't be needing that anymore.'

You know how your adrenalin begins to flow when something like that happens? Well, three things suddenly struck me: *first*, that I was now without a lifeline; *second*, that I was in the presence of a peevish crank who was more than likely going to turn violent; and *third*, that I could do with getting back to civilization pretty quick.

And as for Plan B? Ha Ha!

'What the hell are you playing at?' Outrage! Astonishment!

I was even more dumbfounded when he just shrugged as though I hadn't spoken and sat down again. He splayed his lips at me in a false smile that made his teeth look like fangs, then he carried on talking as though what he had just done was the kind of thing he did every day.

'Was Mr McGovern coming to see Virginia? That's nice. How quaint. But somehow I fear he will be a long while yet.'

I think I muttered something like 'Why', but I was still burning from the loss of my phone. I might have been in shock over his latest revelation about romance as well, but I was wide awake enough to know that he would bar my way if I made a run for it.

'Well, put it this way, Helmsley is in a bit of a panic and he will be up to his ears in police work. There's been a gas explosion, and a leak is affecting the area where he and Ruth live. It was on the radio. He's bound to be busy for a while, but never mind. Think of it this way: you have the pleasure of my company, for as long as it takes,' he added carelessly.

Disinterest and unfocused eyes told me he didn't give a damn about a town full of people who were in danger. I didn't like it one bit.

He didn't know the extent of our plan then.

He sighed. 'Do you want to hear a grisly story? This seems the ideal place for a gloomy tale,' he waved his arm out to the fog, 'so you might as well hear one. It will get it all off my chest and you're not going to tell anyone else. Good for me; not so good for you.'

I still wasn't frightened, more like angry. I don't know, maybe I ought to have been terrified.

'Richard. If you and Virginia are having problems with your marriage, you should go and see someone who can help. It's no good attacking me with your anger: Virginia never confided in me.'

'Problems? There are no problems.'

His scowl told me he was debating whether to tell me what was on his mind. The scales tipped in my direction.

'Let me tell you about the facts of life, Bunty. I shall paraphrase it for you: I wouldn't want any extraneous facts to cloud the story. You being such an intellectual woman and all that.'

A large measure of resentment there, but it turned out that his antipathy was not aimed at Virginia's love interest, but something entirely different and unbelievable.

'You knew my mother-in-law, of course. Flora. An abominable woman. Never a day went by when the old cow didn't find something to argue about. At one point, she promised to move out of the house and leave us alone, but she never did. Lots of mutual hatred there, Bunty: we detested each other.

'Having to put up with one wealthy woman is bad enough, but two—' He shook his head as though to erase the memory.

'It was more than any self-respecting man could take. The pair of them, Virginia and that stupid mother of hers used to laugh at me behind my back.'

'They wouldn't do that.'

His glance might be scornful but the fantasy was too silly to take seriously. I couldn't imagine Virginia ridiculing anyone. He must be imagining it, although it was obvious he believed every word. Flora Winters was a nuisance who still lived within him: you could hear it in his voice and see it in his face. He was coming to the worst part.

'Whether you appreciate my position or not, Bunty, my lovely wife accuses me of killing her mother and that she asked you to go to the authorities.' I held my breath. 'Ghastly woman, Flora,' he said, almost as an aside.

He only knew half the tale then. Virginia may well have laid a trail for me to follow but she had only taken me as far as Silas's doorstep. My head spun.

So that was what this was all about. Nothing about finance, nothing about a bank balance; not even anger about Virginia two-timing him, though I still didn't believe that for one minute. And as for going to the authorities, wasn't that exactly what I had done? In a roundabout way, of course, and not before wandering down numerous dark alleys first.

I hated him more than ever for talking about Flora in this way. She might have been a grumbler, but it was just her way, though I had no personal experience of it. Virginia used to describe her as truculent, but her mother was also non-judgmental and never interfered in family matters.

'You are imagining things Richard.' This man needed the kind of professional help neither I nor his wife could give. 'Flora died four years ago. Why would Virginia want to make up something like that?'

He widened his eyes like a child eager to impart a secret. We could have been talking about a trip to the supermarket, he was so matter-of-fact.
'Because it's true.'

CHAPTER FORTY-TWO

It would have been easy to forget the real reason Richard was here.

I had been sucked into a world of paranoia that was completely alien to me and my brain was having a hard time sorting it all out. He didn't want to talk about old times for conversational amity, that's for sure, and even if I had been unaware of any criminal tendencies before, I certainly knew about them now. Virginia had been right to sow seeds of doubt.

Chessie would be gnashing her teeth somewhere south of here, and Silas would be marshalling his troops in Helmsley, even as I was having this banal conversation with Richard in the fog. All of us might as well be on different planets.

Some inner time-bomb made me think of Turner. If this was to be the last day of my life, I wanted to make amends. I wished I had been nicer to him.

What the devil was I thinking of? I was no weakling and this guy was a psycho who appeared to have no weapons other than fists. I looked round and calculated the odds, seeing wooden walls around me and a patch of wet grass that stretched a few yards in front. Only a few yards, I noted.

He wanted to talk. Not sure that I wanted to listen, but listen I did, because it gave me time to gather together my own thoughts.

'I was there, you know, when my mother-in-law died. I followed her up into the hills and caught up with her sitting on a rock with the lake in the distance. Would have made a nice photograph on your website, Bunty: green hills, beautiful lake.

'I suppose an intellectual like you would want to know exactly which lake and so forth, but I don't remember, even if I ever knew. She didn't hear me coming up behind her until my feet crunched on the gravel and she turned and gave me one of those haughty looks of hers. She was really good at those.'

You could see the hatred in his eyes and smell the antagonism as he recalled meeting Flora's stare over the tufts of grass.

'She knew it was me, you know, even before I came into her eye-line. I think she was expecting me. She looked at me with that contemptuous expression she always plastered on her face. She even had the cheek to tell me that her daughter should never have married me and that I was the one who should leave the house, not her. I was only there because I wanted to get my hands on her money. Stupid bitch! All her millions and she still said I didn't deserve to spend any of it.'

Richard seemed unaware of my presence and stared into the fog as though it were a screen and he was watching and re-living every moment of the action. He was like a tiger about to pounce.

'I walked over to where she was sitting, trying not to let her words throw me. There was nobody around and in any case, it was a sheltered spot, away from prying eyes. A bit like today, really except that we were surrounded by rocks with a sheer drop on one side down to the valley below rather than fog.' The sore humour made him chuckle. 'Then she began to laugh and stood up to carry on with her walk.'

His eyes narrowed in silent antagonism and he waited a moment or two before carrying on. He seemed to be scrutinizing the scene in front of him single-mindedly and measuring the timescale.

'Oh, how I hated that woman, and in that split second I realised this was my opportunity to get away with something I had been dreaming about for months. She had to get past me to walk back to the path, so I blocked her way, making her take a step backwards. It was so easy to give her arm a push so she lost her footing. I don't think she realised just how close she was to the edge of the rock, but one minute she was there and the next she had gone.' He shook his head almost in disbelief. 'No one saw us up there. It was a cold day: just like now.'

The play in front of him came to an end and he gave a sigh of relief and settled back as though he had won a prodigious battle. It meant nothing to him that it was a heinous crime.

'I prefer the mist,' he concluded reflectively.

I was horrified. *Poor Flora.*

'That was one of them out of the way. I haven't managed to get rid of the other one yet,' he smirked across at me with a vengeful wink, 'but I shall when it suits me. But for the moment, my lovely wife is more use to me alive.'

That was something anyway. Virginia was still in the present and he was admitting that nothing sinister had befallen her.

'Not that I can say the same about you, Busy Bee Bunty. You are the only person who knows the truth, or so she says. Not that you will be able to do anything about it.'

'I don't believe any of this,' I said abruptly.

My heart was thudding with vengeance; I wasn't about to let my mother's birthday pass without making the day memorable. Virginia, and Flora, too. I couldn't let any of them down.

He raised a sardonic eyebrow. 'Really?' The word sounded different today: more like an angry animal.

A light bulb moment.

All at once I knew what Plan B was going to be. I would outrun him down the road as far as the village and shout that a madman was after me. Easy. Even if he got to his car and drove after me he would be helpless in the driving seat, though he might run me over. I stood quickly but he got to his feet at the same time and made a grab for my arm.

It would have been a silly plan, anyway. This was where the cavalry was supposed to appear, but, sad to say, there was no sign of brave soldiers in blue uniforms.

When his hand clenched round my anorak sleeve, my automatic reaction was to trip him up and I confess I got a quick burst of oomph when he went sprawling headlong on to the ground. In other circumstances, I would have been sorry about ruining his leather jacket with mud, but not today. I was angry, and right was on my side.

After a moment's fumbling around, he got to his feet and leered unpleasantly at me as I ran back to the road.

I was quicker off the mark in my trainers, but I wasn't prepared for the lightning speed at which he shortened the distance between us. He took hold of my arm and tried to twist it up my back but I was ready for him this time and fought him off. The future might look grim, but I was the fitter. It was questionable who was the angrier.

He was already breathing heavily, this monster who had much to hide from view. And amazingly strong. Most of us have things in our past that we are not particularly proud of, but Richard's past needed a padlock on it to stop them getting out.

Why is there no one around when you need them? I turned slightly to see whether any walkers had taken to the cliff walk this morning but the fog had apparently put them off. We were alone.

He managed to push me to the ground and clumsily dragged me towards the edge of the cliff by my hood, but somehow, I can't remember how, I got to my feet and stood to face him. If my limbs ached, I hardly noticed, but I know I saw red. I would retaliate, for Virginia's sake, if not my own.

Richard's face was contorted with rage as he lunged at me again. I knew I needed to channel my anger into combat and Mingh's words rang in my ears …

Remain tranquil when faced with your enemies …

Move in response to his movements …

Make him lose his balance …

I was definitely an amateur, but one thing I had learned was the value of dodging, and when Richard came to grab hold of me I deflected his arm and moved to one side.

He fell, but I wasn't nimble enough to take advantage and I skittered across the grass as well. I was cross with myself for being so unco-ordinated, and to my horror we both rolled over on the ground towards the edge of the fog. That was when I felt my ankle give way and a nasty stinging feeling shot up my leg. I stood up but my muscles began to complain, muscles I didn't even know I had.

I shall never quite understand what followed, as long as I live.

Everything seemed to happen so quickly, but I told Silas later that Richard staggered to his feet and turned to look at me, his back to the sea, and I braced myself for the next attack. All of a sudden, he seemed to look past me over my right shoulder. There was a look of horror on his face and I heard him whisper what sounded like 'Flora' as he shrank backwards a few steps.

His arms were flailing as he staggered into the mist.

I swung round to look behind me but there was nobody there, and when I turned back, there was nobody in front of me either.

The agony of stepping on my foot sent me slithering headlong along the grass and the last thing I heard was a siren and Ben's voice coming towards me from the road. Welcome sounds that receded into the background as I closed my eyes.

When I came to, I could hear the steady hum of an engine and the gentle vibration of a motor beneath me; it was like returning from the white brightness of one of my dreams. I heard Chessie's voice first. Paramedics had lifted me into the ambulance and she was sitting beside me. I opened my eyes and sighed in relief.

'Well! Good to have you back with us,' she declared stoutly.

Agitated? Concerned? She was both.

'It's been a helluva day, Chessie.'

I tried to move, but my whole body seemed to be strapped down. My left leg, which was now encased in a splint of some kind, felt numb. I stared at it.

'Broken ankle, darling,' she said sympathetically. 'You'll be on crutches for a few weeks once we get you sorted out, but then you'll be fine. Only a few more miles to the hospital.'

'What about Richard?'

It was coming back to me in small doses now, though it could only have been less than an hour since I was in *Dixon's Hut*. I think the paramedics must have given me something because my voice sounded fluffy to my ears.

'Not as lucky as you,' she replied softly. 'The police are down on the beach now that the fog has disappeared, doing what they have to do.'

Something I hadn't done in years. I started to cry.

CHAPTER FORTY-THREE

Silas turned up in Grasmere in the pouring rain. He drove past the church and into the public car park, buzzed a ticket from the parking machine that clocked him in at 10.43am, and pulled his flat cap out of his pocket to cover his head before he stuck the ticket inside his windscreen.

He locked the car and walked quickly along the main street. His mobile phone had been switched on ever since he set off from Helmsley, so he had been one of the first to hear the calamitous news about the explosion and had satisfied himself via Ruth that everybody was OK.

It wasn't, apparently, as bad a situation as the news announcer had made out on the radio. Emergency services had everything in hand and there was no danger to any residents.

Cars swished past him as he made his way up the deserted street. It was quiet for a Sunday morning: the teashop traded busily in bacon sandwiches and pots of tea, and the newsagent's further up offered shelter to those interested in learning what was going on outside their own backyards.

He paused outside the teashop for a moment and stared at one of the window tables where a customer appeared to be reading a magazine. There was an empty plate and mug in front of him, together with a matching teapot; he was wearing black waterproof jacket and over-trousers, golf-style.

The man looked up when he sensed he was being watched and then nodded, whereupon Silas carried on walking up the main street.

The rain would keep residents indoors, which worried him slightly because he knew that when people looked out of their front room windows to see what the weather was doing, they generally noticed who was walking up and down the street as well. On the other hand, this area was always full of holidaymakers, so the curtain-twitchers probably wouldn't care anyway.

It had been sunny back home when he set off earlier, and he now turned into the alleyway that led to the back of Richard Mason's house, noting with relief when he got there that the BMW was nowhere near. So far so good.

He looked round quickly to make sure he was unobserved, and pulled the collar of his black raincoat high enough to cover his ears. Apart from making him less identifiable, it stopped the rain trickling down his neck. He disappeared inconspicuously inside the yard.

He had been there for less than half a minute when the man from the teashop followed him into the yard. He was a stocky man called Ed – at least a foot shorter than the policeman – and probably had a record a mile long when it came to exploring other people's property when the residents themselves were off-site.

On this occasion, for a change, the two men were on the same antisocial side; they communicated with nods and finger-pointing and, with a bit of fiddling with the lock, Ed opened the back door.

They stepped inside.

The door led directly into a small kitchen, sparsely equipped but neat. Ed satisfied himself that there was no security alarm on the premises, and they looked round for a moment, furtively opening doors and trying to get the feel of the place. Silas had convinced himself that he would be aware of Virginia if she were here, but he was wrong. There was nothing.

The three-storey terraced house was tall and narrow, with a sitting room that overlooked the main street, and stairs leading upwards from kitchen to first floor and then up to the attic. They would only need a few minutes to accomplish what they had set out to do, but absolute silence was a necessity in case the neighbours had ears like bats.

Ed pointed to the stairs and noiselessly moved to the top of the house, leaving Silas to examine the ground floor. Keeping a low profile so as not to attract attention from outside, he entered a beautifully furnished sitting room that spoke only of good taste. Again, no sign of Virginia, even though he would have put money on finding something of hers by now.

This was definitely a man's room. Business magazines were stacked neatly on the bookcase alongside car brochures. A state of the art television set and media station that would have cost a pretty penny held a prominent position against the longest wall. An expensive laptop sat over in the far corner.

It was just the same neat affair when the two housebreakers met again on the landing: two bedrooms, one of which contained a made-up bed and dressing table – a room obviously used for sleeping – and another that had been turned into a walk-in wardrobe. There, they found expensive suits and shirts but nothing a woman might wear. The bathroom looked too clean to be used, and there were toiletries in the cabinet.

Ed signalled that there had been nothing feminine on the top floor either. The whole house was a mystery. Everything was too impersonal, so much so that Silas had begun to think it was virtually unused and that it was exactly what the pleasant locality demanded: a holiday home.

It is a depressing feeling: when you know something is wrong, but you fail to find that certain elusive element of proof.

The two men went back downstairs into the kitchen. Silas ran his fingers along the shelves, looking for dust but finding no tell-tale speck on the end of his finger, while Ed methodically and silently opened and closed cabinet doors, as was his wont. Either Richard had an extremely efficient cleaning lady who came in regularly, or he was good at housework.

Silas's mind was alive with questions of the blind-alley type, and while Ed continued to search inside the pantry, he pulled out a stool from under the kitchen table in disgust and sat down. He would simply have to call it a day and report back to Elise that his search had been in vain. But what was the next step? He felt sick.

The weather outside was becoming more atrocious by the minute and had put the small room into darkness. Ed was busy in the pantry with his torch and was on his knees lifting the edge of a carpet square to examine a crack in the floor.

As Silas casually looked over from his position across the room, his brows knitted together. There was a faint glow below the crack that Ed had uncovered, a light so dim that it wouldn't have been noticeable had the kitchen been brighter. Without knowing exactly why, his heart gave a weird and wonderful leap.

The stool fell over with a clatter as he rushed to take a look, but the noise, on balance, seemed immaterial. He bent down to watch as Ed lifted the carpet square completely aside and revealed a trapdoor.

Silas had already been in the pantry earlier, but on that occasion, he had only marvelled at the neatness of Richard's stacking system and had seen cold stone shelves that held non-perishable goods. This time, he could feel the palms of his hands beginning to sweat and his eyes widened as he put his hand on Ed's shoulder.

Ed's face was a picture of complacency coupled with satisfaction at a job well done – or about to be. The trapdoor stubbornly stayed shut as he pulled, but the lock was no problem to a man who had already burgled his way in here in the first place.

A few seconds later there was a click as the flap opened and a bright electric light showed the way down twelve stone steps (Silas counted every single one as he carefully negotiated the tight corners).

Whitewashed walls initially made the place feel cold but as he carefully trod his way to the bottom, air conditioning brought the temperature back to something tolerable. Pleasant, in fact.

This time, Virginia's presence screamed at him and his head drummed with anticipation, though he dreaded what he might find. He, too, knew about her terror of confined spaces. He pointed wordlessly to another locked door ahead, thinking to himself that this place was as good as a prison.

Ed stepped forward and opened up. He put his hand comfortingly on his friend's arm and then stood back to let the instigator of this mission venture inside on his own.

When he entered, Silas was subliminally conscious that he was standing on a thick carpet and that the furnishings in the room were tastefully arranged. A hidey-hole for someone who might be comfortably well-off, perhaps, but who preferred not to be overburdened with possessions? The standard lamp to his right was fitted with a low-wattage bulb and it put the room into what he would have considered to be a seductive glow at any moment in time other than this.

Oil paintings (genuine?) on the wall startled him for a moment, as did the crystal decanter and glasses on the sideboard. He noted the small shower and toilet area that were discreetly set back to one side. As apartments go, it spoke of elegance and finesse; the fact that it was underground added a touch of surrealism.

But his mind was on the bigger picture.

His eyes followed the 'L' shaped room round to what he assumed was the sleeping area, and he thought at first that the body in the bed was a corpse because it was so still. A tea-making machine was nearby and the remains of a meal lay on a small table. The form was covered with a blanket and, when he approached, it moved slightly. He held his breath; there was a quiver in his voice as he spoke softly.

'Virginia?'

The blanket stirred again slightly, making him shudder. He hardly dared to move in case he was wrong; he hardly dared to move in case he was right. Long dark hair splayed out on the pillow and he noted the silver-backed hairbrush on the table next to the bed, together with a few other personal items.

The thin form rolled over to see him properly. The eyes were huge and still beautiful to his way of thinking, but, at first, she showed no sign of recognition and struggled to see him in the dim light.

'Richard,' she whispered. 'Is that you?'

The words came out as a croak: he could hear dejection in every syllable and see hopelessness in her eyes. The person in the bed was not the person he remembered as his best friend's beautiful wife, but more like a skeletal copy. Nourishment did not appear to have been a problem, but she was thinner than he remembered, and her skin was deathly white, having been denied the powerful rays of sunshine for so long.

He almost tripped over the sheepskin rug as he rushed forward, and two faces stared at each other before Silas bent to grasp her in his arms. He hadn't known what to expect, but at least she was alive. He had feared the worst, but this was bad enough – being a prisoner through no fault of her own.

There was nothing squalid about this place and it must have cost a small fortune to construct. Virginia's fortune most likely. Silas himself had locked people up in worse conditions than this without a second thought, but that was when they deserved it. He was at a loss to say anything.

There were streaks of grey in her dark hair that he couldn't remember seeing before, and he stroked the long tresses protectively now, holding her close so that she could not see the anguish in his face.

'My God! Virginia. Let me look at you.' He held her at arm's length.

'Silas?' she whispered when her eyes had eventually focused on his and she realised who it was. The tears uncontrollably began to run down her face and she clung to him almost ferociously as though her life depended on him.

He called over his shoulder. 'You know what to do, Ed. Just be quick about it, will you.'

CHAPTER FORTY-FOUR

I came home with two walking sticks and my foot encased in a solid blue sock. Ben brought us back from the hospital in his car and my leg was now propped up on an old tapestry pouffe that Chessie had miraculously found in the attic. People apparently don't sign plaster casts these days so I had to forgo that little pleasure.

My whole body felt swollen with the bashing it had taken, but the doctor said I would soon be back to normal and that I was lucky not to have ended up at the bottom of the cliff like the poor man who was with me.

I didn't put him right, I just nodded and looked sad. It wasn't difficult in the circumstances.

There was a message waiting for us, which Chessie read aloud, jerkily, because Bella's handwriting wasn't even her best.

'Good news, darling. Listen to this. She says Mr McGovern rang and there's no need to worry about Mrs Mason. She is now *ensconced* ...' she peered closely at the paper, 'I think that's what it says ... in a private nursing home in Penrith. He couldn't reach you by mobile but he will be along later today.'

'Been quite a day for the medical profession, Chessie.'

She had helpfully filled in one or two gaps for me about my own escapade on the way home from hospital, details which had probably made a lot of difference to the outcome and for which, in retrospect, I shall be eternally grateful.

'After I had spoken to you, the traffic miraculously got moving and I tried your number again, but I realised you must have switched your mobile off when I couldn't contact you. I didn't know at the time that it was learning to swim in the North Sea, did I?'

'I wonder whether I shall ever find it,' I murmured unnecessarily, and heard Ben's 'Tsk-tsk!' from the driver's seat. 'God! I feel such a wimp. Just imagine letting anybody do that.'

'Never mind, darling, you can always buy another. So, I rang Ben to tell him where you were and asked him to keep an eye on you. I'd heard the word "Hut", you see, just before our connection blipped, and he put two and two together. He says he got to you in time to witness some of your aerobics on the cliff top.'

'It was T'ai Chi, actually.' Another silly remark of no importance whatsoever.

'I rang Silas, too,' Chessie said, cheerfully ignoring any pedantic utterings from me (perhaps I was a bit spaced out on painkillers). 'He'd already found Virginia and he must have contacted someone over here who turned up almost at the same time as Ben. Talk about sending for the troops, darling. I wish I'd been here to watch; I only arrived for the final act. Your DCI sounds nice by the way, darling. Can't wait to meet him.'

I was beginning to have doubts about whether he was indeed 'my' DCI after recent events, but managed to keep my thoughts to myself.

Chessie stayed with me for the rest of the week. She had 're-scheduled her life' (I think that's how she put it) and told the doctors authoritatively that she would be looking after me for five days and that my uncle and aunt would come and take over when she left.

Business in London was on a long leash. I was amazed how she managed to conduct daily events over the telephone simply by spending at least an hour every morning talking to her assistant.

I have never seen Chessie at work before but she has a handle on every part of the job (and some parts that probably weren't). Must be why she is so successful. She's completely in control, even from a distance. Her checklist seemed endless, and how the poor girl on the other end managed to remain sane was beyond me.

'Right. That's enough,' she said on Thursday morning, when she had broken a call that had lasted a little over two hours. I had been staring at Rosie's portrait, half an ear on Gucci and the other half on Lagerfeld, when she replaced the receiver and put her voice recorder into her briefcase. 'I am now officially on holiday and today is your birthday.'

'Not to mention your niece Amelia's birthday as well,' I said softly to the two-dimensional figure in purple and green in front of me. 'Don't forget that.'

Chessie didn't even raise an eyebrow: she was getting used to these little chats I had with myself. Cards and flowers were spread over every surface of the workroom and I was wearing a pure silk dressing gown, a birthday present she had somehow managed to smuggle into the house without my knowing. Since she hadn't let me take my gammy leg anywhere near the ground floor it could easily have been down there since she arrived.

I was managing quite nicely plodding along the first floor, letting everybody else climb the stairs while I behaved like the invalid I really wasn't.

My monkey friend had been giving me the full maternal treatment, not looking for creepy crawlies in my hair or anything like that, but bringing me food and serving cups of tea almost every hour, or so it seemed. It was nice to be waited on, though I felt a bit of a fraud.

'Did I ever tell you that my mother wanted me to be a doctor, like she was,' Chessie said humorously when I protested about all the energy she was burning up by simply looking after me. She added sternly, 'Don't you dare put your foot on the ground until I tell you.'

I had promised earlier that I would behave myself so long as she persuaded Bella to bake me a birthday chocolate cake that was filled with fresh cream and iced with coffee fudge. After one or two sky-eyes and growls of disapproval, Chessie organized my abominably high cholesterol confection with Bella, and a delicious aroma soon wafted upstairs from the kitchen.

There was a noise down there now and I heard voices at the front door.

'Visitors, Elise!' Chessie called out seconds later from the bottom of the stairs. 'And so many flowers, Bella is weighing up the pros and cons of starting a shop. She's not sure where to put them.'

Then Bella's voice, '… Second on the right … Tell her I shall bring tea and scones up in a few minutes.'

Bella was happy as Larry: a bit like Chessie in that she liked to be in charge. I knew who it was, of course, because Virginia and I had spoken on the telephone just about every day since I came home, but it put a happy grin on my face when she poked her head round the door and I saw her gaunt but still pretty face. Silas was behind her when she rushed over to throw her arms around me. A few tears from both of us were fully justified, I thought.

'Happy Birthday, Elise! I haven't forgotten.' She handed me a wrapped package with lots of ribbons.

I already had piles of presents from friends in the village – books, wine, plants – and I now whipped off the latest wrapper to reveal a leather-bound notebook with the words 'Elise's Journal' embossed in gold on the front. It brought a lump to my throat, but before I could ask how she knew of the significance, she said, 'Francesca gave me the clue; I merely made it happen. I hope you like it.'

Two specials there: the gift itself, which I would treasure, and the name 'Francesca' which had come to mean so much to us all. A couple of recovering casualties hugged, after which I sat down and animatedly thumbed through blank pages of a book that would become number one in a series of, well, probably a dozen. Best estimate.

Silas said, 'Here. You'll probably need this as well.'

His birthday present was a bulky package that contained a brand new mobile phone.

'I've already plumbed in three important numbers, so you can get in touch. Oh, and by the way—' A conspiratorial glance passed between him and Chessie as he handed over a small brown envelope. They had hit it off immediately the first time they met a couple of days ago. 'The sergeant found your battered phone on the beach. It was beyond recognition because it had been mutilated by gulls, but he did manage to salvage this dead SIM card. You could probably have it mounted within a glass paperweight as a souvenir.'

I was overwhelmed by their kindness, but when he bent down to wrap his arm round me, my heart did a confusing dance. Richard's accusations were still fresh in my head and I was at a loss to know where I stood with this man.

Whether he felt the same way, I don't know, but he quickly made it clear that he preferred to be roaming round the garden with Ben, rather than sitting here with a bunch of legendary chatterboxes.

It was understandable, for obvious reasons, that Virginia wanted to spend most of the time by the window and see the natural freshness of things around her that she had been denied all this time. She even moved our chairs over there so the three of us could see my garden, though I noted that she kept her sunglasses on all the time. She was learning to live with sunlight again.

'Ophthalmologist rules,' she explained.

'I'm only glad you will be convalescing at the right time of year. The latter part of this week has been particularly warm and the forecasters say there's more to come. You never did well in a cold climate. Or the dark,' I added pointedly.

'Mmn. Mummy always used to say that I had to put on a woolly hat to walk past an ice cream van. This is wonderful.'

She threw back her head and momentarily lifted her face to the sun. Other than that, I also observed that she never took her eyes off Silas, not for one minute, and my spirits sank.

What do you do when you love two people who show all the signs of being in love with each other?

Not a situation I've been in before and, I can tell you now, it hurt.

We made up for lost time and talked about everything that Virginia had missed. She said little about the entries on the website that had supposedly flown in from Canada, but I noticed she read them avidly and took particular note of the photographs of her supposed house while she was at it.

She would pick up all our other news when she was in the mood, she said, and had no idea why Richard told everyone they were abroad.

'I probably told you this before, Elise, but he lived there for a few years when he was a child, so I suppose he could be quite convincing when it came to describing the place.'

Silas had deliberately left us to our own devices fairly early on, claiming his desk was calling out to him. I think that was the official explanation; he probably understood that we simply wanted to pick up where we had left off.

My inheritance came somewhere in the middle of a mêlée of updates, and Chessie volunteered to act as estate agent and show my house guest around. She told me firmly that I would be a hindrance, so I told them to 'Shoo!' and let me have some peace.

It was lovely to hear friendly feet pattering upstairs and down. I heard them talking to Bella and I heard the back-door close as they wandered into Ben's domain.

With time on my side, I filled it in by setting to work on the manuals James had sent down the line yesterday. It was difficult to concentrate, but I polished the pages nonetheless, and managed to add a few enhancements such as comical caricatures and slick drawings to his words, to make them more user-friendly. I was more drawn to watching my friends through the window.

'Well, Linnet,' I said to the empty room. 'There go my two special friends. Just look at them sitting in the rose garden, not a care in the world; both deliriously happy and both soon to be married, if I'm not mistaken.' Big sigh.

I had so many questions, like, why didn't Virginia choose to marry Silas when Tom died?

What was it Silas had said about his wife? Married already? I can't remember.

Nothing mattered now anyway; they were both free and I was evidently destined to act out Amelia's life for my own, intrepidly eventful though hers may have been.

I can always talk to the portraits, or paint new ones, and I could learn to play snakes and ladders if that's what it takes to be fulfilled. I might even roll my own cigarettes. Now there's a thought!

When they came in, Virginia surprised me by picking out Linnet's painting as the one she liked the most out of my whole collection. She liked everything, including the one downstairs with Amelia's Journal, she said, but the one of Linnet was special.

'It's as though she is listening to what I say,' she murmured. 'It's quite uncanny.'

'What is?'

'This little girl, Linnet, you call her. Your newly-found ancestor. There's something in the way her face watches my lips when I speak. You can tell she is listening. The others don't do that.' She pulled herself together and laughed self-consciously. 'Don't mind me, Elise. I've been cooped up for so long I've lost touch with actuality.'

'Tell me about it, Olive, my girl. I don't need to be holed up for any length of time to obfuscate reality.'

CHAPTER FORTY-FIVE

When Chessie went back home, the plan changed to allow Virginia to stay with me to recuperate for a few weeks.

Virginia was mystifyingly cagey about the future; it was almost as though she had been formulating plans and keeping them to herself for so long that she couldn't let them out. I didn't mind that she wasn't ready to tell me; she would, I knew, when she was ready.

Millie and Charles had graciously decided to leave the two of us on our own, not that Virginia would have minded company, and, let's face it, I had plenty of room.

Before Chessie left, we managed to pull together a few strands that brought a fresh insight into Richard's macabre story and make the facts easier to grasp. Virginia told us how she used to sign cheques and documents in the early days of her marriage so he could have whatever he wanted: a cheque here, a cash card there. Amounts that grew and grew until her mother cottoned on.

During the past two years, though, he had been forging Virginia's signature. I thought about Turner and all the stupid things we do in the name of love.

'You see, he was jealous of our family money, Francesca, and he talked about it incessantly. Mummy grew tired of listening to him. Your inheritance, too, Elise. He told me about that a few months ago. Got it from the website, I suppose. It made him unexpectedly angry, but he had no right to be, having deprived me of mine for the past two years.'

Sex had not been part of the abuse, that much was clear. It seemed that Richard was happy enough to be celibate; it was his ego that had been a lifelong disaster area. At last, Virginia was able to divulge details that she probably wouldn't tell another soul.

'The loneliness was awful. You do realise, don't you, that I haven't spoken to anyone other than Richard for two years. Once he lodged me in the cellar, he used to go over the same ground again and again, the same tales of woe about his childhood. It was like living inside a horror movie, but he romanticised about so much, I shall never know now whether any of it was true.'

I'm no psychiatrist, and I can't say whether it was a good thing or not to let it all out, but Chessie and I listened to a catalogue of atrocities he had suffered at the hands of his parents, and his mother in particular – sexual abuse, being given rotting food whilst being locked away in his room.

Memories like this might help the business plans of soft paper tissue manufacturers, but they make horrific listening; I only hoped Mrs Hanby had plenty of tissues in stock.

Virginia's viewpoint on Flora's accident was as believable as it always had been without Richard's version.

'Mummy lived with us, as you know, but she was seriously thinking about moving out and leaving us on our own. She was frightened by Richard's rages – more for my sake than anything else – and by then she was having doubts about his sanity. She hung in there but he became moodier, and after a while she found his bad-temper intolerable. We had a blazing row on the morning she died, about something and nothing, which was the norm. I remember it clearly.'

She narrowed her eyes slightly as though to hang on to the fragile memory of her mother's final day.

'She said she was going for a walk to give us a bit of breathing space. That was the last time I saw her alive and I have convinced myself ever since that she intended to commit suicide. I ought to have realised she was saying goodbye to me when she left us alone, because she made a big show of putting her arms around me, which she never did in company. Richard left soon afterwards and I think he went out to look for her. I thought at the time that he had gone to apologise in some way, although he says she must have taken another path because he never found her.'

I said nothing. It would serve no purpose to put her right and I knew better than to argue. I think I must be the only person alive to know the truth. I shall tell nobody.

What I did ask, though, was something that had been nagging me.

'I simply cannot understand why you went down to the cellar in the first place. You always hated the dark; you must have been terrified.'

'I had no choice, Elise. After mummy died I had trouble sleeping and Richard was kind enough to get me something from the doctor. He fed me the pills constantly and I slept a lot. I thought I was terribly ill, you know, sliding in and out of consciousness. He must have been preparing the house for weeks because I woke up one day and found myself in totally different surroundings. It was all dark but I had my own things around me and he told me I had been moved to a nursing home. For a while everything was vague, you know, like being in a dream where nothing is clear: mummy, you, friends. Even wonderful memories that I had of Tom and Jennifer were blurred. It was awful. All I could think of was that Bunty wouldn't let me down.'

I had to look at the floor so she wouldn't see my own emotion. Chessie moved quickly round to her side and took hold of her hand. 'You poor girl. Short term memory loss caused by drugs,' she said hollowly. 'My mother says it's a common condition.'

Tears flowed freely, but then Virginia said, 'I hated it at first, and I missed seeing people, but he told me I had been seriously ill and that it would take a long time to recover. He had dismissed all the nurses and was determined to look after me himself. You get used to it after a while. You even forget what the sky looks like. I trusted him so much.'

She kept breaking off for long stretches of time and we could see that she had stepped back in time to her windowless life with only Richard for company. A life without the postman, or newspapers or shops. He told her she didn't need to know what everyone else was doing and that she should rely entirely on him.

'You have to feel sorry for Richard as a child, you know,' she said between tissues. 'With the right kind of help he may well have turned out differently.'

Flora's death had triggered a chain of events that ended on the beach in Wraycliffe, and in that sheep-guileless way of hers I knew Virginia would never stop justifying Richard's abominable behaviour. Her eyes continually welled up as she showed pity for him, though the word I would have used was 'delusional'.

Chessie's stance had the same no-nonsense label as my own.

'He looked almost normal when he came to our reunion,' she said. 'I say "almost" because I am naturally suspicious, as you know, and I couldn't put a finger on what was wrong at the time.

'Something about the way he ingratiated himself all afternoon: you know, endlessly clearing plates and serving food when there was no need. I'm not enamoured by that kind of behaviour at the best of times: it's like the little boy who says, "Look at me everyone. You can't help liking me because I'm good."'

'He's another rat,' I said sourly as though it were the universal answer to every question. 'Charming but ruthless. Just like Turner.'

They both knew what I was talking about, having listened to me droning on for years. Nobody mentioned that we were both better off now, even though our situations were so very different. Turner might still find his way to old age, but death is so final.

'The lousy part,' I thought fit to say, 'is that we all believed you were living the good life in the backwoods: the library work, the dogs. It needs a twisted mind to come up with all that fresh air and peaceful space when the opposite is true. As far as we were aware, you were throwing things at the Internet in your normal fashion.'

'Apart from names,' Chessie reminded me.

'Oh yes. If it hadn't been for your way of handling all our names, you would probably be still underground.'

CHAPTER FORTY-SIX

Personally, I thought the mobility scooter was a bit over the top, but Virginia insisted on having one delivered for me.

She bought it over the Internet and was delighted with the whole process, having never bought anything that way before. She was genuinely on the road to recovery, if only because she was coming around to talking about the last two years without going through so many boxes of tissues.

Most of the time she drove me further afield in my car but being more mobile for short trips meant that I was able to introduce her to Wraycliffe. We spent our days walking through the countryside (she walked, I scooted) our memory cells laughingly reconstructing the long-ago days when two eight-year-olds ran wild through meadows, or raced along the beach and into the sea foam until Mrs Winters sent the limousine to whisk her daughter back home.

We trolled through the village, and there was an ideal moment when I tentatively plucked up courage to broach the subject of DCI McGovern. Nothing heavy, just a light-hearted question or two about his part in the aftermath of recent events. We had been to see Mrs Graham, whom she naturally called by her proper name of Marguerite (I only just found that out – way to go Olive!) and we were on our way home.

'Silas has been so helpful, Elise. You have no idea how much time he's spent looking after the debris of my life; there was a huge amount of paperwork to deal with. Richard ran up all kinds of debts in my name, you see, and Silas has been liaising with my financial manager to sort it all out.'

Silas would have been good at that; a very methodical mind. I could only comment, 'It seems so unfair that Richard took advantage of your family's wealth. I only wish you had confided in me sooner.'

With a shrug and an embarrassed laugh that was more like the Virginia I knew, she said, 'You know I was never very good with money,' (my wheels were slightly in front of her at the time so she couldn't see my grin of agreement). 'Oh yes, I know where every penny goes, but I have never been quite sure where it comes from. Bills just got paid. I only know I'm not bankrupt because I haven't touched any of daddy's trust fund, only mummy's.'

She almost looked embarrassed at the astonishment on my face when I turned to look at her, and simply shrugged it off. There you see; I never knew she still had the odd million secreted away somewhere for a rainy day, but like I always said, she never spoke of money. Too crude to mention, even in an Olive/Bunty relationship.

So, my pal *hadn't* been a complete idiot when it came to divulging the finer points of her background to her husband, after all. Which also meant that my theory about her becoming a pauper was blown sky high.

Hey ho!

The days were warm now, and the rose garden presented a rather better environment for relaxation than being indoors. Tans developed nicely on legs and arms and I was conscious that one foot would be brown and the other one white when I got rid of the sock. Another mildly depressing fact was that I had turned the page on the calendar and was a year older.

Virginia went back to see her ophthalmologist for a check-up, and he advised her to wear spectacles for close work and to use prescription sunglasses all the time when outdoors. Having raided my bookcase and devoured the contents, she then spent a full day in Leeds and came home with a bagful of hardbacks. During her days of forced confinement, she read anything she could lay her hands on and the habit has remained.

Silas came to see us frequently, which would have been great if I'd thought he was coming to see me, but I convinced myself that it wasn't me he had in his sights. In fact, I had mixed feeling about his visits and made a point of leaving the two of them alone as often as I could, without being too obvious about it.

It was around eleven o'clock one morning when I hobbled down the path to sit with them. Bella had done her usual thing with mugs of coffee for everyone, including Ben who was hoeing round the front. I was still unsure whether I would be eavesdropping on lovers' nonsense but it seemed by Virginia's fraught expression that they were discussing matters of a more disturbing nature. I tried (with great difficulty, I might add) to ignore the fact that Silas was holding her hand, but there were tears in her eyes.

'You must listen to this, Elise,' she said, quite calmly as I approached and their hands broke contact. I could tell she was distressed by the way she stared at the ground, immobile.

'What's the matter?'

I sat down and picked up my coffee; Silas leaned back and seemed to take an inordinately long time to organize his thoughts. He took a deep breath.

'It's about Richard, of course. We have been running a detailed check on him back at the office. It's a long and involved story, Elise, but the bare facts tell us a completely different story about the Richard Mason we all thought we knew.'

'About his early life, you mean?'

'It's rather more than that. It's as though we had found a totally different person when we put all the facts together.'

I think Virginia was past the crying stage, and she looked up to take in what Silas was saying. He coughed.

'Richard was born in the Midlands thirty-odd years ago to an unmarried teenager and primarily sent to foster parents. He became difficult to handle and the authorities moved him from one set of foster parents to another as his bad habits came to light. Mr and Mrs Mason eventually took him on as a teenager, and for a while everything seemed to be working out because they were basically religious people who cared about children.

'Eventually, nature triumphed over nurture, as they say, and he began to get into teenage trouble with the police, cruelty to animals in the first instance followed by a nasty phase of bullying and vandalism. Torture was part of his bag of tricks as well, but the Masons never gave up on him, even when he turned on them and physically harmed them, a nihilistic approach to anyone who got in his way by all accounts.'

'We knew so little about him,' my thoughts came out in a bemused jumble. 'I only met him twice. He might well have been unhinged enough to camouflage his past, but he was so self-assured, until the end, of course,' I shuddered. 'So, the Masons weren't his biological parents?'

'No. His birth certificate had him down as Kitteridge. And ...' he glanced across at Virginia again, who had turned into a statue and probably wasn't even listening, 'We uncovered some interesting facts that involve Mrs Winters and Virginia. You see, when he asked Virginia to marry him, he already had a wife in Canada. He knew so much about the country because he had lived there for five years.'

'What?'

My shriek must have echoed down the street. I spilled coffee as I put my mug down on the table but Virginia's tissues were conveniently to hand for mopping up the mess. Silas probably agreed with my outburst but he carried on as though he hadn't heard.

'They had been legally separated for a few years but his wife's religion stood in the way of divorce.'

'You're telling me all that suffering was for nothing? Richard was a bigamist?'

He nodded slowly, eyes never leaving Virginia's stricken face.

'He married Virginia – wrong expression, I know – when he'd been back over here for six months. Probably running out of money and saw Flora as an open cash point.'

'Did his wife know where he was?'

'Says not, but it sounds as though she was past caring by that time.'

Long silence. Hadn't my friend suffered enough without this? I just couldn't tell how she was taking it. She said nothing.

'And what about her now, this Mrs Kitteridge?' I asked. 'Has anyone notified her of his death?'

'Pierre has it in hand. I gather she has even less interest in the events of the past few days than she had four years ago.'

It wasn't only the light breeze that made me shudder, and I wondered whether Virginia had ever suspected Richard had a double life, both of them horrible when you come to think about it. I found I didn't mind in the slightest when Silas took hold of Virginia's hand and carefully watched her face. He spoke almost to himself.

'He needed to control people, you see, and the most effective way to do that is to frighten them into submission. The child psychiatrist said he would grow out of it by his late teens, but somebody would need to work hard in his corner. There doesn't appear to be any record of that happening and when the Masons died in a house fire that was suspected arson, but never proved I might add, he disappeared for a while, presumably to flee the country and find a new life. The remade version turned up and he met Virginia. End of story.'

He let go of Virginia's hand and turned to look at me, waiting for an emotional reaction, I think, but I had none to give. I was treating everything he said as a logical explanation for all that had happened, rotten though it was.

All I said was, 'So, it would have been easy for him to stage-manage the Post Box in Wynyard.'

'My guess is that he planned it all meticulously and went back on holiday to set it all up, after establishing himself over here. Once he had the plan ingrained in his mind, like you say, it would have been simple. He had a calculating mind which, had he used his intellect to better advantage, could have been the foundation of a useful career.

'Not been much of a recuperative holiday for you, Olive, looking after me, I mean.'

We were on our own again that afternoon. The weather had turned cool and we were in the workroom where I was poring through reams of printouts in my rocking chair and she was sedulously cross-stitching a cushion cover for me over by the window.

She may well have been concentrating on what she was doing, but she had been quiet throughout lunch, and even more thoughtful now.

I was purposely feeling my way, but she appeared to have dismissed the latest news as another unfortunate episode which was now behind her. Her calmness put everything into perspective and I think she had come to the point where she was immune to anything else that might happen to her. I had been watching carefully but there were no signs of acute distress and I wondered whether I would be as resilient.

'Two invalids, you mean, Bunty?' Less humour than usual, I thought. 'That's nonsense. I think it's wonderful and, believe me, I am grateful to be here. We are filling valuable gaps for each other. You are providing me with the fresh air I desperately need, and I am delighted to be your chauffeur. There's nothing wrong with that as far as I can see. Foot OK today?'

'Not long to go now before I divest myself of this ruddy thing,' I tugged at the sock. 'I want to scratch my foot all the time but Amelia's paintbrush handle doesn't quite reach.' It was driving me crazy. 'I wonder whether my white leg will be thinner than the brown one.'

'They usually are, according to Francesca. Or rather, that's what her mother says.'

Banal conversation, and in the end, I couldn't resist asking the question that was uppermost in my mind. It came out as a choking noise.

'Will you and Silas get together now? Married, I mean … now that you are both unattached.'

I might not have posed the question very well, but I hadn't thought the words through properly, only the idea. It just came out. Her needle stopped abruptly and she turned to me with puzzlement written all over her face. The smile was bright and genuine this time.

'Good gracious me, no! Whatever gave you that idea? Silas is like a big brother to me, and in any case, he let it slip the other day that he's in love with someone else. He didn't say who it was but I can put two and two together. Francesca agreed with me on the phone; she said that the answer came to four, and that only a dunce wouldn't be able to see it.'

My face felt hot all of a sudden. The electric fire was switched off, but I put my rise in temperature down to a subconscious reaction to a flickering backlight and imitation coal.

'Besides, I had plenty of time to think while I was, well … you know.'

She blushed slightly. Pink cheeks were attractive on the tanned face but I thought she looked suspiciously coy. She carefully cut her thread and folded away her stitching into the canvas bag by her side. Thinking time. She had arrived at a waypoint and was going to tell me about it.

'Well, all right then,' she said impatiently. 'I suppose you might as well hear all about it today. You are my dearest friend and, let's face it, you will find out eventually, anyway.'

Her dearest friend suddenly perked up and waited.

'You see, I met the most wonderful man in Paris after Tom died, just before I married Richard. And I made many plans while I was incarcerated, one of which was to try and see him again, if ever I got out of that place, that is.

'His name's Paul. He's a lovely man, kind and gentle, and he sent me a letter of condolence when mummy died. Mummy always wanted us to get together, she never liked Richard anyway, and she went to school with Paul's mother. I think he's related to a throne somewhere.'

The charms on her gold chain bracelet jingled as she fluffed up her hair and gave me a sideways grin. My mouth opened and remained that way. I knew nothing about this.

It made her gurgle when I eventually asked, 'So why on earth, you little flirt, did you marry Richard when you had already fallen for someone else?'

'Richard needed me,' she said soberly, and the joyful spell was broken.

CHAPTER FORTY-SEVEN

I was on my own again and browsing through one of Amelia's fairy-tale books for pictures that I might caricature for James when I heard Bella's footsteps padding up the stair. It was afternoon tea time and she usually serves pretty good scones with homemade jam around now.

Virginia had removed herself to London and was now in constant communication with Chessie. She had much to do, plans to make, finances to sort and a whole new wardrobe to buy before she flew on to Paris. She looked forward to living at The Dorchester for the time being, she said, and the Grasmere house was already on the market.

A few telephone calls had confirmed that, amazingly, throne-related Paul was not involved with anyone, romantically or otherwise, and certainly not married.

On the contrary, having managed to steer clear of celebrity beauties and titled ladies who would have liked to add him as a notch to their bedposts, this gentle man had sworn to remain a bachelor until he found himself a perfect woman like the daughter of his mother's school friend, Virginia Winters.

Richard's death was devastating, of course, but when Virginia walked back into Paul's life, it could only be Kismet.

The door opened.

'Hi Sweetie. Just put it on my desk will you. I shall be starting work in a minute.'

James's manuals were a regular task and he had emailed three more for checking yesterday.

I loved my new way of working, and I had made a start on the latest one. Casual visitors had eased off, but I knew I had new friends in the village, which meant that Bella still made flapjacks and scones by the bucket load.

'I would if I knew what you were talking about.'

I looked up quickly to see the man behind the deep voice. I had been thinking about him so much recently; Virginia's revelation last weekend still made my toes curl. Well, those on my right foot anyway. He was back to wearing his off-duty fleece and jeans.

Silas's gorgeous eyes, brown as milk chocolate, were full of questions when he came over to me and sank to his knees by the side of my chair. I had grown to like the woody smell of his aftershave.

'And how are you today?'

He had rung my new mobile every day but he had not been to see me since Virginia left. I lifted my poorly foot and gave it a kind of wiggle. Shyness prevented me looking into his eyes.

'Let's just say I shall be glad to get rid of this thing. I shall look really odd, you know, with normal feet.'

'I did warn you it could be dangerous.'

Well-deserved sarcasm, I had to admit. I knew exactly what he was talking about and I muttered something about taking more notice next time. He gave me that eye-nod of his, which this time meant business.

'There won't be a next time. Understood? Leave it to the professionals.'

'And the burglars?'

Mischievous, that. Without giving the man a name, he had told me as much as I needed to know about the break-in.

He suddenly wrapped his arms around me, and I felt the warmth of his chest through the jacket.

For all he spoke in a whisper, I could hear every word over the top of my heartbeat.

'I have been waiting for everybody to leave us alone; I thought they would never go.'

'Silas—' I suddenly remembered. 'Your knee—'

He winced, shifted awkwardly, re-balanced.

'Tell me about it. I probably won't be able to stand, but that's all right because I want to ask you something. This is the recognized position, isn't it?' His eyes twinkled, even though he must be in pain.

'Will you. Elise Kent. Spinster of this parish. Take me Silas Daniel … Oh, you know the rest.'

He backhanded the words to the ceiling and gave me a heart-wrenching kiss that lasted a long time. Our first proper kiss, and one to savour. Out of the corner of my eye I saw that Linnet's mischievous smile was now reflected in her descendants as well.

'Oh yes please,' I replied softly coming up for air but eager to repeat the experience. He didn't really expect me to refuse him, did he? 'On one condition.'

'What's that?'

'Please, Silas, please try to stand up before you do yourself irreparable harm.'

CHAPTER FORTY-EIGHT

We were sitting in the VIP airport lounge at Heathrow a couple of months later, ready to board first a plane that would take us to Toronto for a two-night stopover, and then an internal flight to Regina. Our final destination was to be Vancouver Island, but we were going to stay with Pierre and Joelle for a few days first.

They had been looking forward to meeting Silas's new wife ever since he told them all about me in April. How about that? Now he tells me! He tenderly brushed a tiny piece of confetti from my hair. Even though we had been careful to remove all traces, I must have missed one. I rested my head on his shoulder.

'Are you absolutely certain you never loved Virginia?' I whispered.

'Never did. How many times are you going to ask me? I've told you: I loved my wife, but you know that little story, and there has only been one woman for me since then. Apart from Ruth,' he added indulgently. A sister-in-law I was looking forward to knowing better.

The wedding reception earlier today at *Bolton Manor* had been the best. Friends came from all corners of the country, making it a kind of mini-reunion for chatterboxes and a get-together for both the police force and the legal fraternity. Chessie and Virginia looked fabulous in their designer gear; I met Charlie for the first time, and Paul. Let's just say, they were both magnificent, but nowhere near as handsome as my Silas.

I decided that Ruth was a carbon copy of her brother, blunt and worldly-wise, and you couldn't help liking her. She looked striking in a bright yellow summer dress and matching hat. She already knew Virginia, of course, and was at ease chatting amiably to most of our guests as though she had known them all her life. It was a day to remember.

Charles gave me away. He had written his speech purposely on a scruffy old piece of paper that he held aloft to show everybody, and jokingly said it had been prepared for a very long time. Cheek!

When it was all over, the taxi driver filled his Mercedes boot with enough expensive-looking suitcases to see the newlyweds through their proposed month away. As he did so, he cast a suspicious eye on the best man who was tying a string of tin cans to his back bumper. He didn't mind anything on the outside, he told the groom, but no mess inside his cab. Please. Or else!

Unknown to the taxi driver, the best man also happened to hold the rank of Detective Superintendent somewhere on the other side of the country. He smiled deferentially and mumbled something unintelligible in a foreign language.

In the busy airport, Silas now kissed me gently, which other passengers probably enjoyed as well but pretended to ignore.

'And how do you feel about spending the rest of your life as Elise McGovern?'

I told him all about my longing to be carried off by a handsome prince on a white stallion.

'The only difference as far as I can see is that we shall be galloping thousands of feet in the air and the charger is made of metal. But I dare say I can live with that.'

A voice came over the loudspeaker, announcing that dreams do come true – some of the time.

'Will passengers for Toronto, Flight Number ...'

Made in the USA
Lexington, KY
18 April 2019